PRAISE FOR EVELYN ROGERS'S BESTSELLING ROMANCES!

FLAME

"This one is a keeper. Superb!"

—Rendezvous

SWEET TEXAS MAGIC

"For action, excitement, and adventure, readers will find *Sweet Texas Magic* ideal!"

—Romantic Times

SURRENDER TO THE NIGHT

"Ms. Rogers takes every little girl's fantasy and turns it into a woman's dream!"

—Romantic Times

A LOVE SO WILD

"Readers will be hooked from page one as Ms. Rogers unfolds her memorable tale of passion!"

—Romantic Times

An Angel's Touch

WICKED DELIGHTS

Cad leaned close so that his hot skin touched the cool silk of Amy's gown, his chest brushing against hers. She shifted to an angle; he followed, propping his hands on either side of her.

She fell on her elbows. "Ouch," she said. She was practically lying down, underneath him, which he figured was the best place she could be.

"You hurt?" he said, concentrating on her parted lips, full and rosy. When her tongue flicked out for a second, then disappeared, he almost moved in to suck it our again. "Maybe we ought to get you undressed like me and find out how serious it is."

Her eyes were concentrating on his bare shoulders and arms and his naked chest. "Goodness," she said.

"Oh, it'll be good all right," he said.

WICKED

Evelyn Rogers

LOVE SPELL LOVE SPELL NEW YORK CITY

LOVE SPELL®

March 1996

Published by

Dorchester Publishing Co., Inc.
276 Fifth Avenue
New York, NY 10001

Printed in the United States of America.

This book is dedicated in loving remembrance of my mother
Jessie Reynolds Lay
(November 28, 1915 — April 7, 1995)
and in joyous celebration of my first grandchild
Patrick Reynolds Varner
(born August 17, 1995)

WICKED

Chapter One

Cad Rankin was a dead man.

He caught the big one, a bullet to the gut, outside the Galveston bank he'd tried to rob. Toes-up in the middle of a sunny, crowded street, he made one wish: Let it be over fast.

A boot prodded his side, and fiery pain shot through him. "Hairy thing, ain't he? Can't hardly see nothing but his eyes. Looks like a mean ole grizzly bear."

"More like a long, lean pile of rags. Sorry sonuvabitch."

That he was.

Eyes closed, the pain coming at him in waves, he waited to—what was it the preachers said?—to cast off these mortal coils. Lordy, he hadn't thought of preacher talk since he was a boy.

Anyway, a simple outlaw like him didn't have much in the way of coils.

He held himself still, taking his miserable end as a just reward. What year was it anyway? 1880. That would make a nice round figure on his tombstone. Except he wouldn't be getting anything so fancy in a pauper's grave.

Not that it mattered. No one would seek out his final resting place. Parents dead, and Michael, too. A long time dead and forgotten.

Funny how he thought about them now.

Someone spat on the ground beside him. "Other bastard got away. Too bad we can't hang this 'un twice."

"From the looks of 'im, won't get a rope 'round his neck 'fore he's a goner. Most we can hope for is he burns in hell."

He would for sure. No doubt about it.

Gnats swirled around his face, nesting in his beard. A final ignominy in an ignominious life. All the scene needed was a pile of fresh horseshit upwind to make his death perfect.

One of the men squatted beside him. A hand touched his forehead. "Still warm. Better get him to Doc's office."

"Why bother? The undertaker'll do just as well."

"Ought to be some kind of reward. Is he famous or something?"

"Naw. Just another lowlife trying to steal the money of honest folk. Bank ought to do something for the guard, though. He doing all right?"

"A shoulder wound. He'll be up and about 'fore long."

"The other bastard get away with much?"

Someone chuckled. "They missed the payroll money by a day."

Typical Rankin luck. Rick's fault, thought Cad, for not showing up when he was supposed to. Rick Marsh, who right now was hightailing it toward Houston with the loot, instead of rescuing his sometime partner. Cad couldn't work up much anger. Under the circumstances, he'd have done the same thing.

He heard the rustle of a woman's skirt. He'd always had a hankering for women, and more than a few had returned the interest. Women of a wanton nature, that is. They seemed partial to his grizzly-bear face. And to his . . .

He stopped himself. No need adding to the fire in his gut.

"Junior," a female voice shrilled right over him, "you and Bertie get on back to the carriage and leave vermin like this to the men."

Damn, thought Cad. A respectable woman. He should have known.

Something stung him in the arm.

"Bertie," the woman yelled, "ain't I told you a thousand times not to throw rocks?"

"Shucks, Ma," a boy grumbled, "I was just chuckin' 'em at the bank robber. Don't see nothing wrong with that."

"You might catch something," she said. "Get on away."

She spoke like stealing was contagious, like the boy might splatter himself with outlaw blood and the next thing you knew he'd be taking his mama's grocery money when her back was turned.

Cad opened his eyes. Black silk skirt so close he could almost touch it, meandering on up to a formidable bosom, and higher to a fancy hat that blocked out the sun. Though her face was in shadows, he could make out tight lips and a scowl.

Cad sighed. Gnats, brats, and a prune-faced harpy. Dying wasn't proving a hell of a lot more pleasurable than living. He groaned, as if asking for help. She leaned close. For his last act on earth, he smiled and winked.

"Oh," she gasped, jumping back as if he'd pinched her. "What a wicked, wicked man."

That he was.

Rough hands seized him. The fire in his belly flared into a conflagration. His body gave a mighty shudder, and without a hint of regret he breathed his last.

His next conscious thought concerned why he was thinking at all. He was stretched out somewhere on a hard, smooth surface. The light was dim, but he sensed he was in a small enclosure of some kind. Not small enough for a coffin, though, and not nearly dark enough. And he was thinking, which definitely was the main mortal coil he'd been ready to cast off.

Questions about his condition skittered through his mind like water on a hot griddle. He wasn't hurting anymore. That was good. But he was thinking, and that was bad.

Thinking that of course he wasn't hurting since he didn't have a body. He sat up. *Sat up?* It took a body to do that. He looked down at a familiar woebegone shirt and a pair of Levi's with a bloody bullet hole close to the crotch. His holster and gun were gone, but everything else seemed in place.

Whatever he was lying on, it was too short for his six-foot frame, and his dusty boots hung awkwardly over the end. He put one hand in front of his face, then the other. He counted ten fingers, the same ten he'd been toting all his life.

Next, he poked at his belly. No blood gushed out; but then, dead men didn't bleed. The hole in him was still there, though, surrounded by dark incrustations of matter not meant to see the light of day. Never one to linger on afflictions, he didn't study the wound for long.

He might not be hurting, but something was definitely wrong.

He looked around him. He was in a small room sitting on a table, and nearby another table was laid out with what looked like instruments of torture: knives and picks and a straight-edged razor, along with rags and soap and water, a big pail and jars of some lethal-looking liquid. A white coat hung on a wall peg. He looked farther. Two doors on opposite walls, both closed; one window, shut; and outside, with twilight coming on, all seemed gloomy and quiet.

He shifted his legs to the side of the table.

"Move slowly. You've been through a great deal."

He stared at the man by the outside door. "Where the hell did you come from? You weren't here a minute ago." Without waiting for an answer, he hurried on. "What the hell are you doing here anyway? And while I'm at it, where the hell is *here?*"

"Goodness, Cadmus, you've always been a man of few words."

The man smiled as he spoke, his voice soft and warm, kind of like heated milk. His suit was the color of milk, too, making the comparison easy to come by. He was as furry as Cad, only his hair and beard were neatly trimmed and white as summer clouds, while Cad's were dark as tree bark.

Something about the smile and the voice had a curiously calming effect, as did the light that drifted from him, casting a soft glow across the room.

"How did you know my name? No one's called me Cadmus—well, not in a long time."

"Cadmus Aloysius Rankin, born on a plantation near Lafayette, Louisiana, October 5, 1849, thirty-one years ago today."

"I'll be damned. Killed on my birthday."

"It was a Friday, as I recall."

"You recall?" Cad said in amazement, thinking for a moment how his mother used to say that Friday's child was loving and giving. Mama had been wrong.

He scratched his head and looked closer at the man. He was short and round, his eyes blue and creased with lines, as if he laughed a lot. And his hair looked more silver than white.

"I don't remember you from around Lafayette. Who are you?"

"Dudley will be sufficient. I suppose you might say I'm from everywhere."

"Dudley, is it? Dudley what?"

"Just Dudley. There aren't enough of us to warrant last names." He smiled again. "Actually, we don't need a first name either, but it makes communication simpler when we're dealing with mortals."

Mortals? Something about the word jerked him to the weirdness of the situation. What kind of a madhouse was he in anyway? An Afterlife for Crazies? Or maybe he wasn't dead yet. Maybe he'd just lost so much blood there wasn't any more to lose, and he was a little lightheaded. He tried to stand, but his legs were a mite wobbly and he rested his backside against the table.

"You're the undertaker, aren't you, ready to clean me up for burial, only I fooled you by being alive."

"Oh, you're not alive."

Cad felt unexpectedly sad. "Then I really am dead."

"Not exactly."

"Is this some kind of joke? A man's either dead or he's alive. Everybody knows that."

"An unfortunate oversimplification, Cadmus."

Madhouse for sure.

"If I'm not dead and I'm not alive, then what am I?"

"Somewhere suspended between the two. Undead, if you must put a name to it, although that seems unfortunately negative for your condition. You could go either way."

Cad laughed. It felt good. "This is some kind of joke, isn't it?"

"A natural reaction. Please allow me to explain."

Cad folded his arms across his chest. "Dud, you go right ahead. We seem to have the place to ourselves."

"For a while. I really owe Mr. Stone an apology."

"Mr. Stone?"

"The undertaker."

"Stone the undertaker. I should have known. What's his first name, Tomb? Or maybe Head?"

"It's Walter. Now, shall we get on?"

Why not? Cad had always heard dead men told no tales, but that sure wasn't true of the folks they met on the other side.

"Let's start with a little background. We've already established your name and birth date. You were the firstborn son of Aloysius and Veronica Rankin, owners of a fine plantation west of New Orleans. Your brother Michael came two years later."

Cad came off the table. Shaky legs or no, this Dudley character was going too far.

"Whoever the hell you are, leave Michael out of this."

"Ah, but I cannot, since he is very much a part of our situation. Please, allow me to continue."

The man's words stopped him, made him feel roped and tied and all chilled inside. Wanting to fight or run, to foul the air with some cussing, he could do nothing except sit back and listen, and think how things were getting weirder all the time.

"When set upon by a band of renegade soldiers, your parents faced death heroically. You were but a lad of fifteen. I see no point in dwelling on their demise."

Cad stared woodenly at the stranger. He didn't need details. He carried them in the back of his mind: the Yankee soldiers with the rope around his father's neck, the rape and murder of his mother, and all the while their two sons bound and gagged and watching.

"You acquitted yourself well under those tragic circumstances, getting away as you did, although I cannot condone the taking of life on either side."

"I knifed two of the bastards. I'd do it again."

"Yes, well, I truly do understand."

"I don't give a damn what you understand. Whoever you are, I've had enough."

Dudley's kindly smile carried a hint of sadness. "I am almost done. For the balance of that dreadful conflict tearing your country apart, having lost the home and land that had been yours, you and Michael lived by your wits. In the end it was a representative of the law—"

"A damned carpetbagger sheriff."

"—who was your undoing."

"He chased us into the swamp. For stealing a loaf of bread."

Cad felt a hurt inside, like an old wound was opening up. Once again he was 17, the tough Rankin, the one his gentle brother depended upon. He'd led Michael into the depths of the Atchafalaya, into a nest of cottonmouth water moccasins, into a final agony of death. He could still hear his brother's cries.

"Stop. I don't want to hear any more."

"I'm almost done. Please believe me when I say I share your pain. It is because you can still feel the loss that I am here. Guilt over all those deaths proved too much for your young conscience, and you taught yourself to survive without regard for others. An understandable choice, but regrettable nonetheless, for it led you to a life of crime."

Cad waved a hand in disgust. "What am I supposed to do, beg forgiveness? Forget it. I'll take what I've got coming to me without complaint."

"Matters are not so simple, as you will see. You proved moderately successful on your chosen path, robbing and terrorizing. It is a miracle you never took a life."

"Not for lack of trying."

"Granted. Card playing was another successful enterprise. You became a cardsharp, I believe it's called."

"I became a cheat."

"Yes, well, that, too."

"I gambled and I stole and I whored, and I've known the taste of whiskey on my lips. Anything I've left out? You seem to know me as well as I know myself."

"Better, I believe, for I know there is within you a spark of goodness. You have never assaulted the weak or lame, never harmed a child, a woman, or a helpless animal. There are many of your profession who cannot say the same."

"So you're here to give me angel's wings."

"Hardly that. As you say, you have stolen and gambled and whored."

Cad shook his head. He was practically taking old Dudley seriously. And here he was, feeling stronger by the minute. Must be all the remembering that did it. Undead, was he? Like hell. He ought to be skedaddling through the door and out of town. And he would be, too, except something kept him in place, a force he couldn't see. It seemed like the light coming from Dudley surrounded him and held him down.

He tried to take a deep breath and realized a funny thing: He wasn't breathing. He felt his chest. If his heart was beating, it was mighty weak and slow. He hadn't realized any of this before. He'd felt . . . natural. He didn't feel natural now.

"Tell me, Dud, how come my mind is working and not much of anything else?"

"Simply put, the mind is part of the soul, and that you have not lost. Not entirely. Michael is convinced you are a worthy candidate for redemption."

Cad started. "What did you say?"

"Michael has faith in you. He always has."

"Michael's dead."

"Michael is no longer of this earth. He lives on in another state."

"Not anywhere in Texas."

"I forgot what a literal mind you have. Another condition, I should have said. He believes you deserve a chance at proving yourself. He believes you should be allowed to survive your wound, to continue with your life. In short, he wishes for you the chance he never had."

"No way, Dud. After thirty-one years of hell on earth, I'm ready for a little peace."

"Veracity compels me to reveal that under the present circumstances throughout eternity you would not find anything resembling peace."

"That's all right. It's time someone else made decisions for me. I'm sure as shooting ready for a change."

"A coward's answer. And you have never been a coward."

"Maybe. Maybe not." It was damned sure he was feeling shaky now. He took a minute to think over all the stranger had said. This was crazy, a dream, a nightmare, and yet . . .

"I've changed my mind about my brother. Let me see him: let me hear him say what a good fellow I am."

Dudley sighed. "I'll do what I can. Allow yourself a moment of silent contemplation. Remember the smiling, ginger-haired boy who tagged along behind you, believing everything you said, following your example as best he could."

Cad remembered, all right, and felt a sharp twist around his heart. Damn it, things just kept getting worse and worse. He must be as demented as old Dud to be asking for such pain.

Against his will he closed his eyes, knowing all the while he'd spoken too hastily, thinking only to call the old coot's bluff. What if he got what he'd asked for? What if he saw Michael, and heard him? Impossible, and yet . . .

Cad shuddered. There were things he didn't want to remember, not after a lifetime of forgetting. Already he'd thought of the soldiers and the snakes, and of his own youthful stupidity. He didn't want Michael to appear.

But as he waited he felt a curious thing . . . a presence that was not of this world, like an early morning mist, only not damp in the least; more like warmth from a fire, the heat waves thick enough to touch. Something stirred within him, something gentle that had not been touched in years, something that didn't hurt. He had no will to fight the stirring. If he listened closely enough, he could hear a young boy's voice.

Cad, what are we going to do now? Can I help?

You're running too fast, Cad. I can't keep up.

I love you, Cad. You're the best brother in the world.

His entire being yearned toward the sound, but for only an instant. The good feeling didn't last. With his heart twisting tighter and the voice fading, the gentleness disappeared.

"Get away from me," he growled, as much at the stranger as at the pain, his eyes open wide once again.

"When I have said all that I must."

"Who are you? And don't give me any of that Dudley crap."

"I'm an angel."

"You're a *what?*"

The knob to the outside door turned.

"Oh, dear," said Dudley. "Mr. Stone. Lie still, Cadmus, until I can send him on another mission. He does like to bury his cadavers all tidy and thoroughly prepared, but you have my word you will not be embalmed."

Cad lay stretched out on the table, eyes closed as he listened to the undertaker bustling around him.

Angel? Embalmed? Angels weren't for real,

and embalming wasn't natural. At least, most folks thought so. Right now, Cad agreed.

"Mr. Stone can neither see nor hear me," said Dudley from somewhere close by. "I must return to the preacher. A suggestible man. I shall whisper to him another summons for our industrious mortician."

Cad tried to respond, but he could not move or speak. Somehow he sensed that Dudley was no longer in the room.

Stone moved to the table and proceeded to cut Cad's hair, then to shave him, whistling while he worked. The soiled clothing came off next, and Cad wondered if he planned to use the razor on any other hairy parts.

"Nasty wound," said Stone with a cluck of his tongue. He laid a cloth across his cadaver's abdomen. "Oh dear, he's quite tall. And the coffin I planned to use is rather short. I'll have to break his legs to fit him in."

How tidy, thought Cad with an invisible shudder.

Shuffling with his instruments, Stone sang a chorus of "Bury Me Not on the Lone Prairie." Poking around Cad's chest and arms, he switched to the livelier "Oh Susanna," but Cad was not cheered.

"Strong man. Good muscle structure," said Stone when the song was done. He gave a proprietary pat to the cloth across Cad's loins. "And quite well endowed. Too bad, whoever you are, that you devoted your life to evil."

The door opened. Someone entered. "Ah, Reverend Goodnight," the undertaker said.

"Mr. Stone, it grieves me to bother you again, but the Widow Smathers is in need of counseling as to the preparation for her husband's wake."

"Has she asked to speak with me? I went all the way to the cemetery a short time ago and she was not there."

"My mistake. She is at home. And while she has not asked directly for a meeting, I feel moved by the spirit of God to say that, yes, she wants to speak to both of us."

Stone sighed. "Oh, well, this poor bastard isn't going anywhere. Pardon my language, Reverend."

There was some shuffling about, the opening and closing of the door, and in the ensuing silence Cad opened his eyes. Something about listening to the two men talking over his body convinced him that he really was . . . undead. No matter how weird the word sounded, it fit.

Dudley smiled at him from beside the window, and he felt oddly, unexpectedly comforted. "The good reverend is how I get my messages across on this sinful island. What with the sailors and gamblers and the loose women, there are a great many occasions that call for Divine guidance."

"And that's why you're with me," Cad said, propping himself up on one elbow and securing the cloth across his private parts. "You're an angel who has the ear of God."

"You might say I'm a liaison angel, working between the Divinity and mortals in need of help. Which, I must admit, includes almost everybody."

"*Liaison* sounds like someone in the Army. Whatever happened to guardian angels?"

"They help with those mortals still alive. I hope you appreciate the difference."

Appreciate wasn't exactly the way Cad would have put it. "So you really are an angel," he said, forgetting the eeriness of the situation, wondering if maybe this undead state couldn't work out to his benefit, in ways old Dud wasn't considering. Ever a man to watch out for himself, he couldn't see reason to stop just yet.

"I really am. Now let's get to the particulars of your situation. If you die, you will spend eternity in torment. If you prove yourself on earth, however, you will be allowed a continued life and an eternity of peace. Surely you can see the wisdom of choosing the latter."

"Maybe so and maybe not. Exactly how do I do this proving?"

"By bringing harmony and justice to a place where it does not exist. Rough Cut, Texas, to be specific."

"Never heard of it."

"Forgive me, Cadmus, but I must admit to some surprise. It is generally believed that every rogue and renegade in the state has stayed there at least one night."

"Can't see how I missed it," Cad said flatly.

"It's located far to the west, north of the border town of San Felipe del Rio, near both the Devils River and the Rio Grande. It is, I fear, a place without equal for depravity and violence and general lawlessness."

"Sounds like my kind of town."

"A condition that must be put in the past. Your task is to clean up Rough Cut, as you might put it."

"I shoot everybody and the town can start over, is that it?"

"Goodness, no." Dudley's blue eyes widened beneath his thick white brows. "You must reform its citizens and convince those whose reformation proves impossible that perhaps they had best move on."

"Like I said, I shoot everybody. I'm a damned fine marksman, if I do say so myself. Shame to waste the talent."

"Please, Cadmus. Take this seriously. You must perform your task without bloodshed or violence or revealing the unusual nature of your existence."

"What kind of joy juice they got in heaven, Dud? Whatever it is, you've had a cup too many."

"We get our joy from a sense of goodness," said Dudley, and then he smiled sheepishly. "Oh, my, that sounds a bit pompous, doesn't it? It's one of my flaws."

"I'd say dreaming up crazy notions is another.

How the hell am I supposed to clean up this town without fists or guns?"

"Or cursing, I might add. That, of course, is the challenge."

Cad thought a moment. "It's too much. Count me out."

"You force me to use strong tactics," Dudley said with a frown. "Michael has chosen for you. Good but inordinately stubborn creature that he is, he will not be denied, by you or me. Close your eyes a moment. You will understand what I mean."

Cad had no choice but to comply. Once again he felt his brother's presence, this time more strongly, whispering to him without a sound, enfolding him without a touch. His will to resist, always strong, grew lax. He wanted to hold Michael, but he could not raise a hand.

As quickly as Michael's spirit had invaded the room, so was it gone, leaving in its place a curious and temporary peace. It warmed Cad for a moment, teasing him with the promise of its return, then scaring him with the sense of its power.

Shaken more than he could remember having been since the swamp, he squinted at Dudley. "You're not playing fair." The words sounded childish to his own ears, but he meant them.

The angel's lips twitched within the confines of his beard. "Rather a curious comment coming from you, is it not?"

Something about Dudley's flat tone erased his

sense of loss, and he was once again his old calculating self. "I didn't know angels could be sarcastic."

"When the occasion warrants. I will be present whenever the need arises, but you alone will be able to see and hear me."

Cad glanced around the undertaker's room, dwelling for a moment on the embalming knife and fluid. "What kind of help are you offering?" Not that he needed it. Not that he'd take it. He hadn't agreed to anything yet.

"Advice, mostly, and a sympathetic ear. Not much, I fear."

"Won't these renegades figure out something's wrong when I don't breathe?"

"Oh, you will appear normal in most respects. You can even eat and sleep if you wish, although these are matters of choice rather than necessities. You will also be able to feel pleasure. I'm told it strengthens one against temptation. But you will not feel physical pain, nor can you bleed. And most certainly you cannot die. That you have already done."

Cad felt a vise closing in on him. If he could breathe, he'd be choking right now.

"What about women?"

"What about them? Oh, I see what you mean. Enjoyment of sexual undertakings must be a part of your forsaken past. As must the imbibing of strong drink."

"You sure are a windy angel, Dud. What

you're saying is, if I did it, I'd enjoy it, but since I shouldn't, I can't."

"Confusingly put, but not inaccurate."

Cad scratched his face. Bare as a baby's bottom. Already he missed his beard. "You drive hard bargains; I'll say that for you."

Dudley shrugged, then gestured toward the closed inner door. "Clean garments are in there."

"Provided, I suppose, by the preacher. You were certain I'd accept."

"I knew Michael's persuasive ability."

Michael again. Cad refused to consider so much as his name. "Won't my body be missed?"

"A good question. I've already loaded your coffin with bricks and nailed it shut. Or rather, I inspired a pair of vandals to do so. Mr. Stone is of an absentminded nature. After an hour with Reverend Goodnight and the widow, he'll believe he prepared the coffin himself."

Cad was finally out of questions, and out of protests. He assimilated all he had heard. Whatever the angel was proposing, it was better than lying around here and getting embalmed. Even a hardened outlaw like him could see that.

Within a quarter hour, suitcase in hand, he emerged from the undertaker's parlor, breathing once again, expecting any minute to hear shots ring out and feel another bullet in the gut. All was quiet.

The salty twilight air was cool against his face. Glancing backwards, he saw no sign of

Dudley. He did see, however, the reflection of a clean-shaven, respectable stranger in the window. Tall, lean, and well dressed, with a dark hat worn low on his forehead close to a pair of watchful eyes.

Goddamn, he was looking at himself.

He stopped. *Gosh,* he amended, thinking the mild oath didn't do the job. He'd have to come up with something else. For as long as he went along with this crazy idea, that is.

Right now he'd do what he was told and hit the trail for Rough Cut. Maybe even abide by what old Dud asked, if it was the only way he could get by. Never much on planning ahead, he'd take his undead condition one day at a time.

Dudley had powers, all right. It was Cad's habit to put other men's powers to use. Angels, too, it seemed. The one part of the weirdness he couldn't accept was Michael's presence. He must have been hallucinating back there on the table, thanks to old Dud.

Remembering his brother reminded him how painful caring for someone could be. He wouldn't think of him again.

"Well, hello," a woman said.

He turned toward the speaker, a redhead in a green dress. A good-looking redhead, at that; nicely put together. He was real partial to redheads, right behind blondes and brunettes.

A loner he might be, but he sure as heck wasn't a monk.

"Good evening," he said, tipping his hat.

Her green eyes glinted. He'd seen the look before.

"I'm a stranger in town," he said. "Could you by any chance direct me to the train depot?"

"I'll do more than that. I'll walk with you. It's not far."

"Now that's a shame. I've a notion to stretch my legs a mite."

She looked him over. "Not a bad idea. We could go the long way. By my place."

Cad started to take her arm, but a loud *ahem* stopped him. He recognized the angelic throat-clearing. Gosh darn it to heck. Patience was a virtue he'd never set much store by, but he would have to come up with some now. With more regret than Dudley could ever understand, he backed away.

"Sorry. Maybe the next time I'm in town we'll meet up."

She pouted and turned away, too late to hear his final words.

"And get ready to lift those skirts, honey, 'cause next time I'll be alive."

Chapter Two

"He's here."

Amy Lattimer started, almost dropping the book she had been holding for the past hour. A dozen questions leapt to her mind, but she said only, "Thank you, Sister Bernadette."

"You're welcome." The sister's round face, surrounded by the starched white of her wimple, bore a thoughtful expression. "You're not nervous, are you?"

Amy sat straight in her chair. "Of course not. I trust Mama implicitly."

"Then why," Sister Bernadette said with a glint in her eye, "are you reading upside down?"

Amy glanced guiltily at the volume of love poetry in her lap. While she'd waited in her room for a summons, she'd hoped the romantic verses would establish the mood for this momentous day; they hadn't done a very good job.

She set the book aside, fiddled with a lock of her hair, and smoothed her skirt. "What . . . does he look like?"

"I didn't see him. He's with the Mother Superior."

"Not that appearances matter," Amy said with a little laugh. "Goodness, the man a girl marries has far more important traits than a handsome face."

"Oh, most certainly."

"Like honesty and kindness and intelligence."

"Everyone knows that. Even a nun."

The two women stared at each other, grinned, and after a moment began to giggle. Both had reached the old-maid age of twenty-two. Bernadette was wed to the church, and Amy would soon find herself the bride of a wealthy Parisian.

Pierre Gaston, twenty-five, son of a French merchant who had arranged the betrothal with Amy's long-absent mother, Marguerite, had traveled from his native country to claim her and take her to his home.

Amy would have preferred choosing her own mate, but in the convent school where she had grown up and now served as teacher, her choices were limited. Nonexistent, to tell the truth. She'd already stayed here far longer than other lay residents; it was time to leave. And in her frequent letters from abroad, Mama had promised that Pierre would take care of her.

Foolish romantic that she was, she would have preferred being loved. Perhaps that would come in time.

For now, she knew her duty, and she followed Sister Bernadette into the hall, allowing herself one last glance at her cozy and comfortable room. Mama's money had furnished it with all the creature comforts a bedroom in a convent could provide. Amy would have preferred Mama's company instead of her cash, but Marguerite Lattimer traveled. She had done so since Papa died, when Amy was a little girl.

At first she'd fought her confinement, running away whenever she got the chance, climbing walls and trees, protesting what she considered her mother's abandonment. A real hoyden, the nuns had said, but that had been a long time ago.

The years had worn her down; she no longer allowed herself to feel resentment, to doubt Marguerite's choices or her word. Ergo, Pierre would prove a wonderful bridegroom, keeping at bay the loneliness that sometimes came upon her in the night. Without doubt, he would bring her a lifetime of joy.

A lifetime of joy, she repeated when she saw him for the first time. He stood before the Mother Superior's desk, top hat in hand, along with a pearl-handled walking stick. He wore a gray frock coat over black trousers, a stiff-collared white shirt, and at his throat was a froth of ecru lace.

He didn't exactly wear the coat and trousers; rather, he was stuffed into them. He really should have ordered a larger size, she thought, trying to be charitable. And he was shorter than her five-foot-six by at least two inches. Brown eyes rested like raisins in a round, flat face, his complexion so smooth that Amy wondered if he had begun to shave yet.

A lifetime of joy. Walking into the room, she used the phrase as a silent chant.

He smiled and sniffed. A criticism of her appearance? She wasn't sure. Her gown was a simple gray silk, but finely made, and she thought it showed her long-limbed, slender figure to advantage. As always, she wore her hair in a twist at the back of her head, leaving a few fair curls to soften her face. Her only jewelry was a small silver brooch at her throat.

"Ah, *mademoiselle,*" he said with another sniff. *"Bonjour."*

She curtsied. *"Bonjour, m'sieur."*

Setting hat and cane on the desk, he walked forward, his thighs brushing together in a soft swish, and kissed the back of her hand. His lips were damp and warm against her skin. She pulled free, resisting the urge to wipe away the moisture.

"Madame Lattimer did not exaggerate your loveliness," he said with eagerness, like a puppy offered a bone. "We must wed right away."

Amy glanced in desperation toward the Mother Superior. "Has the ceremony already been arranged?"

A small, regretful smile of sympathy crossed the woman's face. "Monsieur Gaston and I have been discussing the details. It is my heartfelt belief that the two of you should allow time to develop a rapport before the vows are exchanged."

"*Absurdité!*" Pierre grinned from ear to ear. "We will develop this rapport on the sailing ship, *n'est ce pas?* All those weeks, alone, the two of us in our cabin. Oh, I forgive the indiscretions of your family. *C'est possible* you will have inherited the talents of your *mère.*" A shiver shook his portly frame. "*C'est merveilleux!*"

Marvelous? Amy thought not. And what did he mean about her mother? He projected himself so strongly, she could hardly think. If only he could clear his nose. During his strange and altogether unwelcome discourse, she'd counted a dozen sniffs.

An urge to cry swept over her. Not from disappointment, but from a sense of betrayal. Did Mama think Pierre Gaston a suitable mate for her only child? She hadn't seen Marguerite in five years, but her letters were loving and cheerful, always filled with lively descriptions of her travels, with nary a mention of indiscretions. Amy knew little about the world outside the convent, but surely Mama could have done better than Pierre.

Oh, what an ingrate she was, and shallow in her thinking. A husband should be honest and kind and intelligent. Perhaps of the three Pierre would be one or two, but she couldn't have bet on which ones.

Pierre reclaimed her hand and guided her to one of the chairs facing the Mother Superior's desk. Holding tight, he managed to pull his chair close and stroke her palm with his short, fat fingers.

"Papa has provided me with a jewel," he said with a boyish chuckle. "He knows how I like the women—how do you say, with the blonde hair and the blue eyes." His small eyes took in the rest of her. "The wedding must take place at once."

Amy forgot all about wishing for a lifetime of happiness, hoping instead for a few minutes in seclusion to decide what to do. Panic fluttered in her breast. She must get out of this marriage. It was a wicked thought, but it would not go away.

Someone knocked at the door, and a very solemn-faced Sister Bernadette entered with a message for the Mother Superior. Her eyes turned sorrowfully to Amy. Something was wrong, she thought, suddenly alarmed. Something besides her disastrous betrothal.

The Mother Superior glanced at the paper handed to her by the nun, then looked across her wide desk at Amy.

"My dear child, I have bad news." Her dark

eyes barely flicked to Pierre. "Perhaps you would prefer to receive it in private."

"A wife must have no secrets from her husband," said Pierre.

"Go ahead," said Amy with a helpless wave of her hand.

"It is your mother. Madame Lattimer has been struck with a sudden illness. The end came quickly. Her immortal soul now rests in the hands of God."

It took Amy a moment to translate the news. "Mama's dead? Where? In Paris? In Rome?"

The Mother Superior sighed. "No. She was at her apartment here in New Orleans."

"But she didn't have—"

"She did. It was her wish that you not be told of her residence, but of course, under the circumstances, I am relieved of my promise to her."

Stunned, Amy sat back in her chair. "I don't understand. She traveled . . . the letters . . ."

"She was a clever one, all right," said Pierre. "*Père* always said so. Throughout the world, in all of his travels, she was the favorite of his courtesans."

Marguerite Renoir Lattimer's remains were placed in a tomb at St. Louis Cemetery on a rainy October morning. The mourners were a strange lot: a host of nuns from the convent school, led by the Mother Superior; Amy, the lone family member, with an overly attentive fiancé close at her heel; and, in the background, a gathering of the wealthiest men in New Orleans.

Despite her shock, Amy could have named several of them, though none came forward to present a eulogy. More than one cast her an uncomfortably personal glance, as though already seeking a replacement for Marguerite. Why not her daughter? Naive she might be, but she knew the idea was on their minds.

In the middle of the crowd, speaking to no one, Amy stood lost and alone—more so than she'd ever been in her life—but the grief she should have expected refused to come. Instead, she felt a numbness that covered her as thoroughly as the shroud covered Mama.

The ceremony was simple and brief, and then the marble slab was laid in place before the door of the tomb; an anonymous gift, Amy was told, from an admirer. The engraving was equally simple:

Here lies
MARGUERITE RENOIR LATTIMER
deceased October 5, 1880
aged thirty-nine years.
She was a friend to man.
Passersby, please pray for her.

After the funeral one of the men—who identified himself simply as "a friend"—took her to her mother's Vieux Carré apartment, a large second-floor suite of rooms accessible through a private courtyard and secluded stairway off Royal Street. Since he'd freed her of Pierre's presence—insisting she needed to mourn in solitude—she did not question his intent.

"I suppose you will be taking up residence here," her escort said as he led her into the parlor.

She looked around at the red brocaded furniture, at the dark draperies, at the paintings of nudes on the walls. Live here, after the comfortable simplicity of her convent room? She could not answer. She could barely breathe.

He squeezed her hand, holding on longer than necessary for consolation's sake. His eyes roamed her body at will. "Marguerite said you were a child, but you are a beautiful woman, my dear. I would be proud to be your benefactor. Here is my card. You have only to ask, and I will help you all that I can."

With a bow, he departed, and Amy collapsed onto the sofa by the window. As she stared at the vulgar opulence surrounding her, shock gave way to anger, and she forgot the insolence of the man. It was an anger directed at Marguerite, a sense of betrayal that stung more than she could have imagined.

How dare her mother lie to her? She could have been at her side during her illness, could have brought her comfort. But Marguerite preferred to die alone. Because, Amy was certain, of the men who had been her "friends." A grown daughter would have gotten in her way.

Amy, innocent and ignorant, was supposed to know as little as possible, marrying and moving to France. But Marguerite had died too soon, and Amy knew everything.

Worse, she thought, thumbing the calling card, the men were prepared for a similar arrangement with her. Unlike Mama, they didn't consider her at all in the way.

Assaulted by self-pity, unable to consider anything other than her impossible situation, she threw the card aside and drummed her fingers on the sofa's crimson cushion. A righteous, burning rage filled the emptiness inside her. Was she to be a New Orleans courtesan, taking her mother's place in bed, or a bride to Pierre? Neither choice was thinkable.

If only she could remain forever within the convent walls, teaching at the school, accepting the sisters as the family she craved. Unfortunately, the archbishop had decided to employ only nuns in the classrooms. At any rate the cloister had been breached by a worldly knowledge she could not ignore. Even if the archbishop changed his mind, she knew contentment had fled.

Once again she was the hoyden of her early years, ready to jump over those high stone walls.

But not to land in the arms of Pierre.

Unable to rest or think clearly, she decided to investigate this home that had been such a secret. The aura of its late owner hung in the air like heavy perfume; it was an aura she could not identify with the Mama of five years ago. Who had her mother really been . . . the stoic who had advised her to be brave at their last goodbye . . . the loving woman of the letters . . . or the mistress of a dozen men?

Amy began in the bedroom. Her mother's wardrobe and trunk turned up an array of garments the likes of which her convent-raised daughter had never seen: shockingly sheer raiment decorated with feathers and lace, and undergarments lacking what Amy considered rather necessary parts. Little wonder her mother had caught a chill and died.

She thought the words without emotion, as a stranger might. At that moment she scarcely knew herself. In truth, it seemed she had slipped into someone else's skin.

In a bedside drawer she found a stack of letters addressed to her, each purportedly from an exotic locale. The sight of them took her breath away, coming to her as they did from the grave. She knew the route meant for them: from Mama to the Mother Superior, who supposedly received Marguerite's letters in a packet of other correspondence, and then on to her. No wonder her precious messages from afar had never carried foreign postmarks. They had come from New Orleans.

With a shaky hand she put them aside to read later and picked up a small volume that was filled with scribblings. A diary, she realized. Trying to forget her image in the overhead mirror, she settled atop the soft feather bed and began to read.

Two hours later, her cheeks stained with tears, she set the book aside, but the words she'd read burned in her heart. All bitterness, all feelings of betrayal were gone; for the first time she felt the enormity of her mother's death, the tragedy of her sacrifices, and grief for all the years they should have shared.

That she should ever have distrusted Marguerite filled her with shame, and her tears flowed freely, along with prayers for her mother's eternal peace. At last, chilled, the sadness settling into her soul, she pulled the thick satin coverlet to her chin and stared at the woebegone face in the ceiling mirror. Thank goodness for the diary. It told so much she had never known before—of her mother's early life as the pampered daughter of wealthy Creoles, of their untimely death and her schooling in the convent and, in 1857, her marriage to the dashing young gambler John Lattimer.

The description of their first days of marriage was as romantic as anything Amy had ever read. Then a daughter was born, and John began to lose at cards. When the money vanished romance died, and so did love. The war approached and John Lattimer left to make his fortune in the west, promising to send for his wife and child. He never did, and Marguerite had turned to the only kind of life that offered itself to her.

She made no excuses. *I did what I had to do. The years have not been unkind.*

Indeed, her description of them did not seem so. Amy had skimmed them, looking greedily for mentions of her name. She found them often. Her mother had loved her very much, seeing to her care, protecting her from the truth.

"Oh, Mama," Amy whispered to her tear-stained image overhead, "I would have understood."

One thing she did not understand: her father. She had been told he had died, but apparently this was another of her mother's subterfuges, conceived to protect her. When she was financially able to do so Marguerite had hired a detective to find him. He did what she asked, but she received only the one letter announcing his success, three months after he departed New Orleans for Texas. He had promised more details, but she had never heard from him again.

The letter was dated ten years ago. Had Papa moved on? Did he know anything about his wife and daughter? Did he care?

Having lived too long in ignorance, Amy experienced a searing desire to discover answers for all the questions she asked. Mama was lost to her; perhaps Papa could be found. But how? What was she to do?

Darkness came, and she was still lying on the bed. A carriage came from the convent, but she gestured at the window for the driver to leave. She had much to consider, choices that must be made.

One thought occurred to her and would not go away, one even more wicked than her decision to abandon Pierre. Mama had left her a small inheritance, enough to get far away from New Orleans. All the way to—

Lighting a bedside lamp, she found the name in the diary: Rough Cut, Texas, Papa's last known home. Maybe they needed a teacher in Rough Cut. If not, she had another profession she could follow: her mother's.

She should have shocked herself with the thought, but after all that had happened in the past few days she was beyond such an emotion. Marguerite's acquaintances certainly thought her capable of doing a satisfactory job. So did Pierre. If she were going to end up giving her body as a way to survive, in marriage or out, she would prefer that the giving be on her own terms.

Whether or not teachers were needed in Rough Cut, courtesans probably were. According to Marguerite's diary, they were in demand everywhere.

Could she really make her living in such a way? She did not know, but she *was* her mother's daughter. What was good enough for Marguerite must be good enough for her.

Besides, she thought, remembering her mother's wardrobe, she had the clothes for the profession. Always a sensible person, she really could not let them go to waste.

Amy's mind was made up, and she suppressed all nagging doubts. Bolstered by a newfound goal, she found her loneliness fading. Oh, yes, in a far more grown-up way she really was the hoyden of her childhood, the adventuress who'd climbed trees and walls. This time, though, she would make it over the top.

The first order of business would be to write Pierre a letter breaking the engagement, saying that they would not suit. Once he thought over the situation he would surely agree.

Then she would find her father, decide whether to reveal her identity, and take care of herself either by teaching or by following in her mother's footsteps. Marguerite had been a practical woman; her daughter could be the same.

Moving to the window, she stared into the night.

"Rough Cut," she whispered to the stars, "ready or not, here I come."

Chapter Three

"Goodness, I fear he's not going to earn redemption."

Watching his latest charge from on high, Dudley spoke to himself, or to whoever in the firmament might be listening, which probably wasn't anyone, busy place that it was.

With one exception, of course . . . the companion who was always with him on this difficult campaign.

Far below, Cadmus was stretched out on a bedroll beside the Devils River, head and shoulders resting against his saddle as he waited for dawn to finish its work. And what a glorious dawn it was, drifting over the limestone walls of the surrounding canyon, scattering pink light to dance on the surface of the water, bringing life and promise to a rugged land.

The West Texas desert wasn't godforsaken at all, though many called it so. Cadmus Rankin was not one to notice the beauty of nature, however, concentrating as he was at the moment on whiskey and women. Or rather, the lack thereof.

"He hasn't reformed in the least," Dudley said. "At least not in his heart, and that's where reformation has to take place."

Cadmus hadn't actually done anything wrong, but he had considered it for most of the three weeks since leaving Galveston. Dudley didn't talk to him often, choosing to appear briefly at irregular moments as a reminder of his situation. But he could read his mind, something the unfortunate soul had yet to figure out.

Poor man. He had a great deal to understand over the next few weeks. Dudley couldn't allow him any longer than that. Given the hardness of Cadmus's heart, he might not last that long before he broke too many rules.

Maybe it was time for another talk. Dudley dropped down to the riverbank, materializing at the water's edge.

Cadmus barely flicked him a glance, shifting only slightly on the bedroll.

"You're back."

"I told you I would never be far. Is something troubling you?"

"I should have been here two weeks ago. And

I would have, if you'd let me cheat at cards in San Antonio. Instead, I had to play honest . . . and sober."

"The expedient way is not always the right way."

"Yeah, I know. You already told me."

"You were the one who wanted money. I'm not sure you really need more than the necessities, which I had already provided."

Dudley hoped he didn't sound miffed, although that was his unangelic attitude at the moment.

"You never know what I'll need," Cadmus growled.

But, of course, Dudley did.

"About being a beer salesman—"

"We went over that," Cadmus said. "They won't be buying Bibles in Rough Cut. I've got enough going against me, riding in there without shooting or fighting. Give me a profession they'll understand. I got all the literature I need at the Menger Brewery in San Antonio."

"You know, of course—"

"Yeah, I know. I won't be sampling the product myself."

Dudley understood everything, but he liked to hear his charge go over the stipulations of his redemption. Such rules simply had to remain in his mind.

Cadmus stood and bundled the bedroll.

"I'll leave you to your journey," said Dudley, wishing he didn't have so many misgivings.

"You do that, Dud."

With a rueful and sadly skeptical smile, he dematerialized and drifted back to his watchpost on high, looking on as Cadmus took a quick dip in the river, shaved, and then saddled his horse. His charge thought his liaison angel came and went, tending to other mortal souls, but in truth Dudley had decided from the first that this particular mortal would need all the help he could get.

"Don't worry so much."

Dudley glanced at his companion. "I can't help it, Michael." What a dear being Michael was, a boy who would for all eternity remain fifteen. In his human form, which was the way Dudley liked to view him, he was dark like his brother, except that his hair had a touch of red he'd inherited from their mother. And he had her gentle ways, too.

Cadmus was more like the father, quick-tempered and physically tough. Both parents resided in heaven, but it was their younger son who had fought to save his brother's soul.

He kept Michael with him as an inspiration for Cadmus when his faith and determination lagged. The condition was occurring far too often the closer they got to Rough Cut, but as of yet he'd held off using the youth's presence, saving him for the difficult times ahead.

Cadmus would never be able to see Michael—that was forbidden—but he would feel his proximity, as he had in Galveston. And, Dudley knew, he would be moved.

"He'll be all right," Michael said, his gaze on his brother. "You didn't see him suffer when I died. Or maybe you did, but you didn't feel it the way I did."

Dudley had to agree. He couldn't, however, go along with the lad's confidence in his brother, try though he might. At first he'd shared Michael's hopes, but doubt had intruded outside the undertaker's parlor the day Cadmus entered his undead state, when he'd lusted after the first woman to come along. An unrepentant mortal he'd been, and so he was likely to remain for his last days on earth.

With an angelic sigh, Dudley looked down the road toward the east, toward Rough Cut, toward the site of his charge's hoped-for epiphany. A detail far out in the desert gave him pause, and for the moment he forgot the town.

"My, my," he said to himself. "Here's something I hadn't anticipated." He'd been concentrating too hard on Cadmus to see the overall picture of his redemption. The narrowness of his focus had been a mistake.

He looked solemnly at Michael, his skepticism relieved. "It's just possible that in this situation you are right and I am wrong. Whatever happens," he said, glancing once again at the distant sight, "it will be most interesting to observe."

* * *

Cad was relieved to find himself alone. For one thing, angels moved too slowly. He should have been here weeks ago. Honest, sober card-playing cramped his style.

Besides, old Dud was sounding more and more like one of those talky preachers who visited jails.

Cad hated jails, hated crowds, hated being beholden to anyone. He was a loner by choice and nature, a man who looked after himself, and here he was saddled with a chaperone. And a mission not of his choosing. A recluse, a drifter, an outlaw, he could give up liquor and women if he had to, but he hated giving up control. At the outset of this craziness, he'd planned to do what he wanted every chance he got, but the first chance had yet to appear.

Still, he had little choice but to go forward. The San Antonio–San Diego stagecoach had brought him as far as the border town of San Felipe del Rio—Del Rio for short. Within sight of the Rio Grande, he'd bought a horse for the final three-day ride.

He didn't need sleep, but since he didn't care for traveling through strange country in the dark, he'd camped beside the Devils River in a rugged ravine known as Rough Canyon on his first night out of Del Rio. A passenger on the stage had said it gave the town of Rough Cut its name.

"Don't know why you'd be going there," the man had said with a shudder. "Ain't nothing within fifty miles but scorpions and rattlers and two-legged killers looking for a fight."

Cad hadn't come up with a response, not for the passenger and not for himself.

Devils River, running clear and fast over bed-rock, provided water for the last two days of his journey. His horse, a strawberry roan he simply called Horse, was proving a worthy mount over the rugged desert hills.

The second day out of Del Rio passed with no untoward events, the morning October sun bright in his eyes as he traveled due east, and warm against his back in the afternoon. The land was harsh and forbidding, so different from the Texas he knew close to the Louisiana border, but the longer he rode, the more he liked its openness and solitude.

Gradually the hills lengthened, turning greener, almost welcoming, except for the rat-tlers and scorpions lurking beneath the rocks. Killers of the two-legged variety he saw not at all; they'd be waiting for him on down the road. He was packing both a rifle and a pistol, but they'd do him little good.

"I need them for authenticity," he'd told Dud-ley back in Del Rio. "And for the rattlers. Surely they don't have a liaison angel protecting them."

The final night of his journey he camped in a grassy valley beside a thick-leaved tarbush. The shrub's tarlike aroma perfumed the cool desert air. Cad liked the scent far better than that of smoke-filled rooms. He had a long time to enjoy it, too, going sleepless as he did, spending the dark hours remembering Galveston and the strange hallucinations about Michael and trying to understand the magnitude of his undead state, gradually forgetting all his sacrifices and thinking instead of what he was supposed to do. He'd never been one for reflection, but in the night he could engage in little else.

Strange it was that he found himself out here seeking salvation and a long and happy life. Or so Dud had promised. Cad had never cared about such things. Temporary pleasure was about all he'd sought. That, and being left alone.

He'd made a big deal about giving up alcohol, but the truth was he could take it or leave it. Wanting it too much—wanting anything, whether it be women or beer—called for passion, for caring. He'd left such feelings in the fetid bog of the Atchafalaya Swamp.

Such morbid musings were burned away by the sun, making the daylight hours pass more easily. Cad, the temporary man, could accept his strange situation, if not exactly understand it. On the last afternoon of the ride he was enjoying the peace of the countryside, not having to think about robbing or thieving or watching his double-crossing partner Rick Marsh, when suddenly a big round rock came from nowhere, landing directly in his path. Horse reared, pawing the air and snorting like he'd seen a hellhound. It took Cad a minute to get him under control.

Another rock fell. This time Horse wasn't so skittish, but Cad was. Habit sent his hand to the holstered gun. His eyes darted to the only place the rock could have come from, a roadside hackberry rising thirty feet above the surrounding sage and mesquite.

"Anybody home?" he yelled, feeling foolish talking to a bunch of leaves.

"Depends," a sweet voice called back from the high branches. "Are you friend or foe?"

Goddamn. Oops, gosh darn. What the heck was a woman doing out here in the middle of nowhere, perched on a limb like a mockingbird? Whoever she was, she packed a powerful arm.

He guided the roan a half dozen yards to the base of the tree, thinking all the time that nothing after Galveston ought to surprise him.

"Don't get too close," the woman said. "I've got more rocks."

"You've got me shaking in my boots, honey."

His eyes trailed up the hackberry's trunk, through the thick dark-green leaves, to a branch almost at the crown. He stopped at the sight of a well-turned ankle above a tightly laced boot. The ankle curved into a calf, then got lost in a swirl of white petticoat.

He tipped his hat to the leg. "Good afternoon, friend. Would it be too bold of me to ask why you're chucking rocks at my horse?"

"I wanted to get your attention."

Cad stared at the ankle. "You've got it."

"I picked you because you're the first person who's ridden by since yesterday who looks halfway civilized."

Unconsciously he brushed at the lapel of his black gabardine suit, all the while thinking that bathing and shaving had finally paid off. Or maybe it just looked like it had. Mustn't jump to conclusions based on a well-turned calf. Besides, he reminded himself, all he could do was look.

"You've been up there two days?" he asked, wondering why he hadn't passed her on the trail, then remembering he'd traveled cross-country a spell to pick up some time.

"More like twenty-four hours. I come down every now and then to . . . well, never mind. But my water jug's almost empty and I've been out of food since early this morning. I knew to travel with supplies, but I didn't bring enough."

Cad thumbed back his hat and scratched his head.

"If you think you're explaining things, little lady, think again."

"It's kind of complicated, and—"

She broke off with a sigh. "To tell you the truth, my arms are tired from holding on up here."

"My neck's getting a crick too. Come on down. I promise not to harm you."

And he meant it too. Women usually invited all the fooling around he wanted without his suggesting a thing.

All was silent for a moment. Then a second ankle appeared, and some more petticoat and skirt, gray shiny material he took to be silk. Expensive duds to wear for tree climbing. Hell—heck, that was a piss-poor consideration, given the circumstances.

He'd have to ask Dud if *piss-poor* was profane or not. Heck, he had to say something.

He forgot all about cussing when he saw through the branches a tiny little waist and a pair of tits just crying out for some stroking. The leaves in the trees shifted with the woman's descent, but no more than his private parts.

He got off the horse to help her to the ground, looping the reins over a low limb, straightening his suit coat as if he was some kind of lover waiting for his intended.

"I can do it myself," she said, reaching the last branch, but when she tried to swing free she fell hard against him. Caught unawares, his mind where it shouldn't be, he fell backwards, landing on the hard ground, his shapely tree bird stretched out on top of him.

He felt no pain from the rocks beneath him, but he sure felt the softness on top.

He looked up into a pair of blue eyes the color of the sky. They were accompanied by thick black lashes, a pert nose, and sun-yellow hair. Dudley had lied about his condition; he'd died and gone to heaven, and this was his reward.

Maybe old Dud had sent her down as a sort of incentive to do as he was supposed to. No.

More than likely she was just another temptation thrown in his path as a test.

If so, she was a potent temptation indeed. Lying beneath her like this was better than lying under a tarbush, her lavender scent being sweeter than tar.

She blinked. "I'm sorry." She tried to pull away.

Cad's arms encircled her, his hands feeling the curve of waist and itching to move on down. She'd have a nice backside; he could tell from the quality of her front.

"Just wait a minute," he said, giving in to weakness. "We need to catch our breath."

Her eyes narrowed. "No, we don't. I may seem crazy to you, but I'm not a fool."

She scrambled to her feet, hands brushing at her wrinkled dress then working to arrange the fallen curls that must once have made up a fancy coiffure.

She was taller than most women, and slender without sacrificing any curves, and her arms were long, like her legs. She reached to the ground and came up with another rock. Like she'd said, she was nobody's fool.

"This is the only weapon I've got, but I can take out an eye if I have to."

Cad stared at her breasts. She was armed more than she knew. Lordy, he thought, looking was torture, but it was sure better than staring at Horse's ears.

He held up his hands in surrender.

"You got the drop on me, miss."

"Don't be patronizing. You could shoot me if you like, or far worse. But you promised not to harm me and I believe you. Besides, if I spent another night in that tree, I'd probably just expire on my own. I don't know why people say there's no life in the desert. I heard rustling and cat cries and I don't know what else every minute it was dark."

For just a second she glanced past him at a stretch of rolling land that went on forever. Cad caught a lost look in her eyes, and a hint of fear she was trying hard to control. The look came and went so fast, he could have blinked and missed it.

Scooping up his hat, he slapped it against his thigh and dropped it on the back of his head. She was watching every move he made, looking cautious and interested at the same time. It made for a nice combination. It was clear she was a respectable woman, though not the least prune-faced.

And not nearly so confident as she was pretending to be. If she had any idea what she did to a man, she would be scurrying back up that tree.

"I've got some vittles in my pack, and some water. Why don't we pick us out a patch of shade and eat?"

A timid smile broke out on her face; it was like a chorus bursting into song.

Warning bells went off in Cad's head. She was

trouble, fragile and tough at the same time, and more than likely a little deranged; otherwise she wouldn't be here. Whoever she was and wherever she was going, she would get in his way. If he had any sense, he'd toss her back in the hackberry and light out alone.

Instead, being a little deranged himself since Galveston, he went for the food, which he carried more out of habit than hunger. They settled in a crop of shady grass beneath the tree, her skirt billowing up around her as she wolfed down most everything he'd brought. Cad took off his coat and string tie, rolled up his sleeves, and watched, taking an occasional swallow of water to keep her from getting suspicious.

A pink tongue caught a bread crumb at the corner of her mouth. Cad had considered catching it for her, but figured either she or Dudley would object.

"I hadn't climbed a tree since I was a little girl. Funny how things like that come back to you."

Cad leaned back on one elbow and did the only thing he could: He kept on looking at her. "Is that why you climbed this one? To see if you still knew how?"

She giggled. It was a very feminine sound, and Cad groaned. She was Trouble, all right, with a capital *T*.

"I made it all the way from New Orleans to that border town just south of here without any problems. At least nothing I couldn't handle."

For a woman alone she was speaking brave

words, but it was possible she was trying to convince herself as well as him. Before he could ask her which one it was, she hurried on.

"The trouble started when I had to hire someone to take me to Rough Cut. I picked the wrong man. We had a little disagreement, you might say, about how I should pay him for the wagon ride, and I ended up walking."

Cad sat up, the warning bells clanging louder than ever, and he forgot all problems other than his own. "You're going to Rough Cut?"

She looked him straight in the eye. "I heard they needed teachers there."

She was lying. Cad had done it often enough himself to know.

"They need teachers in Rough Cut?" he said.

"Right."

"Where did you hear that?"

"Around. I don't remember exactly where."

"What if you heard wrong?"

She swallowed. He liked the play in her throat. He liked, too, how the gray silk lay against her body, shimmering over the valleys and peaks. He might not be alive, but he wasn't nearly dead enough not to notice.

He did not, however, care for being taken for a fool.

"If the schools are adequately staffed," she said, "I have alternate plans."

He tried to think of what they might be. Snaring a husband came to mind, but even considering her equipment it was an iffy prospect.

Besides, why look for a groom in Rough Cut? She could have had her pick of half the men in San Antonio.

Another idea came to mind. There was one profession outside of marriage a woman might follow in the wild west, far out where family and friends—if she had them—would never know.

He studied her again. No way. One of his finely honed traits was recognizing experienced women. His mystery companion was a virgin through and through.

"This man," she said, her pert nose wrinkling, "claimed he was the sheriff, but he was so drunk I don't see how he could be. Anyway, he didn't seem too encouraging about the school situation. He did mention another business that might hire me: Kate Cassidy's Pleasure Parlor. It's right on the main street."

Cad stroked his whiskery chin and considered the growing possibility that she was more deranged than he was. She didn't look it, but where a pretty woman was concerned a man could be fooled.

"You got any idea what kind of place this pleasure parlor might be?" he asked.

"Oh, yes, Mister—"

"Rankin. Cad Rankin. And you are—"

"Amabelle Latourre."

Another lie, he figured. She didn't say the fancy name like she'd toted it all her life.

"Anyway," she went on, "I've already told you

I'm not a fool. If no one will hire me as a teacher, then I'll just have to take up business as a courtesan."

Amy waited for his reaction. This playing innocent and ignorant was getting old, but for all his good looks, Mr. Rankin didn't seem overly bright.

He certainly did have the looks, though . . . hair and eyes the color of hackberry bark; leathery, bristle-shadowed skin with fine lines at the edges of his eyes; strong, even features with a chin maybe a little too firm; and a long, lean body that had felt hard as rock when she landed against him. The falling had not been entirely an accident. She'd wanted to knock him off his feet and grab another rock before he could go for his gun.

Heavens, she'd scrambled up and down that tree a dozen times since yesterday. He should have been on his guard.

Right now he was regarding her like something that had drifted down from the moon. He really did have unsettling eyes. They reminded her of the way his hands had rested on her body; they turned her jumpy inside.

She studied the folds of her skirt. Had she thrown her rocks at the right man? She'd been so frightened up that tree, and hungry and cold, wishing she hadn't left her cloak in her trunk, that he'd looked like a welcome rescuer riding by.

Civilized was what she'd called him, but from a distance he had looked harmless. Up close, his harmlessness was hard to detect.

"Are you talking about being a whore?" he said.

She flinched. "If you insist upon calling it that."

"Most men would. You had much experience along that line?"

Amy stirred restlessly. "In a way." *I've read my mother's diary.*

"So why did you take objection to the sheriff's suggestion?"

"He was drunk and he smelled. I have my standards, Mr. Rankin. Would you bed a beer-soaked woman who hadn't bathed in days?"

He grinned. Her heart turned flip-flops.

"I may have done it once or twice. In my younger days."

"I suppose that's the difference between men and women."

His lips twitched. "One of 'em," he said, taking a long, lazy time to look her over.

Amy was finding it hard to breathe. She turned her attention to a turkey vulture circling overhead. Somehow the sight was less unsettling than Cad Rankin's scrutiny.

"He took all my belongings into town. He said they would be waiting for me if I decided to claim them. I don't believe he expected to return them for free."

"I don't expect he did."

Amy tried to get control of herself. The longer she sat beside Cad Rankin, the more flustered she became, talking too much, thinking that for a not-so-bright stranger, he had a way of confusing her thoughts. She hadn't been half so bothered by the men of New Orleans.

He wasn't harmless at all. From the start she'd known he wasn't exactly an intellectual, but there was something about him, a wily wariness, that said she shouldn't judge him too soon. And, of course, there was also the power of his looks.

How much easier it would be in this harsh and desolate country if she were a man. From her observations, men never felt scared and alone.

But enough self-pity, that maudlin feeling that weakened her whenever she thought too much. She stood. "Is there any way you can take me into town? I'll pay you. In cash."

He pulled his long, lean body up beside hers, moving more gracefully than a man had any right to.

"No need. I'm a civilized man, remember? If that's where you're headed, then I'll go there, too. Horse here can ride double. You don't look too heavy for him."

From the way he was studying her, he ought to be able to guess her weight within two pounds.

"I'm crazy to do this," he added, "but I suppose you're just another part of the challenge."

"What are you talking about?"

He shrugged. "Nothing. Don't pay me any mind, Miss Latourre. Out in the desert, a man's likely to say most anything."

Easing into his coat and thrusting the tie in a pocket, he mounted, then pulled her up in front of him without the least sign of effort. She ended up sitting across his legs, her feet dangling to the side, her hands fluttering from the saddle horn to her skirt to his very solid arm. She'd never sat in a man's lap before, but that was basically what she was doing now.

She tried to ignore him, to concentrate on the land, to remember how much she missed the lush, humid country that had always been her home. At the moment he rode into view along that winding desert trail, she'd been thinking how much she would give to be in a dark, murky swamp.

But she was a woman who'd been raised in a convent, her companions nuns and orphans, the only men a few kindly—and elderly—priests. And here she was, her backside resting on a pair of very solid and very male thighs. It was one thing to imagine being a courtesan and something else to count the bristles on Cad Rankin's lean cheeks. He hardly seemed a member of the same species as Pierre.

Amy sighed. At the moment her dream swamp seemed an eternity away.

Could she really follow through on her courtesan plans? She'd been thinking that no matter who she entertained—a term Mama seemed to favor in the diary—she could keep her true inner self apart. Marguerite wrote that she had done just that before she was able to choose her own clientele. What worked for Mama ought to work for her.

In a way she was doing this *for* her mother; carrying on the search for Papa that she had begun long ago.

She'd been so sure of herself and her cause, but such was no longer true. First there had been the boorish sheriff. And then she'd met Cad, for all his smoother ways a man she suspected could live up to his name.

They rode along for a quarter of an hour, each lost in separate thoughts, when suddenly a shot rang out and she found herself falling to the ground, Cad wrapped around her like a blanket. They landed hard, and the breath went out of her.

"Keep still," he warned. She did what he said, lying on her side, scrunched into the protection of his body, staring up at his dark eyes scouring the countryside. The horse had galloped on down the trail; it was just the two of them . . . and whoever had fired the shot.

When he drew his gun her eyes settled on the bullet hole in his sleeve and she pushed aside her own personal terror and the sting of the fall. He'd been shot, poor brave man. Without thinking, her heart pounding, she touched the wound. He didn't flinch or seem to notice, and for just an instant she entertained a foolish thought.

If he were wounded, why wasn't there any blood?

Chapter Four

Cad studied the surrounding hills, guessing where the gunman might be hiding. Having been shot at a time or two in his thirty-one years, he knew the likely places to look. Thinking Dudley wouldn't mind his shooting *back* at someone to protect a woman, he hoped the bastard was within pistol range.

He searched the hills in vain. Except for the roan grazing a few yards to the west, in line with the afternoon sun, all was still across the rolling, rocky ground. Other than a few restless birds, all was quiet in the clumps of scattered brush.

A warm, soft body stirred against him.

He stared at Amabelle Latourre, her face so close to his that he could see the faint sprinkle of freckles on the ridge of her cheeks. So close he could tell every place where her body touched his.

"Don't do that."

"Do what?" she asked in a shaky voice.

"Move." In the mood he was in, if she asked why, he'd tell her that whatever was undead about him, it wasn't the equipment between his legs.

"I'm sorry," she whispered. "I've got a cramp."

"Yeah. So do I." And, as an afterthought, "You all right?"

She nodded, but he could see the fright in her eyes.

Letting her go, he risked sitting up; only it wasn't much of a risk, he reminded himself, since he couldn't be hurt. If it hadn't been for the woman—and if he'd been thinking clearly—he could have ridden right into the firing.

"Be careful," she warned.

He didn't bother to answer, waiting instead for another shot that didn't come.

"Have they gone?" she asked.

"Looks like it." If, that is, they'd been gunning for him, or maybe they were just being ornery, stirring up trouble on a quiet day. It was possible, however, that whoever was out there was waiting for a better shot at the fair Miss Latourre, self-proclaimed teacher and whore.

Who was she really, and why was she here? He eyed her with a new suspicion, cursing himself for abandoning his cautious ways and taking her at her word.

She looked innocent enough, her blue eyes darkened with fear and her yellow hair half falling down and her full lips trembling. But women could be as conniving as men, and a hell of a lot sneakier.

"Anyone know where you are?" he asked.

She shook her head.

"And if they did, any chance they'd be gunning for you?"

"Of course not," she snapped, the fear turning to indignation. "What do you think I am? A fugitive from justice? Why, I'm no more an outlaw than you."

Cad didn't find much comfort in that declaration, but he let it go with a shrug. Instinct told him that whoever had fired the shot was long gone, anyway. Which didn't, of course, mean she hadn't been the primary target. It only indicated that for the time being they were safe.

Sitting up beside him, she touched his sleeve. "You've been hurt."

He stared in surprise at the hole in his coat. By damn, he'd been shot and didn't feel a thing. It was the first real test of old Dud's promise—at least the first since the angel had rescued him from the undertaker's knife. Not needing to eat or drink or sleep was all well and good, but taking a hit this way was something else entirely.

Cad felt proud, as though he'd done something brave and strong instead of getting in the way of a shooter's bullet.

Speaking of the bullet, where was it anyway? Must have bounced off him and fallen to the ground.

He shrugged against Amabelle's scrutiny. "It's nothing."

"That's not true." She grabbed his lapels, like she was planning to undress him.

She had long, supple fingers, surprisingly strong for such a slender woman, and a determined glint in her eye. Cad's mind worked fast. "It's an old hole."

Her eyes narrowed. "Doesn't look it. Besides, I didn't notice it before, and I looked you over carefully."

"Liked what you saw?"

Her cheeks turned pink, and he couldn't see the freckles anymore.

"I was trying to decide if you were an honorable man," she said, scooting backwards until they no longer touched.

"I'm not." He tossed his gun aside and shrugged out of his coat.

"What are you doing?" she asked, sliding further away.

"Showing you I'm not injured."

And maybe showing her just how *dis*honorable he could be. Throw a little scare into her so she wouldn't be so brazen. Teach her she needed to stay out of his way.

He tugged his shirt free of his trousers.

"I believe you," she said in a small voice, but

she didn't say it very loud and she didn't look away from his hands.

He unfastened the buttons all the way down. His shirtfront fell open. She stared at his hairy chest.

He eased the shirt back over his shoulders, hurrying so she wouldn't see the bullet hole in the sleeve. The day was warm for late October, practically like summer, and he took the shirt off, letting the sun warm him to his bones.

He flexed the muscles in his arm where the flesh ought to be torn.

"No blood. No wound," he said. "Satisfied?"

At last her eyes moved to his. "I—"

He leaned close so that his hot skin touched the cool silk of her gown, his chest brushing against hers. She shifted to an angle; he followed, propping his hands on either side of her.

She fell on her elbows. "Ouch," she said. She was practically lying down now, underneath him, which he figured was the best place she could be.

"You hurt?" he said, concentrating on her parted lips, full and rosy. When her tongue flicked out for a second, then disappeared, he almost moved in to suck it out again.

"Maybe we ought to get you undressed like me and find out how serious it is."

Her eyes were concentrating on his bare shoulders and arms and his naked chest.

"Goodness," she said.

"Oh, it'll be good, all right," he said, bothered

with a heat that had nothing to do with the sun, and feeling sure of himself, the way he always did around women.

Bawdy women, that is. Whatever Amabelle Latourre was, it wasn't bawdy, no matter that he'd found her alone in the wild, and no matter her declared ambition to be a whore.

His suspicions of her returned like thunder. He wasn't so far gone he'd lost all sense of self-preservation. When the rattle sounded just past her head he scooped up the gun an arm's length away and fired, all in one motion, taking no more than a second to blast off the snake's head.

She screamed and buried herself against him, the high pitch of her cry blending with the roar of the gunshot. He pulled her to her feet, the two of them standing there holding on to one another, Cad with a smoking gun in one hand and a soft shoulder in the other, as he stared down at the bloodied mess spread against the hard dirt.

He hated snakes, feared them as he feared no man. For a moment he wasn't in the desert but in a dank, dark swamp, trapped by thick cypress and ghostly Spanish moss, breathing in the stink of rotted vegetation and primal bogs, listening to the hiss and slither of a hundred water moccasins and the agony in Michael's screams.

The woman's slap brought him back to the desert. He shoved her away and shook his head to clear the ringing in his ears. What in the hell had sent him back in time? He was hallucinating again, that was all, for which he blamed Dudley. And Amabelle Latourre.

"What the hell you do that for?" he growled, not caring that he was cussing.

She rubbed at her shoulder. "Because you were hurting me. Why did you fire the gun? To scare me out of my wits? Didn't you know I was barely controlling myself already? I'm so close to crying right now, I almost can't hold back the tears, and crying is the last thing I want to do."

Cad stared at her for a moment and tried to figure her out. Helpless as a kitten one minute and bold as a wildcat the next, stranded in the middle of nowhere, claiming to be a whore but putting out the signals of a lady, though not the kind he'd ever met before. True, he didn't know much about ladies, but he knew something about women. At least he used to.

Amabelle Latourre, teacher and courtesan, had more complications about her than a dozen stagecoach holdups. For a minute there he might have wanted her, but he didn't need her, and he damned sure better not want her again.

He holstered the pistol and reached for his shirt. "If you're afraid of me, lady, you sure have a strange way of showing it."

Her chin tilted, and he would have thought she was losing her fear if he hadn't seen the quiver return to her lips.

"I was trying to decide what made you different."

For a moment he thought she'd figured him out.

"From the sheriff, I mean," she explained.

"Well, I'm stone cold sober, more's the pity, and I took a bath two days ago."

She brushed the dust from her skirt. "That's not what I meant." She turned from him, trying to pin up her fallen curls and looking, in truth, just the least bit bawdy. And sexy as all get out. She was muttering something about men and New Orleans and he could have sworn he heard the word *convent* whispered a time or two.

Even something about a father, but he wasn't sure.

Then she saw the scattered carcass of the snake.

"Oh," she said. She kept on staring at the mess, as if she could have looked at it forever.

At last her gaze moved to him. "That's why you fired the gun. I . . . didn't know." She bit her lower lip. "And I slapped you. Can you ever forgive me?"

Cad couldn't bring himself to say the hard words on his tongue. Something about her held him back. "Sure," he said, forgetting for the moment that he'd been about to rub his hands over her silk-covered breasts and try to lift her skirts. Instead, he felt noble, having saved her twice—once from her hideout in the hackberry and now from a rattlesnake.

He wasn't used to feeling noble. He wasn't sure he liked it—not half so much as being horny—but it was the way things were.

Then he remembered Dudley, who was no doubt watching and listening.

This redemption business was hard as heck on a man. Irritation took the place of nobility. He turned and stepped away.

"Where are you going?"

"To take a leak. You want to watch? Maybe study me some more?"

The chin went up again, and he wondered whether she got cricks in her neck. "You don't have to be crude."

"Oh, yes I do," he said, thinking that if he was to hold on to anything of himself, crudity was his handiest weapon, and the least likely to get him in trouble. "You need some privacy, best find you another bush. Just watch out for snakes."

Behind a clump of scrub oak he took care of business, pissing because of the water he'd drunk, then tucking in his shirt, smoothing his hair, making himself presentable for the ride into Rough Cut. He was a respectable businessman, after all, a purveyor of beer and ale.

"You enjoying yourself, Dud?" he asked as he was working.

"Not especially," came a disembodied voice.

"Well, neither am I."

"That is not the impression you have left."

"You mean when I had her down on the ground? I was testing you, finding out how far you'd let me go."

"Haven't I mentioned the stricture against lying?"

"Don't change the subject. Why didn't you cough? I've come to expect it when I don't do as I'm told."

"You are not a child, Cadmus. From now on you must make judgments on your own. If they are right, you will benefit. If not . . . well, I've adequately explained your fate."

"Yeah: eternal damnation."

"The loss of a rich, long life filled with love and happiness is more what I had in mind."

"You're talking a language I don't understand."

"I know. It is my deepest wish, and that of Michael, that you learn the true meaning of love."

Cad stared at the empty air, all the argument gone out of him. He didn't like being reminded of his brother, didn't like having the old hurts stirred up over and over, but his liaison angel didn't seem concerned about what his latest victim liked.

Leaving the brush, he grabbed his coat and snapped it in the air, removing as much dust and debris as he could from the black gabardine. His hat was in no better shape; he settled it low on his brow and looked at his unwanted charge.

"Do you often talk to yourself?" she asked, hands on her hips, looking for all the world as if she was the one in control.

"When I want a sensible conversation I do."

He whistled for the horse, which to his surprise came at a trot. It was nice, he decided, to be obeyed for a change.

He mounted, then pulled Amabelle up in front of him. He didn't look at her, though, instead keeping his eyes on the winding trail before them. Trying to ignore the body resting against him, he thought of Rough Cut and its thieving, rotten inhabitants. Until recently he'd been like them, and contented to be so. Truth to tell, he still was, and old Dud knew it. That was why he kept giving him warnings and bringing up the past.

More than anything, Cad wished he could take a long draw on the unopened whiskey bottle he had stashed in his bedroll. Temporary pleasure though it was, it might help him forget his circumstances, including the presence of Miss Latourre—or whoever the heck she really was.

"I'm leaving you at Kate Cassidy's Pleasure Parlor," he growled. "After that, lady, you're on your own."

Kate Cassidy's Pleasure Parlor. Amy fought a sigh. It sounded fancy enough, if she thought about the *parlor* and forgot the *pleasure* part. And Kate Cassidy was a pretty name. True, the only Irish she knew about in New Orleans lived in a squalid section of town across Canal Street, but a few of the women had worked for brief periods of time in the convent and had been tireless, cheerful sorts.

Now was not the moment to be fainthearted, she told herself, and she conjured up quarters somewhere between her modest convent bedroom and her mother's brocaded apartment. Too, she reminded herself, she was here on a mission. Her personal safety and comfort should be of no concern.

What she tried to forget was the man who was taking her to her chosen destination. She'd made a fool of herself, telling him she was experienced, then scrambling away from him like a demented fool. But the sight of his muscled chest had completely unnerved her; her fingers had burned from wanting to trace the sinewed contours, to explore every inch of his manly torso. Not for enjoyment, of course; the tightness in her stomach hadn't been enjoyable in the least, no more than the strange warmth between her legs.

At least not what she defined as enjoyment, which under normal circumstances included things like a cool spring breeze and a good book, and all the pralines she could eat.

No, the sight of Cad Rankin's naked body was far from a comfort. She hoped she never saw it again. Even as she thought it, Amy chastised herself. She was supposed to like men, not fear them. She was at least supposed to pretend to like them, in the way her mother had described.

But pretending meant she was in control of

her thoughts, and ever since he'd first pulled her up to sit on his lap her mind had been befogged. When she should have been planning her arrival in Rough Cut and deciding how to meet John Lattimer, she'd been thinking wicked thoughts about wicked things . . . like Cad Rankin's hard, spread thighs.

And then when he did make overtures she'd wanted to run like a rabbit instead of finding out more about this thing between men and women. Didn't she need to be prepared? Wouldn't stroking the tight skin across his shoulders have helped her out?

Amy sighed. Fool described her well indeed.

Ordinarily she was a good girl, possessed of a charitable heart, but she hadn't even thanked him for his rescue, nor for saving her from two brushes with death. Three, really: starvation in a tree, a gunman, and a rattlesnake. He seemed to bring out all the worst in her. Somehow she'd have to show him she was grateful for his help; just how, she didn't know.

Like make him her first customer? Like letting him put his hands on her and undress her the way he'd suggested, and sleep with her all night long?

She shuddered at the thought, but it wasn't a shudder of repulsion, no matter how much she wished it were. *Au contraire,* as her ersatz fiancé Pierre might have said. For just a moment she contemplated isolation in a ship's cabin with Cad Rankin, all the way from New Orleans to a port in France. What would he do to her? What would she do to him?

Amy dabbed at the perspiration on her upper lip, her eyes on the strong tanned hands at the reins. He fascinated and frightened her, all at the same time. But those weren't the only effects he had on her, she realized with surprise. Since she'd been with him, she hadn't felt lost and alone.

Who was this Cad Rankin? Sun-kissed and hard-bodied and sharply hewn, he wasn't at all like the men she'd peered down on from the top of the Ursuline Convent wall. When she was young that wall was where her education on the opposite sex had begun. It had extended to Pierre and her mother's friends and now all the way to Cad. She saw she had a lot to learn.

This courtesan business was far more difficult than she'd realized from Mama's diary, and she hadn't even gotten into town. She couldn't decide if she wanted the men of Rough Cut to be like the sheriff or like Cad. Repulsive or strangely appealing, either type had its dangers for a girl trying to make her own way in the world.

Despite their contrasting outsides, at heart they weren't all that different, she told herself, both of them being men and therefore lustful; according to the diary, all men were so, and her personal experience was bearing that out.

One was just a little leaner and a lot cleaner than the other. After all, he'd bathed in the last two days. When compared to the men she'd been around on the crowded stagecoaches he was as pristine as a nun's new wimple.

He was sober, too, although, remembering a thirsty look about him, she wondered how long that would last.

All right, so he brought her comfort. But not very long ago so had thoughts of marriage and living in France.

Trying to ignore him as best she could, she studied the endless land, one hill leading to another, turning greener the longer they rode. Off to the left, the horizon was pink and gold and purple, offering the prettiest sunset she'd ever seen. This time of day the desert seemed restful; she'd noticed it even from the tree.

So much land, she thought, so much open space. She felt lost in its vastness, alone despite the strong body behind her. Contrary creature that she could be, she also felt exhilarated. For the first time in her life she was truly on her own. Without walls. Without rules, except those she chose to recognize. It didn't make much sense to be beset by such conflicting emotions, but that was the way things were.

Exhilaration, she soon found, could be an enervating state. Weary from two days without much sleep, she dozed against the solid strength of Cad.

In the twilight, with a hawk circling overhead, they topped a hill and he reined to a halt, stirring her to wakefulness. She stared into her rescuer's eyes. Their lips were almost touching; she had only to shift ever so slightly and she'd be getting her first kiss.

In her dreamy state she couldn't speak, couldn't breathe, couldn't even manage to be unnerved. She just kept staring into his bark-brown eyes, welcoming danger, waiting for him to make the first move. She needed to start with a man sometime. Why not here and now?

His lips parted and all her insides tingled in response, her stomach tight and jittery, her hands clinging to his coat for dear life. Was that a shudder that raced through him? She hoped so.

"We're almost there," he said, his voice thicker than she remembered it.

It was a definite dismissal. Embarrassed, disappointed, hoping beyond reason that he hadn't seen her weakness, she eased her grip on his coat. She must have grown overconfident in New Orleans, too sure of her charms. She wouldn't make that mistake again.

"Good," she said too brightly, turning her head so he wouldn't read anything in her eyes.

That was when she got her first look at Rough Cut. Her heart sank, and she forgot all else but the sight stretching out in the valley below them. A row of ramshackle buildings on either side of a rutted road, smoke coming from the chimneys as though it couldn't wait to escape, a few horses tied to front posts, a couple of wagons jouncing through the ruts. Nothing pretty or painted or in the least bit inviting. Nothing that brought the word *parlor* to mind.

Off the main road a half dozen squat adobe houses sat in gloomy squalor, so dark it was as though they didn't hold a single kerosene lamp, much less a living, breathing, civilized human being.

Was John Lattimer ensconced in one of those dreadful places? He'd left a loving wife and daughter and the lush beauty of New Orleans for *this*?

"It all looks so . . . bare," she said, wishing for a single window box of flowers to break the desolation.

"It's what I expected."

"Then why are you here?" she asked, surprised the question hadn't occurred to her before. "Surely it's not just to deliver me."

"I'm a salesman. Beer and ale. I imagine Rough Cut has a few saloons."

Why she didn't believe him she didn't know. But then, he probably didn't believe her story about seeking employment as a teacher. Or as a courtesan. Probably still suspected that whoever had fired the shot back on the road had been firing at her.

It was just as well he hadn't wanted to kiss her, since they didn't know each other at all.

He flicked the reins against the horse's flanks and started their final descent. An apt direction, she thought, dark forebodings overtaking her, overpowering her exhilaration of a short while ago.

In more than just a biblical sense, they were riding into hell.

Chapter Five

Cad guided the roan slowly down the narrow road toward Rough Cut, each step rocking his passenger's rounded bottom against his private parts. Torture, pure torture. He should have left her up that tree.

Back on the hilltop he'd almost lost control and given her the kiss she was asking for. It would have been a good one, with tongue and hands getting involved. She'd looked so innocent and eager when she awakened, his body had hardened like one of the rocks she liked to throw. A quarter hour later it was still hard.

Temptation was supposed to make him strong, was it? And he wasn't supposed to feel pain. Wrong on both counts. He'd tell old Dud the truth of matters when next they met.

Did she know what she did to him? Possibly. She was holding herself as stiff and still as she could manage, but the movements of Horse undid her best efforts.

The roan stumbled, throwing her solidly against him. "Put your arms around me," he said, submitting to the inevitable, "and hold on tight. With night coming on it's hard to see the path."

She did as she was told, adding the pleasure and the pain of her breasts rubbing against him with each jounce. It took all his self-control to keep his hands on the reins.

Under a gray-blue twilight sky, with the early stars poking like small candles through a layer of thin, drifting clouds, he got his first up-close look at the notorious desert hamlet that he was supposed to make safe for decent folk. As they rode slowly down the lone street, there wasn't much to see. Except for an occasional drunk stumbling down the way, and a few horses tied to posts, the street was deserted.

He counted no more than two dozen buildings in all, including a livery stable, a hotel, and, at the north end of town, an adobe building that labeled itself BANK. He picked out only one saloon, big and crowded and noisy, its yellow light spilling onto the deep, dark ruts outside. Over the swinging doors hung a crudely painted sign—THE INSIDE STRAIGHT. The scene had the effect of a cold shower on him; at last his body relaxed.

Cad didn't like towns of any size. Except for poker and bank robbing, he couldn't see any purpose to them. He especially didn't like Rough Cut, and not because of his mission. It had the smell of rot to it, of decay at its roots, like a town born to be bad. Give him the open road anytime, and a lone hideout in the woods.

He spared a glance at Amabelle. Most of what he'd been thinking was reflected in her eyes. Close to panic, she gazed from one side of the street to the other, her lips squeezed tight.

Panic showed she wasn't stupid; but then, being here without anyone dragging her said maybe she was. As much a puzzle as ever, she wasn't his problem, he reminded himself, although the thought brought surprisingly little comfort.

He allowed himself a private moment of cussing, and then, true to his word, he took her to the pleasure parlor door. Sitting next to the saloon and facing the Rough Cut Hotel, the place wasn't much to look at—two stories with dimly lit windows opened to the street, a clapboard front with the name of the establishment painted at a slant over the closed portal, not so much as a walkway or overhang to offer shelter from the elements.

It was, in short, little better than any other place in town, for all its fancy name. It did, however, have curtains at the windows, a detail Amabelle mentioned after he'd set her down in one of the deep trenches close to the door. He didn't bother to dismount, choosing instead to keep as much distance between them as he could. She'd felt light as air and soft and rustly in her high-necked silk as he lowered her to the ground. Helpless, too, like a kitten abandoned by the road.

But she wasn't his kitten, or his responsibility. He would be better off if he never saw her again.

From the looks of the one-street town, however, that would be impossible if clearing up Rough Cut took more than a day. Which seemed likely, since he hadn't yet worked out a plan.

She glanced up and down the street, squinting into the gathering dark.

"I wonder where the sheriff's office is," she said, with only the trace of a quaver in her voice.

"Looking to get started right away?" he asked, irritated at himself for being irritated with her. She had a right to live her life as she saw fit.

Another thought occurred to him. As part of the deal with Dudley, was he supposed to make whores give up their livelihood? If so, he'd get more resistance from the men than he could handle, liaison angel or no.

Amabelle shot him a blue, icy stare.

"I was thinking of my belongings. I'd like to get them as soon as I can."

A drunk staggered through the swinging door of the neighboring saloon and stumbled in the uneven street, managing after much effort to right himself.

Cad flicked an idle glance in his direction. A snot-nosed kid, he thought in disgust, shirttail dragging, cheeks fuzzy, a rank odor somewhere between an outhouse and a moonshiner's still rising from him and fouling the evening air.

In his staggering, he caught sight of Amabelle. "Hot damn," he said through a snaggle-toothed smile, "we got us some fresh meat."

Cad glanced at her, expecting to see revulsion and fear on her face. Instead, he saw the same disgust he was feeling.

"Don't be ridiculous," she said, speaking up boldly like she had good sense. "You're just a child. And a very dirty one at that."

The boy hiccoughed. "I'm man enough." He hiked up his britches. "Why don't you just lick me clean?"

He shifted his dusty boots in her direction. She glanced around the street. Searching for rocks, probably. Found one, too, from the looks of it as she scooped up something close to her feet.

"Don't come any closer," she said, "or I'll have to hurt you."

The would-be lover giggled. "I like it rough." He slapped the pocket of his dirty trousers. "Got money, too."

"A hundred dollars?" she said airily, like she was the queen of Rough Cut. "It's what I charge."

That stopped him. "A hundred dollars?" He scratched the peach fuzz on his face. "Damn, woman, what you got beneath that skirt?"

"I'm from New Orleans," she said, like that explained the fancy price.

It seemed to satisfy him, for he turned and lurched up the street, muttering beneath his breath, taking his odor and his fast-dying lust with him.

Amabelle dropped the rock, her shoulders sagging, and Cad saw she wasn't nearly so sure of herself as she'd been pretending.

"You better get an arsenal of those," he advised. "He's probably one of the prime customers you'll have."

A sniff was her only response.

"Wouldn't have done much," Cad went on, unable for some reason to let the matter go. He didn't like the idea of her entertaining such a lout, but he couldn't have put words to his objection if he'd tried.

"What are you talking about?"

"Not able to get it up, I don't imagine. You could have rolled him for whatever was in his pockets."

Her bemused expression said she didn't understand a thing he said. "He probably would have fallen asleep before getting what he was after," he explained by way of translation, "and you could have robbed him."

She stared at him in surprise. "Is that what courtesans do?"

"When they get a chance. But then, you ought to know. Didn't you claim to be experienced?"

Ignoring his sarcasm, she said, "Have you ever been rolled?"

"Once," he said, remembering his twentieth birthday, when he'd felt lonely and let an East Texas whore liquor him up. Two days later, sober and in the righteous rage that only the young can manage, he'd gone looking for her. She'd been apologetic, explaining how the money was already spent on her five children, saying that he should learn from the experience, or words to that effect. He had taken her advice to heart and hadn't been rolled since.

Amabelle's sigh brought him back to Rough Cut. "I'll just have to develop a reputation as an honest employee, then."

Cad spat in the dirt. "I don't think honesty's what men are looking for, Amabelle. Least it's not high on their list."

She started to respond—always quick with an answer was Miss Latourre—but gunfire erupted behind them in the saloon, ending their little chat. It was followed by shouts and what sounded like the crashing of chairs. Two men fell onto the street, light from the saloon falling on their scuffle a few feet away.

"Oh!" she cried out.

The roan stepped nervously, but Cad did not flinch. As far as he was concerned, if they killed each other, there'd be two fewer rascals he had to reform.

"Get on inside," he said, "and I'll get your things."

"But I haven't—" she began.

More bodies flew through the swinging doors, turning the fight into a major brawl, and with a quick, regretful glance in his direction she hurried through Kate Cassidy's door.

Cad reined Horse around the fracas. By rights, the sheriff ought to be coming to stop it, but more than likely he'd be the kind to hide when duty called.

Cad found the jail at the far end of town, on past the bank, sitting quiet and separate, like it wasn't much used. Probably wasn't, he thought as he swung down to the ground. He was supposed to clean up Rough Cut without using violence, and now it looked like it would also be without help from the law. Dudley might be an expert on the rules of heaven, but he didn't know beans about the ways of the world.

Where was his angel, anyway? Except for that brief conversation behind the bush, he hadn't visited since the Devils River. Not that Cad missed him. He'd been given a task, and no matter how high the stakes were, he'd get it done on his own, the way he always managed. Only now he was invincible; couldn't be shot, couldn't be cut. It was something he had to keep in mind.

Looping the reins around a post, listening to the fight in the distance, wondering how he'd gotten roped into such a fool mission for a woman, he stepped into the sheriff's office. To most folks it was the center of law and order, a source of comfort for good citizens, a place of punishment for the bad. But not being one who voluntarily visited such an establishment, he had to force each step.

He found himself in a small, dimly lit room, an empty, bare cell at the rear, a splintered desk at one side, a gun rack at the other. In the chair behind the desk slumped the sheriff himself, gnarled hands resting on a rounded stomach, the bald dome of his head nodding in sleep. Scraggly gray-brown hair grew in a circle beneath the dome, hanging over his ears and shirt collar. His snores shook his short, fat frame, as well as the window at his back.

What caught Cad's eye was not the rumpled, smelly lawman but the open trunk on the floor beside his chair. And the lacy garments strewn across the desk, the feathers and the shiny red and black satin thingamabobs Cad couldn't begin to identify, scattered in a colorful heap around the sheriff's sweat-stained hat.

At the front edge of the desk rested a long triangle of wood with the name SHERIFF HICKOK BOWLES burned into its rough-hewn surface.

Ignoring Bowles's snorts and sniffs, Cad picked up one of the intriguing items, a filmy piece of flesh-colored nothing that wouldn't have covered the wearer's essentials if she'd been a midget. He imagined it on Amabelle Latourre.

In his mind, the garment fit her just fine, but there was still something wrong with the picture, like she was wearing someone else's clothes. Crazy idea, he thought, and then he sensed someone behind him. Reaching for his pistol, he whirled, stared into the business end of a rifle, and dropped his own weapon back in its holster.

His eye traveled along the barrel, past the skeletal hands holding it, past the long arms, to the thin neck and the narrow face of the meanest-looking bastard he had ever seen.

Not hot mean, the way a man with a hair-trigger temper might look, but cold and ruthless. A killer without purpose; the worst kind. Colorless slit eyes, sharp nose, thin lips . . . everything about him looked bad.

"Thought I got you back on the trail," the man said in a voice as sharp and thin as a knife. His eyes found the bullet hole in the suit-coat sleeve, and his lips twitched, as if he was fighting a smile.

Against the background of snores, Cad kept his hand close at his side where he could go for the gun, not because he needed it for protection but because it was what the stranger would expect him to do. Besides, it was habit. The old ways were dying hard.

"Why the shooting?" he asked, tossing Amabelle's flimsy piece of clothing back on the desk, acting like he hadn't a care in the world.

"Target practice. You rode into view kind of

unexpectedly and got in the way."

A lie. Cad was getting good at picking them out.

Behind him, the sheriff snorted awake.

"What the hell," he murmured, still sprawled in his chair, his hands fumbling for the hat. Slapping it over his bald spot, he focused his eyes past Cad. "Fike, what's going on?" He rubbed a sleeve across his mouth, catching a trail of drool. "Did you find the woman?"

"No, but I caught us an intruder," Fike said. "Trying to steal her clothes."

"Trying to return them to their rightful owner," Cad said. He gave both men the most innocent look he could manage. "The way any law-abiding citizen would."

That brought the sheriff to his feet. "You know where she is? Like to took my head off with that right fist of hers. Against the law to hit an officer of the law. Alls I was doing was helping her out."

Studying the sheriff more closely, Cad detected a faint bruise beneath one of his bleary eyes.

"So now you want to throw her in jail," he said.

"Thought we might have us a little talk." Bowles opened a desk drawer and pulled out a bottle of whiskey and took a long swig; then, with more reluctance than grace, he offered it to Cad.

"No, thanks. I'll just bundle up these things and get them back where they belong."

The rifle barrel nudged his arm. He looked over his shoulder at Fike. "Either pull the trigger or put your play toy away," he said. "I've got more on my mind than bothering with you."

The pale slit eyes widened slightly. Whoever he was, Fike wasn't used to being talked to like that. But Cad was tired, even if he'd lost the ability to get sleepy, and he still had all the impatience of when he was alive.

"Don't want no trouble in here," said Bowles, taking another draw on the bottle. "This is my deputy, Wiley Fike. Just doing his duty as he sees it."

"Then tell him to stop the fight down the street. Or can't he handle anyone he doesn't get the drop on?"

Was that a growl he heard coming from the deputy's skinny throat? Maybe he had a temper after all.

Fike's eyes were razor thin as he studied this unexpectedly fearless enemy. Cad could almost hear his mind grinding through choices of what to do. There wouldn't be many: take him out now, without knowing much about him, or get him in ambush, the way he had tried a few hours ago.

He must have settled on the ambush, for he lowered the rifle barrel and shifted his gaze to Bowles. He made signs of speaking but caught himself. With another hard look at Cad he turned on his heel and was gone.

In the silence that followed his departure, with Bowles giving his attention to the bottle, Cad gathered up Amabelle's garments and tossed them in the open trunk. He snapped the lid shut, glad to get them out of sight, ready to quit thinking of her wearing them for horny men. They were her clothes, all right. Who else could they belong to?

Grabbing the handle, he hauled the trunk toward the door.

"Get her to wear one o' them things, why don't you?" the sheriff growled over the lip of the whiskey bottle. "Charge just to look. Men'll be shooting each other to get at her. Clear a few of these rascals out of town so a man can get some peace."

Walking into the night, the trunk lifted to his shoulder, Cad wondered if maybe Bowles didn't have something there. He pictured Amabelle's long legs encased in a pair of those fancy stockings he'd fingered, a see-through piece of nothing riding high on her rear and low on her breasts.

Men had killed for less reason than a chance at a woman like that.

It certainly was a way to clear up Rough Cut and settle his problem without lifting a hand. The trouble was, he didn't think his angel would approve.

* * *

Amy sat in a broken chair and waited in what passed for a parlor while Kate Cassidy finished with a customer upstairs. The bottom cushion canted so sharply, she fought against being pitched onto the worn and dirty carpet. She'd lose the battle if she had to wait awhile.

It shouldn't be long, according to the blowsy brunette who had been walking down the hall when Amy entered the pleasure parlor. Her red gown was drab despite its color; like its hard-eyed owner, it had definitely seen better days.

"Kate don't never take much time." The woman had looked Amy over, shaking her head as though she didn't understand what the world was coming to, and made her way slowly up the rickety stairs at the back of the hall, her full hips swaying from side to side. It seemed to Amy a wearisome way to walk.

Without any guidance, she had taken refuge in the lone downstairs room. Hands folded in her lap, she tried not to look prim, but it was either that or look as lost as she felt. Glancing at the bare walls, the sprung, dusty sofa, and the general air of gloom that surrounded her, she felt the urge to run after Cad. Only noise from the street fight kept her in her seat.

"Mama," she whispered to the stale air, "I'll bet New Orleans was never like this."

Heavy boots thundered down the stairs and along the hall toward the front door. She glanced up to see a man striding by, a hairy creature who was buckling his pants and adjusting his gun holster as he hurried along.

Behind him, walking more quietly, was a woman of middle years, her red hair piled neatly atop her head, her low-cut black gown showing to advantage her full and formidable figure. She watched the front door close, then glanced into the parlor, kohl-darkened lashes widening as she caught sight of the pleasure parlor's visitor.

Amy stood, more nervous than she'd been as a child when called before the Mother Superior because of some forgotten infraction.

In a way, despite the paint on her face, the madam of Kate Cassidy's Pleasure Parlor reminded her of the Mother Superior . . . solidly built, blessed with an air of authority, a not unkind glint in her eye.

Amy almost smiled to think of the nuns' likely reaction to such a comparison.

The sound of gunfire erased all comforting thoughts. She jumped and wondered if maybe she shouldn't be hiding behind a chair.

"Don't fret," the madam said. "They're just about done. Boys having a little fun, that's all. Not that there won't be a body or two for the undertaker, but you're safe enough for now. Any bullets fired in here don't have gunpowder in them, if you know what I mean."

Amy did not, but she kept her ignorance to herself.

"Dora said you wanted to see me," the madam said.

Amy cleared her throat. Not used to small talk, she stood straight, threw out her obviously inadequate chest, and got to the point. "My name is Amabelle Latourre, Miss Cassidy, and I'm looking for work."

The woman's green eyes narrowed. "It's Mrs. Cassidy, but everybody calls me Kate." As she spoke, she gave Amy a perusal that was as thorough as Cad's.

It made her just as nervous, too, but not in the same way.

"Ever been with a man?" Before Amy could lie, Kate hurried on. "Didn't think so. I can tell a virgin a mile away."

She circled Amy, walking slowly, silently, and when she was done she headed for the hall. "Come on up. We need to talk."

Gathering her courage, Amy followed her up the stairs to the pleasure parlor's back room, which served as Kate's office and private quarters. Here the walls were papered, the chairs neatly cushioned, the desk orderly as a banker's; the office part occupied one end of the room, a single bed and wardrobe the other, and the floor was covered with a floral rug.

Here, too, the noise from the street faded, as if it did not exist.

"I sleep alone," Kate said to Amy's unasked questions. "There's usually an empty bed somewhere when I need to work. Sometimes one of the boys wants to double up. They pay double, too, or maybe more, depending on how much cash they're carrying."

She might as well have been talking about selling books for the emotion in her voice. Amy sat in one of the chairs facing the desk and wished she could be as detached.

Kate settled in the leather armchair where she obviously took care of her records.

"There some crazy-eyed papa looking for you? One that's likely to shoot up the place when he finds where you've run?"

"No," said Amy.

"How about a fiancé?"

"No." More emphatically.

"Mother, sisters, brothers?"

"I'm alone in the world."

"So are we all, honey. So are we all."

Conscience pricked Amy. "I guess I ought to tell you the sheriff might be after me."

"Thought there had to be something wrong. Which one?"

"The one here in Rough Cut, according to what he said."

"What'd he look like?"

Amy had no trouble being succinct. "Short and smelly and drunk."

"That's Hickok, all right. Hickok Bowles. Where'd you run into him? You're new in town; I would have heard about you otherwise."

Something about Kate made her want to tell all. But she couldn't, her mission to find her father being a secret in case things didn't work out. She told what she could. Describing her ride out of Del Rio, she put in all the details she recalled about the sheriff, and left out most everything about Cad, other than the fact that he'd ridden along and brought her into town.

Kate laughed, and she made Amy laugh too. Now that her adventure was over she could see the humor in it, and it felt good to do something besides frown. It helped, too, that the gunfire had ceased.

"Why Rough Cut? Besides a few outlaws and bandits up from Mexico, it's not on anybody's beaten trail."

Amy had been dreading the question, but she had an answer ready. "I was born and raised in New Orleans. In an orphanage." She said a private prayer that the nuns might forgive her for her half-truths and outright lies. "It was not a happy experience. I wanted to get as far away as I could."

"You did that, all right," said Kate, looking skeptical. "This Rankin fellow: Tell me more about him."

Kate, Amy was reminded, proved herself again and again a shrewd woman. She got right at the empty parts of her tale.

"There's nothing to tell, except he looked safe enough and I had to take a chance. It was either that or starve to death."

"He try anything?"

"No. He just looked."

"Been dead not to." Kate thought a minute. "You sound disappointed. I'll bet he's good looking, someone that might turn a girl's head."

"I—"

"Don't be embarrassed. Men and women liking one another is what gives us a job." She thought another minute. "Why do you want to take on strangers?"

Because I'm my mother's daughter.

"It's a way to make money and have a roof over my head," was all that she said.

"If you're thinking it's an easy way to earn a living, think again."

"Maybe there's a need for a schoolteacher in town. If this doesn't work out, I mean."

Kate laughed, but it wasn't nearly as pleasant as the last time. "These bastards don't tolerate children. If they had any, the kids'd be bastards, too, and on their own. Prudence Thor runs a kind of orphanage on her ranch for the few youngsters we've got. She's a widow, but she gets by on her own. A tough woman, like me. You've got to be tough to survive out here."

She said it as though she doubted her would-be employee could make it in the West.

"I'm learning," said Amy. "I've made it all the way from New Orleans to Rough Cut, haven't I?"

"Yeah, that you have. How old are you?"

"Twenty-two."

"And a virgin. Amazing, with looks like yours." Kate tapped her fingers on the desk. "You sure you want to do this?"

Amy thought of her mother's diary and all her

mother had sacrificed for her; she thought, too, of the man who had run out on them. She had to find him. She had to.

All right, so working in the trade wasn't the same in Rough Cut as it would have been in the rooms on Royal Street. But she was too far along now to go back.

Besides, if she did, she would probably end up with Pierre.

"I'm sure," she said, and at that moment she meant it with all her heart.

"I give my girls a third of what they bring in, minus room and board, of course. It's a better deal than you'd get down on the border."

Ignorant of all business matters, this one most especially, Amy could only nod.

"You'll bring a pretty penny the first time; all that yellow hair and those blue eyes. A real innocent. Only one man around here might pay what I'll be asking—a rancher who lives on out past Prudence's place. Owns half the county. Used to have him a Mexican woman, but she upped and ran away not long ago. If I know John, he'll be getting real horny about now."

A common name, Amy told herself, but still she could barely breathe. It couldn't be. It simply could not be. "John?" she asked, using the last reserves of her courage.

"John Lattimer. He's not a good man, but he's a rich one, and in our business that's just about the same thing."

Chapter Six

Cad spent his first night in Rough Cut roaming its lone street on foot, Horse having been lodged with the sleepy young hand at the livery stable.

He kept to the shadows, observing the movement of men in and out of the saloon, occasionally watching an intent customer enter the pleasure parlor, wondering which of the whores would satisfy him. He told himself it wasn't any of his business, at least not yet. The more he thought about closing down the parlor, the more he thought it might be a good idea, no matter what additional trouble it brought.

He'd left Amabelle's trunk with a black-haired, round-hipped woman named Dora, who'd met him at the parlor door. She was just the kind who would have serviced him without any problems a few weeks ago. Tonight, even without Dudley's restriction against fornication, she struck him as a little too tired to work up much enthusiasm for her job, a practiced woman who'd been practicing too long.

Not fresh and fair and filled with spirit . . . like no one Cad could bring himself to name.

Miss No Name, that's who she was, all right. She sure as heck wasn't Miss Latourre. Cad kicked at a rock. Something about the woman caused him more distress than dealing with outlaws and sheriffs had ever done. It was like she'd stirred up something inside him, something with sharp little claws that was scratching to get out.

He kicked another rock. Never needing sleep surely had robbed him of those few hours that used to bring him peace. And wasn't peace what old Dud had promised? Only after he'd done his duty, he reminded himself . . . a difficult feat, he'd decided after looking over the town. A worse bunch of thieves and cardsharps and no-good drifters he'd never seen collected in one place.

In ordinary times he'd have fit right in, not making judgments, playing some poker, cheating the cheaters, then bedding Dora before riding out of town for the comfort of a solitary camp.

Now he was in the judgment business. And the staying around one, too.

An eternity of damnation was beginning to

look better—and more likely—all the time.

Just before dawn, when he'd managed to forget a blue-eyed female with more complications than she had curves, he found her walking in the dark down the side of the street. The saloon was closed, and except for an occasional drunk passed out in a rut the town appeared to be deserted.

Like the creatures of the wild, he'd always had good night vision; he hadn't lost it along with his life. Wearing a cloak against the early morning chill, she'd let her hair down, but he recognized her right away. The hair, pale in a mist of moonlight, fell past her shoulders halfway to her waist. She walked slowly, kicking at the dirt, missing the piles of horseshit, not seeming to search for rocks. Everything about her said things weren't going too well.

Let her go, his good sense told him as she walked past. But Cad had never put much stock in good sense.

"Morning," he said softly as he stepped into a shaft of silvery predawn light. Amabelle jumped a foot and whirled.

"Oh, Cad," she said as she got a look at him, a hand pressed to her heart. "You frightened me half to death."

"You needed a good scare," he said, suddenly pricked with anger. "What the heck are you doing out here alone?"

"All my servants were otherwise occupied,"

she said with a wave of her hand. "Besides, I'm not alone. You're here."

Cad didn't try to follow her logic.

"I'm here, all right," he said, ambling closer, wanting to give her the scare she deserved. "Thing is, you don't know whether that's good or bad."

Darned if she didn't almost cry, eyes all blurry beneath the thickest natural lashes he'd ever seen. She was helpless again, and knowing it this time. Needing someone. Needing him.

The trouble was, she aroused a few needs in him. By the time he'd convinced himself that the fires of hell awaited if he put his hands on her, she leaned against him and burst into tears.

Cad couldn't stand a woman crying. He wanted them strong and willing, and then he wanted them gone. Amabelle Latourre wasn't any of those things. So why did he hold her kind of gentle-like and pat her on the back?

Touching her in such a way felt awkward at first, it being his first attempt at tenderness when he and a woman were both upright and dressed. And then it didn't feel so awkward anymore. Her crying stopped, and she held so still, he wondered if maybe she hadn't fallen asleep on her feet. She stirred a little, rubbing her breasts against him, giving him another rush of forbidden ideas.

He didn't stop her until the pounding of horses's hooves vibrated under his boots. He could hear them too. More than a few, and they were coming into town fast.

He jerked her back into the shadows as a passel of riders came into view, shouting things like *vamos!* and *anda!*, which was about all the Spanish he recognized. They reined to a halt before the darkened saloon, so close he could smell the sweat on their mounts. He counted a dozen men, banditos from across the border by the looks of them, what with their silver spurs and fancy saddles flashing in the moonlight. A thirsty lot, too, as they dismounted, their leader pounding on the saloon's locked door.

Clinging to him, Amabelle choked on the dust kicked up by the horses. He buried her head against his chest to muffle the noise. If he had been on his own, maybe he could have handled them, maybe not, but once they got a look at the woman's long yellow hair, and one or two more particulars about her, he wouldn't stand a chance.

It wasn't long before lights flickered inside the saloon, and a sleepy-eyed bartender in long underwear opened the door, scratched himself, and jumped out of the way as the *banditos* stormed past.

One was left behind to tether the horses; Cad watched in silence until he'd joined his *compadres*, then nodded for Amabelle to come with him.

"Where are we going?" she asked in a loud whisper.

"To my hotel room," he said, thumbing at the

ramshackle structure behind him.

Which was the last place he wanted her, but he didn't care to risk a showdown right away by getting caught crossing the street to Kate Cassidy's.

They slipped inside Rough Cut's only inn. As far as Cad could tell, he was the lone customer, most of the town's visitors choosing to sleep in the street or out in the hills. Smart men, thought Cad. The hotel smelled of old sweat, smoke, and whiskey, with a few other rank odors mixed in to foul the air and make breathing hardly worth the effort.

"Is that the innkeeper?" Amabelle asked, gesturing to a scrawny, bearded codger sprawled in an armchair behind a small table.

"That's him, all right, guarding his post."

He hurried her up the stairs to a room at the back. Inside, he opened the window looking out on the hills. She joined him in gulping the fresh air, standing close by his side. Neither spoke for what seemed an hour or two.

"Rough Cut certainly lacks the finer amenities, doesn't it?" she said at last, sighing.

He glanced down at her. She was staring at the edge of pink light shaping the horizon. Tears stained her cheeks and her hair looked a mite untidy, but she had that fine chin raised and she showed few signs of the troubles that had set her to crying down on the street.

His hands started itching, and so did a few other parts. Much as he liked the morning breeze, he backed away and sat at the edge of the bed. Something creaked ominously beneath the bare mattress, but the slats held. Loosening his gun holster and setting it aside, Cad took off his coat, stretched out his legs, his boots crossed at the ankles, and studied his guest.

She took off her cloak and laid it over the windowsill. He wished she hadn't done that. In profile he could see the curves beneath the silk gown all too well. If he wasn't mistaken—and he rarely was about such matters—those were taut little nipples pressed against the fabric, practically crying out for a man's tongue.

He sat up and bent one leg over the other, hiding the evidence of his reaction.

"This country is so big, isn't it?" she said. "It goes on for miles and miles and miles."

"Is that what has you so upset? The big country?"

"No," she said, unable to stifle a sigh. "It was just an observation." She looked at him straight on. "We need to talk about a much more practical matter. If I'm going to get into the courtesan business, I'll have to get started before long. I've decided my first customer ought to be you."

Amy thought he took the news fairly well—not exactly grinning with pleasure, but not crying out *no,* as if she would give him a disease.

He just scratched his chin and kept on looking at her. The longer he looked, the more nervous she became. She really was demented to think she could attract a man like him. He was so much leaner and darker than she remembered, more ominous in a way, more attractive, and more manly than any other man she'd ever observed. It was altogether possible she wouldn't be woman enough for him.

She stopped that line of thought. He would help her. He had to. When she'd heard his voice down on the street, at one of the loneliest, darkest moments of her life, she'd never experienced such relief. Holding on to that sensation and trusting in his basic goodness were all that kept her sane.

"You don't have to pay me if you don't have the money," she assured him, thinking maybe finances were causing his hesitation.

"How do you figure we'll get away with that? You're working for Kate Cassidy now, aren't you? It's my experience that madams are shrewd businesswomen."

"I can spare enough cash for a few visits, at least until I get used to . . . everything."

"You do the paying," he said, and she saw he didn't believe her. Of course he wouldn't. He'd probably never heard of anything like this.

"As I said, I'll pay as long as I've got the money."

He leaned forward, putting his weight on his bent leg. "You sure you still got the money? It's still inside the trunk?"

"I sewed the packets into the underside of my petticoat."

His lips twitched. "You're pretty shrewd yourself, Amabelle Latourre. So why are you out here making such a proposal to a stranger?"

"Because I had a whim to go west and do things I'd never do at home, and because you're the least strange man I know. At least in Rough Cut."

She spoke lightly, hiding the desperation that tore her heart. So much more she could have told him, especially how, when he was near, she didn't feel quite so alone.

As her first customer, he was also infinitely better than John Lattimer. After Kate Cassidy had suggested him, Amy hadn't been able to breathe right, not until she stood at Cad Rankin's hotel window and stared out at the dawn.

Knowing her father was alive and prosperous had brought a sense of satisfaction; thinking about what Kate had suggested, an act against the laws of God and man, had set her to pacing in her tiny new room and at last walking outside in the street.

She wasn't ready to reveal her true identity, not until she'd seen her papa and learned what kind of man he was. Kate had told her little, other than that he was rich and powerful and likely to be lonely out in the country since his latest mistress had headed south.

"She was a pretty thing," Kate had said, "but I guess she got lonely out on that ranch with only John and a Mexican cook and a pack of no-good cowboys to keep her company."

Papa could have sent for his wife and child, Amy started to say. He wouldn't know Mama was dead.

The thought of Marguerite had brought tears to her eyes. She'd pleaded weariness and gone to the room Kate said would be hers. Unable to sleep, she'd taken to the street . . . to Cad Rankin's comforting and blessedly familiar arms. In his embrace she hadn't gotten all fluttery inside—at least not until her tears were spent. Just as the flutter was returning, along with the strange hunger she felt when he touched her, those dreadful men had come riding into town. And here she was telling him the idea she'd decided on if she ever saw him again.

"You're awfully quiet," she said, smoothing her gown over her hips. "I know I can't compare to Dora or Kate, so if the idea's repulsive to you—"

"It's not that."

"So what is it?"

"You wouldn't believe me if I told you."

"Try me."

"It's just that I've . . . been injured."

"Injured?"

"Yeah. In the place a man values most. If you get my drift."

Amy blushed, glanced out the window, and decided that was being cowardly. She met his gaze, thinking he had the darkest, most penetrating brown eyes she had ever seen.

"You mean you can't get it up?" she said.

"What?" he said, so loud he made her jump.

"Didn't I say it right?" she said, feeling very much the fool. "It's what you said about that drunk young man who accosted us outside Mrs. Cassidy's. You said he wouldn't be able to get it up and so I could roll him."

Cad scratched his chin. "You remember everything I say?"

Amy nodded. "I haven't had many conversations lately. And you were talking about my line of work."

An uncomfortable silence fell between them. He was embarrassed, Amy thought, and it was all her fault for being so bold.

She'd always been a sympathetic sort, patching a scraped knee when one of her students fell, kissing the tears away, weaving fanciful stories to ease the pain. She felt the same sympathy for Cad, except that his injury was far more delicate.

"You're not just lying to make me feel better about being turned down?"

"Sugar, the last thing in the world I would do is turn you down. If I had the choice."

He sounded sincere enough, poor man. And she had thought him so virile . . . so strong.

"You were teasing me out there on the trail, weren't you? When you made me think you wanted . . . to do something to me."

"That's right. I was teasing."

"To make me understand how dangerous my situation could be with someone not . . ." She broke off, afraid she might embarrass him. Her eye fell to the juncture of his thighs. "How did it happen?"

"I was shot. A couple of no-good rascals were trying to rob a bank, and I got in the way of the gunfire."

"I'll bet you were trying to be brave, weren't you?" She hurried to his side and sat on the bed beside him, her hand resting on his sleeve, her thoughts going back to Mama's descriptions of how men were built.

"Was everything just blown away? Did it leave a scar?"

He dropped his hands to his lap, in the process brushing aside her hold on his arm. "The equipment's still there. It just doesn't function the way it used to do. And yes, there's a scar."

His voice was thick, and she could see there was perspiration on his brow.

"It's nothing to be ashamed of," she said, fighting disappointment. She'd been so sure her first time would be with him.

What a selfish idea. She shouldn't be thinking about herself.

"My guess is, you were trying to stop the bank robbers. It's a brave wound, that's what it is. Like a badge. Would you mind if I looked?"

She had no idea where the question came from. It startled her as much as him.

Fiddling with her hair, glancing out the window at the rising sun, running her fingers over the faded blue ticking that covered the mattress, she waited nervously for his response. She tried to rationalize: He'd bared his chest and arms to her on the trail, hadn't he? Somehow, though, this display wasn't the same thing.

But wasn't she supposed to know what men looked like? Mama had been quite explicit when one of her friends was excessively endowed, but Amy didn't see how a man could walk straight with such an appendage dangling between his legs.

"It's all right if you're embarrassed," she said, thinking more of her own reactions to this strange conversation than of his.

"That's not the problem."

He shifted his hands, and she looked between his legs. His trousers had a bulge to them she hadn't noticed before.

"I thought you said—"

"Oh, I can get it up all right. But having sex hurts."

Amy jumped to her feet, her cheeks burning. "I'm sorry I mentioned such a painful subject."

He pulled her back down beside him. She sat hard, sending up a puff of dust from the mattress. "It's something we were bound to talk about since you settled on me for your first."

She stared at her lap. "You're being very understanding. When I dropped down from that tree I thought you weren't very bright, but I've changed my opinion. You're really very smart."

"You want me for my mind?"

Amy looked into his eyes, caught the heat in their depths, and gazed down at the strong, tanned neck, the chest hairs visible at his shirt opening, the flat abdomen, the strong thighs, the bulge . . .

"I suppose," she managed, feeling tight and hot inside. "And your kindness."

The voice she heard didn't sound like hers, but she knew it was.

Cad chuckled. It was a kind of low, deep, rolling sound, as though it didn't come out very often. "Smart and kind, am I? You've earned a peek at the scar. But remember, you asked."

Amy thought about running for the door. But that would be cowardly. This was a course she had chosen, and while it didn't exactly bring her to exhilaration, it came frightfully close.

"I'll remember," she said.

She licked her lips and watched as he unbuckled his belt. Her stomach turned somersaults, her breasts grew too tight in her clothes, and something strange started happening between her legs.

All of it was very startling, but she didn't look away. His fingers worked at the trouser buttons. Her heart fluttered and panic set in. "I've changed my mind," she said, admitting to cowardice.

"No, Amabelle, you asked and you have a right to see. I won't charge you a thing."

She barely heard him, what with the roaring

in her ears. Did all parts of the body get involved in sex? It was clear she had a great deal to learn.

Rooted to the bed, she kept on watching as he eased his trousers and long underwear toward his hips. She saw an abdomen so flat, she could have bounced a coin on it, and a sprinkling of dark hairs that grew thicker the lower he went. She hadn't known men grew hair in private places like a woman.

It was the only resemblance to herself she could see.

And then she saw the scar, obscenely white and jagged against the pale flesh and black hairs. It was low on his stomach, covering a vital part of the body. Forgetting the bulge at its base, still hidden by the folds of his trousers, she marveled that he had survived.

"You poor man," she said, her heart going out to him. "Does it hurt?"

"Like the very devil."

"Oh." She reached out to touch it. He caught her wrist.

"You better not do that."

He spoke with startling urgency.

"Of course," she said, pulling back her hand, feeling like a fool. "I wouldn't want to add to your pain."

"No, neither of us would want that."

She had to show him her sympathy. Unable to touch him anywhere else, she rested a palm against his cheek and felt a fiery warmth. Whether the heat came from her hand or his taut, bristled skin, she didn't know.

Then she kissed him. Lightly, just brushing her lips over his, but it was the sweetest experience of her life, and she trembled down to her toes.

Afraid of what else she might do, of the demands she might put on him in her ignorant enthusiasm, she stood and returned to the window, waiting while he pulled up his trousers.

If only she were more experienced, she wouldn't be making such a fool of herself. She certainly wouldn't be so distracted by him as a man. Mama hadn't been, not at first, but of course Mama had not been a virgin.

Amy saw her condition as a definite handicap.

"Amabelle," he said at last.

"Amy," she said. "Most people call me Amy." She forced her eyes to his. "I understand now why you don't find me attractive. You can't find *any* woman attractive, can you? And I understand why you didn't kiss me when we were out on that hill. I was expecting too much of a very brave man."

Cad covered his eyes, then looked at her again. "I guess that's it."

She tried to read his expression, but he was more clever than she at keeping his thoughts to himself. Clever, yes, and skilled in ways she could not comprehend. In that instant, she saw what she must do, for him as well as for herself.

"You have been with lots of women before,

haven't you? Women like me."

"Amy, I have to say that in all my life I've never met anyone quite like you."

"I mean courtesans." She shuddered. "Whores."

"A few."

"So you can tell me what's expected of us, even if you can't demonstrate the particulars."

It seemed to her he took a long time in answering.

"I could do that."

She breathed a sigh of relief. He had not rejected her, as she had feared, and her confidence grew.

"You can't make much selling beer and ale, so I'll pay you."

"You'll pay me?"

"That's right. Don't forget, I've got money. Not enough to live on forever, but enough."

Enough, she hoped, to last until she'd done what she had come to do. John Lattimer was either a father she wanted or someone she had to reject. If it was the former, she would identify herself and let him become the papa he should have been.

And if it was the latter . . . Why, then she would have to make other plans.

In the meantime, she would get to know Cad, before he finished his business in Rough Cut and she had to tell him good-bye. The thought made her feel hollow inside.

"I think we'd better get started right away,"

she was quick to say before the aching loneliness returned. "Kate Cassidy has provided me with a room. I'll see you tonight at eight."

Dudley watched from on high as Cad escorted Amy back to her new home. For a change, it was Michael's turn to be worried.

"I hadn't considered such a complication," the youth said.

"Neither had I. Not at first."

"There's something about her that's very appealing. Even to me."

"She's a good woman, and lovely, too, by all your human standards."

"Yes. Despite what she's trying to be."

"Not despite, Michael, but because of. She's doing it for her mother and her father. Besides, for all her intentions, she hasn't actually done anything yet."

"But sex outside of marriage is a sin."

"Sex outside of marriage if one or both of the parties is married to someone else. Or if there is no love. Theologians have been arguing the fine points of such matters since Adam and Eve."

"It's true Cad and Amy aren't married to anyone. But they aren't in love, either."

Dudley smiled at Michael. "You think not?"

"I know not. As much as I have faith in my brother, I understand his attitude toward women. Amy Lattimer almost got raped on his bed."

"Ah, but she wasn't. Don't you see the importance of that?"

Michael wrinkled his nose. "Not exactly."

"That's your youth showing. In the thousand years I've been watching the human species I've learned what to look for and what to ignore. In his altered state, your brother has a destiny that he knows not of. As does Miss Lattimer. Their fates are inescapably entwined."

"A happy ending is ensured," said Michael with a smile. "That's a relief."

"I wish it were that simple. Amy Lattimer is a good woman, and thus far in his life Cad Rankin has been a bad man. If truth and goodness always triumphed in the world, theirs would be a satisfactory story. But too much has happened through the centuries for even an angel to make such a claim."

He stroked his full white beard. "We can only hope and pray that fate will run its proper course. Because of the personalities involved, and the problems they will undoubtedly face, their situation will need all the hope and prayers we can give."

Chapter Seven

Mornings in Rough Cut started slow, with the sun coming up gold and soft and mistless over the dry land. Cad liked the empty street and the quiet, but he wasn't in town for solitude. Besides, he'd had all he could expect of being alone during the few sleepless hours after leaving Amy once again at the pleasure parlor door.

Good riddance, he'd told himself when she was safely inside. Amabelle Latourre was a subject he didn't want to have anything to do with, day or night; getting back his life, miserable though it was, would be difficult enough without a blue-eyed blonde messing up his mind.

Women *never* messed up his mind, and he wasn't about to get bothered by one now. Especially not in his condition. If he felt those tiny little claws scratching at his insides every time he thought of her, it was because he knew nothing could happen between them. Nothing. She wanted talk, and that was the most she would get.

Redemption was his only goal. Getting a life and doing what he wanted to do were worth a little sacrifice. Besides, he thought, remembering the embalmer's knife, Dudley had given him little choice.

So why did he let her touch him? Why let her look him over as if he had something between his legs to be proud of? What he had was equipment he couldn't use.

The fact of the matter was, her kiss, light as a butterfly's wing, had gotten to him as much as her reaching for his scar.

Butterfly wings and kitten claws. He must be losing his mind.

Dressed in his respectable duds, he started what ought to be his primary efforts at the Inside Straight Saloon.

"You look like a whiskey man," the bartender said when he walked inside.

So he didn't look so different from his old self after all, despite the suit and the string tie and the almost white shirt. He'd toted up water from a cistern behind the hotel for a morning bath, just to keep looking respectable. He was glad he hadn't gone too far.

Rubbing at his freshly shaven face, he looked around the long, narrow room. Through the dimness and the smoke, he spied a couple of the *banditos* slumped over one of the tables at the back. Otherwise the place was empty. He saw no need to keep his back to the wall.

He dropped his hat on the bar. "A little early for liquor."

The bartender shrugged and wiped at a glass with a rag as soiled as his shirt. "We don't go much by time around here."

In days past, neither had Cad. He eyed the man carefully. Early forties, dark hair and eyes, thick mustache, his body squat and square, his expression flat, he looked like a man who had seen more of life than he wanted to and was keeping his feelings to himself. His shirtsleeves were rolled back over hairy forearms, and he had the biggest hands Cad had ever seen.

"Got any coffee?" Cad said.

Without a word the bartender poured him a cup from a tin pot stored beneath the bar. The brew was thick and black, the way he used to like it. But he didn't need the jolt anymore, and after a taste for his observer's benefit he left it alone.

"You had a noisy crowd in here a few hours ago," he said, feeling foolish making small talk.

"Yep."

"Up from Mexico, were they?" He nodded toward the back table. "I see a pair of 'em didn't make it out."

"Nope."

Cad reconsidered the whiskey. It would certainly make the words come out easier. Later, he thought, in a few weeks when all this was done.

"Guess their *compadres* hightailed it for the hills."

"Could be." The bartender set down the glass he was wiping and took a swipe at the bar. "You thinking about joining 'em?"

A good man sure did have to put up with a lot of sarcasm. But Cad wasn't all that good, at least not yet. Just for show, he eased his pistol from its holster and rested it next to his hat. Without seeming to, the bartender watched his movements, but Cad could read his mind.

"You know much about guns?" he asked.

"Some."

"This one, for instance." Cad stroked the blued barrel, eased his fingers around the walnut grip, then picked it up to aim it at a bottle on the wall directly beyond the bartender's head. "Nothing special about it. Single-action army revolver; the Peacemaker, it's called. Around these parts they must be common as dirt. You can get pearl handles, or ivory, with silver or gold finish, if you lean to fancy ways. Nickel's good enough for me." He cocked the gun, his thumb resting on the hammer; the click sounded like an explosion in the quiet saloon.

The bartender kept watching, kept on wiping at the splintered counter, but his eyes had narrowed to hardness.

Cad eased back on the hammer and returned

the gun to the bar, positioned where he could reach it fast. "Now then, about those *banditos*. You see many of their kind around here?"

The bartender sucked on a tooth before answering, and Cad got the feeling he was being sized up.

"Every few weeks sometimes, or maybe a month or so goes by before we get a gang riding through. They drink and shoot up the place, then keep on riding. No one bothers 'em and as a general rule they don't bother us." He glanced at Cad's gun. "If we didn't have bullet holes in the walls, mister, we wouldn't have no decoration at all."

A practical man, Cad thought, and introduced himself as he holstered his gun.

"Welcome to Rough Cut, Mr. Rankin. I go by Amsterdam."

"Amsterdam?"

"My dear old ma, may she rest in peace, read it in a book. Some folks try to shorten it to Dam, but it ain't something I encourage."

Cad wasn't inclined to say more about the name, having sported *Cadmus* all his life.

"Well, Amsterdam, tell me more about the town. Not much threat from Sheriff Bowles or his deputy, is there? About keeping the peace, I mean."

"Why? You planning on robbing the bank?"

"Not anytime soon."

Amsterdam managed a smile. "Sounds like an honest answer."

"It is, Amsterdam, it is."

The two men eyed each other for a minute, and Cad got the feeling that while he wasn't exactly making a friend, neither was he making an enemy.

"I gotta give the sheriff credit," Amsterdam said. "He's what keeps the drifters and the bushwhackers and their kind riding through, and dropping a few coins on the way. They can get a drink and a woman and a place to lie low if they need to without trouble from the law. As for Deputy Fike, he ain't been around long enough to figure out. Most folks just stay out of his way."

Cad saw the wisdom in such a course. He gave another look at the saloon, and at the *banditos* still sawing logs. "You own this place?"

"Nope. Just about everything in town belongs to a rancher lives out in the county."

"Every place but the jail."

"Oh, he owns that too, in a way."

"You care to explain?"

"Nope. And you can wave that gun around all you want. I've said all I've got to say." He spread his huge hands flat in front of him. "You sure do ask a powerful lot of questions. What's your business here anyway?"

"Beer."

"Shoulda said so. Supply's running low up here, but if you're real thirsty, I got some kegs up from Del Rio just last week. They're out back. Take just a minute to haul one in."

"I'm selling, not drinking." Cad had a hard time getting the words out, and when he did he could hear the lie in them plain as the bullet holes in the wall.

"Mr. Lattimer does the buying," Amsterdam said.

"Lattimer?"

"John Lattimer; that rancher I mentioned. Owns the Rocking L ten miles to the east, and most of the land in between. Not much goes on around here Mr. Lattimer don't have a hand in."

"Including Kate Cassidy's Pleasure Parlor?" The question surprised Cad as much as it did his listener.

Amsterdam grinned. For a coarse-bodied man, his teeth were surprisingly white and fine. "Miss Kate's about the only independent businessman around here. And she sure ain't a man."

Cad didn't know if he wanted to hear more or less about the whorehouse. Less would be better. It might keep a certain woman from slipping into his mind. Here, he'd just about forgotten her, but after one mention of the parlor—which he'd brought up himself—he was wondering what was happening to her on this quiet day.

Sleeping, that's what she was doing. Had to be after what she'd been through lately. And sleeping alone. Waiting for her first customer, which she'd asked him to be. Showed what a foolish female she was.

Coming to his room without much of a fight, sitting on that bare mattress so close he could smell the lavender over the stink of the room, then asking to see his wound. Kissing him, too, like she'd never done such a thing before. Maybe she hadn't. Virgin lips, that's what she had; sweet with a light, warm touch to go with her virgin eyes.

In his past life she could have put those lips anywhere she wanted. Hell, with those white little teeth of hers, she could have given him a wound of her own.

Cad cursed himself for where his mind was headed. While he was at it, he cursed himself for cursing, too. Life—or whatever his existence could be called—was sure as heck hard.

He caught the bartender looking at him and cleared his throat.

"If I'm going to do business in Rough Cut," he said, tossing a coin on the bar and slapping his hat on his head, "looks like I'll have to meet this John Lattimer."

"You'll have to go to him. He don't come to town all that often. Matter of fact—"

He broke off at the sound of heavy boots stomping through the door, and Cad turned to watch a surly quartet of trail-dirty men enter the saloon. On past them he caught a glimpse of horses out on the street. He hadn't heard them ride up. Such a failure wasn't like him. He'd probably been thinking of Amabelle at the time.

Amsterdam set a bottle of whiskey on the bar. Eyes on Cad, the man in front grabbed the whiskey. He looked much like his companions: heavy in his movements, solid in his build, his leathery face bristled and deeply line-cut, his clothes rough and made for hard riding across the hard land. There was something about his eyes, however, something wary and sharp, that set him apart from the others, that labeled him *boss.*

After a long, slow look at Cad, he turned his attention to one of the back tables. "We'll need a fresh deck of cards," he said. "Got an itch in our britches and it's too early for Miss Kate's."

"Sure thing, Sonny."

The four settled heavily in one of the tables close to the *banditos*, making more noise than was strictly necessary, but the Mexicans kept right on snoring. Amsterdam delivered the cards and four glasses, then returned to his post behind the bar.

"There's some of Mr. Lattimer's men," he said.

"I would have taken them for a pack of outlaws," Cad said, "more than ranch hands."

"I didn't say what they did out on the Rocking L."

Cad met the bartender's eye. "No, you didn't. This Sonny—I take it he's the lead dog."

"You might call him that. Not to his face, understand. Sonny's got a mean temper, and he don't worry much about what he does when he's riled."

Cad studied the men, studied their holstered guns, their broad, powerful bodies, the cold look in their eyes. He'd seen their kind in renegade gangs often enough, hard-bitten men no older than he but aged beyond their years. Ranch hands, were they? Like heck.

Just what kind of a man was this rancher? Old Dud hadn't mentioned him in particular, but maybe he was the evil that needed to be exorcised.

Lordy, thought Cad, he was sounding more and more like a jailhouse preacher. He'd have to watch himself.

Leaning against the bar, he watched the card game from a distance. It didn't take much time to get a feeling for the rhythm of their play. They bet wild and high, and the money shuffled around the table, no one much of a winner for a while until the one called Sonny began gathering a pile of coins in front of him.

Accepting a beer, Cad paid the bartender and took a center table where he could watch both the game and the door . . . and keep his back to the wall.

They'd be easy to cheat, more foolhardy than cautious; he'd seen Sonny deal from the bottom of the deck a time or two without getting caught. Too bad he was out of the cardsharp business, or he'd show him a few subtle tricks.

But he wasn't out of the playing business, he

reminded himself, and besides, this was research, learning the nature of the men he had to reform.

He made his move when one of the players threw down his cards in disgust.

"Deal me out," the man growled. "I gotta take a piss."

"Coming back?" Sonny asked.

The gambler scratched his grizzled face. "I'd sooner shovel shit than pick up the hands you been dealing. I'll see you boys back at the ranch."

As he strode past Cad, he spared him a quick sidelong glance, then a closer look, but he didn't quit walking and he didn't look back as he went out the door.

Cad picked up his beer, showing anyone interested that his gun hand was occupied holding his drink, and strolled back to take the quitter's place.

"Mind if I join you boys?" All polite like, almost humble, like he'd be easy pickings.

Sonny looked him in the eye. "This is a friendly game."

Cad glanced at the pile of coins in front of him. "I can tell."

No one spoke for a moment. "You got the money, stranger, we got the time," Sonny said at last, without consulting his silent companions.

Cad took the empty chair opposite him, thumbed his hat to the back of his head, and pulled out a fistful of cash, a mixture of coins and bills.

"We're playing draw," Sonny said as he dealt the cards.

Cad shrugged, as if it made no difference, but he put in a frown, as if he would have preferred another game.

Sonny won the first hand, and the second, Cad the third, and one of the other men a pair of small pots. Cad participated in the play without comment, forcing himself to keep quiet when Sonny resorted to his bottom-dealing ways.

Funny how playing honest made a man downright cranky when he watched an opponent cheat. Made him want to get even, too.

Cad might not always have been an honest player, but he'd been a good one, and he took advantage of the bluffs that an overconfident Sonny couldn't resist. Slowly the money changed sides of the table.

The more he won, the more still the air became, until it seemed as if no one was breathing. Even the *banditos* ceased to snore, and after a while they sat up, looked around cautiously, and made a hasty departure.

A few observers ambled into the saloon, and then a few more, but as far as Cad could tell without looking around they chose to watch and to wait until Sonny decided what to do about his losing ways. The other players dropped out after an hour, and then it was just the two of them, no one bothering to step up and take an empty chair.

Cad's course was plain: He'd take the cheater for everything he had. If he pushed him into doing something foolish, it was hardly his fault. And it for darned sure wasn't going against any of old Dud's edicts.

Trouble came at the end of a hand Sonny was sure he'd won. The pot must have held a couple of hundred dollars. He spread out his cards—a full house, jacks over threes—and started to rake in the money.

"Hold up," said Cad, dropping the winning hand, four twos and the final jack.

"Goddamn!" Sonny jumped to his feet. His chair crashed to the floor behind him. "Ain't no sonuvabitch cardsharp gonna rob me like that."

The crowd scattered, and Cad began pocketing the money.

Sonny reached for his gun. Cad looked up into the business end of the barrel, but he kept on gathering his winnings.

"Didn't you hear me, you no-good son of a whore?"

"Loud as you are, Sonny, I imagine the dead themselves could hear."

When he'd taken all he had coming to him he shifted his hat low on his forehead, being careful to keep his hands away from his gun. "Now listen carefully," he said, standing. "I'm leaving. I wasn't the one cheating, and you know it. So does everyone here. But if you still think you've got business with me, let's settle it outside. Seems to me this saloon has all the decorating it needs."

With that, he turned his back, sent a message to Dudley that he hoped his liaison angel was keeping his end of their bargain, and started toward the patch of blue he could see through the open doorway. He wasn't quite sure how he would play the scene awaiting him, given his restrictions, but he was hoping something came to mind soon.

The crowd scattered in front of him, getting out of the line of fire, and he was reminded of Moses parting the Red Sea. He hadn't thought of the Old Testament story since he was a boy, but somehow the biblical comparison came to mind.

Cad and Moses: not exactly two of a kind. But they were both fighting evil in the desert, and they both had Divinity on their side. If Moses had a sense of humor, wherever he was right now he ought to be laughing out loud.

Whisperings stirred like leaves in a breeze as he walked through the swinging doors and into a sunlit day. He was surprised to see it was not yet noon. In the street he turned to watch his adversary standing just outside the saloon door. Sonny blinked against the brightness, a puzzled look on his face. It was plain his threats had never been ignored before, not as Cad had just done, coolly, without a worry in the world.

Sonny was the kind who got his way, no exceptions. And here was a stranger, standing in a circle of hard-eyed men that Sonny probably knew, showing him out to be a fool.

Cad could have shot the band off his hat or the fringe off his leather vest without wounding him, but he didn't want to demonstrate his prowess, not just yet.

"I didn't ask for this showdown," he said, keeping his hands open and away from his body. "I'll play you a hand or two, anytime you say."

"So you can cheat me again, you lying bastard?" Sonny took a step forward. Cad held his stand, looking around at the crowd. If he'd been trying to round up a gang of outlaws, he could have stopped right there. Wary and watchful, they looked as kind as cactus and as rootless as tumbleweed. Drifters and thieves from both sides of the border, enjoying someone else's troubles for a change. Only Sonny's two companions, the ones who had stayed around for the game, showed any sign that they would help their comrade in a fight.

And even they didn't look all too sure as they watched to see what this crazy stranger would do.

One observer in particular caught Cad's eye. It was Deputy Wiley Fike, standing away from the action, gaunt and pale as a skeleton, trousers hanging loose on his hipless frame, a holster riding low against each leg. He made no move toward his guns; nor did he give any sign that he was stepping forward to uphold the law.

A commotion outside the pleasure parlor next door brought little attention . . . until Cad heard an all-too-familiar voice cry out in anger.

"Put me down, you oaf!"

Cad rolled his eyes. One of the onlookers, a burly and bearded brute, pushed through the crowd, an arm wrapped around the waist of a struggling and very angry woman who was kicking and flailing her arms and doing what she could to give him a hard time.

The man paid her no mind. "Caught her outside the whorehouse. Had a rock in her hand, like she was getting into the fight."

He set her on the ground. She swayed once, then got her footing, just standing there, the only woman in a gang of unprincipled men. Too bad, Cad thought, she was wearing one of the fancy nothings from the trunk, although, given her looks in general, she would have stood out in her high-necked silk.

He looked her over, starting with the high-heeled boots, black and laced up to the ankle, her exposed legs encased in red-striped hose, fancy black garters holding them around the sweep of her thighs. Instead of a dress, she wore a bit of flesh-colored chiffon over her vital parts, the rise of her breasts full and milk-white, the way he'd pictured them, her shoulders bare, her yellow hair wild, as if she'd combed it in a tornado.

He couldn't see her nipples exactly, nor the

dark between her legs, but he almost could. And so could everyone else. Glancing around the suddenly quiet crowd, she crossed her arms in front of her, shifting them about, but there were too many places she needed to cover and she ended up with her hands at her side.

"I saw you from the window," she said to Cad, trying to tilt her chin and sound brave, but she didn't meet with much success.

"You should have stayed up there."

"But you were in trouble. I thought if I threw a rock—"

Cad shook his head in disgust.

"Honey," someone in the crowd yelled out, "you can throw one of your rocks at me anytime you want."

The offer was met with raucous laughter, and then a few specific suggestions as to what else she might throw.

"Hot damn!" said a man at the edge of the crowd. Cad recognized one of Lattimer's men, the one who'd left the gaming table first. "Sonny, I'll bet this is that hundred-dollar whore Billy was telling us about. The one from New Orleans."

He dragged out the name of the city, giving it several syllables, making it sound obscene.

Amy's flinch was strong enough for all to see. She gave no sign of the bravado that had sent the drunken youth on his way last night.

She'd managed to draw attention away from the card-game confrontation, but, while giving her credit, Cad couldn't claim to be pleased. She looked as enticing as any woman he'd ever seen, but his enforced goodness had taken the pleasure out of the sight. Especially since he wasn't the only one looking.

Two strides closed the distance between them, and he scooped her into his arms. "Gentlemen," he announced to one and all, "the lady and I have made prior arrangements for an assignation."

"Ass what?" someone said.

"Assignation," he repeated. "That means the woman is mine."

He didn't ponder on the significance of his announcement, except to think that his reformation was bringing out words he hadn't used in years. Association with his garrulous angel, no doubt.

Amy's arms went around his neck. Her lips were pulled tight and she had a trapped-animal wildness to her eyes, but she didn't whimper and she didn't shed a tear.

She made him proud. Darned if he knew why.

Scratch, scratch. He didn't even mind the claws.

He started toward Kate Cassidy's and again, like the Red Sea, the crowd parted.

"What about me?" Sonny yelled out from the front of the saloon.

"Sorry," Cad said over his shoulder, "but I prefer women. If you're hankering for a fancy man, you'll have to find your pleasures with somebody else."

Chapter Eight

Amy held on for dear life as Cad carried her past what seemed like a thousand staring, drooling men. She'd been trying on some of her mother's clothes in preparation for his lesson tonight, thinking of his wound and how brave he was to try to hide it . . . and then she'd glanced out the window onto the street.

Why she'd thought she could save him was beyond her, but the idea had struck with a surprising force, and without grabbing so much as a wrapper, she'd tromped downstairs as though she had Divine protection. Absurd though it was, she'd thought someone in heaven was looking out for her and guiding her path.

She'd found out different right away, about both his rescue and her state of salvation. Much as she needed one, there hadn't been an angel in sight.

And here was Cad, irritated with her again. They entered the brothel—Amy's new designation for her abode—and stopped at the foot of the stairs. She was holding on to him so hard, she felt something trembling inside him. He must be furious with her; he had every right. For someone intent on taking care of herself, she was making every mistake that she could.

She eased her hold on him and looked into his eyes. Eyes lit with a glint of definite pleasure. His trembles turned to rumbles and he threw back his head and laughed.

Laughed! She couldn't believe it. She'd scarcely seen him smile.

Indignation replaced chagrin. "What's so funny?"

He grinned, and her heart turned flip-flops.

"You and me and Sonny boy. I haven't seen anything so ridiculous in years."

They stared at each other for a while, and the light in his eyes turned to something far more solemn, far more intriguing, far more disturbing than anything she'd seen outside. She felt hot all over, and restless, too, for something she couldn't describe. Something to do with her and Cad.

Just when she felt she might melt in his arms, he turned hard and cold; she didn't know how she knew it, but she did. Somehow he was distancing himself from her, though he held her in his arms.

Last night . . . this morning . . . she'd experienced a surge of sympathy for him, and a kind of communication she'd never felt with anyone else. They both had troubles; they could help each other out.

In the bright light of day things were different. Unwanted baggage, that's what she was; more trouble than she was worth. An amusement, an irritation, a bother, like a troublesome child.

And here she'd been swept with emotions quite different, feeling the way she had when she'd sat beside him in his room. Not sympathy, exactly, but something warmer and deeper and more basic—and more unsettling too.

She flushed with embarrassment, and indignation as well.

"Put me down," she ordered. "See if I ever try to save you again."

"Is that a promise?"

"Oh!" she said in exasperation. "Just put me down."

"Where you staying?"

She clamped her mouth shut.

He kissed her, the way she'd been wanting him to, only he picked a time when she was in a rage. At least she was attempting to be. She tried to stay tight-lipped, but he had a very insistent way of rubbing his mouth over hers, and she felt herself softening all over. He took advantage of her vulnerable condition, touching her with his tongue, playing inside against her teeth, then returning to a simple kiss.

The cad! He was, indeed, well-named.

The trouble was, she didn't want him to stop. When he broke away without any urging she almost went after him with a kiss of her own. This kissing was a fascinating undertaking. Mama hadn't written much about it. She should have. A girl could lose much of her will from just touching lips.

It was certain Cad knew it, and he was rascal enough to use the knowledge against her. Summoning her dignity, she tried to sit straight in his arms, but there were too many bare parts of her and she felt the roughness of his clothes and the heat of his body almost everywhere. And where she didn't feel him, she wanted to. Even angry and embarrassed and knowing she was being manipulated, she wanted his touch more than anything.

She looked into his eyes, asking unspoken questions about what was happening to her. Then she remembered his injury, and she felt ashamed. *She* was the rascal, not he, for forcing her attentions on him when they could only bring him pain.

He looked past her to the top of the stairs, where Kate Cassidy stood watching.

"Her room's up here, the right front," Kate said.

"I can walk," Amy said, squirming to get free.

He paid her no mind. He moved up the stairs with ease, as though she weighed no more than his hat, sparing a quick, knowing glance at the brothel's madam as he passed. He didn't set Amy down until he was in her new quarters and the door was closed behind them.

Through the open window could be heard the noises from the street, men and horses and a wagon creaking by; inside the room, except for the pounding of her heart, all was quiet.

She looked around, seeing the place through his eyes . . . the simple bed with the plain oak headboard, the old-fashioned quilt, the rag rug, the bare walls—except for a single mirror over the bed—and the chest with its basin and water pitcher. Her trunk was on the floor in the corner, open, its contents in disarray.

When she looked back at him he was looking at her . . . rather, at parts of her: the half-exposed breasts, mainly, with glances at her fully exposed legs.

"That's what you picked for tonight?" he asked. She thought his voice sounded a little thicker than it had a minute ago.

"I was considering the ensemble. Isn't it all right?"

He let a perusal stand as his answer, a look so thorough that she felt her nipples tighten. Apparently the outfit would do.

"Where did you get it?" he asked.

She swayed toward him, then got hold of herself, resting her sweaty palms against her thighs. "I didn't steal the clothes, if that's what you're thinking."

He tossed his hat on the bed, as though he were marking his territory, and glanced back at her with a thoughtful look on his face. His very lean and interesting face, his tough-and-tender-at-the-same-time face, she thought, at the same time she decided she was losing her sanity.

Why else would she want to be in his arms again? He couldn't do much, and even if he managed to work through the pain, she would be the one to pay.

In more ways than one, she decided, with cash and, far more importantly, with whatever emotions he left tearing through her. Why, even her heart might get involved. What if she were fool enough to fall in love? He would never love her in return, and she didn't mean just in a physical sense. For certain he would never give her the home she craved. If she knew nothing else about him, she knew that much.

Caring for the enigmatic Cad Rankin, she thought with a sigh, could prove very expensive indeed.

She simply had to be strong and keep her heart uninvolved. Mama was clearly right when she said a courtesan wasn't supposed to get emotional about her patrons. She should rejoice that this one, her first, could do no more to her than instruct.

"Amy," he said, giving her another long glance, "I'm sure those clothes are yours. Whatever you are—and I haven't figured that one out yet—it's not a thief."

So he thought she was enigmatic, too, did he? She had enough of her mother in her to know that keeping a man guessing was a good thing.

Standing there with him so close, tall and lean, with his hair thick and dark and his eyes deep and searching, she felt her knees give out. She sat on the edge of the bed, prim as she could manage in her getup, deciding she needed a lot of work on her strength.

She'd done a lot of thinking since she and Cad had parted, remembering all they had said and all they had done . . . and all they'd been unable to do. She'd even managed to put a favorable twist on things.

Her foolish heart notwithstanding, Cad offered her the perfect delaying tactic in her professional pursuit. He could keep meeting with her at night, not doing much but talking, and her, of course, not wanting him to do more. Kate would be satisfied she was bringing in money, and all the while she would be working during the day to find out about John Lattimer. It might just be that she could settle on whether to stay with Papa or leave Rough Cut before she lost her virginity.

Why, if she didn't know better, she'd think she was getting some more of that Divine guidance in her what-she'd-thought-of-as sinful plans. All she had to do was stay in control.

"I was hoping to see you this morning," she

said, "so I guess things worked out all right."

"I didn't get shot, and you didn't get raped. That what you consider all right?"

"In Rough Cut, yes," she said, avoiding his eyes, hearing something in his voice she didn't like.

"What kind of stupid thinking sent you outside dressed like that to protect me with a rock?"

Amy's cheeks burned with embarrassment. "I don't know. It wasn't anything I thought out. One moment I was trying on clothes, and the next I heard something outside, and when I looked down there you were, surrounded by what looked like enemies, and all I could think of was getting down there to help you. The idea hit me out of nowhere and it wouldn't go away."

He looked at her strangely, more puzzled than angry. "The idea hit you?"

She nodded. "It was like a voice speaking to me. I didn't seem to have any choice."

Now that, she decided, really did sound stupid. "Have you eaten yet?" she asked, desperate to change the subject to what had originally been on her mind. Control, she reminded herself; dealing with Cad was a matter of control.

He didn't try to hide his surprise. "What difference is it to you?"

"I worked out an arrangement for you with Kate. If you'd like some decent food, that is. There's some kind of soup kitchen down by the stable, but from Kate's description it didn't sound too appetizing. Unless you care for maggots and weevils in your diet."

"Maggots and weevils?"

"Something like that. I forget exactly what she said."

"I've eaten my share of weevils, but I draw the line at maggots. A man can stand only so much."

He leaned against the door, his arms folded, staring at her in a way that made her feel more naked than she already was. He unnerved her so much, she crossed one leg over the other and began to jiggle her foot. It took him a while to say, "What's the deal?"

She told him.

She expected an argument. To her surprise, he agreed, and with practically a smile. "You'll have to get out of those clothes, though," he said. "We need to get started right away."

Within a half hour they were in the pleasure parlor's mule-drawn wagon, Cad's strawberry roan tied to the rear as they headed out of town. Amy had changed to another gown, this one gray like the first, maybe a shade darker, but just as high-necked and just as finely tailored to her body. She'd thrown a cloak around her shoulders for the ride. Her hair was pinned into some kind of bun beneath a high little hat, but a few yellow curls kept pulling loose around her face, and she had a gleam in her eyes that said she was enjoying the ride.

Cad held loosely to the reins and tried to feel the same. Trouble was, too many unknowns faced both of them. Going for food was their mission: fresh vegetables and meat provided on a regular basis by a widow rancher a couple of miles out of town. In return for fetching the goods, Cad could take his meals with the whores. Amy had been so proud of the arrangement she had made, keeping the maggots from interfering with his insides, he hadn't the heart to tell her he didn't need to eat.

He went along for the ride, planning to leave her and the wagon at the widow's place and ride farther east, for a meeting with Sonny's powerful boss.

Silently he sent a message to his angel, demanding that they talk. It seemed unlikely Saint Dudley had pushed Amy out on the street half-naked, but she *had* talked about a voice urging her on, and he really didn't know Dud's capabilities all that well. Back in Galveston, he'd made the reverend do his bidding. Amy was probably just as suggestible.

Throughout most of the bumpy ride she sat still and quiet, holding on to the seat, studying the rolling hills, the thick brush, the small crops of yellow and purple flowers growing bravely in the dry, hard dirt. Occasionally they caught sight of a jackrabbit bounding through the grass, or a hawk swooping overhead. But mostly they were alone, listening to the creak of the wagon and the clop of the mule's hooves against the rock-strewn road, and breathing in the dry, sweet air.

After a time of riding and bouncing she hugged herself. "I grew up in sight of the Mississippi. There were so many trees, and so much water, and so many people all around, I never could see much of the land." She looked at him. "Does that make sense to you?"

"If you're saying all those things made you feel closed in, then it makes sense."

"I didn't look at it like that, at least not consciously. But I can see how it might have made me feel that way." She stared up at a sky that matched the color of her eyes.

"Out here, I feel so . . . insignificant."

She smiled at him, but it was a self-conscious, not-quite-happy kind of smile, and it made him feel uncomfortable, as if she was about to confide in him and make him feel more obligated to her for the sharing of secrets. "In New Orleans I had walls to keep me from doing foolish things. Out here, I seem to be on my own."

"You miss those walls?" he asked, feeling at least obliged to respond. He wanted to hear her answer, too, he admitted to himself.

"I don't know that I miss them so much as I realize that maybe I need them."

"To keep you from doing anything foolish?"

She shrugged; a slight movement, but it made her look younger and more alone and helpless than ever, and brought out a protective nature in him that he didn't know he had.

"It's a little late to keep me from being foolish, don't you think?" she said

Cad studied the rump of the mule ambling along the uneven trail. "If you want to back out of tonight, no problem."

"I don't . . . unless you do."

He felt her eyes on him. "I said I'd teach you to be a whore, and I will."

Even looking straight ahead, he caught her flinch. She'd never be a success at the poker table, that was for sure.

"It's kind of you to keep to your word, but would you mind calling me a courtesan? I know what I'm planning to be, but I'd like to ease into the name."

She'd never make it as a whore, either, he thought. No more than he would stay celibate if she kept looking and sounding and behaving the way she did.

The trouble was, he understood what she was feeling, with her talk of walls and open spaces. She was learning to live by new rules, or maybe no rules at all, and it was frightening to her. He'd been through the same thing a long time ago.

Hell, she'd adjust, he thought, feeling angry at both of them. He really did need a word with Dudley. Old Dud had talked about cutthroats and thieves, but he'd never said a word about a situation like this.

Two miles out of town, they turned onto a smaller road, just a pair of wheel tracks really, and after a short distance he reined to a halt in front of a closed gate. THUNDERCLAP RANCH was burned into a wooden sign overhead. He hopped down to open the gate, and Amy bravely took the reins to guide the wagon through the narrow opening.

The ranch house sat in a green valley a quarter of a mile from the gate. It was a beautiful sight, sprawling and whitewashed, with a picket fence close to the house, smoke curling from a stone chimney, a scattering of adobe outbuildings, and a red-roofed barn nearby to make it seem not so alone.

Around the front of the house was a neatly tended flower bed with a mass of flowers Cad remembered from his youth as chrysanthemums. Between the house and the fence was a stretch of freshly trimmed grass.

He urged the mule closer. A herd of sheep grazed on a hill to the east of the valley, adding to the pastoral scene, and there was a corral of fine-looking horses beyond the barn.

Since the war Cad had never wanted a place to put down roots, but if he had thought of one, it would have looked like this.

He glanced at Amy. She met his eye, and he thought she was about to cry.

"Have you ever seen anything so lovely?" she asked, and he saw her tears were happy ones.

"No," he said, speaking the truth, wondering whether he meant the spread or her.

Growling to himself, he looked back toward

the house. A woman came out the front door, strode across the lawn, and halted by the closed picket gate. She appeared to be in her early thirties and sturdily built; not large, but solid in her cotton gown and apron, and handsome, too, with her sun-browned face and hands.

The hands especially caught his attention, since she was carrying a shotgun and she had it aimed at him.

"Mrs. Thor," Amy said, "we're from Kate Cassidy's."

"Thought I recognized the mule. It's the critter at the reins I'm not so sure about."

Cad tried to look innocent, but he hadn't enough experience to pull it off. No matter how pure he tried to be, he got the feeling the widow would see through his pretense.

"This is Cad Rankin," Amy said. "He's helping me and the other women in exchange for his meals."

"You're one of Kate's women?" She shook her head, as if to say the world was going to hell faster than she'd supposed.

"Never known Kate to need a man's assistance," she added.

"She's letting Cad help as a favor to me," Amy said.

Cad wasn't used to having women dicker over him—at least not as to whether he was harmless or not—and he didn't like it much. Securing the reins, he jumped to the ground and helped Amy down beside him.

He looked past the widow to see a face staring through one of the front ranch-house windows, and then another and another, and then a head peeked through the front door. His hand went toward his gun, and the widow's shotgun shifted in line with his heart.

For a moment no one moved, and then the head at the door became a body, and Cad watched as a little girl walked onto the porch.

"Lenoma, you get back in here," a voice said, and the girl was joined by a little boy.

"I'm not hurting anything, Amonel," she said in a soft voice that just managed to carry to the wagon. "We got company."

Another child joined them, and then another, until Cad counted a dozen of them on the front porch, a mixture of boys and girls, ages ranging from toddler to maybe ten or twelve. They stared at him and he stared at them, while Amy whispered, "Oh."

"They're not mine, if that's what you're thinking," said the widow. "Lost two boys at birth, and then my husband. These are abandoned tykes, some of 'em orphaned. They make their home here."

She glanced at Cad as if he'd done the abandoning, or maybe was the one who killed their folks.

Cad didn't have much use for children, but neither did he mean them harm. He'd felt the same when he was alive.

Grinning at them, Amy showed a more positive attitude. "I used to teach in an orphanage," she said. "I love children."

At last the widow lowered her gun. "Come on inside and rest a spell. I've got some beans on the stove, and some fresh-baked corn bread. Bet you worked up an appetite riding out from town."

She led them past the children and into a big, open parlor right inside the front door. The over-abundance of furniture had a comfortable, used look to it, without a pattern to the distribution. Lace curtains hung at the windows, the fire was low but put out a welcoming glow, and the air held the scent of beans and bread.

The memory of good vittles made Cad hungry, and he joined Amy and the widow at the long kitchen table at the back of the house.

"The tykes have eaten," Prudence said as she dished up their plates. "Did most of the cooking, too, and the cleaning. We take care of ourselves around here."

She said it defensively, daring him to disagree. He'd done nothing that he could remember to put her on edge. Maybe she didn't like men.

They ate for a while in silence, the sound of their spoons against the china plates setting up an uneven rhythm.

"This is wonderful," Amy said at last.

The widow nodded her thanks, and Cad showed his appreciation by cleaning his plate. All the while he felt young eyes watching him, as if he was some kind of freak. If only they knew, he thought. If only they knew.

"You must not get many men around here," he said, pushing away from the table.

"I've got a few hands that help out with the horses and sheep, and a couple of women, too, to help with the chores. Don't run many cattle. Land's not suited to 'em. We raise what we eat, and what we can sell in town."

Cad sipped at the water she'd served them and took in everything she said. The Thunderclap seemed so peaceful, he couldn't figure out why she'd met them with the gun. Just being cautious, probably. It must be her way of life.

Amy got up to clear the dishes, paying no mind to the widow's protest. "Please," she said, "I'd like to help."

"Kate tell you much about the Clap?" she asked Cad.

He choked on the water, and Amy, scraping one of the plates into a bucket, said innocently, "You mean the ranch?"

"I do." Prudence watched Cad carefully through a pair of steady green eyes. "That's what folks around here call the Thunderclap. My husband, the late Ralph Thor, was an educated man with a sense of humor to him. Used to get a big laugh out of men saying they wanted the Clap."

Amy looked perplexed, and Cad put the pox and related diseases on his list of subjects to cover tonight.

"Is the ranch in much demand?" she asked.

"You might say that," Prudence answered in a voice turned slow and wary. She didn't take her eyes off Cad. "There's creeks a-plenty in these parts, run right well most of the time because they're spring-fed and don't need the rain. The wellhead of all that water is on Thunderclap land."

"You control the flow of the creeks—is that what you're saying?" asked Cad.

"You got it right. But then, I suppose you knew that already. Most men come out this way do."

"I'm new to the county, Mrs. Thor. I've never heard of the Clap before."

She didn't look as though she believed him.

"He's telling the truth," said Amy. Cloth in hand, she picked up the pot of beans and headed toward the stove. "We rode into town together. We . . . met yesterday out on the trail."

Cad didn't bother to expand on Amy's explanation; he liked the brief puzzled look that flashed across the widow's face.

"You saying you weren't sent by the Rocking L?" she asked. "Could have sworn you were. You look the type."

Cad came to attention. "Why would I come from there?"

"Because of the no-good, murdering, thieving snake that owns the L. If I thought you came from John Lattimer, I'd shoot you between the eyes."

Just then a gangly youth burst through the back door, waving a shotgun around the kitchen.

"He's here, Miss Prudence," he yelled in a squeaky voice. "That bastard Lattimer is at the gate."

"Oh, no," the widow said.

Behind her, Amy cried out and dropped the pot of beans.

Chapter Nine

Cad accompanied the Widow Thor to the picket gate where the infamous John Lattimer awaited them on horseback. Behind him were a half-dozen riders, as tough, grizzled, and mean-eyed as the cheating Sonny, and carrying enough weapons to start a war.

Could be that's just what they were about. Every one of the bastards wore a leather duster, as if it was some kind of uniform. Except that the uniforms weren't Yankee blue, and they lacked insignia—

He broke off the thought. He had enough to deal with in the present without dealing with the past.

For once Amy took the cautious path and stayed inside. Insisted on it, as a matter of fact, claiming she and the children had to clean up the spilled beans in the kitchen.

Such discretion wasn't like her. He glanced over his shoulder; she stared back at him from the front window, watching everything going on.

Warning himself to stay cool, to ignore the anger that had begun to burn in him, he studied Lattimer. Mid-forties, holding himself straight in the saddle, he wore a suit not much different from Cad's, but of a better cut of cloth. Gray streaked the dark, short-trimmed hair visible beneath his hat. He looked more like a banker than a rancher, a town man who took care of himself.

Except for the face, the hard-bitten look around the mouth, and the crafty squint to the ice-blue eyes staring down from beneath the wide-brimmed Stetson. His weathered skin showed he rode the range as much as his men, and he sat astride the horse as easily as a town man might ride a chair.

As far as Cad could tell, he was without a gun. He didn't need one, with gunpower equal to the U.S. Army riding behind him.

For backup, Cad had a shotgun-toting widow and a tow-headed boy of thirteen, both of whom were, unlike him, vulnerably alive. And, of course, there was the ever-watchful and strong-armed Amy ready to rescue them, although her rocks didn't seem like much of an asset against a passel of guns.

Cad didn't feel afraid of the man—he'd ridden down too many dark trails ever to feel fear again—but he sensed Lattimer's strength and his ruthlessness, rising from him like a stench. Evil authority: that was what he represented, its power used to crush and subdue. The old rage churned in Cad's gut, surprising him with how quickly and unexpectedly it had returned.

"Get off my land, John Lattimer," the widow ordered, her shotgun held steady. If she was frightened, Cad couldn't hear it in her voice.

"It's that *my land* I've come to discuss."

The rancher's voice was unexpectedly soft, holding traces of a southern upbringing. Cad thought of water moccasins in the swamp.

"Not much of a surprise," the widow said. "Land's all you ever want to talk about."

Lattimer glanced at Cad, lingering for an instant on his holstered Peacemaker. "You hired yourself a gun?"

"Do I need one?" she asked.

The rancher smiled, but there was no humor in it. "Not if you'll be reasonable."

Cad thought of several comments he might toss in, but for now this was Prudence Thor's show.

"I'm as reasonable as most folks," she said. "I don't care to do business with lying, thieving bastards who'd kill women and children if they got the chance, only they're afraid of the circuit judge down in San Felipe del Rio, who happens to be the woman's brother-in-law, and who just happens to be ready to call in the marshals if anything happens to me."

"Oooo-whee, Prudence, that's a mouthful."

She shifted her shotgun in line with his head. "Mrs. Thor to you."

"Of course, Mrs. Thor," he said, a thin line of impatience taking the softness from his voice. "I'm a sensible man."

"And I'm Cleopatra, Queen of the Nile."

Lattimer shook his head in disgust. "Your problem, Cleopatra, is you got too much education and too little sense."

"Maybe. But I've also got a heart and I've got a spine, which is more than I can say about those brave men of yours ready to shoot us all down. I'll bet they've got little private parts the size of mesquite beans, and they're just about as much use."

One of the men snarled, and a couple edged their hands toward their guns. Cad did the same, but the rancher gave no sign that he noticed.

"Now Widow Thor, is that any way to talk around children?"

"I ain't a child," the boy snapped, tossing a lock of hair from his eyes.

Lattimer settled cool blue eyes on him, taking in the too-short shirtsleeves and the ankle-length trousers hanging loose on his gangly frame, showing that he'd grown up way before he'd grown out. "You're not a man, either.

Never much cared for tykes; they're more trouble than they're worth."

He looked back at Prudence. "Hear me out. There's no need for gunplay on anyone's part. I've come to double my offer for the Clap. It's my last one. You take it and that's the end of our differences. Settle down in Del Rio with that brother-in-law you're so proud of. The children can go to school, and you'll have the money to build the biggest house in town."

"And if I don't take it?"

"Why, then, that's another matter entirely." He glanced past her to the house and to the outbuildings, and on to the surrounding hills. "Nice spread you got here," he said, his voice back to being soft, close to a hiss, and again Cad thought of snakes. "Be a shame if anything happened to it."

Several of his men grinned.

"I've heard your threats before, John Lattimer. They didn't frighten me then and they don't frighten me now."

They ought to, thought Cad. Long years on the trail had thrown him into contact with a thousand badmen. The rancher had shown himself as mean a bastard as he had ever encountered, on a level with Deputy Fike, only more dangerous because he was rich and powerful, and way too sure of himself.

"You've got your answer," Cad said, speaking just as softly as Lattimer, dredging up the accents of his youth. "It's time you and your men rode on home."

Lattimer slowly turned his attention to Cad. "I was wondering if someone'd cut out your tongue."

"Sometimes a man learns more when he's listening than when he's talking."

"Is that what you're doing? Learning?"

Cad didn't bother with a reply. Instead, he turned to the widow. "Those beans were so good, Mrs. Thor, I was wondering if maybe you didn't have a pie hidden in the larder. Seems to me we've taken care of business out here."

Cad turned to the click of a gun. One of the men aimed a shotgun at him. It seemed to be the habit in these parts. He had a strong urge to show them all what he could do with a pistol, but he had the widow and the boy to consider, and Amy and the other children watching from the window. Burdens one and all, but he couldn't forget them. Dudley sure had gotten him in a mess.

"Why don't you and the boy go on inside, Mrs. Thor? I'd like to teach your visitors some manners. I'll be along shortly."

"I'm staying here," the widow said.

"So am I," said the boy, red-faced, his hands clenched at his sides.

Cad shook his head in disgust. Goddamn heroes, that's what they were, he thought, giving up on the cussing rule. There were times cowardice came better advised.

"Stubborn, isn't she?" said Lattimer. "I keep telling her what she needs is a poke or two from a real man, but she won't listen."

The boy growled; she waved him back. "When I find a real man," she said, "I'll consider the suggestion."

"I'm man enough, Cleopatra. I'm just not interested."

"What you are is a pantywaist, coming here with your big brave men with their big brave guns, making threats you're afraid to carry out because you don't know for sure where the spring's located and you're afraid I might poison it for everyone. Thinking, of course, I'm as mean and no good as you."

Lattimer's face twisted into an ugly sneer, and he came halfway out of the saddle. "See here, bitch—"

"You leave her alone," the boy cried, rushing the gate and slamming through, heading for the rancher as he pulled a pistol from inside his oversized shirt.

"Tommy!" the widow screamed.

Taken by surprise, Cad sprang after the boy. The click of a gun snapped his attention to one of the riders. His gun leaped to his hand. Lightning fast, he fired, striking the rider's weapon too late to stop the shot but deflecting it all the same. The bullet slammed into the boy, jerking him backwards, and he fell to the ground.

In the dying roar, a half-dozen hammers snapped, ready for fire.

The widow hurried to the fallen boy. Lattimer raised a hand and the guns behind him lowered. Suddenly Amy was there, kneeling on the ground beside Prudence and the pale, still boy. A spreading stain darkened the top of his shirt.

For a moment Tommy took on the features of another boy, ginger-haired and heartbreakingly familiar as he lay helplessly on the ground. Tearing his eyes from the sight, Cad looked from man to man, imagining their chests exploding under the force of the Peacemaker's bullets, bodies jerking in death throes, the air filled with their cries.

Shaken, he fought for control, swallowing the bile of anger and clenching his shaking hands. He caught Lattimer staring at him. Could he read his thoughts? Cad hoped so.

The widow looked up. "Shoulder wound. He'll live." She spoke calmly, but there was twisted pain beneath her words.

The boy moaned, and she returned to her ministrations.

Lattimer's eyes remained on Cad. "Neat shooting," he said, as if that was the only issue. "Another half-second and the little bastard would have been gut shot."

Amy just sat on the ground, the life seemingly taken from her, the gray skirt billowing around her in the grass and Tommy's gun within reach. She stared at the weapon. Knowing her proclivities, Cad felt a sharp alarm. Slowly she raised her eyes to the rancher, the gun apparently forgotten. Watching her instead of the men, the way he ought, Cad caught a look of dark despair wash over her, soul deep, heart-rending. He recognized it for what he'd once felt himself and, in truth, what he was feeling now.

Goddamn it, he wasn't supposed to feel, not for himself or anyone else, but Amy's expression shook him as much as anything that was happening. It didn't seem to fit what was going on, bad as it was. After all, she didn't have memories like his, remembrances of a life torn apart by demons like Lattimer.

"You wanted him dead," she whispered.

"He's a child. A pest," the rancher said. "He tried to kill me."

A small cry escaped her, and she clamped a hand over her mouth.

Cad's rage burned brighter still, awesome because it came in someone else's defense. Forgetful of salvation, he itched to put a bullet between Lattimer's eyes. But he couldn't take them all down at once, and while he couldn't die others were not so protected.

Amy dead because of him . . . like Michael.

The comparison was insane. She meant nothing to him. Nothing. She never would.

Holstering his gun, he saw that his hand still shook.

Lattimer noticed, and a smirk tugged at his thin lips. "Not so tough after all, are you, stranger?"

In that moment Cad knew that someday the

two of them would face each other again, would test each other's mettle, and only one would survive. A darkness in the rancher's eyes said it clearly enough, and he understood.

"Let's get Tommy inside," Cad said. "The air's too foul out here."

Lattimer chuckled. Cad used all his will to ignore him.

Tucking the boy's gun beneath his belt, he lifted him in his arms and was rewarded with a stirring and a low moan. The women stood back, Prudence watching Tommy, Amy staring up at the rancher, her expression cold and blank and lost.

"You wanted him dead," she whispered again. "Because he was a child."

Lattimer stared down as if seeing her for the first time. She stood tall, the wind catching wisps of golden hair and blowing them against her lips and lashes. Her back was straight and her chin at a tilt, her dress wrinkled and stained from the dropped pot of beans.

"What kind of monster are you?" she asked, her voice torn with anguish.

"The surviving kind," Lattimer said without blinking an eye.

Her breast was heaving, as if she was having trouble drawing breath. Cad watched the men watching her, taking in the shifts in her figure. He wanted to pick her up along with Tommy and drag her back in the house. If he were alive, she'd be the death of him yet.

"You got you some new help, Prudence?" Lattimer said, keeping his eyes on her.

"She's the new whore I was telling you about," one of Lattimer's men offered.

Amy blinked once at the description, but she didn't flinch and she didn't lower her gaze.

"Do we know each other?" Lattimer asked.

She shook her head.

"You look familiar. Seems I would remember if I had you in bed, good-looking woman like you."

She shuddered and squeezed her eyes closed for a moment. "I don't know you. And you don't know me."

She seemed to be expressing more than she was saying, as if she was pulling the words from a pool of pain roiling deep inside her. Cad stared at her in puzzlement. Hadn't she said she liked children? Was Tommy's wound what this was about?

The air around them crackled with tension, the way it did before an electrical storm, and Cad looked toward a line of black clouds on the far horizon. Overhead a hawk circled as it waited for something to die.

"Get inside, Amy," he ordered.

She started to speak, then unexpectedly did what he said, running ahead of him through the gate, shooing the children gathered on the porch back into the house, with Cad and Prudence and Tommy hurrying in her wake.

It was the widow who had the last word, stopping on the steps and looking back at Lattimer and his men.

"You're a mean man, John Lattimer, and a coward too. If there is any justice in this world, your soul will burn in eternal hell."

The boy didn't have much flesh on him, and the bullet had passed right through his shoulder, narrowly missing bone. Having tended a few such wounds in his day, Cad took care of the cleaning and patching, glad of something to do. He'd left his rage and memories at the front door. Tommy was Tommy, not anyone else, a foolishly brave lad who, like Amy, meant nothing to him.

He gave the boy a hefty swallow of whiskey from the flask he carried in his saddlebag, half expecting Amy to protest, but she held her tongue. Tommy sputtered and choked, but he kept the liquor down and tried to brag how it didn't seem half bad and he'd take another swig, if it was all the same to Cad.

"We'll go with what you've got," he responded. "Can't have you drinking all my firewater. Might need it someday myself."

The ranch hands came in from the hills, and a pair of Mexican women watched in silence from the boy's bedroom door as Cad cleaned the wound and doused it with carbolic acid. Tommy cried out at the pain, tossing in some cussing that was beyond his years, reminding Cad of himself when he was a boy.

Throughout the procedure Amy had held Tommy's hands, and Prudence had wiped his sweating brow, the two of them casting encouraging glances at Cad as he worked. In the hall outside the bedroom, the other children waited in worried silence.

Cad bandaged the shoulder, put the arm in a sling provided by the widow, and stepped back, letting the women take over. He figured it would be Prudence to step up first, but Amy started right in straightening his pillows.

Tommy kept his eyes on her, but he never looked higher than her throat.

Just like me, thought Cad. The boy's already half a man.

He didn't much like observing the two, especially the way Amy was fussing over her patient, but he couldn't put a name to his irritation except to think she was overdoing the sympathy.

When she started to back away Tommy moaned. The little rascal. The widow was watching, and Cad could tell by the glint in her eye that she understood what was going on.

As for Amy, Cad didn't know what was on her mind. He never did.

She looked down at the boy and smiled. "You want me to stay?"

"I'd take it as a favor," Tommy said. The weakness didn't sound faked.

"I could read to you." She glanced at Prudence, who nodded and glanced at a shelf of books over the dresser.

"That'd be real nice."

She made her selection quickly, then settled on the bed beside him.

"You were a real hero out there. I'll read about another hero, one who lived more than two thousand years ago. The story's called Jason—"

"—and the Argonauts," Cad finished.

Amy glanced up in surprise. "You know the Greek legends."

"I wasn't raised in ignorance," he said.

Afraid he might say more, fearful of revealing something about himself, he stormed from the room, scattering the children in the hall. He didn't stop until he was standing at the parlor door. He needed air. Everybody had been looking at him as if he was some damned doctor, or a savior. The truth was, if he hadn't been there, maybe the widow wouldn't have spoken up so boldly, and the boy wouldn't have been shot.

He didn't like feeling helpless. He didn't like feeling responsible. Most of all, he didn't like the change that was coming over him. What the hell did he care about these people? He had enough problems of his own.

He heard the rustle of silk behind him.

"I never said you were ignorant," Amy said. "I might have thought it once," she added, with her usual overabundance of honesty, "but I never said it."

She managed to sound contrite and contrary at the same time, and too sympathetic for her own good. He didn't need sympathy, and neither did the misguided people at the Clap.

He whirled on her. "You're the ignorant one, Miss Amabelle Latourre, or whoever the hell you are. You think that boy was a hero? He was a fool. He could have gotten you all killed. Where did he get that gun? Is the good widow arming the children so she can keep her precious ranch?"

Amy looked as though he had struck her.

"She . . . thinks he got it from a man who used to work here." She spoke in a soft, uneven flow, but she didn't back away from his rage, a fact that ate at him all the more. What the hell did she mean by answering him so reasonably, and looking so hurt? He didn't feel reasonable in the least.

It certainly wasn't reasonable to want to take her in his arms. What good that would do he couldn't imagine. Any comfort he brought her would be only temporary, and he would get no comfort at all.

Still, he wanted to, and he wanted to take back his words.

But she needed to hear them; they all did. They needed to get the hell out of the county—the women and children especially—and leave the Clap to Lattimer's kind. The survivors. The rancher had said himself that's what he was.

The urge to touch her, to make her understand, became so overwhelming that he grabbed her by the shoulders and shook her.

"You could have been killed," he said in a voice torn with something that approached anguish. The tone, the words, the fearful anger were so unlike him that he let her go, as stunned by his sudden action as she. But he could still feel her soft, warm shoulders crushed in the curve of his hands, and he could still see the shake of her head and the thick lashes lowered in shock over high-boned, freckled cheeks.

She was a woman made up of details, and he saw them, every one.

He raked a hand through his hair. He was the cool and controlled one here, the one who kept to his own business and let the world wend its way to its own perdition. A long time ago he'd taught himself not to care; the lesson had been dearly learned and forever remembered.

Dudley had made his heart function again, but it beat in familiar rhythms that were once again selfish and cold.

And there was nothing Amy could do about it, even if she cared to try.

"There aren't any heroes out here," he continued, needing to go on so that he didn't have to think. "There's only the quick and the dead."

She blinked once, but he didn't see any tears, nor did he see the spirited anger he was trying to arouse.

"The quick and the dead," she said. "That seems almost biblical."

She spoke as if from a distance, and all the intense emotions were gone from him as quickly as they had taken hold, leaving him with a tiredness that reached his soul.

"I've been sounding that way lately," he said.

They looked at each other for a moment, neither speaking, and he saw the blank, lost look return to her eyes. He felt a little lost himself.

"Maybe there aren't any heroes out here," she said. "I don't know what to expect anymore. I don't understand you people, any of you. You live by rules I never learned."

The bitterness in her voice tore at his insides. Before he could formulate a response she left the room, and thunder rolled across the distant hills.

Chapter Ten

When Amy went one way Cad went the other, walking out the front door and into the grassy spread of yard between the house and the fence. Staring at the clouds moving in, he tried to keep her from his mind. He concentrated on what should have been his central concern all along: how to bring John Lattimer down without killing him. He studied the scene of their first meeting by the gate, recalling details of the rancher and his cold-eyed killers.

The heat of his earlier anger had settled into cold resolve. If a man wanted to destroy a snake, he took off its head. Lattimer seemed to be the head of things around here.

The decision should have been giving him peace, but even while he focused on the business at hand, Amy's lost look seared its way into his thoughts. Her stillness, her quiet didn't fit the woman who'd run practically naked into the street in Rough Cut, ready to throw rocks in his defense. And they didn't fit the woman who'd run from the ranch house toward a half-dozen armed horsemen thinking only of an injured boy.

I don't understand you people.

Of course she didn't. And if he had his way, she never would.

Who or what she was didn't matter to him, he told himself. Still, thoughts of her stayed with him. Worst of all, she made him think of other times when he'd felt as lost as she looked.

Thunder sounded again in the distance. Just what he needed, a desert storm.

Prudence came out to say they'd best spend the night. Declining supper, he stayed in the barn while the elements poured their worst onto the tiled roof and the horses stirred restlessly in their stalls.

He used to like sleeping during storms, during the times he could boast a dry bed. Not anymore.

The next day, with a quilt of clouds hanging low but holding back their rain, he kept his distance as the ranch sprang back to life. Staying well out of his path, which was fine with him, Amy tended the boy, who'd turned cranky to show he was on the mend.

Cad sought refuge by the corral, watching

four spirited Arabian mares prance in the mud. A stallion, one of the hands had told him earlier, was staked out in another corral over the hill, waiting for breeding time.

He felt a tug at his trouser leg and looked down to see a yellow-haired little girl staring up at him with eyes as brown as his own. Six years old at the most, he figured. He remembered her from yesterday, the first child to come out and greet them. Ordinarily he paid no attention to children, but this one, as bold as another fair-haired female he could name, was hard to ignore.

Without a word she held up a biscuit.

"What's this?" he asked.

"It's for you." She continued offering it as if it was some kind of gift, and he got the feeling she was thanking him for something.

He felt awkward; he hadn't talked to a tyke since he was a tyke himself, and he didn't know what to say. So he took the biscuit, although he didn't want it, and ate it, although he didn't need the food.

Her small, pink mouth curved into a grin, revealing that she was missing a front tooth. Inside him, prickles bothered the area around his heart.

"Don't you ever smile?" she asked. "Amonel says if you did, your face would break, and I told him he was wrong."

Cad could have faced a gun-toting marshal

more easily than answer her. A call from the back door saved him.

"Lenoma," her brother yelled, "you get back in here. You're in big trouble."

Lenoma rolled her eyes. "Boys sure are a pain," she said and then, over her shoulder, she yelled, "I'm coming."

He watched as she scurried toward the house, her cotton dress catching between her skinny legs as she ran, yellow braids bouncing against her back. She passed the widow, who was coming out to take her place, and Cad decided the Clap was a poor place for a man who liked solitude.

"She bothering you?" Prudence asked as she took a place beside him at the corral fence.

"No," Cad lied.

"The twins haven't been with me long. Couple going through from Tennessee caught a fever, and the children were left down in Del Rio, with no one to look after them. My brother-in-law told me about the situation, and here they are."

"That's the judge you threatened Lattimer with?"

"The same. Don't tell the bastard, but neither my sister nor her fancy-dancy husband would care much if I lost everything up here. Fact is, they expect it. They wouldn't have told me about the twins except the family had been staying with them and they were afraid they might end up with 'em."

"And Tommy?" Cad asked, not knowing he'd

been thinking about the boy.

"His ma was one of Kate's women. One day she just up and disappeared. Must have been five years ago. He's been here ever since. Tries to be a man, and at thirteen in some ways he is. Mostly, though, he's still a boy." She sighed and looked toward the hills. "It's hard to grow up out here."

Cad thought of Louisiana and a few of the tragedies that had happened there. He could have told the widow it was hard to grow up anywhere.

Instead he sought a safer subject. "Fine animals," he said, gesturing toward the mares.

"They were the late Mr. Thor's pride and joy. Not having children, you understand, he felt the need to breed something. He was shot down by the creek one night, just before Tommy moved in. Everybody believed it was rustlers, but I'm not so sure."

"Are you blaming Lattimer?"

"I blame the bastard for most everything." She hesitated for a moment. "It's no secret, Mr. Rankin, that I had my suspicions about you when you rode up yesterday. You had the look of one of Lattimer's gunmen. No offense intended."

"None taken," he said.

"But you proved yourself right brave when you needed to. Showed some real *cojones.* Not many men would have stood up to that band of bastards the way you did. Looked for all the world like you weren't afraid of getting shot."

"Maybe I'm not."

"Only a fool would feel that way, and you're not a fool."

Cad could have disagreed.

"Anyway," she went on, "I wanted to thank you for what you did. And for taking care of the boy. He's got too many women hovering over him. That's part of his problem."

"What about your hired hands?"

"That's all they are. When I take someone on with some gumption they either go over to Lattimer's side or they ride on. Sometimes they just disappear. I don't like to think about what happens to them, but my conscience makes me. I pay good wages—the best in this part of the state—and that's why I'm able to keep finding workers. But I don't blame them when they make themselves scarce, the way they did yesterday."

"Lattimer sure wants your land. Is the water problem around here so bad?"

"There's more creeks than you'd think, being this close to the real desert. Lattimer's problem is, he wants to be boss. Can't stand it that a woman is keeping him from owning the entire county. He brought in a drunk for a sheriff to keep a genuine lawman from taking the post. He's the one who runs the town. Except for Kate Cassidy's receipts, the bank holds nothing but his money. And there's plenty of that."

Cad remembered days when banks were very

much on his mind. "Anybody ever try to rob it? Looks easy enough."

"In a way it is; dumpy little adobe with one rabbity teller. I could open everything inside it with a kitchen knife. One man tried a year or so ago. They rode him down before he got a mile out of town, drawing and quartering his carcass in the old way, dragging what was left of him up and down the street to make an example of him."

"That would tend to discourage another thief."

"John doesn't mind cardsharps, and he doesn't mind killers and robbers and drunks passing through, long as they understand what they can get away with and what they can't."

"The bartender at the saloon told me much the same thing."

"Bet that was Amsterdam. He's one of the few outside the pleasure parlor can put a sentence together to make some sense."

They watched the horses for a time, while Cad put thought to what she was saying.

"What would happen if Lattimer lost control of things?"

He felt her eyes on him. "Can't see that happening anytime soon. Unless you've a notion to take him down."

"I'm just saying *what if.*"

"You're talking about Utopia. Good people would come to settle the land. They'd put down roots, have kids, start schools and churches."

There was a dreamy quality to her voice. "It would give my children someone to play with. It would show 'em not everybody in the world is a rotten, no-good—"

Her voice broke off, and he could see she was thinking hard thoughts.

"Sorry to get you involved with my problems," she said, embarrassed. "What about Amy Latourre? She said you rode into Rough Cut together."

"That's right."

"Yesterday sure did upset her. Know anything about who she is or where she comes from?"

"Just that she wants to be a whor—a courtesan."

"You can say it, Mr. Rankin. She wants to be a whore. She says it with about as much conviction as me saying I want to be Queen of England."

"Or Cleopatra."

"Yeah." She smiled, and Cad saw what a pretty woman she was, solid and strong and good, of hardy pioneer stock. It was the good that made him uncomfortable.

"Think I'll take me a walk around until she's ready to leave," he said, shoving away from the corral, making for the herd of sheep on the hill without another word. He returned when he saw the widow waving to him from the back porch, gesturing that the wagon was loaded and ready to go.

They got under way after lunch, Horse tied to the rear. The food supplies for the pleasure parlor were neatly packed away in the wagon bed, along with a couple of squawking chickens who didn't much care for the ride, seeming to know what lay ahead for them.

Smart chickens, Cad thought. He should know so much.

After a while the animals settled down, and he heard only the squeak of the wagon and the creak of the traces as they rode along. Amy sat quietly beside him on the hard, narrow seat as he urged the mule down the trail, going slow, picking out a grassy path to keep the mud from building up on the wheels. Not so long ago he wouldn't have believed they could ride so far without Amy saying a word, but that was the way it was today.

The distress of yesterday was gone, but so, too, was the easiness that had settled between them in the past. They could have been at opposite ends of Texas for all they were communicating.

He couldn't keep from stealing an occasional glance at her, but she kept on looking straight ahead. He remembered the scared, lost look on her face when she'd stared up at Lattimer. Traces of it still lingered in her eyes.

Who was she? Where did she come from? They were good questions asked by the widow, but damned if he knew the answers. He could have said she was brave, for all she was delicate-looking; that she had more gumption than good sense. She was a liar, too, covering up worries that lay as deep as his.

The liar part he could take, but not the courage. He didn't like that trait in the fairer sex; it led to too much trouble, and he had troubles enough.

Worst of all, she had all the assets that kept a man thinking about a woman . . . a curve of cheek and a tilt to her chin, and a pair of tits—

He stopped himself. Somehow calling 'em *tits* didn't seem quite right, now that he knew her better. She had a front to her that never quite left his mind, he amended, though calling her figure a *front* was about like saying *heck* instead of *hell.*

Her hair was bound up beneath her foolish little bonnet; he would have liked to see it blowing in the breeze.

But that was because he was a fool. And being a fool, he asked, "You feeling all right?"

She kept looking straight ahead. "I'm feeling just fine."

"Then why are you so quiet? It's not like you."

"You said some harsh things yesterday, Cad. I guess I'm trying to take them all in." She looked across the rolling landscape to the horizon. "Mostly I'm trying to remember how excited I was when I decided to come out west. How determined I was to see that all went well. I don't know if I'll feel that way again."

She spoke flatly, her tone telling him she was done with talking, and he made up his mind to leave her alone—in more ways than one, he decided, but the determination gave him less comfort than he'd hoped.

He didn't speak again until he'd reined to a halt at the pleasure parlor. She looked at the door, sighed, and, before he could help her, scrambled down to the street, not paying attention to the once-dry trenches now turned to muck. The landing jarred her bonnet to an angle atop her head, and he remembered the way her loose hair flowed down her back.

"We missed the lesson last night," he said, wondering where the thought came from.

She looked up at him. "I'm sorry. I forgot." For the first time in almost twenty-four hours her eyes lost their bleak stare. "Before you get away I'd like to tell you something, and I'd appreciate it if you'll let me have my say."

Reluctantly, Cad nodded.

"You made much yesterday about there being no heroes, but that's not true. You were heroic in going out to the gate with Mrs. Thor, and you were especially fine in the way you took care of Tommy."

"I didn't keep him from getting shot."

"No one could have. You were outnumbered, remember."

In the old days, meaning a few weeks ago, that wouldn't have mattered, but that was for him alone to know.

Cad wasn't so sure he liked her praising him, especially since she didn't know what she was talking about. He ought to tell her he couldn't be hurt, couldn't be killed. But that was supposed to be a secret; for the time being she'd have to go on thinking he was brave.

Cad saw with disgust the way things were. For most of his life he'd been a cheat and a thief and generally he'd kept to himself, but he'd always been honest about the kind of man he was. Now he was nothing but a lie.

"Maybe we better forget about getting together for that lesson," he said. "I wouldn't do you much good."

She started to say something. Darned—damned—if she didn't look regretful, but all she said was, "I guess that's best."

She looked behind her at the entrance to the parlor, but she made no sign of moving. She didn't seem to know what to do.

The chickens chose that moment to renew their squawking.

"Go on inside, Amy," he said. "I'll take care of the supplies. You take care of yourself."

"Yes," she said. "I will."

Like some kind of guardian, he watched until she disappeared through the door; then he left the wagon and mule at the livery stable, along with Horse, made arrangements for the food and chickens to be delivered to the parlor, and, on impulse, strode through the mud to the sheriff's office. Bowles was inside alone, bleary-eyed and nodding over his desk.

Briefly he described what had happened at the ranch.

"He shot a boy?" Bowles said, momentarily stirring himself from his stupor.

"One of his men did, and he didn't object. Thought you might want to do something about it."

Defeat sat on the sheriff's shoulders, heavy as an anvil. He opened his mouth to speak but instead reached for the whiskey in his bottom drawer. Cad left without another word.

In the privacy of his hotel room, the window open to the cool, damp air, he remembered the emotions of yesterday: the anger, the worry, the hate that had been stirred. He remembered, too, his gentler feelings when he'd looked at Amy Latourre. At last he spoke to an invisible Dudley, who he figured was hovering just outside.

"I want out. Bring on the hellfire and brimstone. I don't care anymore."

"I can't do that, Cadmus."

The voice came from behind him, and he whirled to see the white-suited, white-bearded angel standing by the closed door, looking much the way he'd first seen him in the undertaker's office.

As before, light emanated from him, brightening the gloom and somehow clearing the air of its rank smell.

Cad ignored all of his angel's glories. "Why can't you do it? You're my liaison angel, aren't you? Liaison me right into my grave."

"We have an agreement."

"What if I went down and shot me a few people? How about clearing out the saloon?"

"You are not capable of such an act."

Cad laughed. It came out a hard, bitter sound. "Try me."

"That is unnecessary. I know you better than you know yourself."

"I came close to taking out a few of Lattimer's men. Were you watching? You should have been."

"I'm always watching."

"Hell of a lot of good it does me. Did you see that band of bastards he calls ranch hands?" Cad raked a hand through his hair. "I could imagine them in soldiers' uniforms. I wanted to kill them one by one."

"It was a natural reaction. It shows you are capable of caring."

"I don't want to care. Get me out."

"What about Miss Latourre? Could you really leave her to the citizens of Rough Cut?"

"She chose the place."

"Ah, so she did."

"A couple of times I've come close to raping her, or didn't you notice?"

"Oh, I noticed. The important thing is that you decided to leave her alone. Besides, you're too harsh on yourself. Rape? Never. It would have been by mutual consent."

Cad felt as if he was talking to the wall. He glanced out the window at the gray day, then back at Dudley. "You know what she wants me to do."

"I know."

"And you have no objections?"

"Your sessions will be no more than discussions."

"Don't bet your wings on it, Dud. No, I want out. I'll never reform, and you ought to know it. The truth is, I don't want to."

The angel smiled sadly at him. "You are a stubborn mortal, Cadmus Aloysius Rankin. You make me do what I've avoided doing since Galveston, but I have no choice."

"What's that?" he said, and then the realization of Dudley's meaning hit him like one of Amy's rocks.

"Don't," he said, walking toward him, desperate to make him understand.

"You give me little choice. My powers of persuasion having failed me, I must call upon Michael to show you the way."

"You're not being fair."

"As a poker expert, Cadmus, you know I must play my best cards."

Just like before, when his brother's spirit had wafted upon him, Cad fell helplessly backward, this time landing on the bed, unable to fight, unable to move.

And just like before, he felt the warmth and the love of a lad who'd died because of his carelessness. He knew, too, that, long dead and gone, the forever-young Michael was in control.

Chapter Eleven

Amy sat at the edge of her bed, her back to the door, and stared out the window, letting the cool night breeze ruffle her loose hair. After returning from the Clap she'd spent the afternoon alone, trying to start a diary like Mama's, describing her travels up to yesterday, in case she ever had a daughter of her own. She'd ended up with little to show for her time.

Someone cursed out on the street, and in the not far distance she heard gunfire, rapid for a moment, then stilled.

The sounds of Rough Cut, Texas. No music as she had been wont to hear from the streets of New Orleans, no flute or hand organ putting out a lively tune, no tradesman singing of his ripe red strawberries, no gentle laughter from passersby, no clop of horses' hooves against a brick street.

Everything out here was hard and harsh and tasted of grit. Even last night's storm had been fierce and loud and thick with threats. Huddled in a narrow bed with Lenoma and another of the orphan girls, listening to the torrent and the thunder, she'd felt foolishly frightened . . . she who was raised in such rains.

But rain was as much a part of New Orleans as the Mississippi itself; at the edge of a great desert, it seemed as alien as she did herself.

Staring into the blackness outside her window, remembering matters far, far worse, she held inside herself a rising panic and a sense of despair.

Never cared much for tykes. They're more trouble than they're worth.

Her father's words echoed in her mind, louder than any gunfire. She'd been a tyke when he left, half the age of Tommy. He hadn't cared for her.

He's a child. A pest.

And not worthy of living, he might as well have added. He'd shown no remorse over the boy's wound.

There were other things to remember from yesterday: the way he'd talked to Prudence, the coldness in his eyes. This was the man she had traveled to perdition to meet.

The widow had called him mean, and he was. The news shouldn't come as a surprise; any man who would desert his wife and young daughter, leaving them to a life of poverty, amassing for himself a fortune without once finding out how they fared, should indeed burn in hell as Prudence had said.

Amy shuddered and rubbed her hands against the sleeves of the neck-to-toes white nightgown that had traveled with her from the convent. She was talking about her father, the man who had given her life, talking in ways she would have once thought impossible.

The nuns had taught her to honor her father and her mother. Honor for her mother was easy because her mother had been filled with love for her. Her father cared for no one but himself.

Worse, he seemed to enjoy inflicting pain and suffering on those who crossed him. He seemed to need it the way she needed love.

Had he always been so? Amy thought not. Marguerite had cared for him once. Had the hard times before the war changed him so much? Did she want to know? Thinking him dead, she hadn't spent her life missing him, or grieving for him. She didn't even remember him, for during her first six years, before he ran out for good, he hadn't spent much time at home.

Yesterday, as she'd watched him and listened to him and seen the meanness of his soul, she'd been hurt and angry, and she'd bitterly regretted leaving New Orleans. In comparison to the greedy rancher, even Pierre Gaston didn't seem so bad.

The panic tightened in her throat. She had lived more of a cloistered life than she ever realized. Her parents had lived in the real world. She had the diary to understand Marguerite; with her father, she had only what he did and what he said.

Since first looking through the ranch-house window at John Lattimer, she'd fought to keep her stubbornness, her resilience, her strength, if not her sense of excitement. She'd almost succeeded, until Cad Rankin told her good-bye on the street.

Cad, with his hard face and harsh words about how everybody on the Clap was a fool, including her.

She'd managed to rationalize away all he said, telling herself she understood him. He feared for their safety, though he wouldn't admit it. She should have told him how much she feared for him, facing all those men as he had.

Feared didn't quite seem adequate; *terrified* came closer to the mark. Burning with the need to meet her father, shaken by the sight of Cad and a woman and a boy against all those armed men, she'd stayed inside as long as she could, but then the gunshots had sounded and she didn't know who had been hit.

No heroes on the scene? Cad Rankin was hero enough for her. He'd shown her how she ought to behave.

But she didn't understand him in the least, not when he could so coolly tell her good-bye and ride away, leaving her alone once again. How had she let her fate get so entwined with his? He had nothing to do with her or her quest. He had problems of his own, and secrets too.

She thought of the jagged scar that had robbed him of his manhood. And then she laughed, a nervous sound because he was more man than anyone she had ever met. He could not enjoy a woman, but oh, how a woman wanted to enjoy him.

What a shameless creature she was, a convent-raised innocent craving the first real man she'd ever met. She had to stop feeling so much. If she did pursue her investigation of her father—if she could figure out a way to do it without disaster resulting—she must make it purely an intellectual pursuit. Rather like the way she had researched facts in the Ursuline library during her school years.

But, hundreds of miles from her cloister, how was she to survive? After the incident at the Clap, which she had reluctantly related to Kate, the madam had ordered her to rest. But she wouldn't hold to that order for long. She had agreed not to arrange for a tryst with Lattimer, but she would be sending someone up before too many nights went by.

Amy looked around the room, settling her attention on the trunk in the corner. She thought of the clothes inside—the whore's clothes; no need to put a nice name to them. She'd planned to wear them for Cad. Not anymore.

She hugged herself. Brave, tough-talking Cad wanted nothing more to do with her. *That* was the part of all this that stung the most, that weighed on her so heavily she could barely draw a breath. She shouldn't have pushed him so far, demanding more of him in her innocent hunger than he could deliver.

But he had his pride; she could see that now. Since she'd thrown that first rock at him she had not done one thing right.

She jumped at a knock at the door. "Who is it?" she asked, wishing she weren't undressed and already in bed. Surely Kate hadn't already . . .

The door creaked open, and Cad stepped inside. Impossible, incredible, yet he was here, as though she had conjured him up from her need. All considerations save him fled her mind. She could have jumped with joy; instead, warning herself not to frighten him away, she forced herself to stay seated where she was on the bed, her hungry eyes feasting on every detail of him.

He wore a black shirt, sleeves rolled back from the wrists, dark trousers, and polished boots. His legs were long and lean, and she wondered what it would be like to see below his scar. Her timid mind skipped past his manhood and rushed to his thighs. They would be hard as his callused hands.

Blushing, she tore her eyes away and moved

them up to his face. He wore no hat, and his hair, the color of desert shadows, was combed as neatly as she'd ever seen it. Until he raked his fingers through its darkness and ruined the smoothness.

She liked him better mussed.

There wasn't much light in the room, but it was enough to show he was clean-shaven. She also liked him better a little bristled, a little trail-weary. It seemed to go better with the little she understood about him. Mostly she thought of him as brave.

And manly and strikingly appealing too. Her stomach twisted into knots.

He closed the door. "I changed my mind."

Her fingers gripped her nightgown as she shifted on the bed to get a better look at him. "Oh?" she said, wondering if he could hear her pounding pulse.

"About the lesson. I spoke to Kate. We made a deal."

Flustered, Amy tried to concentrate on financial matters and not the shuttered look in his velvet-brown eyes.

"I'll give you the money," she said.

"This one's on me. I've already paid."

"Why?"

"Because I can darn well afford—"

"Not the money," she said, interrupting, feeling like a fool. "I mean, why did you change your mind?"

"Let's just say I was inspired to do so."

"I see," she said, but she didn't see in the least. He might inspire her to wild considerations, but she couldn't see herself inspiring him.

In truth, he didn't look as though she had charmed him into the room. He certainly didn't look particularly pleased to be there, much less joyous and excited, as she was. So much for her allure.

A small voice reminded her of his injury, but her pride was not consoled.

Her hand rose nervously to the buttons at her throat and her gaze trailed down the fullness of her gown, all the way to her bare toes, peeping out at the hem. "I'm not dressed for it."

"You'll do just fine, Amy." His voice was deep and low and determined; the sound of it flowed through her veins like a drink of heady wine, but that was impossible. Sound didn't flow.

Except when Cad talked to her.

She curled her feet beneath her to hide their bareness and scooted back against the headboard. Cad sat on the bed by her bent knees.

The mattress sank beneath his weight, and she felt herself leaning toward him. She forced herself to sit straight.

The implications of all that this lesson might include hit her like a warm ocean wave. It was the teacher in her, she thought, that cared about procedures. But it was the woman in her that was growing hot.

If he wanted her to, she could undress quickly enough. The problem was, she had nothing on under the gown. Beneath the thin white lawn, the nothingness felt like warm hands against her skin. And not just anybody's warm hands. Only Cad's.

He gave her long and thorough consideration. "It doesn't matter too much what you're wearing. The woman doesn't usually keep her clothes on for long."

Could he read her mind? She wanted to dive beneath the bed.

Either that or work fast at the tiny pearl buttons that ran from her throat to her waist.

"Who takes them off?" she asked, trying to approach the situation as she might have a history question, or a new knitting stitch.

She'd never had an instructor look at her the way he was doing. And she'd never felt her intellect tingle the way several segments of her were tingling now.

"Depends on the situation," he said. "Depends, too, on what the woman looks like."

He spoke the way she imagined whiskey tasted, dark and rich and dizzying.

"I don't understand," she said, figuring she would be saying the same words over and over if he stayed very long.

"Some women a man would just as soon fu—visit in the dark."

"That doesn't seem very gentlemanly."

"Tsk, tsk, Amy. I've heard that's what most ladies prefer."

Irritated, she looked him in the eye. "I

wouldn't know. It wasn't a subject that came up at the—"

She stopped herself just in time. He'd laugh enough at her ignorance without knowing she was raised by nuns.

"At the what?" he asked.

"At the orphanage where I was raised."

"Ah, yes, I had forgotten you were an orphan."

"Well, I am." The lie slipped out easily. She could not let him know she was daughter to the meanest man in the county. He would hate her, attributing the sins of the father to the child.

If she were to commit any sins on this or any other night, she preferred them to be her own.

"We're straying from the subject," he said.

"So we are." She tried to remember details from Mama's diary. Strange how she had been able to recall whole passages until now, when she needed them most.

Tucking her knees beneath her chin, she tried for a provocative smile. She had to test her skills sometime, but she was very unsure of herself and perishing from alarm that he might sense it.

"Do you want to turn out the light with me?"

He let out a long, slow breath. "No."

He stood, and for a moment she feared he would leave. She'd been provocative, all right. She was provoking him right out the door.

Instead of walking out, he went around the bed to the window and closed the curtains on the night. "Never cared much for audiences, unlike some men."

Mama had written something about voyeurs, but she hadn't thought about running into any in Rough Cut. Men were the same all over, she reminded herself.

He stayed by the window, just watching her. "You've let your hair down."

"I was just about to braid it. I usually do that before I go to bed."

"But you're usually in bed alone. From now on you'll have to keep it loose."

"I suppose most men like it that way."

"Let's forget other men for a while." He sounded angry. "I can only speak for myself."

Her eyes met his, and her body heat rose a dozen degrees. "All right," she said, unable to speak above a whisper. "We'll pretend it's just you and me."

"Remembering we're not going very far. Talk, mostly, and little of that."

"I won't forget."

She wished she could forget the tightness of her breasts, the hunger skittering through her, the dizziness from her thundering heart. She wished she could ignore the urge to jump across the bed at him, to throw herself in his arms and kiss his cheeks, his lips, his throat. She wanted to run her tongue over his tight, hot skin. She wanted to . . .

Amy stopped herself. These ideas hadn't come from the diary; they'd come from somewhere deep inside her, and she didn't know how long she could ignore them. Only the fear of rejection kept her at the head of the bed.

He said sex was painful to him. Not having sex was equally painful to her.

With Cad she was truly a wanton, hungry for the world's wicked ways.

"Do whores and their customers kiss?"

He hesitated, sounding almost wary. "Sometimes."

"Teach me how. You kissed me once before, I know, but I didn't exactly participate."

Unless he considered melting in his arms participation. Tonight she had something more active in mind.

"No." No hesitation there, and certainly no wariness.

"But kissing wouldn't involve your . . . injury."

"It might."

"I don't see how."

The scowl that darkened his already grim face should have frightened her. She suspected that it was meant to do so. Instead, it made her feel powerful, because she could make him react in such a forceful way.

She even went so far as to wonder if he weren't staying close to the window to make a quick escape. For the first time she thought she just might already have a bit of the courtesan inside her. Or maybe the coquette.

"We'd only be touching lips," she said with a

wave of her hand, trying to sound nothing other than reasonable.

"You think so? I must not have done a good enough job the first time."

He came to the bed fast and pulled her to her feet, holding her by the shoulders to help her stand with her bare feet on the rug. She expected him to do something rash if not out-and-out violent; instead he stroked her arms and back and her free-flowing hair, then lifted her chin so that she looked up at him.

His lips brushed against hers. She came close to collapsing at his feet.

Only touching lips, were they? Such touching seared her to her toes.

"Put your arms around me," he ordered. "Hold on."

Amy had always been a good student. She did as her mentor said.

She'd never felt anything more wonderful in her life than Cad's strong body in her embrace. She rubbed her cheek against his, breathing in the scent that was his alone.

She felt his hands in her hair and then on her back, shifting lower, settling at her waist, the callused toughness of his palms taunting every nerve ending as he stroked. She wanted to press her body into his, to rub her aching breasts across his strong chest, to thrust her thighs and all the private parts of her against all the parts of him that she could reach.

But this was supposed to be only a kiss, and

she wasn't supposed to act out of her own needs. So she kept herself a whisper away from him, her arms resting lightly on his shoulders as she waited for whatever he chose to do.

"Are you naked under that gown?"

She nodded, looking up at him through thick lashes, watching the dark glint in his eyes. She could have sworn she heard a feral growl rumbling in his throat.

What would he choose to do? He touched her with his tongue. In feather-light strokes he outlined her lips, then touched her teeth, and, as she lost all sense of decorum, dipped inside her mouth and touched her tongue.

Like a child, she whimpered, except that she didn't feel like a child. She felt like a woman, and he tasted like a man. She held him as tightly as she could, sucking at him, wanting more intimacies than she could name, knowing they would be as sweet as this.

He broke away so fast, she cried out in pained surprise. And humiliation. Had she done something wrong? She asked him, and he took a minute to respond.

"No, you didn't do anything wrong." He took a dozen deep and ragged breaths; she counted them with ragged breaths of her own.

"Tell me how it felt," he said.

She buried her face against his shoulders to hide her burning cheeks. "I can't."

"Yes, you can. I want to hear you say the words."

"It felt good," she managed.

"That's all?"

Forgetting humiliation, moving beyond shame, she shook her head. "It felt better than anything I've ever felt in my life."

"Where did you feel it?"

"Everywhere."

"Tell me exactly."

What kind of torturer was he? Did he know what he asked?

"I touched your lips. Did you feel it in your breasts?"

He knew, all right.

"Yes," she said, the word muffled against his shirt.

"And lower?"

She nodded.

"Did you feel it between your legs, Amy? Are you pulsing still?"

He knew, and then she saw the message he was trying to get across. What a selfish creature she was, as well as being demented.

She forced herself from his embrace, staring at the fine, dark body hair that dusted his forearms where the shirtsleeves had been rolled back. His skin was the color and texture of aged leather, and she wanted to lick it very, very much, to learn if it tasted as sweet as his tongue.

It wouldn't. He would be salty, and she would need to slake her thirst with his kisses.

She closed her eyes, seeking self-control. "You feel it there, too. It hurts you to kiss me, doesn't it? And here I am forcing you to do it."

She hugged herself, trying to hold in the wantings that he aroused. She knew she wasn't supposed to feel anything this strong when she was with a customer, but she didn't know how to stop.

With a low curse, he pulled her back in his arms. "You're forcing me, all right. Let's keep telling ourselves that's what's happening here."

He kissed her again, and this time he didn't stop with simply plundering her mouth. His hands, his magic, trail-hardened hands, rubbed her in a hundred places. He stroked her back, her shoulders, and down to the tight mounds of her rear, cupping her hard against him so that she knew his wounds didn't keep him from being aroused.

Her hands sought his throat, playing in the hollow, feeling his pounding pulse. His skin burned as hot as hers. When she rubbed her breasts against him the taut nipples grew tauter still, and her breasts swelled with desire.

Men paid for this? If he would only continue, she would pay him everything she had.

He was the one who stopped.

She couldn't believe it. Not at first, not when his hands stilled against her bottom and eased to her waist, not when he broke the kiss and rested his forehead against hers.

She knew it when he muttered a very vile curse and backed away, leaving her swaying without support, abandoning her to again take his post by the window. He parted the curtains slightly to let in a wave of cool air.

The breeze wasn't enough. She would have needed to sit in a bath of ice water to still the conflagration he had begun. Shameless, shameless, shameless. And so shaken with wanting his magic again, she could barely breathe.

She brushed the strands of sweat-damp hair from her face. "I'm sorry."

He looked over his shoulder at her. She caught her breath, unable to see the sharp lines of his rugged face or the soul-deep brown of his eyes without a bitter regret for what could not be.

"Sorry for what?"

"For—"

She broke off, unsure what to say. Sorry for enticing him too much? That was absurd.

Sorry for being a woman when a woman was what he couldn't want?

She had too much pride to admit that another woman—any woman—could have aroused him the same way, although she suspected it was true.

"I'm sorry for not believing you about the kiss. You said it involved more than just touching lips, and you were right."

He studied her for a moment, then returned to looking down at the street. When he looked back there was such a hardness in his eyes, she took a step away. She felt the change in him, from teacher to almost-lover to someone she didn't know.

"There's no need for any more lessons," he said. "You know all you need to know."

"I don't know anything."

"Oh, yes, you do. Just fake what you've been feeling tonight and you'll do just fine as a whore."

She gasped and covered her mouth to keep from crying out. Pain squeezed her heart and would not let go. To her eternal shame, tears welled in her eyes and trickled down her cheeks.

He muttered another curse.

"That's what you wanted to be, wasn't it?" he asked.

She managed to nod.

"Then grow up. This is what whores do, only they don't usually start crying."

She brushed the dampness from her cheeks. "I'm not crying."

More tears proved her lie.

"And I am grown up. I'm twenty-two."

"Then prove it by getting the hell out of Rough Cut. Go back where you belong. Go back to New Orleans."

But she didn't belong there. Impossible as it was to admit it, she belonged close to Cad.

It didn't make sense. He didn't want her. She didn't know anything about him, and if he had his way, she never would. He couldn't use her in the way men used women, and he didn't seem to draw much pleasure from whatever she had to say.

An image flashed in her mind of a lone rider moving down the trail, a man in a black hat and a black suit sitting tall and somehow graceful in the saddle, riding inexorably to her rescue. Or so she had told herself. She'd thrown rocks to stop him, and now she'd thrown her whole self. He'd reacted more favorably to the rocks.

Why did she want this hurt? No answer occurred. She was fascinated by him, tempted by him, aroused by him. But that was all.

It was enough. If the fascination, the temptation—yes, even the arousal—brought her a strange kind of comfort, the cause lay in something needful in her. It was a need he did not share.

"I'm staying," she said, but even as she made the declaration she knew it made no sense.

"You're a stubborn woman."

"I've become that way."

"And what else will you become?"

She had no answer, but she saw in his eyes what he believed. She would become a whore.

Against all common sense and practicality, against all her rationalization, she knew that a courtesan was the one thing in all the world she could not be.

He pulled out a fistful of gold coins and tossed them on the bed. "Here. That should pay for a few nights of your time. Maybe you'll get some sense into that head of yours and hire someone to take you to Del Rio. Someone besides me."

He looked at her a long time without speaking, and she got the feeling he was trying to put his thoughts into words.

"I'm not a man for hanging around or being someone to depend on. When I'm done in Rough Cut I'll be leaving. And I'll be leaving alone."

"She's crying."

Dudley nodded, moved as much by the sounds of Amy's quiet sobs as was Michael. He looked from his youthful companion down through the walls of Kate Cassidy's Pleasure Parlor to a small front room, to the still, slender figure lying beneath the covers of a single bed, and to the tears dampening the pillow on which she lay.

"Mortals weep when they're distressed."

"Not Cad."

"Your brother has forgotten how."

Michael sighed. "Is that what we're bringing him to? Such sadness?" His brows furrowed. "I meant to bring him happiness."

Dudley could have told him that mortals could not have one without the other, but it was a fact of human life the youth must learn for himself.

"I didn't mean for him to make her cry," Michael said.

"Neither did he; not really. He thinks what he wants is to make her angry enough to go away."

"That's not what he's after?"

"It's what he thinks is his goal. It's just not what he wants."

Michael shook his head in puzzlement. "I guess I haven't been up here long enough to understand."

"Rather, I'd say you weren't on earth long enough to understand the human heart."

"I know there is goodness in my brother."

For the first time in Dudley's acquaintance with the boy he sounded resentful.

"Of course. But I speak of the relationship between men and women. Nothing in all the universe is more simple or more complex, and in that enigma lies a multiplicity of problems. Love changes mortals, even those who do not wish to be changed."

"So she loves him."

"That is for her to say. She is certainly standing on the threshold of a strong and very natural feeling, and I do not mean solely her physical attraction for your brother. Her feelings are complex. He fascinates her, he frightens her, he awakens those instincts within her that are the basis of womanhood. The instincts to nurture, to soothe, to love, and, yes, to arouse."

"He gives her no encouragement."

"You think not?"

"Why should he? She angers him and defies him and will not do as he says."

"Another instinct of womanhood."

"And he doesn't yet know she is John Lattimer's daughter. He will not be pleased."

"A point well taken. I ask that you observe and remember: Cadmus entered our agreement thinking it the best way to take care of himself. Since your untimely death, self-interest has been the essence of his existence. Now he finds himself considering others. He rebels."

"Like a mud turtle out in the swamp. His shell has been cracked."

"Just so. He wants to crawl back in the mire to heal and become once again the familiar, selfish creature he was. Except that his undead state has rendered such a retreat impossible."

Michael sighed. "Did I make a mess of things in pushing his redemption? I can't believe so, and yet, listen to the woman's sobs."

"Remember, Michael, you had nothing to do with her coming out here. This was her decision, made separately from either of the Rankin sons. Were Cadmus not present, I dread thinking what might have already happened to her. And consider that their life stories are not yet done."

"You told me earlier a happy ending was not assured."

"I spoke the truth. Their situation, already complicated, will grow yet more complex."

Stroking his thick, white beard, he looked past the bedroom, the parlor, the town, and down the trail, to a horse-drawn carriage wending its way across the hills, and he looked farther east, to a lone horseman riding through the brush. Both carriage and horse moved in a path that would bring them to a wild and wicked West Texas town.

He looked, too, to the sleeping children at the Thunderclap Ranch, to the worried widow who tossed restlessly in her bed, and then to a ranch lying deep in the hills, to the avaricious owner who sat nursing a glass of brandy before a solitary midnight fire.

So many people with so many separate ambitions, newcomers and old-timers alike. Complications, indeed. They were enough to shake the faith of the staunchest angel.

And yet . . .

Dudley ventured a secret smile. It was because of these complications, and not in spite of them, that the matter of Cadmus Aloysius Rankin's redemption might yet turn out all right.

Chapter Twelve

Cad threw himself into his mission that same night, gambling at the Inside Straight Saloon throughout the long, dark hours that crept their way into day. The cool, smooth flatness of the cards against his hands came as a relief. He'd had his fill of warm, rounded flesh.

Right away he discouraged cheating by shooting the outline of a hangman's noose in the wall behind the table where he played.

"We'll be dealing from the top of the deck tonight, gentlemen," he said, his voice sounding strange in his ears as he gave the order. "And keep those aces up your sleeves."

Giving orders wasn't in his nature, but he decided he'd much rather give them to men than women. Men didn't show pluck by lifting a brave chin or blinking back tears or staring at him with soulful blue eyes.

At least, none of the men at the Inside Straight did; if anyone was so inclined, he kept it to himself.

Cad didn't eat, didn't drink, didn't rest, just kept on winning, letting the coins pile up in front of him, every hour or so passing them on to the bartender Amsterdam to guard while he gathered in more.

"No need to stay in the beer-selling business," Amsterdam said as he eyed the money.

Cad started. He'd just about forgotten the story he'd come up with to ease him into Rough Cut. So much for planning ahead.

"Looks like you're right," he said.

Working at it with everything he had, he managed to keep a particular woman from his mind.

A woman he had been trying to help. A woman with something she regretted in her past, a woman on the run. She'd asked for his services, and he'd given them without straying beyond the bounds of rectitude. At least he hadn't strayed too far. Strange, that when a man was trying to be good he could still feel like shit.

So he kept dealing and concentrating on how to play his hands, thinking that maybe he ought to put the philosophical question about guilt feelings to Dudley. But old Dud didn't play fair. He'd be better off leaving his angel alone.

You'll make a good whore.

He heard his own voice more than once. All he'd been doing was laying out the facts, in language even an innocent like her could understand. Trouble was, he'd lied. She wouldn't last a week in the trade, fragile creature that she was.

For sure, she'd have to get rid of that god–awful nightgown. It made her look like a nun.

It was a sign of his volatile state that he'd found it enticing, promising treasures that put a man's mind to work, treasures like high, full breasts and rounded hips and long legs that could wrap—

He broke off the dangerous thoughts. The trouble was, he'd been without a woman too darned long. Putting him in close quarters with Amy and a bed was like striking a spark to gunpowder. He'd gone up as soon as he stepped into the room.

"Gawddamn," growled a gunslinger who sat across the poker table from him. "The sonuvabitch don't never have to piss."

Cad almost thanked him for the interruption, since it jolted him back to important matters.

The gunman had ridden down from New Mexico after shooting up a few towns, or so he bragged. They'd been playing for the past two hours, along with a pair of drifters, and Cad had kept to his winning ways.

He raked in the gunman's stash and shuffled the cards. "You in for another hand?"

The man stood and threw his chair back,

sending it crashing to the floor. "Hell, no. This used to be a town where a man could enjoy a friendly game. I'm riding on toward San Antone."

The drifters mumbled their agreement and left with him. Replacements settled at the table. Cad saw they were confident they would be the ones to break him. He would let them try.

Throughout the night and into the next day he played, betting cautiously until he sized up his opponents, then upping the bets and winning far more than he lost. The crowds came and went, but there were two regulars among his audience: Amsterdam and a bleary-eyed, bearded resident of Rough Cut known as the Professor.

Amsterdam introduced him early as the town drunk. "Every place has got to have one, kinda like a church. The Professor used to teach at some fancy university back east, until he caught his wife in bed with one of his students, doing some teaching of her own."

"Life's like that sometimes," Cad had said, giving the rumpled, beaten man a quick glance, deciding he was harmless.

"Rumor is he killed them both, then skedaddled out here. Disappears from time to time, either drying out or drowning hisself in whiskey; never know which. At the Straight he just nurses one drink for the night, then heads back to one of those adobe huts about when the sun comes up."

Proving the bartender right, when daylight began drifting through the saloon's swinging doors the Professor abandoned his table and disappeared without a word. He returned in a couple of hours, but throughout both his presence and his absence Cad just kept on playing.

And winning. He managed to gather a cheering section, which had not been his intent.

Some of the women from the pleasure parlor joined them as the morning wore on. There was Dora and a companion she called Lilly Mae, a frail-looking mouse of a woman with brown hair worn twisted at her nape and brown eyes she directed to the floor. She reminded Cad of a quail more than she did a whore.

Two others who plied the same trade joined them, a redhead and a black-haired señorita, showing Kate offered variety among her girls. She even offered a virgin blonde.

Neither Kate nor her virgin made an appearance at the Straight, which was fine with him. He didn't need the distraction of Miss Amabelle Latourre. She made him think too much, about himself as much as her. About things he'd said and done to her, about how being undead hadn't given him the gift of words.

He was a man for action, not orating or cogitating. So he just kept on dealing the cards. As the day wore on, he saw a few of the men take long looks at the women. He didn't have to be a professor to know what was on their minds. He signaled for Amsterdam, whispered some instruction to him, then settled back to the game.

It took a half hour for the results of their conference to hit the saloon.

It came in the form of Sonny, John Lattimer's would-be cardsharp and sore-losing ranch hand. He slammed through the swinging doors in a shower of obscenities that Cad would have admired for their variety if he hadn't already met their inventor.

Sonny thundered his way through the crowd to the poker table, where he let loose an assessment of Cad's ancestry that went way beyond the bounds of good taste. In life Cad might have taken offense. Undead, he stifled a yawn, which, he admitted to himself, was more for show than from necessity.

"You got a bee in your britches?" one of the onlookers asked when Sonny paused for breath.

"I sure as hell ain't got anything else in there to do me much good."

Dora laughed. Sonny shot her a warning scowl. She fell quiet, but she didn't drop the smile.

"I planned to get me a woman, paying for her as is a man's right." He glanced around the crowd. "Any of you got any problems with that?"

None did, with the possible exception of the women, but they kept their eyes directed to the poker table and their mouths closed.

"Kate's done gone and closed the parlor."

His announcement brought an uproar.

"For the duration," he yelled over the crowd, and the protests gradually ceased.

"What the hell's a duration?" someone asked. "Is it anything like the pox?"

"You ignorant pisspot," Sonny snarled. "For the duration of this poker game. Seems the stranger here done bought the women with the money you've been losing to him."

For the first time since entering, the mousy Lilly Mae looked directly at Cad. "You did?"

"Yes, he most certainly did."

It was Kate herself speaking from the door. With her red hair tucked neatly into a bun and her green kohled eyes taking in the room, she stood about as militantly straight as a woman with her buxom figure could manage. Cad glanced her way and saw she was alone. Good, he told himself, ignoring the small twist of discomfort that was akin to disappointment.

The pleasure parlor's madam swished into the saloon, her full skirt brushing men and furniture aside. She came to a halt next to Sonny and looked across the table to Dora and Lilly Mae and the other two whores.

"Paid prime rates, too, girls. What we've got here is a vacation."

Dora had to explain to her companions the definition of the word.

"You mean we don't have to lie on our backs for the rest of the day?" Lilly Mae asked in a small voice.

Kate surveyed the cash piled in front of Cad. "For the rest of the week, it looks like from here."

"Hell's fire," someone shouted. "A man's got his rights."

A chorus of rough voices rose in agreement, and in an instant the mood around Cad turned ugly.

A gunshot exploded in the saloon. Amsterdam stood on the bar, gripping a shotgun in his oversized hands. "We got us a friendly game going on here," he yelled over the echoing roar. "I intend to keep it that way."

"You're a good man, Amsterdam," said Kate.

"He sure is," said Dora.

If Cad hadn't known better, he would have sworn the swarthy bartender actually blushed.

Hands on hips, Kate smiled the smile of an innocent. "Now, boys, you're acting like maybe there's a law says we've got to service you. If that's the way you feel, you ought to take it up with Sheriff Bowles."

The suggestion was not well received, especially by Sonny, who drew his gun on Cad.

Cad stared into the barrel. "You know how to shoot that thing?"

"Damned sure do. You're about to find out how good I am."

Cad drew the Peacemaker. The crowd moved back. Slowly he flipped the handle over until he was holding the Colt by its business end. He held it up beside Sonny's gun.

"I do believe mine's bigger than yours. Longer and thicker. What do you suppose that signifies?"

Dora snorted in laughter, and Kate shot him a knowing look.

Sonny growled a few more obscenities, but they were poor imitations of his earlier eloquence.

"You shooting real bullets in that thing, or just blanks?" asked Cad.

Sonny pulled back on the hammer. "Like I said, you're about to find out."

Cad looked at the three cowboys at the table, then around the room. "You'll be robbing these gentlemen of a chance to get even."

"Damn sure will," said one of the gamblers.

"First the women, then the cards," another said. "Ain't like the good old days."

Cad assumed—and hoped—those good times had started slowing down about the time he came into town. If Dudley was listening, he ought to be pleased.

Considering the situation, feeling closed in by the smoky surroundings, Cad came to a decision. What he needed was an old-fashioned showdown to get rid of some kinks. Knowing Dud's peculiarities, however, he saw the importance of changing the usual rules, at least the one about shooting to kill.

He spied one of Lattimer's men in the crowd. "Sonny here a pretty fine marksman, is he?"

"Ain't seen none better."

"Say we were to have a shooting contest. Who'd you put your money on, Sonny or me?"

The ranch hand scratched a grizzled cheek. "I seen Sonny shoot the horns off'n a bull at fifty yards. Ol' Toro went plumb crazy, running around and all, but that didn't stop Sonny from leaning down and taking off his balls. Never seen no castrating quite like it."

"Heard about that," another man said, and several swore they'd been witness to the double feat.

"And the bull survived?" asked Cad.

"Nope. Just keeled over and died, like being without balls was more'n he could stand. A shame, too, considering he was one of the boss's prime studs. But Mr. Lattimer decided this land weren't too good for cattle anyway, and damned if he didn't give Sonny a bonus for being such a good shot. My money'd go on my buddy here, that's for sure."

Holstering the Peacemaker, Cad stood and settled his hat low on his forehead. "Seems like Sonny is a winner, then. Fool like me doesn't know any better than to challenge him, though. To a sharpshooting match, that is. Any of you men want a chance to get your money back, now's your chance. I'm covering all bets."

He might as well have announced free beer, considering the cheering that went up. Even Sonny managed a smile, which was a pitiful sight as it broke the line of bristles on his cheeks and showed a row of yellow teeth behind his twisted lips.

Smooth as a Gulf tide, the crowd surged out of doors. Cad and Sonny took their places in the center of the street. Bets were placed, most of them going against Cad. They started with tin cans and beer bottles as targets, tossed in the air by Amsterdam from the front of the Inside Straight. Neither marksman missed a shot.

They looked at the saloon's sign hanging crooked over the door. Sonny dotted the *i* in Straight with a well-placed bullet, and Cad put a hole in the *g*.

"This is getting boring, Sonny," Cad said as he reloaded the Peacemaker. "You've got to pick out something more challenging."

Sonny spat in the dirt. "Got just the thing."

Cad didn't care for the meanness in his voice. He followed Sonny's eyes and saw he was looking at an upstairs window of the pleasure parlor next door. Worse, he was looking at a woman watching the goings-on. The sun fell directly on her. She was wearing a high-necked gown and her hair was flowing long and golden against her shoulders. Truth was, she looked golden all over; Cad wondered if she ever looked bad.

He muttered a curse. He should have tied her to her bed.

"Want to help out your man here?" Sonny yelled up at her.

"He's not my man," she yelled back.

Shut up, Amy, and go away.

She didn't seem so inclined. If anything, she leaned a little farther out the window.

"Come on down," urged Sonny.

"No!" Cad ordered.

Of course she backed away from the window, and before he could think up a suitable substitute for *damn* she appeared on the street. The crowd parted to let her through. She walked without looking down, and he realized something else about her besides her golden qualities. She never seemed to step in manure.

She avoided his glare, instead turning her wide blue eyes onto Sonny. "You two certainly are making a lot of noise."

Sonny flashed her his yellow smile. "We're almost done. You like to help?"

"Leave her be," said Cad.

Her chin went up a notch. "What did you have in mind?" she asked.

Sonny flipped her a coin. She caught it with a quick swipe of her hand.

He whistled his admiration.

"We used to toss pecans where I was raised," she explained.

Cad grew restless with the chitchat. "This isn't a kid's game, Amy. Get back inside."

"You're spoiling our fun," Sonny whined. He looked around at the crowd. "Ain't he? Looks like he's ready to call it quits."

"I am."

Amy's eyes met his. She seemed to be studying him for something she wasn't sure was there, something good and noble. Darn it, she was making him out to be a hero again.

"You're using your winnings to keep the parlor closed, aren't you?" she said.

He didn't like the question, knowing as he did the way her mind was probably working.

"You've bought us all," she went on, "even when you can't—"

"That's enough," he said, breaking in.

She looked at him with growing admiration, when what she ought to do was kick him in the balls for the way he'd treated her. Didn't the woman have any sense?

She glanced back at Sonny. "What do I do?"

Showing off, Sonny twirled his pistol a few times, then shined the barrel against his shirtsleeve, before checking the gunsight. "Hold up the coin and I'll shoot it out of your hand."

She stared at him in disbelief.

"She's not going to do it," Cad said, taking a step toward her. A dozen men edged forward. He spied Deputy Fike at the edge of the crowd, his pale skin and sunken cheeks making him look more than ever like the corpse of a mean bastard who'd died bad. He stared at Cad without blinking, getting across in his cold, menacing way that he was enjoying the proceedings.

"Either she holds the coin or we shoot you," one of Lattimer's men said, and Cad forgot Fike. He recognized the speaker as one of the four gunslingers who had backed up Lattimer at the Clap.

He'd shoot, all right, just like he claimed, along with twenty others. Amy would probably get caught in the crossfire, bullets whizzing at her like the fangs of a dozen cottonmouths. Coldness took hold of Cad, and for a moment he could smell the swamp.

He looked at Amy, at the fright she was fighting, at the admiration she was trying to maintain. He forced his own chilling fear from his heart, from his mind, from the slight tremor that threatened his hands. He even managed a smile.

"I'll do the shooting," he said. Cocking the Peacemaker, he aimed at Sonny's heart. "You got any objections?"

"Nope." The reply came quick, and Cad got the feeling this was what his opponent had been planning all along. "Twenty paces oughta be just right."

He went to Amy and took her in his arms, ignoring the catcalls around him.

She returned the embrace. Her slender body felt good against him, and right. Most of all, she felt too cursed vulnerable for the place and the time.

"Don't worry," he said, sounding sure of himself, as if he was feeling that way. Then he kissed her, and she kissed him right back. With more reluctance than good sense dictated, he pulled away, but the sweetness of her lingered on his lips.

She was putting on a show, he told himself,

acting brave and even forward in front of so many men. But they couldn't see the beads of perspiration on her brow.

"Just hold the coin by your fingertips and put your arm straight out to the side. I'll aim wide."

She didn't say anything, just kept staring up at him. With the crowd behind her scattering, he backed away. Vaguely he heard more bets being placed against him, and a couple of the women urging him to give up, but he kept on counting the paces. When he came to twenty he halted, thumbed his hat away from his eyes, and lifted the gun.

Amy stood down the street, her head high, and held out her hand as he had instructed. From this distance the coin was just a dot at the end of her fingers. He gave a brief thought to Dudley and Michael but decided he was in this alone. Emptying himself of feeling, he took aim and fired.

In the echoing roar no one moved, no one spoke. Cad lowered the gun and stared at Amy, who stood straight as ever and stared right back. He'd never seen a more beautiful sight than that soft, golden woman with a backbone of steel holding herself apart and yet part of the strange gathering of outcasts lining the street.

An uncharacteristic tremor shook his gun hand; he ruthlessly shoved the Peacemaker back in its holster. Slowly the hollowness inside him filled with relief, and his heart began once again to pound.

"You did it," she said, so softly he could barely hear her. "You hit the coin." She cradled her hand against her bosom. "It stung," she added, surprised.

In a flash he covered the distance between them and claimed a victor's kiss. This time she didn't respond, but grew limp in his arms.

"Are you all right?" he asked.

Her eyes looked like shiny blue pools as she stared up at him. "You said you would aim wide."

He tried for a cocky grin but wasn't sure he made it. "I lied. If I missed, Sonny would have claimed a shot." Holding her close, he looked at his opponent. "Match is over. Ride on back to the ranch."

Sonny started to protest. Kate stepped to his side.

"The man's right," she said, with a quick, warning look at Cad. "But you did right well, Sonny. Tell you what: Come on in to the parlor and I'll give you a little reward. No charge."

"You don't have to, Kate," said Cad. "Your time's paid up."

"Yes, I do," she said, her jade-colored eyes darkening with resolve. "You'll be moving on one of these days, and I'll be here dealing with Lattimer. It's best I stay on good terms with him and his hirelings."

Sonny holstered his gun and took Kate by the arm, swaggering as if he had done something noteworthy. A few of the men started for the other whores, but the sight of Amsterdam holding a shotgun gave them pause. "Come on into the Straight," he yelled. "Drinks are on the house."

With a cheer, they changed direction toward the saloon. The sound of a carriage clattering up the street stopped them. It was a fancy rig, with a high perch for the driver, and the top rolled down behind the two-passenger seat. A pair of fine bays sweated in the traces under the whip of a formally clad man in a top hat. A lone passenger, also in top hat, rode in the back. As the carriage halted in front of the saloon, Amy dug her fingers into Cad's arm.

"No," she whispered. She looked the way she had when he'd shot the rattlesnake.

The passenger stood, swaying to gain his balance. He was short and overweight, his dark suit tight and trail-dusted, but he had a big smile on his smooth, round face.

"*Enfin! C'est merveilleux!* I have found my little pigeon at last."

He hopped from the carriage, stumbled, then, with the aid of a pearl-handled walking stick, righted himself before stepping in a pile of horseshit. He didn't seem to notice, intent as he was on Amy.

"Pierre," she managed in a shaky voice.

"*Oui,* it is your very own Pierre."

He hurried toward her, his legs swishing against each other as he walked, and his eyes gleamed like oiled raisins as he looked her over.

"I have come to rescue you from this terrible place. The *billet-doux* you sent me in New Orleans came from a distressed mind. Not suit? *Absurdité!* Both the fates and our families have decreed that you must be my bride."

Chapter Thirteen

Speechless, Amy stared at her rejected fiancé. How determined he looked, how proud, how smitten. He was, above all, a man who would not be denied.

Once her stunned mind accepted his presence—his inevitable presence, she saw now—she tried to say something, anything to fill the silence and deflect the strange look Cad was giving her. Here she'd decided that being the target of gunfire would be the low point of her day, but, as in other matters lately, she was proved wrong.

She swallowed and took a deep breath. Neither action helped ease her paralyzing panic. She thought about grabbing Cad's gun and shooting herself, but that seemed a bit drastic.

It wasn't in her to shoot Pierre, although, she admitted shamefully, the idea did flitter through her thoughts. Anyway, she would probably miss and shoot a horse.

"Your bride?" Cad asked, breaking the silence. She should have known he would be the first to speak.

"Oui," Pierre responded. "Allow me to introduce myself." He attempted to click his heels together, but the manure on one boot detracted from the sharpness of the endeavor. "I am Pierre Gaston of Paris, and this is George, my valet, my driver, and, how you say, my bodyguard in this strange country."

Cad tipped his hat. "Cadmus Aloysius Rankin."

"Mon Dieu!"

"I go by Cad."

He waved a hand at the motley collection of drifters and gunslingers standing on the street, at the whores and the shotgun-wielding bartender in front of the saloon. He even included in his gesture the pale, cadaverous onlooker with the badge pinned to his shirt. Kate had called him Fike and warned Amy to avoid him at all costs.

"And these are the people of Rough Cut, Texas," Cad concluded.

"Mon Dieu!" Pierre repeated with increased feeling as he stared around him.

The men spoke as if Amy were incidental to their conversation. She considered retreat, then abandoned the idea as hopeless. Instead she kept looking from Cad to Pierre and back again, telling herself that she ought to join in the conversation; and she would, as soon as she was inspired with what to say.

"You caught us by surprise," said Cad. "Your woman forgot to mention you were coming."

"For her, this is the little surprise. She is the naughty *Américain*, playing—how you say—hard to get. *Mon père* and the mother of the beautiful mademoiselle were the best of friends, if you understand what I mean, but my beloved and I have yet to grow close."

"Your beloved?"

"Mademoiselle Lat—"

As her name rose to the Frenchman's lips, Amy found the inspiration she required.

"Oh, Pierre," she cried out, and promptly swooned to the ground. Neither man caught her before she hit the mud and manure. Her luck, never the best lately, had definitely made a change for the worse.

Cad was the first to reach her. He swept her into his arms and held her close, ignoring her filthy state. "Amy," he whispered in her ear, "is this any way to greet your beloved?"

He didn't sound particularly pleased over the turn of events. Neither was he fooled by her fake faint.

She cocked an eye at him. "Please don't give me a hard time."

He smiled, but there was no humor in his

eyes. "I never cared much for women who played games."

"This isn't a game," she hissed.

"I will take the mademoiselle," Pierre said, swishing up to Amy. She started to protest, but then he signaled for help from George, who was taller and clearly more muscled than his employer.

Without so much as a twitch of his lips, Cad shifted her to George's arms, then stepped away, as though he were delivering a portmanteau. Somehow the valet's support wasn't nearly so strong or so pleasantly disturbing as Cad's, but when she tried to look at Cad she turned coward and stared instead at her soiled gown.

Beset by a feeling of helplessness, she directed the two Frenchmen through the crowd, into the pleasure parlor, and upstairs to her room. She told herself all the while that she ought to be glad to leave the disastrous scene down on the street, but a small voice reminded her that she was also leaving Cad.

Leaving him to his thoughts, his assessments, his condemnation of her. She stopped herself. Condemnation would mean she was important to him, and of course she was not.

This last was the most lowering thought of all.

Pierre and George waited in the hallway while she cleaned herself and changed into another gown. She moved slowly, methodically, letting each task fill her mind. By the time she allowed Pierre to enter his valet had disappeared to care for the horses and to inquire about lodging and a decent meal.

Pierre closed the door behind him, looking both sulky and spirited, like a puppy let indoors after too long a stay in the rain. He started for her. She backed away and in that instant chose her course. Reversing her recent behavior, she decided to tell the truth.

"Please, Pierre, we must talk."

"First the kiss."

He was, she saw, a very stubborn puppy as well. She held up a hand. "No. I am not worthy."

A weak line, but it stopped the Frenchman's progress and brought a warm chastisement to his eyes.

"Indulge me," she said, fluttering her eyes, "while I have the strength to speak." She swayed for emphasis and prayed she was not overdoing her weakness. Pierre might be the sort of man who would take advantage.

"But of course," he said, showing little enthusiasm. Setting his hat and cane on the bed, he rested his arms around his plump middle and nodded encouragement.

"When I left the letter for you," she said, "I was not distressed. I truly felt we would not suit."

"*Absurdité.*"

"It's not absurd. Please, allow me to finish without interrupting."

His shrug indicated he would try to cooperate.

Pacing back and forth across the room, Amy related how she had learned of Marguerite's profession after her sudden death, had learned, too, that her missing father still lived, and had decided to find him.

She halted in front of Pierre. "You would have stopped me. That's why I communicated by letter and why I ran away."

"And have you found M'sieur Lattimer?"

Amy nodded, unable to speak. She'd found her father, all right, and wished with all her heart that they had never met.

Better the devil you know than the devil you don't know, Sister Bernadette had said on occasion. Amy knew now what she meant.

Moving to the window, she looked out on the street in time to see Cad walking with that long, graceful stride of his away from the pleasure parlor, away from the saloon, away from her.

She reached out toward him, wanting more than anything to call his name. But it would serve her little good, and she pulled back her hand, holding it against her breast. He was done with her; she knew it in her heart.

Her cold, heavy heart. She'd never felt such loss, such desolation, even at the Clap. If she managed to live into her dotage—an occurrence that seemed highly doubtful given her penchant for getting into trouble—she would never forget the look in his eyes when Pierre claimed her as his bride.

He'd just performed heroics with a gun—after she had intruded herself into a shooting match that was none of her affair. Her reward to him had been a limpid kiss. He *did* like kissing her, she knew, even though it brought him discomfort.

If she didn't know better, she would think he was hurt by the Frenchman's arrival, but it was probably just his masculine pride acting up. Mama had written that men did not like to be fooled.

The trick was, Mama said, not to let them know it.

Mama must have been better at it than she. Mama was better at several things. Cad said she would make a good whore, but he'd never been more wrong. Whenever a man touched her—more truthfully whenever *Cad* touched her—she got too involved. Thinking of Pierre standing patiently behind her, she knew that for the opposite reason neither would she make the Frenchman a very good wife.

Down the street, Cad stopped at the livery stable and went inside. Almost immediately he rode out astride Horse and headed at a gallop toward the trail winding north. She watched until he was out of sight; then, squaring her shoulders, she turned back to the room to continue her tale.

"I found my father, all right. He's one of the meanest men I have ever met."

"Incroyable!"

"It's worse than incredible. It's disastrous. He came here poor and now owns most of the county, except for one lone ranch owned by a widow who uses her home as an orphanage. He wants to throw them all out, and I wouldn't be surprised if he shot each and every child to get his way."

Pierre drew himself to as dignified a stance as he could manage and waved a determined finger in the air. "I will stop the m'sieur from this terrible deed."

He sounded both brave and foolish, and oddly romantic, like one of the French knights of old. For the first time since he'd arrived at the convent, she felt kindness toward him, and regret for what could never be between them. She felt, too, a frisson of fear for his safety. There was no telling what his idea of honor might lead him to do.

"John Lattimer is too strong. Too tough. Too mean."

"I have George, a marksman nonpareil."

Amy's heart sank lower. "Please, Pierre, no. Twenty Georges might do it, but none fewer. My father surrounds himself with men who would shoot down innocent children without a qualm." Her eyes teared, and her fingers stilled her trembling lips. "I saw them myself."

He stepped toward her but halted when she held up a hand. This demonstration of weakness would not do. More than anything else, she must show Pierre she was strong and without need of assistance, for the good of them both.

"I'm all right," she lied. "Just weak from the surprise of your arrival." She managed a conspiratorial smile. "I do request one favor of you."

He gestured broadly. "You have but to ask."

"Don't call me by my real name. And do not reveal what I have told you. No one knows who I am or why I am here, and I would like to keep it that way. Everyone thinks my name is Amabelle Latourre, and that I came here to"—this part was harder—"to follow in the path set by my mother."

Already pasty, Pierre turned whiter still.

"And have you . . . succeeded? With perhaps this man named Cad?"

"No. I tell you in all honesty that you should not fear my deflowering from that particular source."

"But he is so—" Pierre gesticulated to show what he meant.

"Manly? Yes, he is. And quite attractive. But he is not interested in me. Trust me on that.'

"Perhaps he is a man who prefers the men."

"Perhaps," said Amy, deciding that was as good an explanation as any for Cad's affliction. "Sometimes we pretend to . . . you know. But I promise it is just pretense, so that I will not be bothered by others. Despite my surroundings," she said, trying to keep dissatisfaction from her voice, "I am as pure as the day I left the Ursuline nuns."

She did not count lascivious thoughts as sullying that purity, or even the way Cad's hands had stroked her eager flesh. He hadn't touched the really vital parts, she told herself; yet it was true that everywhere he touched took on a new import.

Pierre's round, smooth brow furrowed in disbelief. Amy changed the subject. "You're not sniffing."

"In this land with the dryness, the nose behaves itself. This is truly *incroyable.*"

Amy agreed.

George knocked on the door, then entered, top hat in hand. He was taller than his master by a foot, his face sharply Gallic where Pierre's was pudding soft, but he bore a deferential air that said he knew his place. He bore, too, signs of a difficult afternoon, his clothes having picked up an extra layer of dust, and one cheek a streak of dirt.

"Mademoiselle Lattimer, forgive the intrusion."

Amy glanced at Pierre, who said, "We will call her Mademoiselle Latourre."

"But of course," George said, without so much as the lift of a brow, as always the well-trained servant. "Mademoiselle Latourre." He bowed slightly to Pierre. "I have found us quarters."

"In the hotel?" Amy asked, unable to imagine

them in a room as bare and rank as Cad's.

The valet's nose wrinkled in distaste. "*Non.* M'sieur Gaston has a delicate constitution. I am considering a small fire to bring this public accommodation to the ground."

"So where are you staying?"

"With a m'sieur who calls himself the Professor. I have been preparing our room. He knows the French literature, and the history and language as well. This is a beginning. In time I shall teach him to bathe."

Claiming a headache, Amy convinced Pierre to retire early. Reluctantly he admitted he, too, was worn by the long journey, and he retreated to the sanctuary of the Professor's adobe hut, where, he assured her, George was attempting to assemble a decent meal.

"I will give much thought to our dilemma," he said as he prepared to leave her room.

"*Our?*" she asked.

He kissed her hand fervently. "But of course. I will not desert you, my beloved, in your time of need."

Ah, the French knight. Amy wondered what she might do to discourage him.

Afraid of thinking too much, she sought company with the other women. The mood in the pleasure parlor's downstairs kitchen, where they were eating an early dinner and talking over the shooting match, was festive on this rare surcease from work, but a silence fell as she entered, and she felt all eyes on her.

"Are you all right?" asked Kate. "You look a little pale."

"It's the excitement of the day," she said as she took her place at the table.

This was the first time she had seen all the women together. At least two or more were usually with a man. There was Kate, dignified but with the wisdom of hard experience in her green eyes; Dora, who'd clearly been in the business a long time; Lilly Mae, the sparrowlike young woman who clearly had not; Sal, who'd arrived at the parlor only a few days before Amy, her body bruised by the man she'd been traveling with; and Carmen, who came from a brothel across the border, claiming that Kate's establishment was the best place she'd ever worked, despite the quality of its clientele.

"So you're gonna get married," Dora said.

"No. I broke the engagement before I left New Orleans."

Dora snorted. "Pierre don't seem to know it."

"I'm working on that," Amy said. "He's very young and . . . innocent."

"I think he's sweet," said Lilly Mae, her eyes downcast. "He called you his little pigeon. And he came all the way from France."

She looked up to find all eyes on her. Her cheeks turned pink, giving her thin face a needed splash of color. "Well, he did."

"Yes, he did," agreed Amy. "And it was very brave of him to travel all this way to find me.

But it was also needless. We will not be wed."

"Why not?" asked Sal. "He looks like money to me, and he don't look like a bastard who'd beat you."

"I don't love him." Even as she said the words, Amy knew how foolish they must sound. To these women, love was a commodity bought and sold in bed.

Carmen let out a spate of Spanish, Dora shook her head in disbelief, and Lilly Mae smiled sadly, as if she thought Amy expected too much.

Only Kate watched without expression, but her eyes were sharp as ever. Amy found her stillness more disturbing than the open reactions of the other women, and she felt like the fraud she was.

I left Pierre to find my father, John Lattimer, and now that I've found the kind of man he is I don't want anyone to know.

What would Kate say to that? What would they all say? She knew in her heart that accepting though they were of human weaknesses, they would not be pleased by her deception.

She stood. "I think I'll go on up. It's been a long day."

In truth, she did have a headache. Accepting the offered sympathies, she sequestered herself once again in her room.

Unable to sleep, she braided her hair by the window and watched the setting sun, the rising moon, the twinkling of a million stars. Never had she seen such a glorious sky, but she could not find it in her heart to enjoy the spectacle.

The sounds of Rough Cut drifted up to her, but she ignored them. But then the sound of one particular horse brought her to full alert, her heart pounding. How she picked out Cad's horse she did not know, but it was certainly him riding back into town in a wash of silver moonlight. He was dressed all in black, and she could only imagine the grim set of his mouth and the taut pull of bristled skin against his lean cheeks.

Cadmus Aloysius Rankin: a name she would never forget, and also one of the few facts she knew about him, details she gathered as though they were precious jewels—the courage he denied, his skill as a marksman, and, sadly, the tragedy of his wound.

She suffered for him, and she suffered for herself.

Leaving Horse at the stable, he made his way down the street to the hotel. Toward her, too, though she knew the parlor was not his destination.

Or at least it wasn't at the moment.

Bending forefinger and thumb between her teeth, she let out a whistle that would have awed the children back at the convent. It was a skill learned in her hoydenish youth; she hadn't tried it out in years. Proudly she saw Cad's head whip around in her direction. Unfortunately, he wasn't the only man looking the same way.

Billy from the Rocking L, the boy who had

accosted her that first night in town, staggered on the street beneath her window.

"Hot damn," he called out. "I'm coming, honey."

"Oh, no you're not," said Cad. "The woman's taken."

He steered Billy toward the saloon, thumbed his hat to the back of his head, and looked up at her. Even in the pale moonlight she could see the anger in his eyes. She shrank back into the room and began to loosen her braid, mindless as to why. She was fingering her hair about her shoulders when he slammed through the door.

She closed the curtains and turned to face him. "I remember you don't like onlookers."

"There's not going to be anything for them to see. What the hell are you doing, whistling like that?"

His anger stirred her own. "Why, isn't it ladylike? Are the men of Rough Cut likely to think I'm a whore?"

She hadn't planned to challenge him in such a way, but when he attacked like this he brought out the worst in her.

He looked her up and down. Once again she was wearing the neck-to-toes nightgown, and nothing else. And he was the way she had pictured him, scowling and bristled and more arousing than a man had any right to be. The anger fading, her nipples puckered into hard little nubs and her stomach pulled tight as a drum.

She smoothed her hair, aware of why she'd loosened the braid. Cad liked her hair this way, and she wanted to please him in every way she could.

"Isn't being a whore what you want?" he growled. "Or is it marriage to the fancy Pierre?"

Neither. But she kept the thought to herself.

"Where did you go?" she asked.

"You're evading the question, Amy."

"I'll answer you if you answer me."

"Do you think you're in a bargaining position?"

"I just want to know where you went."

"Horse needed a ride. I went nowhere."

His harsh tone hinted at several meanings, but she knew he would tell her nothing more.

She held her hands tightly at her waist. "Let me explain about Pierre."

"I've decided I'm not interested."

"Oh, yes you are."

"Oh, no—"

He stopped himself, shook his head, and tossed his hat on top of the quilt. Did all men do that? Was dropping apparel on a woman's bed the same as making a claim? In Cad's case she would like to think it so, but she knew such a thing was impossible. She picked up the hat and walked past him to hang it on a hook by the door. Turning to face him, she stood close by the room's only exit. Not that she was afraid of him exactly; but with the piercing hardness of his eyes and the grim set of his mouth, neither did she feel completely safe.

For more than one reason, Cad Rankin was a dangerous man. It was one of his many charms.

Her breasts continued to swell, and she wondered if he could see their tips through the soft gown. He certainly was staring in that direction. Instinct inspired her to straighten a fraction and give him a better look.

She cleared her throat. "I broke off my engagement to Pierre before leaving New Orleans. The whole thing was arranged by our parents. I met him for the first time only a month ago. The fifth of October, as a matter of fact."

Cad's eyes widened slightly. "The same day I—" He broke off. "Never mind. So you have a family."

Thrusting her hands behind her, she crossed her fingers. "My mother was widowed."

"Weren't you raised in an orphanage?"

"She couldn't afford to keep me."

Uncrossing her fingers, she shrugged. "All right, Pierre has already hinted at the truth, and I'm sure you understood. My mother was the one who was kept. She was his father's favorite courtesan. I didn't know how she earned her living until he showed up in New Orleans. She died from a fever the day he arrived."

Cad eyed her with more skepticism than sympathy. "You must not have known her very well."

"I thought I did, but I was wrong."

Cad's sharp eyes cut to the trunk in the corner. "And the clothes?"

"They were hers. Part of my inheritance, which I used to run away. Rather than marriage to a man I didn't love, I chose to follow in my mother's profession."

His gaze returned to her. "Of course. It's what any sensible young virgin would do. But why Rough Cut?"

Goodness, he could be sarcastic. "Why not?" she asked, lifting her chin, defying him, and wanting him, too, despite everything.

"Anybody ever call you contrary?"

"You taught me well."

The air between them crackled, and Amy felt herself being sucked toward him. She clutched the doorknob at her back to keep away.

"That's not what I was supposed to teach you," he said, his voice low and again full of hidden meanings, but this time she caught them all.

"You taught me how to kiss," she said, barely above a whisper.

"I had an eager pupil."

"Yes, you did." She saw little use in denying what he had so easily found out. "I've done some teaching too. Different subjects, but the methods are the same. Like repetition. It's one of the best tools of the trade."

"Is it?"

Amy could have sworn she saw fear in his eyes. Impossible; Cad wasn't afraid of anything.

She took a step forward; he took a step back. She felt a devilish urge, and a sense of power that was new to her. "Would it be too painful if I demonstrated what I learned?"

"Depends on how rough you are."

"You know what I mean." She swallowed nervously. "I don't want to hurt you down there."

Her gaze fell to the only useless part of his anatomy that she had discovered. Except that it was pushing hard against his trousers and looking as far from useless as it could get.

Instinctively, she reached out to touch it. He caught her wrist. "What do you think you're doing?"

She kept her eyes downcast. "I thought I might make it feel better."

Something sounded in his throat, more animal than human, and he pulled her against him. "What the hell. Old Dud should have known I've got no character."

"Old Dud?" she asked, puzzled even as she welcomed the sensation of his lean, firm body pressed into her curves.

His answer was a kiss, and she forgot the question.

Opening her mouth, she thrust her tongue out to touch him, lest he back away before she got the chance. Quick to respond, he sucked her inside him. His mouth was sweet and warm and wet, and she could taste the desert breeze when his tongue danced with hers.

If she didn't know better, she would swear a thousand birds sang their night song right outside her window, and the scent of springtime blossoms sweetened the air. But Cad alone was the song and scent; he filled her senses until she thought she might explode.

Wrapping her arms around his neck, she rubbed her breasts against the broad expanse of his chest, seeking release from the demands that her body was making. Everywhere she touched him she wanted to touch him more.

She was a tart, no other way to describe her, but it wasn't only her body that became involved. Her heart, her soul were swept with the warm wonder of being with Cad. She felt alive in his arms, and complete, as if the world could hold nothing more important for her than this man. The power of the feelings confused her, even as they made her spirit soar.

He broke the kiss, but instead of backing away he swept her in his arms and moved the short distance to the bed. He laid her down on top of the quilt, then pulled back to stare at her as though he had never seen her before.

The look he gave her should have heated her bones, but he was much too far away for sufficient comfort.

It was wicked of her to taunt him so, but she couldn't stop. In Cad she had found a part of herself she'd been missing, and she was lost in the need to hold him close.

"I'm cold," she whispered. "Cover me."

She left it up to him to decide with what.

Chapter Fourteen

Cad saw right away what Amy wanted. He saw, too, that no threat of eternal hellfire would keep him from giving it to her.

Undead, was he? He'd never felt more alive.

Pulling off his boots, he covered her with his body and proceeded to demonstrate a few more details about kissing. Beneath his added weight she sank into the soft mattress, but she wrapped herself in his embrace and gave as good as she got.

As far as he could tell, she didn't have much more to learn about this particular activity. Truth was, she was teaching him a thing or two, such as how, with no more than a touch of her tongue, she could shred his mind.

How could someone so soft and pliable be

tearing him to pieces the way she was? He broke the kiss, then shifted to lie beside her and run a finger down her cheek. If he was to burn in hell for this, he didn't want to rush it. Still, he shook from the control it took not to mount her right away.

She ran a hand through his hair. "I'm bad," she whispered, and he thought maybe those were tears making her eyes so shiny. "Hurting you, I mean."

Worried about him, was she? A momentary uneasiness took hold of him. He didn't want to make her cry, except maybe in pleasure, and he sure as heck didn't want her drawing away as a sacrifice.

Was he doing the right thing in bedding her? After the life he'd led it was a strange time for conscience to start pricking at him. Besides, he told himself, she wanted this as much as he did. He'd be hurting her worse if he got up and left.

Taking care of her; that's what this was about. If he was also taking care of himself, that's the way things were between a woman and a man.

Cad looked at the spray of golden hair against the pillow, at her thick-lashed bluebonnet eyes, at the sprinkle of freckles across her nose. Her lips were full from the kissing, and her cheeks were roughened to pinkness by his bristles.

The picture softened and hardened him, making him feel tender and horny all at once, making him know this was right. He thought of the parts of Amy he couldn't see, imagining them the way he thought they'd look. It was time he found out for sure.

"Anybody ever tell you you're beautiful?" His voice was husky. He wasn't used to this kind of talk, but she *was* beautiful, and he didn't think she knew it.

"Only—" She broke off and lowered her lashes.

"Pierre. You can say his name."

Her eyes flew to his, panic flashing in their blue depths. "I don't want to." She kissed him. He let her, for a long, long time.

Cad had never been one for lingering over the preliminaries, but with Amy he saw a purpose to them. She was a sweet one, all right. No, more than that; nestled against him, warm and soft and eager, she was driving him loco.

He unbuttoned the top of her gown and kissed her throat.

"Cad," she whispered.

He mumbled something that was close to *what*, but he didn't stop what he was doing. Her skin was as warm and honey-sweet as her lips, and he could feel her pulse pounding like his. She was loco, too, and he was motivated to run a hand down her side and back to the curve of her breast. She filled his palm just the way he'd been imagining on his long evening ride out of town.

She stiffened. "Be careful," she said.

"You sore or something?" he asked, thinking maybe Pierre had tried some things with her.

An image of the Frenchman's hands on her sent anger burning through him.

"I'm thinking of you. You know, your injury."

Couldn't she just forget it, he asked himself, at the same time cursing the story he'd come up with. It was sure getting in the way.

He flicked a thumb back and forth over her nipple as it poked through the cloth. "I'm doing just fine."

"But you said—"

"Hush, Amy."

"I'm only—"

He caressed her breast. "Trust me," he said.

She closed her eyes, sighed, and did not speak again.

Not until he kissed her breast through the nightgown.

"Oh," she said, eyes flying open.

Cad grinned. She still had a lot to learn, and he was hot to teach it all.

With their gazes locked, he unbuttoned her gown and fingered her smooth skin. She was hot too. Innocence warring with instinct was commencing some friction inside her. Which was where he would be before long.

Exposing her breasts, he stared at them for a moment. She held herself very still. High and full for such a slender woman, they had hard little peaks that begged to be kissed. He licked one tip and then the other, trying not to show partiality. He felt her tremble, but she didn't pull away. Not Amy. Instead, she arched her back, holding herself up to him. With a low moan, he examined her with his tongue and a touch of teeth; nothing to hurt, just to give her a little thrill. Funny thing; from the tasting and the nipping and the way she was offering herself, he got the same charge.

He moved slowly, not rushing, wanting this to be as good for her as for him. Not taking time, either, to think about how unusual this extended lovemaking was. He'd been a long time without a woman. He ought to be stripping off his clothes and applying himself to business.

Then he'd get the hell out the door, back to the street, back to his solitude. Except that was not what he wanted, not even afterwards. For the first time he could remember, solitude held no charm.

The thought of needing someone else brought with it a dreadful fear, the worry that forces he couldn't control might take her away. He stopped himself and held her tight until the dread thrummed into desire.

Directing his lips to her throat, he sent his fingers to the skirt of her nightgown, tugging at the soft, thin material, easing it up her legs until he could feel the firm, satiny sweep of her thigh. She stiffened and he paused, not wanting to frighten her.

She hugged him tighter. "Don't stop."

Ah, Amy. She was a constant surprise.

Stroking his hair, she kissed his ear, letting her tongue do some of the work. It was his turn to stiffen. His whole body felt like a rod, hot and ready.

She backed off the kissing. "I'm not supposed to do that?" she asked.

"You can do anything you want," he rasped, and meant it. Anything, that was, but tell him to leave.

He bent her leg and ran his hand along the underside of her thigh, playing at the back of her knee, then returning to her leg, stopping high and close to where his tortured shaft wanted to be. His fingers edged under her hips, and he cradled her buttocks. Round and firm, like her breasts. They'd be cream white too.

Raising his head, he stared down at her. Her eyes were closed and her cheeks were bright with the same heat he was feeling. Shallow breaths lifted her breasts in a rhythm that matched his own inner pulse.

As if he'd called to her, she stared up at him. He felt the slight rotation of her hips under his hand, as if she was saying a few things of her own, using the kind of silent words a man liked to hear.

Cad had never wanted anything or anyone more than he wanted Amy. He felt like a schoolboy experiencing sex for the first time. With excruciating gentleness he came to her womanly treasure from the back, the wet warmth of her tingling against his hand. Uttering a low cry, she buried her head against his shoulder, but her unspoken words, the slight lift-and-lower of her hips, kept urging him on. She raised her knee against her stomach, giving him better access to her damp sweetness. It was like she was crying out for him, her body weeping woman's tears for him to make her feel good.

He gave her what she wanted, easing his fingers across those milky teardrops, asking himself when he'd turned to such fanciful language, then forgetting everything but how making her feel good made him feel the same.

Dipping into her tightness, he felt her muscles tense around his finger, and he almost lost control. Still, he just kept stroking, holding himself rigidly away, wanting to pleasure her first.

And that's what he did. As if he'd designed her himself and knew where all the important parts awaited, right away he found the hard little nub that was wanting attention. He gave it, rubbing and stroking in small circles, letting the rise and fall of her hips direct his pace, hearing her soft little cries, her gasps, feeling her breath hot against his neck.

She came fast, with more violence than he'd thought her slender body could manage, and he knew it was her first climax. Her trembles eased their way through his clothes, his skin, to the heart of him, and he welcomed them as though they were his own. For a brief, bewildering moment she *was* a part of him, and he saw himself as more complete than he'd ever been.

He pressed his palm hard against her, willing

her to experience the sweet downward spiral of satisfaction, not wanting her to come out of it too soon.

Holding tight to him, she gradually grew still. In his arms she felt vulnerable and innocent, too, not like a woman who had given herself to intimate exploration, but more like one who was giving herself to his care.

Quit thinking, he warned himself, but his mind wouldn't listen. Now was the time to take her quickly, show her how far the exploration could go. He knew it because that was the way it always was with him. From the moment he'd heard her whistle, he knew how the night would end.

All he needed to do was pull down his trousers and mount her. But something held him back, an unseen force, a sense of wrong that fed a conscience he hadn't known he had. He fought to clear his mind and let his body take control. He throbbed for her, hurt for her, his blood hot, his heart pounding, his chest so tight he couldn't breathe.

One thrust, and then another and another; he'd be fast, too fast, but the hurting would be gone.

He would take her innocence but not without giving her a woman's understanding in return. It was what she had begged for, and what his body was begging him to give.

But his brain—the half that kept on functioning—wouldn't let him be. What would he do afterwards—tell her she'd been violated by a ghost? Tell her that needing her was sending him straight to hell?

He fought the questions. Where were they coming from, anyway? She wanted him as much as he wanted her. He *had* to have her, and he was a man used to taking whatever he could.

The truth uncoiled within him like a lead-tipped whip, striking out at the remnants of his tattered soul. He'd left guilt behind him in a Louisiana swamp, but somehow, against all his efforts, it had caught up with him again.

And it wasn't guilt alone he was feeling. Tenderness, too, began its curious assault. Useless emotions both of them, but they gave him the strength to stop.

With Amy, wanting wasn't enough. A temporary man was all he was, and she deserved better. Taking her would be wicked, to use a term Dudley might have chosen; if she was reasoning things through the way she would later, she would agree.

His own salvation wasn't his concern. He figured he was already pretty well damned. The angels themselves must know it was true.

Holding her like this, feeling her eager body pressed against him, he cursed the two of them; her for giving in to her weakness, him for not being weak enough. He thought of harsh things to say, like how she sure was hot for a man and better take Pierre as fast as she could. He'd been cruel to her before; why not now? That way he'd make sure she didn't whistle for him again.

But he couldn't make a sound, and he found himself lowering her gown, protecting her from his hard need, as well as from her own, and giving himself torturous time for his blood to cool.

He thought a minute of Dudley, wondering if maybe his liaison angel hadn't interfered in some way, but he knew that wasn't so. This decision he'd made on his own, a temporary man being temporarily good.

He let her go on holding him, embracing her firmly in return while his various parts experienced the pain of frustration. He'd never been much for suffering, and never anything like this.

At last he broke the embrace and lifted her chin. Her eyes were shiny again, and her cheeks were streaked with tears.

He thumbed the moisture away. "You don't exactly give a man confidence."

Her lips trembled. "Oh, Cad, you were wonderful."

He didn't feel wonderful; he felt like hell. And yet there was a curiously uplifting feeling within him for having done the right thing. He wasn't used to being uplifted, and if it wasn't exactly enough to substitute for sex, it was all he had and so would have to do.

"I kinda thought so," he said, trying to sound like nothing was wrong. He'd been downright angelic, he could have added, although he wasn't sure under the circumstances whether the description fit.

"I didn't know . . . that is, it was so much more involving than I imagined."

"I guess that's one way of describing it."

"And personal."

He could see she was warming up the discussion.

"Hard to make it otherwise."

"But what about you? You've lost so much. That is"—she fluttered her lashes, stumbling for words—"I guess it's the same for a man."

Better, he could have said. He'd always thought so. But Amy had lost herself the way he did when the sex was good, taking the pleasure but still thinking about him.

"It's the same for a man," he said, keeping the answer short. No telling what he might say if she really got him to talking.

She stroked the dampness at his throat, then kissed the hollow where his pulse was pounding. Bullets might not hurt him, but one particular woman's lips were laying him low. He'd rather face a dozen posses than get in a trap like this again.

John Lattimer was his challenge, not Amy Latourre. The two had nothing to do with one another, and he'd better not get his priorities confused.

What he and Amy needed was some distance between them—like maybe a county or two.

Guilt he might feel, but he was human too. At least he was in a way.

The longer he held her, the harder it was to remember his resolve. It took some potent willpower to pull away, and a reminder or two of why he was doing it. Sitting at the side of the bed, his back to her, he pulled on his boots. Her hand pressed against his shirt for only a moment, but it felt like a brand touching his skin.

He stood abruptly, as if she'd catapulted him from the bed, and made for the door, barely remembering to grab his hat. Slapping it low on his forehead, he turned to look at her, lying in wanton innocence against the bed, her hair spread wildly across the pillow and her eyes darkened in puzzlement. She'd closed her gown, but he could see the dampness where he'd kissed her nipples through the soft cloth.

The sight was almost his undoing.

He thought again of a parting line, like *hope you liked it,* or *want me to send up Pierre?* What he wanted to say were tender whisperings, silly things he'd never known were in his mind.

And then chuck his clothes and get back in the bed.

Instead, thinking how he'd like to get his hands around the neck of a white-bearded angel, he left.

Amy stared as the door closed behind him. A cold wind stirred the curtains. She moved beneath the covers, holding them tight against her chin. And she kept on staring at the door as she remembered the way Cad had looked with his dark eyes studying her from beneath the brim of his hat, his bristled cheeks in sharp outline, his body tall and strong and invincible to all who didn't know the burden he carried.

Her body tingling from his touch, she closed her eyes and relived all he had done. How skillful he was, how gentle, how perfect. The memories alone made her feel like dancing around the room. Though he'd pulled away more abruptly than she'd wanted, and the soft longed-for words had gone unsaid, she would not allow a moment's disappointment. He had done all he could.

And he'd done it very well, changing her forever, taking her ignorance, showing her the world as it really was.

"I love you, Cadmus Aloysius Rankin," she whispered to the fast-cooling air.

The admission startled her almost as much as it would have him, had he been present to hear it. He wasn't at all the man she had imagined as her true love. In the convent, waiting for her unseen fiancé, she'd pictured someone honest and kind, someone who would bring her a lifetime of joy. Looks hadn't mattered at all.

Cad had more secrets than any honest man could carry, and he could be harsh, even cruel. Too, he wasn't a man to stay around for a lifetime. He hadn't even been able to stay with her the night.

As for looks, he was the handsomest creature she'd ever seen; not in a pretty-boy way but in the rough-hewn manner that said, despite his wound, that he was a man.

Would she have told him how she felt if he had stayed? No. Theirs was not a love fated to thrive. Besides, it wasn't *their* love; it was hers.

The thought should have made her sad, but her feelings were too newly realized for pain. Let the suffering come later. Right now she would rejoice in her budding devotion; she would hold its warmth close to her heart.

Her state of bliss was another secret to put beside the fact of her parentage, except that the bliss was different. Someday she would more than likely reveal the truth about her relationship with John Lattimer; her feelings for Cad would never be told.

Despair threatened but she thrust it aside. This night she would accept nothing but happiness. True, she couldn't continue dwelling on the physical aspects of the evening. The discovery of passion was too raw for any more dissection than she'd already given it. The knowledge and the joy he'd brought her would be like a precious pearl she would pull out for inspection later, when she no longer felt his hands on her skin . . . his lips, his tongue, his fingers . . .

Stop, she warned herself. Otherwise she would know the same painful frustration he must have felt at being unable to join her in rapture.

Rapture, passion, joy; such strange words for a woman so recently removed from behind the Ursuline walls. But she hadn't been a woman then; she'd been an ignorant girl.

Hugging herself, wishing she could hold in all that passion and feel it again and again, she at last fell into a deep sleep. When she awakened shortly after dawn thoughts of Cad immediately flooded her. Her lips curved into a smile as she pulled out her pearl of memory and remembered all he had done. The images heated her almost as much as the reality had inflamed her last night. She had been shameless in letting him do what he wanted; she hoped only to have a chance at shamelessness again.

Pangs of hunger struck her, driving her from the bed. Desire, it would seem, increased all the appetites. She dressed in one of her gray gowns, thinking it far too dull for such a glorious day. Feeling noble and good and wise beyond her years, she fairly flew from her room and down the stairs. When she joined the other women in the kitchen she thought that surely they could see a difference in her, could sense the euphoria that kept her feet an inch above the floor; other than the usually watchful perusal from Kate, no one paid her much mind.

Over the next week she had a thousand opportunities to ponder her situation. Cad didn't come near the parlor; she told herself it was because being close to her hurt him too much, but after a day or two of rationalizing she found the argument growing thin.

Euphoria, she discovered, needed more than memories to flourish in the heart.

Not that she didn't see her true love entering and leaving the Inside Straight, or sometimes riding out of town, past the soup kitchen, the bank, the sheriff's office, looking neither to right nor left, certainly never glancing back toward her room. Kate must have sensed something was wrong because she didn't push her about taking on customers, even though, from time to time, when Cad's poker money didn't buy them, the other women went back to work.

After a couple of days Amy was no longer able to hold off the pain. Love wasn't joyous; love wasn't grand, at least not the unrequited kind. It left her feeling hollow and lost, and more lonely than she'd ever been in her life, as unworthy as something she might step into on the street.

It might be noble to give love to a man who could not give it in return, but nobility carried with it no warmth or comfort or joy.

She tried to compensate her ought-to-be employer Kate by taking on the cooking, but she wasn't much good at the task. After eating a plate of burned beans and raw cornbread, George suggested she let him teach her a kitchen trick or two. Reluctantly she agreed.

Surprisingly, Pierre didn't bother her much,

claiming she needed some time to adjust to his presence. Once he and George escorted her out to the Clap for a supply of food, and she saw how gentle he was with the children. A good man. She ought to accept his proposal, but she couldn't, when she loved someone else.

On a few occasions she caught him talking with the usually reclusive Lilly Mae, who actually smiled when he was near. Both seemed a little flustered when she came upon them, but so wrapped up in her own situation was she, she gave it little thought.

George struck up a friendship with Carmen, teaching her French while she taught him Spanish. Amy suspected they continued the lessons in bed.

A week after Cad's last visit, she awoke to the pop of steady gunfire. She realized it was a sound she hadn't heard in days. Too, there had been fewer cutthroats and thieves riding into town, with the exception of a dozen *banditos* who spent a few hours at the saloon and, of course, the men from the Rocking L.

The shots seemed to come from somewhere behind the pleasure parlor. Thinking she might see Cad—demented woman, she *always* thought she might—she brushed her hair a hundred times and left it loose against her back. No one else in the parlor seemed to be stirring, and she realized it was still early.

Grabbing a couple of cold biscuits and ham from the kitchen, she strolled out the back door and headed for the noise, which came from the small adobe hut twenty yards away from Kate's.

It was the Professor's place, where Pierre and George had taken up residence. It seemed natural to see Lilly Mae standing behind the parlor and staring toward the hut. The young woman started guiltily as she passed and cast her eyes to the ground. Granting her the privacy she obviously craved, Amy hurried on.

It was Pierre she found, not Cad, and she fought a bitter disappointment. Would she never learn?

The Frenchman was beside the Professor's home in a field of weeds and hard-packed dirt, firing at a row of bottles lined up on a distant rail. After a brief observation she decided the bottles were in no danger of being hit.

What was he up to now? Still trying to play the part of the French knight?

A momentary silence fell on the scene as he paused to reload. "Pierre," she called out as she hurried to his side.

He lowered the gun and watched her approach. *"Bonjour,"* he said without the usual smile. "I see you have heard what has happened."

Amy felt a sinking feeling. "What?"

"I speak of the Thunderclap Ranch. A rider arrived early with the news, but he departed for Mexico before he could be questioned. George has gone to discover all that he can."

He turned back toward the bottles. Remembering Prudence and the orphans and the injured boy Tommy, Amy grabbed his arm.

"What about the Clap?"

"The terrible fire. Did you not know?"

"The house—"

"It is not known what has been lost." He looked past her. "Ah, the efficient George returns."

In cold dread she turned to watch the valet approach. Unable to speak, she awaited the tragic news.

George bowed crisply before he spoke. "M'sieur Amsterdam—a curious name, *n'est ce pas?*—reveals that only one structure has been lost."

"Which one?" Amy managed to ask.

"I know not the name in *anglais,* but it is the home of *le cheval.*"

Le cheval. The horse. It was the barn that had burned. Amy let out a deep sigh of relief and murmured a prayer of thanks.

"So no one was hurt," she said.

"This is what M'sieur Amsterdam said is believed."

Gunfire boomed behind her and Amy jumped. Ears ringing, she barely heard Pierre say, "And so I learn the way of the gun. Your father must be reproved."

"What do you mean?"

"This conflagration was not an accident. *Père* Lattimer is the villain."

"John Lattimer did this?" she asked, wanting

to disbelieve what she already knew was so.

Pierre nodded. "This is what the bringer of the news reported."

"Oui," said George in agreement. "This was the part of the report M'sieur Amsterdam most reluctantly supported."

"I will stop him," Pierre announced as he let off another round of shots. This time he actually grazed one of the bottles, which teetered on its perch but did not fall. With something close to a flourish, he proceeded to reload.

"That's nonsense," said Amy, but he paid her no mind. She looked to the valet for help.

"You must stop him."

George's Gallic shrug told her that he could not.

"Then maybe Cad can do it." How easy it was to think of him in times of trouble . . . how easy it was to think of him at *any* time.

"M'sieur Rankin has departed for this Thunderclap," George said. "M'sieur Amsterdam reports that when the unfortunate tidings arrived he left the town. 'Like a bat out of hell,' the man said. A curious expression, *n'est ce pas?"*

Amy's hands twisted at her waist while her mind raced. She couldn't just stay here in Rough Cut and watch Pierre assault bottles while her true love rode to avenge a wrong. For that was exactly what he would do, if any lives had been lost. He'd admired the horses; she had watched him from the ranch house when he stood by the corral. Maybe one of the children had wandered inside the barn. Maybe little Lenoma, who showed such courage and curiosity for her young years.

Tommy could have risked his life to save the stock. He'd shown such foolish bravery before when he tried to shoot a man.

That man being John Lattimer. Her father. Amy shuddered. John Lattimer was the villain here.

And who better to tell him so than the daughter he didn't know he had?

While Pierre concerned himself with target practice, she took George aside. "Keep him here at any cost. If you have to, tie him down. He will thank you later."

George must have heard the urgency in her voice, for he offered no argument. She hurried away, her destination the Inside Straight Saloon. Without a glance at who else might be inside, she made for the bar.

"Amsterdam, I need help."

The bartender spread his huge hands on the counter and studied her with a pair of unnervingly watchful eyes. His arms and shoulders were massive, and she could see dark hairs curling from beneath the wrists of his shirt. A brute of a man, she thought, but she didn't see cruelty in his stare.

"Please," she added when he didn't speak.

"That *please* usually get you what you want?"

"Hardly ever."

His mouth twitched beneath his coarse mustache. Could that have been a smile?

He picked up a cloth and began to wipe the bar. "What you got in mind, Miss Latourre?"

"A ride to the Rocking L."

If the request surprised him, he gave no sign. "It'll take more'n *please* to get it."

Money, perhaps, or did he refer to something else? What did he take her for, she almost asked, then remembered where she was residing. She remembered, too, Pierre preparing for battle and Cad riding out to God-only-knew where. She had to get to that ranch, no matter the cost.

"What exactly will it take?"

"Help from one of Mr. Lattimer's men. They're the only ones can escort you onto the property without bullets flying."

He gestured toward the back of the saloon. She saw the man called Sonny slumped in one of the chairs, a half-empty glass of beer in front of him.

"Drowning his sorrows because the pleasure parlor's temporarily out of business for him," Amsterdam explained. "Kate threw him out last week when he got rambunctious and there weren't no other whore to take her place. Didn't let him back, neither. He passed out before dawn."

Amy looked around the room, seeking help from another source. The Professor sat at a side table, staring into an empty glass. Something about him cried out *helpless,* and she looked back at Sonny. Now was not the time to be faint of heart.

"Ain't much of a choice, is he?" Amsterdam said. "Strange thing, with the whores not working full-time and with word spreading down to the border about how Cad Rankin takes everyone's money and then shoots up the town, riding-through business has dropped off considerable. Mr. Lattimer ain't likely to be pleased."

It was another reason to keep Cad away from the Rocking L. Thanking the bartender, Amy approached the back table with caution.

"Mr. Sonny," she said, too softly to cause a stir. She cleared her throat and repeated his name more loudly. Then, when he didn't stir, she emptied the remains of his glass over his head.

Cursing, he came out of the chair swinging, but she was nimble enough to get out of his way.

When he got tired of hitting the air he lowered his fists and stared at her with beady, blinking eyes. "What the hell you do that for?"

"I need your help."

He smirked. It was not an encouraging sight. "You got it."

Refusing to be intimidated, Amy proceeded to tell him what it was she wanted and what she was prepared to do to get it.

Sonny didn't interrupt.

Chapter Fifteen

"We've got to stop her."

Dudley wholeheartedly agreed with Michael. Unfortunately, interfering with Amy Lattimer in her present state of mind was beyond the power of the Archangel himself, much less a humble liaison angel known lately around the firmament as old Dud.

Simply put, the woman wouldn't be receptive to suggestions. He'd wafted her out of her room once when Cadmus had been close to a gun-fight, using her as a distraction to save his soul. Since then, however, she'd been hard to control.

Cadmus would probably agree.

That was the problem in dealing with mortals; they behaved in unpredictable ways.

How could he have known his latest charge—

and greatest challenge—would get involved with a woman like Amy? He corrected himself: To his knowledge, there *were* no other women like her. At first, when he spied her in that tree, he'd been pleased, thinking she would influence Cadmus's reformation to rectitude.

Instead, she'd influenced him into bed.

Not that Dudley disapproved exactly. He'd known she loved Cadmus long before the realization came to her. And Cadmus was being as much a gentleman as he could manage, given his past proclivities.

Still, it wasn't their amorous inclinations that had him and Michael worried. It was the woman's journey to her father's ranch.

He watched from on high as the wagon she'd rented made its way down the dusty trail. Riding ahead, where his horse could kick up more clouds of dust for her to consume, the villainous Sonny led the way.

Like most angels, Dudley did not like to label a man villainous, but in this case the word suited.

"Will she be harmed?" Michael asked.

"Sadly, I cannot see into the future. We can only hope and pray she is not."

"She gave so much of her money for this escort."

"That she did. Sonny was most insistent on the sum, especially when she showed her distaste for any other form of payment."

"Of course she did," said Michael, wrinkling

his nose. "He put the ideas to her so plainly, even I understood what he meant." The youth shuddered. "Do women really do such things to men?"

Dudley nodded, hoping his companion asked for no further details. He did not, instead concentrating in silence on the progress of the wagon.

"You seem more concerned for the young woman than you do your brother," he said.

"She loves him the way I do."

"Not exactly."

Michael cast him a sheepish glance. "You know what I mean. You heard her."

"Heard, yes. After Cadmus had departed. It is to our credit that we did not observe the entire evening in Miss Lattimer's room. Even mortals have a right to privacy."

"Did he hurt her?" Michael asked in a small voice.

"I don't believe she sounded hurt."

Michael sighed. "I wish we could help her when she meets her father."

Dudley felt the same, but he had no desire to share his concern.

"We can observe, and put thoughts into any suggestible minds that might be on the scene."

"Do you think her father is suggestible?"

"Perhaps."

It was as close to a lie as he'd ever come in his angelic career. John Lattimer had become obsessed with property, with possessions, with power. He hadn't considered the rights or problems of other mortals since New Orleans, and he would most certainly not respond to angelic whisperings in his ear.

There was more Dudley could have told Michael about the man, particulars even his daughter did not know, but nothing that would put his companion's mind at rest. Already he worried too much.

Michael shifted his gaze to the Thunderclap Ranch, a half dozen miles away, and to the smoking ruins of the barn.

"The loss of the mare was a shame."

"That it was, but it might have been worse. Prudence Thor's quick-thinking bravery and the cooperation of her workers helped save most of the stock. I fear, however, that the destruction of her property and the threat of more to come will drive her to rash action."

"Cad, too."

"It is a possibility." He should have said *certainty,* but why disturb the lad more than was necessary?

"Come, Michael, let us draw nearer to the wagon. Miss Lattimer now rides onto Rocking L land, and already the men who serve her father are alerted to her presence. Cadmus, remember, cannot be injured. Our fair lady does not share such protection. She is most vulnerable. We must help her all we can."

His words rang hollow, although he spoke with all sincerity. If only John Lattimer had not trained himself to be a man unmoved by a woman's tearful appeal.

Even if the woman was his only child.

The instant Amy guided the wagon through the gate of her father's ranch she felt enemy eyes on her. Listening to Sonny's leering suggestions had been bad enough, and then having to choke on his dust throughout the long ride, but at least those discomforts had been obvious.

Unseen eyes were proving far more unsettling.

The hills of the Rocking L bore more vegetation than the surrounding landscape. It was as though her father willed the oaks, the mesquite, the shrubs, and the juniper to grow. A pair of hawks circled overhead, and higher in the sky a flock of wild geese flapped in formation on their journey to the south.

It should have been a peaceful scene, but she was terrified. If only she knew how to approach Mr. Lattimer—she could not call him *Papa,* even in her mind—she might find a moment's peace. But she hadn't yet decided whether to reveal who she was.

How would he take the news? Would he care?

She thought not. The conviction was lowering, but she told herself she was doing this for Cad. There was so little she could do for him otherwise, staying out of his way having proven distinctly unrewarding. Though he denied it vehemently, he'd been a hero for her; today she would be a heroine for him.

The thought of him bolstered her spirits, and she straightened on the hard, narrow seat. Next time she made this ride—if there was a next time—she would bring a cushion to sit on, or perhaps the mattress from her bed.

When at last she looked down on the ranch house she reined the horse to a halt. Clouds blocked the sun, and she had to estimate the time. Shortly after noon, she thought. Mr. Lattimer was probably inside having lunch.

His home was built in hacienda style, with adobe walls and a red tile roof that suited the green valley where it had been built. Octagonal in shape, it was constructed around a central garden area. Even from the hill on which she had stopped, she could make out little else except that the house was surrounded by cactus plants.

Spiky gray-green vegetation that would discourage picking. Not at all like the azaleas and magnolias her father had left a long time ago.

The air was chill and, even this close to the border, she felt a hint of winter's bite. It must be well into November already; she'd lost track of the date. How long had she been in Rough Cut? How long had she known Cad? She was shocked to realize she'd thrown those first rocks at him less than two weeks ago.

Things happened fast out west. It was another change from her slow-paced Louisiana life.

Fast and frightening. Pulling her cloak tighter around her, she snapped the reins and began her descent down the hill.

A half dozen horsemen appeared from nowhere to join Sonny as her escorts.

"I brought the boss a woman," he said, and all eyes shifted to her. She attempted an innocent smile but feared she looked sickly instead. She thought she recognized some of the men she'd seen at the Clap, but that could be because they wore similar leather dusters and stared with the same hard eyes.

Remembering how they'd pulled their guns on a boy, she knew they'd shoot her down if the need arose.

The wagon creaked and rumbled down to the house. No one offered to help her alight, and she had to jump awkwardly to the ground. Straightening her bonnet, she made for the entryway.

"Hold up," one of the men said, and she imagined she heard the click of a gun. Right away she held up as Sonny preceded her, knocking first, then disappearing inside when a Mexican housekeeper opened the door.

He returned quickly. Too quickly. Her brain had not yet worked out her approach, and her heart was still shifting between the pit of her stomach and her throat.

Hurrying after Sonny along a corridor that wound around the inner courtyard, she caught glimpses of the passing rooms. Dark, massive furniture filled the tiled spaces and seemed to leave no room for people.

Did John Lattimer ever have visitors? She thought perhaps not, and she felt an unexpected sadness grip her heart. She feared him—oh yes, despite all the silent lectures to herself, she was terrified—and doubted they could ever forge a father-daughter bond.

But that didn't keep her from regretting the way he was, for his sake more than for hers. Mama had loved him once; for her to do so, there must have been goodness in his soul.

When she at last entered the room where he waited, the look he gave her drove the sadness from her mind. It was an openly insolent perusal, as if she were a piece of goods he wasn't sure he wanted to buy. She felt dirtied by his consideration, and at the same time emboldened to wipe the insolence from his face.

She was his daughter, his equal, whether he knew it or not, and for her mother's sake she must act the part. It was clear she was meant to cower, and in truth she might do that yet, but right now she met him with an open consideration of her own.

Standing before her, he looked shorter than he had appeared on the horse—at least three inches under Cad's six feet—but he looked just as strong as she remembered, his body square and straight. She doubted there was much lax flesh beneath the black vested suit and pristine white shirt he wore. At his throat was a string tie with a fancy silver-and-turquoise clasp. His dark hair, combed slickly back, was streaked with gray, his face strong and leathered, the skin around his eyes and mouth deeply lined.

The eyes caught her the most, narrow and coldly blue beneath thick black brows. Eyes that must have chilled many an opponent. But that wasn't what she was, unless he made her so.

She saw nothing of her own features in his face, nothing at all that suggested he was her sire. And yet, there was something about him that she could not name, something that told her she'd found the right John Lattimer. Perhaps time would reveal what that something was.

Shaken by his cold silence, she turned her attention to the room. He stood in what was obviously the library, although the books on the shelves looked far too new and untouched to have been read. Here as in the rest of the house, the furniture was big and dark and forbidding, and the two windows that flanked the hearth were heavily draped, closing off the view at the back of the house.

Only a leather armchair facing the fireplace promised comfort. One comfortable chair in all this massiveness. No, he did not entertain very often, or at least visitors he considered his peers.

He glanced past her. "That will be all, Sonny."

"I'll be close by, boss," the ranch hand

growled. The door to the library closed, and they were alone.

"Did Kate send you?" he asked. His voice was brusque, his meaning clear. He viewed her as a whore sent from the pleasure parlor to service him. She burned with a mingling of embarrassment and shame.

"I came on my own," she managed, more strongly than she would have supposed.

"Going into business for yourself?"

"No!"

He almost smiled. "You seem quite adamant."

She swallowed. "I am." Her hands felt clammy, and she fought the urge to wipe them on her cloak.

He studied her more closely, his sharp eyes taking in her features. "Do I know you?"

"I'm—"

Her voice broke. Now was the time to tell him the truth, but the words would not come to her lips.

"I was at the Clap when the boy Tommy was shot."

He gestured impatiently. "I mean before that. Haven't we met?"

Again the opportunity arose. She looked past him to the smoldering coals in the hearth, praying for the courage to do what must be done. Oh yes, they had met, but she had no memory of how close they had been. Had he held her when she was an infant? Had he ever taken her upon his knee and sung childish songs?

Of course he hadn't. He'd been gone too often from their home, and then he'd been gone forever.

For a moment she felt sad for herself, as if she'd lost out on a part of life that should have been hers. She ought to tell him what was in her heart, but what could she say?

I'm your daughter.

And his response? *You're nothing to me.*

She couldn't bring the words to her lips. Not now. Perhaps not ever.

A poor sort of heroine she was proving to be. Heroines thought of others, not themselves. Heroines steeped themselves in courage, never fear.

"You don't know me," she said, shamed further by her weakness. "My name is Amabelle Latourre."

The name sounded absurd to her ears. Why hadn't she picked something less fanciful? Something that didn't sound so dangerously close to the truth?

"No," he said. "We've never met. Amabelle Latourre is a name I'm not likely to forget."

He strode to his desk, poured himself a drink from a crystal decanter, then sat to stare across the room at her. No offer of refreshments for her, no suggestion that she, too, sit down. Amy felt more and more like a fool, and with that feeling some of her shame and terror died.

She remained, however, miserably aware of

her cowardice. Uninvited, she moved closer to him and sank into a straight-backed chair facing the desk. Unable to be brave about her own situation, she must summon strength in the cause of Prudence Thor.

"I came about the Thunderclap," she said.

His thick brows lifted slightly. "You do surprise me, Miss Latourre. What business of yours is the ranch?"

"It's not exactly mine."

"But still you're here. Prudence sent you."

"She doesn't know about my visit."

"How plucky of you to ride out to the ranch on your own." He sipped at his drink, his cold eyes on her over the rim of the glass. "And how foolish."

More foolish than you will ever know.

"I'm not the issue here. Did you set the fire?"

He did not so much as blink at the audacity of her question. "I've not left the Rocking L since that unfortunate day the boy was shot."

"The day your men shot him," she corrected.

"You take me for a heartless villain, do you?"

"I do," she said, choosing to be as forthright as he. Like father, like daughter, at least in certain ways.

"Yet you think to dissuade me from further villainy." He sat back in his chair. "Why?"

Amy's wish for forthrightness abandoned her, and her gaze shifted toward the hearth.

"I thought it was worth a try. To keep anyone else from getting hurt."

How weak she sounded. Cad would do better at this if he were here. Or else he might get himself shot. Thank goodness he was far away, safe at the Clap.

"I doubt you set the blaze yourself," she added with more force as she looked back at him, "but you've a dozen men who could have done it."

"Two dozen, at least. Don't doubt my power."

"All those men against a widow and children?"

He waved her words aside, as if they held little import for him. Could he truly be the monster he presented to be to the world?

Suddenly she wanted very much to understand him, not for herself but for the wife he'd abandoned long ago. Somewhere Mama was listening—she knew it in her heart—listening and probably still hurting, even in death. Her own sensitivities faded as she thought of Marguerite.

Sitting at the edge of her chair, she gripped the corner of his desk. "Why harm the innocent? What's so important about the Clap?"

"It's none of your business," he snapped.

"Is access to the water so vital that you would kill for it?"

"I told you it's none of your business."

"That's no answer. Are you afraid to say?"

He slammed down his fist on the desk, and the decanter rattled on its silver tray. "There's nothing in this world I fear," he said, hard anger in his words.

What had she said to upset him so? Conscience sometimes drove a man to extreme emotion. Did he have a conscience? Was he perhaps not such a monster after all?

"Everyone is afraid of something," she said.

He stared past her, as if he looked into another place and time. "I left fear and regret behind me long ago."

This time his voice was flat, his words hiding more than they revealed, and she saw the cold fury evaporating from him like a fog. She could not breathe, knowing she edged close to discovering the truth about her father, a secret he kept in his heart. For he *had* a heart. She knew it must be so. A heart and a tortured soul; she sensed their existence without knowing how or why. Hope warmed her and gave her courage. Perhaps he could be her Papa after all.

Instinct moved her to stand and walk around the desk. Stopping beside his chair, she touched his arm. He jerked away. "You must be insane to be here," he said.

He spoke harshly, but she could not back away.

"What's happened to you?" she asked. "I want to understand."

"You're crazy," he snarled. "A crazy whore."

She barely heard him. "I'm someone you can talk to," she said, reaching for him again.

He stood so abruptly, she stumbled backwards and fell to the floor. He raised a fist;

thinking he would strike her, she waited for the blow.

He wanted to. She could see it in his stony eyes, and in the lips pulled back into a feral snarl. He was like no man she had ever seen. No man with a soul would look at another human being that way.

Hope died within her, as suddenly as it had been born. She'd been wrong, deluded by her own needs and wants. As much as she wished it otherwise, there was no chance for them to make amends.

"No," she said softly, putting a great deal of meaning into the single word. But she did not cower and she did not cringe.

His eyes bored into her, and then he stared at his curled fist, as if realizing for the first time what he was about to do.

"Goddamn," he muttered and reached out to help her to her feet.

Amy lifted her hand to him, certain that while he would never love her, neither would he purposefully bring her harm.

His fingers reached for hers. The crash of glass stopped him, and a figure hurtled through the closed draperies of the hearthside window.

Father and daughter stared at the intruder.

"Cad!" Amy cried, just as a pair of the ranch's henchmen burst through the library door.

Chapter Sixteen

Cad ignored the gunmen. Steeling himself to coldness, he stared at Amy. Weight on her elbows, her bonnet resting at an angle on her forehead, she stared right back.

"Are you all right?"

She nodded quickly and scrambled to her feet, cloak and gown rustling in the silence of the room. Despite the whiteness of her face and the stricken expression in her eyes, she didn't look harmed. The bastard hadn't had a chance to hurt her yet.

Whatever happened to her now was up to him.

The rage he'd been fighting on the long ride from the Clap took hold of him with such force he couldn't speak. He wanted to hit something, someone, and Dudley's rules be damned. Without a qualm, he could tear Lattimer and his thugs limb from limb before he threw himself at the woman.

More than anything, he wanted to grab her, to shake her, and, Lord help him, kiss her until neither one of them could breathe. Afraid of himself, of the emotions racing through him, he shuttered down everything inside.

"Get behind me," he said.

"But—"

"Now!"

She did as he ordered, her shoes crunching against the broken window glass. He raised his hands. "I'm not drawing a gun," he said, directing his words to Lattimer. The head of the snake. The one he had not only to convince, but eventually destroy.

And destroy him he would, no matter what it took.

"A mistake," the rancher said, as coolly as if Cad had entered invited. But his mouth was tight. He wasn't unmoved.

Cad glanced at the two men, recognizing one as Sonny. He shifted back to Lattimer. "Call off your dogs."

Sonny growled.

"I won't call them off just yet," said Lattimer.

"Don't know how he got around us, boss," said Sonny. "Sneaky bastard, that's what he is."

"We'll discuss it later," the rancher said. If Cad got any pleasure from the scene, it was knowing Sonny would catch heck before long.

Amy tugged on his shirtsleeve. "Let me help," she said in a small whisper.

"Perhaps you ought to stand behind her," Lattimer said.

"Please, Cad," she said, straightening her hat and brushing a tendril of hair from her cheek. "I'm not afraid anymore."

Cad shook his head in disgust, grateful that at least Amy's ridiculous offer cleared the cobwebs from his mind. He had some fast decisions to make, but he wasn't sure if bullets went right through him or simply bounced off.

This was a piss-poor time to check out the particulars of his condition. His trigger finger itched to take out every bastard in the room, but he had Amy to consider, as usual. He could hardly wait to get her alone.

He glanced at Sonny. "You tell your boss here about our shooting match?"

"I heard," Lattimer said. "You're quite a marksman."

"That's right," Cad said as he looked back at the rancher, matching his cold stare. "But I'm not shooting now. All I want is to get Miss Latourre back to town."

"How brave of you."

"Yes," said Amy over his shoulder. "He's very brave."

Shut up, Amy.

"Look," Cad said, "we've got a barn destroyed, and one of the mares down, but no loss of human life. I want to keep it that way."

"Thank God," said Amy, clearly not getting Cad's *shut-up* message. Then, to Lattimer, she added, "You must let us go. We all know my coming here was foolish, but I've done you no harm." Her hands pulled at Cad's shirt, and when she spoke again her voice was thin and tight. "If you let Cad leave, I never will. I swear it on my mother's grave."

Her vow fading to a whisper, the rancher stared at her, and she stared right back, as if no one stood between them. Lattimer's eyes narrowed. "Amabelle Latourre. You can't be—"

He didn't finish the thought.

Cad felt a new tension in the air, a danger he didn't understand and could not fight. He got the feeling something was happening between the two, something they would leave unsaid. Nothing in the man's expression indicated sex had anything to do with it, but what else could it be?

And why in hell should he care?

Damnation! Here he'd been crazy with worry for Amy, feeling tender, too, the way he'd felt for the past week while he was fighting to keep his distance, and she was working out everyone's problems for herself.

He felt like a fool, jumping through the window the way he had, finding her lying on the floor at Lattimer's feet. He put a new twist on the scene he'd interrupted. Maybe he was jumping to conclusions about her and Lattimer, but again, maybe not.

What had she done, come to the bastard offering herself in order to protect the Clap? Making good on her plan to become a whore? He ought to leave her to whatever deal she'd been making. He ought to tell her she'd got herself into this mess and she'd have to get herself out.

The hell of it was, even thinking ugly thoughts the way he was, he was still loco enough to want her in his arms, to make sure she was all right. And if the situation got any worse than it already was, he'd cut down every man in the room to get her away.

His hand hovering close to the Peacemaker, he spared her a quick glance. Under the rancher's glare she looked pale as porcelain.

Cad concentrated on Lattimer, who kept staring at Amy, his lips growing tighter all the while. A cruel hardness settled in his eyes.

"Get her out of here," the rancher ordered. "I don't know who the hell she is, but get her out." He looked at his two men. "Let them go."

"But boss—" said Sonny.

"Let them go!"

Both gunmen scrambled away from the door. As puzzled as Sonny by the unexpected order, Cad was quick to move. Grabbing Amy's hand, he headed across the library.

"One thing more," said Lattimer. Cad stopped in his tracks. "Come here again, or interfere with me in any way, and you're a dead man."

Amy gasped.

"I'll keep it in mind," Cad said, glad to get the war between them out in the open, at least as open as he could let it be for now.

Keeping a tight grip on his charge, he let his instincts guide him down the winding corridor. He didn't look back, didn't put the issue of the burned barn before the rancher, didn't pause until he had her outside and perched in the wagon. He whistled for Horse, who came around the house at a run. Tying him to the back, he climbed up beside her and snapped the whip in the air.

Around them a dozen hard-eyed men watched, but no one made a move to stop them as the wagon lurched up the hill in front of the hacienda. Neither did Amy move, except to bounce around on the seat, brushing against him and pulling back as if she'd been scorched.

When they were well down the trail, past the Rocking L gate, she finally spoke. "How did you get in without being seen?" Her voice was flat, as if the question were the only issue between them.

"They were watching the front. I came in the back."

"You knew I was there?"

"Let's say I had a hunch."

Which was about as clear as he could put it. He'd been at the Clap, helping to corral the horses who'd scattered into the hills, when an image of Amy had struck him. Put there by

Dudley, no doubt. His angel hadn't instructed him to save her, but he'd let him know she was at the Rocking L. He'd figured out the danger for himself.

Or what he'd taken at the time as danger.

Old Dud had probably done something to distract the ranch hands, maybe planting an idea or two in what couldn't be very smart heads. Conditioned as he was to criticize his heavenly liaison, he decided this time Dud deserved some thanks.

Right now he needed to concentrate on Amy Latourre, on getting her back to town, on getting her out of his life. Or what might once again be his life if she left him alone.

He'd have an easier time of it all if he could get his heart to slow down. It hadn't quit overworking since he'd left the Clap.

He watched her for a moment, sitting still and straight as she could manage on the swaying seat, her eyes staring blankly ahead, her absurd little bonnet sitting uselessly atop her head. She gave no sign of wanting to talk. It was as though she'd cleared up the one point that puzzled her—his sudden appearance in the library—and had nothing else to say.

He sure as heck did, and she'd listen, whether she wanted to or not.

He looked at the hills around them. This time of year, the sun set fast. They'd never make it to Rough Cut, or even the Clap before dark. In riding cross-country from one ranch to the other, he'd passed a place that might do for a camp. She would be cold and hungry, but he figured she would survive.

As he turned the wagon toward the site, he felt her questioning eyes on him, but she had the good sense to keep her thoughts to herself. He reined the dray mare to a halt in the protection of a stand of cottonwoods close by a creek. The trees cut off the wind that was picking up, and gave them privacy from anyone who might ride by.

"We'll stay here for the night," he said as he helped her to the ground. She felt light and vulnerable as usual, but he stiffened himself against her appeal.

At least he tried, but he couldn't quite forget the last time they'd been alone. The time they'd spent in bed. The time she had bared herself to him with an innocent passion he still couldn't believe. In the past week, even though he'd kept himself away, he hadn't gotten the picture of her, nor the feel of her, from his mind for more than a minute at a time.

Was she remembering it too? Was that the reason for her stunned expression? He doubted it. She looked more worried than hungry to get inside his britches. Which she would consider useless, anyway.

The fury that had never quite left him twisted into something else, not pity and certainly not a return of tenderness. Frustration was what it was, an admission of weakness where she was concerned.

He'd never let anyone get to him like this, and he didn't like it one damned bit.

"It's talking time," he said when she started walking away from the wagon.

She halted but kept her back to him. "What do you want me to say?"

Were you fixing to spread your legs for Lattimer? That's what he wanted to ask, but she looked so helpless, with her hair half down and her bonnet perched at an angle and her shoulders slumped beneath the dark cloak.

So what if she had done just what he'd been picturing? He had no hold on her, no more than she had on him.

"I changed my mind," he snapped. "We'll talk later."

"No," she said, turning her wide, pain-filled eyes on him. "You're right. You deserve an explanation. You've earned far more than that, risking your life for me the way you did."

She sure had a way of making him feel like dirt.

"I didn't risk anything—"

"You're just too modest to admit it."

Cad ran a hand through his hair. "I've been accused of a lot of things, but modesty's not one of them."

She ignored him, as if he hadn't spoken. "I heard about the fire and thought maybe I could face Lattimer without anyone getting hurt." She hugged herself, rubbing her hands over her arms.

"Did you have a plan in mind?" He put the question to her gently, giving her a chance to confess.

"I wanted to reason with him," she said, looking away, and he knew she was holding something back.

"Like maybe the Widow Thor hadn't already tried that."

"I was stupid, I know."

"So what was happening when I came through the window?"

"I'd tripped and fallen. He was helping me up."

It could have happened that way, Cad told himself. Sure it could, just as he could walk on water.

Why he was getting so worked up over all this he didn't know, except that Amy was a distraction he didn't need.

"Don't go out there again."

"I won't."

"Seems to me you promised Lattimer the same thing."

She nodded.

"On your mother's grave. What was that all about?"

Her eyes filled with tears. "It seemed the thing to say."

Cad felt all twisted inside. She was good at slippery answers, and at looking helpless, too, making him forget all about the talking, making him think it was a waste of time. They were out here in the middle of nowhere. A man of his nature ought to be kissing away that helplessness and taking off her clothes.

She'd want it, too, the kissing and the naked bodies. Probably already did. He got the feeling that in most ways Amy was far ahead of him.

Trouble was, thinking he was damaged, she didn't know the way things really were. He wished she did; he sure wished his various parts understood the situation too.

"Let it go," he said, not knowing exactly what he meant. "Just stay away from the Rocking L. I'll do what has to be done."

With her standing to the side and watching, he threw himself into the care of the horses with a vengeance, leading them to the water, then tethering them in a stand of grass. As soon as he began to gather wood for a fire, she joined in to help, and they soon had a blaze going at the edge of the trees. Taking off his holster, he spread his blanket roll close to the warmth, then dropped down to enjoy what used to be his favorite time of day.

He didn't get much enjoyment, though, from her sitting at the edge of the blanket, more off than on, her stomach growling over the snap of the twigs.

Muttering a few choice phrases from the old days, he got up to get her some food. From his supplies he dragged out a string and a hook, and he had little trouble digging up a worm for bait. By the light of the moon he caught a couple of bullheads, so small he normally would have thrown them back, but not tonight. He cleaned and gutted them, used a stick for a spit, and soon slapped the sizzling repast onto a flat stone not far from the fire.

Stretching out on the blanket, pulling off his boots, he gestured for Amy to eat.

"What about you?" she asked.

"I'm not hungry."

"But you have to be."

"Eat!"

She jumped, blew on the fish to cool them, and devoured every bite. Licking her fingers, she thanked him.

Weak creature that he was, Cad couldn't keep from watching her pink tongue. Firelight flickered over her features, and the silver moonlight settled in her eyes.

Lordy, she must be a witch, sent not by Dudley but by the devil himself.

He propped his head on the saddle and tried to ignore her. This was the life he was used to, listening to a creek trickling its way over a pebbled bed, staring up at the stars, taking pleasure from the crickets as they sang their nighttime song. Simple things a man could lose himself in when he was alone.

Instead he heard Amy's slow, deep breaths and her occasional sigh. Every time he tried to pick out stars through the overhead tree limbs he imagined her wide blue eyes watching everything he did.

"You could have been killed," she said at last, and the softness of her words startled him like a shot.

"Forget it, Amy. I already told you I was safe enough."

She turned her wide, warm eyes to him. "I can't forget it. I almost caused your death. And there's nothing I can do for you in return."

Cad came dangerously close to telling her different. And he wouldn't need many preliminaries to demonstrate what she could do. Just sitting by her like this, catching her scent, hearing her breathe, had him as hard and hungry as he had ever been.

He needed to cool both of them, and keep her from feeling so grateful to him. He saw a way.

"There's something you can do: Tell me the truth. Did you offer yourself to Lattimer?"

She stared at him openmouthed, as if he'd hit her, and he hurried on before he changed his mind.

"Don't look so innocent. It occurred to me you could have put your new trade to use so he'd back off from the Clap."

She jumped up and backed away from him. "That's a terrible thing to say."

The hurt in her voice tore through him, but he found himself wanting an answer. If he didn't know himself better, he'd think he was jealous of Lattimer. He stood and moved close, wishing he could intimidate Amy into backing away, angry because she held her ground.

"I'm only going by the evidence. You're the one who rode out there alone. I figure the only ammunition you had was yourself."

She slapped him. The blow was strong and sharp and would have stung like heck if he could feel pain. It seemed to surprise her as much as it surprised him.

"Oh," she said. "I hit you, and you could have been killed."

Cad couldn't see how the two were connected, but why should he? She thought like a woman, and he was a man.

She touched his cheek. The sensation was more powerful than the slap. "Everything I do is wrong."

In an instant Cad's anger burned to ash. How could he go on blaming her when she did a better job of blaming herself?

"Not everything," he said.

"Don't try to make me feel better. You hate me, don't you, for causing so much trouble?"

Her wide, wet eyes and trembling lips were almost his undoing. "I don't hate you, Amy. It's none of my business what you've got going with Lattimer. You're not my woman and I'm not your man."

"I know," she cried and, whirling, ran from him, disappearing into the trees before he could stop her. Cursing, he pulled on his boots, balancing awkwardly at the edge of the fire on one foot at a time, and then headed after her, grateful for the clear night and the light from the moon and stars.

She wasn't much good at sneaking through the woods. He followed the sound of her thrashing, then turned up the speed when he heard her cry.

She'd stumbled to her knees at the edge of a clearing. He came close to careening into her but stopped himself in time. She stared straight ahead. At the sound of a familiar hiss, he turned cold inside.

The rattler sat coiled and ready at the end of a fallen log, its fangs a scarce foot from her hand. He must have been headed for hibernation when she'd disturbed him. Cad slapped his thigh, then remembered he'd left the Peacemaker back by the fire.

The silvery scene was unreal, beautiful and deadly at the same time, shadows playing across the wild grass and trees, the snake's flat head lethal and still. Sweat beaded on his brow. He kneeled slowly, inch by inch, and eased his arm around her waist. Jumping back and taking her with him, he kicked out and took off the rattler's head with the toe of his boot.

He stood there for a minute, unable to move, then put Amy on the ground beside him. She hugged him tight, her cheek warm against his chest, then shoved herself away.

"I did it again!" she cried.

Before he could reassure her she took off

once more, heading back for the fire, beckoning in the darkness. Cad rolled his eyes. Didn't the woman ever slow down? He took off after her. He found her at the camp, down by the creek.

"Stay right there," he ordered, and came up on her slow.

"Why don't you ride on back to town?" she said as she watched the water dance in the shallow shadows of the rock-strewn bed. "Leave me the wagon. I'll be all right."

"Don't be stupid."

"I can't help it; that's the way I am."

Cad ran a hand through his hair. "I didn't mean it that way."

She moved closer to the creek, where the bank was wet and slick. Her foot slipped out from under her; she fell against him and they both went down.

Unfortunately, his boot caught in a tree root and twisted at an awkward angle. When she landed on top of him he heard the snap of bone and knew what it meant.

She heard it too. "What was that?"

"Nothing," he said.

He wasn't hurting. All he had to do was get her up and straighten out. . . .

"It's not nothing."

She eased off him and rested a hand on his trousers.

"Oh, Cad. This time I've broken your leg."

* * *

Amy brushed away her tears and accepted this latest horror. Crying would do little good now. She ought to get Cad's gun and put a bullet through her heart, ending the misery of them both. How could such good intentions go so wrong?

She thrust aside self-pity as the wasteful emotion it was. Forgotten, too, were all regret about her father and the kind of man he was. Instead, love thundered through her, filling her heart and soul. She was Cad Rankin's woman, whether he knew it or not, and for the rest of her life she would call him her man. More than once Cad had thrown himself into the face of danger to help her; she must do whatever she could to help him in return.

She'd once given emergency care to one of her students who had broken her arm. She knew exactly what she had to do. Set the bone, fix a splint, and keep the patient warm and calm.

The child had had such a little arm and Cad had such powerful legs. Not that she'd seen them exactly, but she'd imagined them often enough. She'd have to see them now.

The thought was not entirely unpleasant. Oh, what a wanton creature she was to get pleasure from his pain.

"You're wet and cold. I have to get you back on the blanket by the fire."

"Listen, Amy—"

She kissed him, longer than she'd intended,

and with more enthusiasm than was called for at the time.

"Why did you do that?" he asked when she eventually pulled away.

"To keep you quiet. It's what you do to me."

"That's not all I've done."

She blushed. Her gaze fell to where it should not have gone. Astonished, she saw he was aroused.

Why wouldn't he be? She was so hot she wanted to rip off her clothes and do unspeakable things to him, things the terrible Sonny had suggested back at the Inside Straight. She could be almost grateful to the villain for putting the ideas into her mind.

Maybe she could do them later . . . a week, a month from now, when he was healed. If, that is, he let her near him again.

He couldn't make her go away right now, no matter how much he ordered or cajoled. She was selfish enough to draw satisfaction from being in control.

"Do you think you can scoot back with your good leg? I'll help you."

"No," he said, rather more sharply than she liked. "That is, I'll scoot back by myself."

She stood aside while he did just that. The mud he'd picked up on his backside rubbed off as he eased across the grass. How brave he was being, holding his injured leg above the ground, using the powerful muscles of his arms to pull himself closer to the fire.

When he was once again on the blanket she stoked the embers, tossed her bonnet and cloak aside, and rolled up the sleeves of her gown.

"Let down your hair," Cad said as he leaned back on the saddle, his arms beneath his head.

"Why?"

"I like it down. You need to humor me, don't you? Make me feel as good as you can?"

The trouble was, she didn't know how good that could be. She did, however, intend to find out. In a flash she followed his order, shaking her head until the curls tumbled loosely down her back.

"Is that better?" she asked.

"It's getting that way."

He spoke as if he had other orders in mind.

She kneeled beside him. "Take off your pants."

"Why? Because you like them off?"

"I've never *seen* them off." She remembered his hotel room and the way he'd shown her his scar. "At least, not all the way."

"And you're prepared to do so now, when I can't defend myself."

If getting hot and flustered was being prepared, that was exactly her state.

She had to bring a semblance of sanity to the occasion. "How can you be so indifferent under the circumstances?" she asked.

"I'm not indifferent, Amy. Undressing right now is not a good idea."

Something in his voice twisted her insides

and set her heart to racing. Glancing at the tight fit of his trousers, she gestured toward his private parts. "Doesn't that hurt you?"

"In ways you can't imagine."

His dark eyes glinted. A reflection from the fire? No, it was an inner spark.

"I'm sorry," she said, and meant it for both of them.

"Don't be."

He stared into the night, as if he could see something or someone invisible to her. "We've got forces throwing us together, don't we? Good or bad, it doesn't make much difference. I should have seen it before."

His dark gaze returned to her. "I surrender. Take off my pants. A man can fight some things just so long."

He sat up, his lips dangerously close to hers, and her heart thundered faster and louder than ever. "The underdrawers, too, don't you think?" he added. "If you're going to care for me right."

Chapter Seventeen

Amy began by stripping Cad of his boots and socks. Unable to think about the body parts awaiting her, she concentrated on his feet, callused but high-arched, a trait the nuns called a sign of high birth.

"Amy, are you all right?"

She started and realized she'd been caressing his toes. Unable to look up, she nodded.

"Good, because I'm not."

"Oh, I'm sorry. You must be in terrible pain."

"I'm ticklish."

Her eyes darted to his. He was grinning, but lurking behind the grin, like a hungry, warm-blooded beast, was a wilder response to her touch. It glinted in his eyes and pulsed in the tightness of his body. She knew because it pulsed within her too. She almost threw herself into his arms.

How brave he was being. If she didn't know better, she would think the broken bone didn't bother him at all, nothing like the other wound, with its unthinkable, crippling consequence. Meeting his gaze, matching his smile, she felt consumed by her love and, more, by pride in his courage and wonder at his unselfishness.

Consumed, too, by hot, humming urges to give herself to him in every way.

With renewed diligence, she threw herself into her work, folding his shirttail high so it wouldn't get in the way. He didn't flinch when she unfastened his trousers—well, maybe just a bit—and he held himself stone-still while she eased them down his taut, lean hips, past the hard wall of his abdomen, to his equally hard thighs. She felt both grateful and frustrated because his undergarment protected him from complete nakedness. A small, insistent voice inside her whispered that he wouldn't be protected for long.

A poor angel of mercy she was turning out to be.

Somehow she managed not to stare at anything but her hands gripping the waistband of his trousers, and in the feat demonstrated a strength of character that surprised her. The nuns would be pleased, she thought, and then decided that perhaps, if they knew exactly what she was feeling, *pleased* was not the appropriate word.

She treated his right leg, the broken one, with great care, expecting at any moment to hear him cry out, to protest, at least to moan. As she set his trousers aside, he kept his silence, and she heard nothing but her own unsteady breath over the rustle of dry leaves in the wind.

Even her breathing stopped when she took a thorough look at his long underwear. They fit him like a second skin, and his arousal thrust straight up at her, like the convent flagpole, she thought with some irreverence, or a mast on the ship that had taken her from New Orleans. She closed her eyes for a moment and let the sweet, slow heat build inside her. If her character had slipped beyond recognition, so be it. For all her determination to keep her ministrations impersonal, there were some things that even the strongest of women could not ignore.

Cad's erection was definitely one of those things.

She stifled a nervous laugh. It would have been a release from all the tension she'd been feeling since she found Pierre shooting at those bottles, but she feared Cad might not understand.

Men didn't like to be laughed at concerning their private parts, Mama had written. Amy couldn't imagine her humiliation if he had laughed at her breasts.

But she wasn't laughing at him; she was adoring him, and she was terrified that in her care of him she would behave badly and disappoint him once again.

She touched his thigh and felt hard muscle twitch beneath her fingers. He groaned, and she jerked her hand away.

He was in pain; she knew it. The memory of how he'd eased the wounded Tommy's discomfort came to her. "Do you still have that whiskey you were carrying at the Clap?" she asked.

"In the saddlebags. But I don't think—"

She stopped him with a wave of her hand and went to get the liquor. Kneeling on the edge of the blanket, she thrust the flask into his hand. "Drink."

He straightened against the saddle, his powerful arms and shoulders shifting his weight, and she wished with all her being that she had removed his shirt when she'd had the chance.

"I can't," he said. "That is, I'm not supposed to."

"Do you have a drinking problem? I mean, like the Professor? I'll understand if you do."

Cad looked from the flask to her and back to the flask again. "I guess there's only one way to show you I don't. You're making me do this, remember."

He took a long drink.

"Another," she said. "This may take a while."

"I'm counting on it," he said, following her orders for a change. She watched the muscles of his throat work with each swallow. Beads of sweat formed on her upper lip.

"Better?" she asked when he had finished off the whiskey.

"Getting better all the time. I'm ready for my drawers."

His voice was thick; she attributed it to the liquor and wished she'd taken a sip or two. Hot though she was, she feared he would get a chill, and she took time to build up the fire. When she began the final disrobing, easing the undergarment down his hips, the light from the rising flames flickered over his exposed skin and turned it to gold. She paused to drink in the sight, caught in an agitation that no liquor could have aroused.

The flash of his gaze over her said she must look golden too. Instinct drove her to unbutton the top of her dress and to flick her long, free hair against her shoulders. Slowly she rolled up her sleeves and with hungry hands returned to her task.

The scar on his abdomen was the way she had remembered it, jagged and puckered until it disappeared into the thick black patch of hair close to his thighs. As she neared his . . . flagpole, she decided to call it . . . she hesitated. In truth, she panicked, fearful that in her wantonness she might touch him in places she had no right to see.

It was bad enough that her fingers dragged unrelentingly across his exposed skin.

"You'll get cold," she said. "I'll cover you with my cloak."

Despite his protests she did just that, letting her fingers feel their way unseen to his underclothing. At first she brushed up against something hard and slick. He caught his breath and so did she, but she kept on with the disrobing.

Needing to see his injured leg, and being the good girl she didn't want to be, she folded the cloak so that it covered only his private parts, and gave her full attention to the rest of his undressing. At last she set his underclothes aside, but she couldn't move right away or even shift her gaze. He didn't have an ounce of fat on him; just skin over muscle and a dusting of dark hairs, light on his thighs, heavier below the knees.

His legs were much longer than hers, bigger and harder, yet bearing a graceful sweep of tight flesh, even the right one, despite the twist. Stroking his calf, she could feel the broken bone through the skin.

"I need to make a splint."

"Don't bother. I heal better without one."

"That's impossible."

"I've done this before, Amy. Trust me. All you need do is straighten my leg."

She trembled at the thought.

"Trust me," he repeated. "Do it."

"I trust you," she said, trying to mean it, and popped his leg before he could give further instructions. Cringing, she waited for his explosion of pain.

There was no sound. She opened her eyes slowly and saw him watching her with great care, the firelight giving his features a wicked look. Sensations of heat and hunger swept through her, and she cared not if he read the love in her eyes.

"That must have hurt," she said.

"It didn't."

"Because of the whiskey, I suppose."

"The company."

She knew he teased her, and she regarded him with open skepticism. "Liar."

"Sometimes. Not now."

He was flirting with her gently, insistently, and she felt a new kind of joy in being with him. She wrapped her arms about her middle, fighting a thousand wild urges. Everything about Cad beckoned, from his dark, unruly hair to his high-arched feet.

Why was she fighting? Why was she holding herself back? Smoothing the cloak over his hips and thighs, easing around the arousal that even thick folds of wool could not hide, she smiled to herself. For a change she had him in her power. If she couldn't tell him what was in her heart, she could show him in other ways.

In his weakened condition there was little he could do to stop her. He couldn't go all the way, but he had already gone a long distance in making love to her. He could go that distance again.

She unbuttoned the front of her gown.

"What are you doing?" he asked, but he didn't sound displeased.

"If it was my company that held off the pain, I thought you might need a stronger dose."

Shifting her gown from her shoulders, she eased out of her chemise, then sat back to let him see her bared breasts. He'd liked the sight of them before, when she'd been lying in bed. Maybe he would like them as well in front of a flickering fire.

He brushed his thumbs across her beaded nipples. She stopped his hands, pressing them against her fullness, then moving them to the blanket. It was the hardest thing she'd ever had to do.

"My turn," she said. "You mustn't exert yourself."

Without a thought for the diary's instructions, she did what came naturally, unbuttoning his shirt and dragging her breasts across his muscled chest, then lying gently against him and stroking his throat with her tongue.

With a shudder, he lifted her chin and kissed her. The whiskey on his breath shot straight into her bloodstream. She felt drunk with excitement and longing. Weak woman that she was, she forgot all about his leg.

He embraced her; their tongues danced together, and Amy was lost in her love. The fire's warmth licked at her back; Cad's body heat seared her front. Unmindful of the harsh

November chill, she fell headlong into a magical, verdant spring. For her it was a night of birdsongs and babbling waters that stirred the scented air. If a thousand blossoms had rained upon them, she would not have been surprised.

Astray in this sweet new world, she forgot all unnecessary matters, such as the inhibitions of innocence and the strictures of common sense. She felt Cad's hand on her hair, stroking, caressing, then easing through the long locks to make lazy circles on her bare back. Like a cat, she curled against him, then grew impatient with the clothing bunched at her waist.

Pushing away, trying to remember his injury and doing a very poor job of it, she helped him out of his shirt, then finished her own disrobing. All the while his dark eyes watched with piercing thoroughness, but she was beyond questioning anything she did. If he wanted her to stop, he would have to say the words.

All she heard was his uneven breath, which drifted to her over the crackle of the fire and the sough of the wind in the trees. Pulling her cloak over their naked bodies, she nestled in the crook of his arm and kissed his neck, his chin, his eyes, his lips. Her body burned everywhere she touched him . . . her breasts, her thighs, her lips. Eager hands ruffled his hair and played at his ear.

Fevered, shaking, her body a mass of gooseflesh, she experienced all the signs of illness, but she'd never felt healthier or more alive than she did out here in the wild.

He shivered, she hesitated, and he took command, covering her mouth with his, hands roaming down her back to her buttocks, cupping her against his leg. His broken leg. She tried to pull away, but he was so strong, so determined, she feared doing him a greater injury if he did not have his way.

And his care was her greatest concern. She let him touch where he wanted, kiss where he wanted, her eyes, her throat, her hair, stirring to life a side of her nature she had never known existed, a wanton eagerness that went beyond even the one time he had lain with her in her bed. All her body hummed in rhythm with his ragged breaths, and he became her everything.

"Do you always smell of lavender?" he whispered in her ear.

"Always," she whispered back. "Unless you don't like it."

"I like it."

She licked his lips. "You taste of fire and whiskey," she said, then added hastily, "I like it."

She thrust her tongue inside his mouth to show him just how much.

His hand moved to her thigh; she touched his leg, wondering how she could help him share her pleasure. Sonny's suggestions, so abhorrent to her in the saloon, beckoned softly in her mind. Did she dare try them out? She did.

Lying on top of Cad, she settled her body between his legs and felt his sex against her stomach. Slowly she kissed her way down his chest, licking at his nipples the way he had licked at hers, circling her tongue in his navel, feeling his scar beneath her lips, hearing his gasp, waiting yet not waiting for an order to cease her descent.

"What are you doing?" he asked.

"Experimenting," she said from the dark beneath the cloak. "Don't let me hurt you if I get carried away."

His hands stroked her shoulders in a sure and steady massage, the pads of his fingers rough yet soothing against her skin. Her tentative fingers touched the tip of his manhood. He didn't feel at all like the cold metallic flagpole she remembered from the convent. He felt warm and slick and pulsing with life.

She touched her tongue to where her fingers had been.

"My God," he said hoarsely.

Taking the ground-out words as encouragement, she licked him again, then wrapped her lips around his sex and slowly took him deeper into her mouth. Sonny hadn't been specific; she was acting on urges that went beyond knowledge. In the dark beneath the cloak, pressing her breasts to his thighs, she loved him with the wild abandon she could never display in the light.

With a thick moan he dragged her away from him, ending their primitive contact too quickly, easing her upward over his body until his eyes met hers. In swift, smooth movements, he turned her on her back and lay on top of her. She no longer held control.

He stared at her with wild intensity. She burned with shame. She must have heard Sonny wrong; men did not like to be kissed in intimate ways; or maybe it was just Cad and his injury. It could be, too, she'd done it wrong. He hadn't let her do it long enough.

She cursed his wound as though it were her own, for in truth it was. "I'm sorry—"

He swallowed her words, covering her mouth in a kiss that was the glory of all kisses, his hands at work in equally glorious ways on her breasts, her stomach, her hidden thatch of hair.

Fingers eased between her legs and stroked in the dampness that he so often caused—sometimes when he wasn't even present. She had only to think of him, especially when she lay in bed at night, and a strange wet, private thrumming struck her like a ravenous rage.

But he was here now, and he didn't find the dampness strange at all. Continuing the delicate, savage massage, he lifted his head and stared down at her, his eyes dark as the night, his face shadowed and feral and dear to her beyond words.

His touch aroused such hot longings within her, she bit her lip to keep from crying out.

"Now," he whispered, and then again, "Now," as though he were warning her of some terrible happening about to take place.

She touched his cheek in reassurance, her eyes glittering in eagerness up to his. He settled his body between her legs and thrust inside her. The pain was unexpected, but nothing she couldn't keep to herself. What was he feeling? He'd said sex hurt him. If he could hide discomfort, she could do the same.

It took no more than a second or two for her to forget the hurt. With walls of night surrounding them, she knew only the natural joining, the thrusts, the sighs, the heady thrill of a thousand raptures coursing through her heated veins.

The pleasure centered in one place. She rubbed that place in wild abandon against his probing shaft, crying softly in what must sound to him like whimpers for a sweet release from this ecstatic torture. If her frenzied response surprised him, he gave no sign except to meet her eagerness with a frenzy of his own.

Gripping him with arms and legs, she felt the stars explode . . . in her body, her heart, and throughout the universe, though she held her eyes tightly closed. Sweet violence shook them both, and in that moment of supreme pleasure, wrapped in her true love's arms, Amy left all innocence behind. In its place she gained the secrets of the world.

With the last tremors of passion fading, Cad held Amy tight and waited for the fires of hell to consume him. If they did, he would die contented.

Damned . . . darned if he wouldn't. Maybe he wasn't thinking things through—he always lost his reason when she was near—but he knew he'd never before had sex to compare with tonight. He'd never been with a woman like her, either, a woman who gave herself so completely, holding nothing back.

When she'd gone down on him he'd almost exploded in her mouth. She had no idea what she was doing to him. The act itself came from experience, but she did it so tentatively and then so eagerly, he knew she was learning as she went along.

And teaching him that virgin passion was the most erotic passion of all.

When the hellfire did not materialize, he waited for Dudley's scowling face to form in the stars. Old Dud wouldn't likely accept the argument that she'd gotten him drunk and done the ravishing.

Old Dud would be right.

Nothing happened, except that Amy kissed his chest and the hollow of his throat, not seeming to mind the fact that he'd worked up a sweat over the past half hour trying to keep up with her.

He stroked her arm and kissed her hair. She sighed, her breath soft and warm against his neck. A precious woman, like no other he'd ever known, delicate and ornery and more loving than any man deserved.

She sure had something better coming to her

than a lying, thieving bastard who'd soon be six feet under the ground.

His conscience ought to be hitting him any second, but being the lying, thieving bastard that he was, he kept on hugging and kissing and wishing the night would never end. He didn't even bother with worrying about the tenderness she stirred inside him, a feeling that usually struck fear in his heart.

Letting her go—tonight, tomorrow, whenever the judgment bell rang—would be as hard as anything he'd faced in a long time. He'd better arrange things before he went toes up, or else she would be blaming herself for whatever happened to him.

But they still had tonight.

She stirred. "You did it."

"Did what?" he said, teasing, knowing what she meant.

"Did *it*," she said, hitting his chest. "You know."

"Yeah, I know. We did it all right. Thanks to you."

She pulled back to look up at him. She still had the signs of recent lovemaking on her face: deep, rounded eyes and swollen lips and a satisfied air about her that could break a man's heart.

Cad didn't have a heart, leastwise where women were concerned, but something was pounding away inside his chest, and something was making him want to laugh and sing.

Lordy, that would be a pitiful end to the night, him bursting into some off-key, bawdy saloon song, which was the only kind he knew.

She kissed him, her touch light as the breeze. "The whiskey must have cured you. It couldn't have been me. I wasn't sure what to do."

"Then you've got some smart instincts, Miss Latourre."

Something in what he said caused her to frown, and the brightness dimmed in her eyes.

"What's wrong?" he asked. "Did I say something I shouldn't have?"

She laid her head on his chest. "It's just that my name's not Latourre."

"I never believed it was."

"You know who I am?" She sounded afraid, as if she had secrets about as bad as his.

"A woman who ran from commitments she didn't want. You're like me, Amy. You've got a need to be free."

She held herself so still, he thought for a minute she'd fallen asleep.

"You're right," she said, not putting much conviction in the words. "It would take someone like that to do the things I've done. Running away, getting myself stranded up a tree, taking up residence in a whorehouse."

"But not being a whore, remember."

"Right. Not being a whore."

He didn't like the flatness in her voice. He lifted her chin and stared into her eyes, thinking what a delicate, fine-looking woman she was.

Thinking, too, that she had more gumption than any man he'd ever known.

The combination was enough to start a man considering possibilities he had no right to, for her sake as well as his. The old fears threatened, but still he couldn't stop the thinking.

"Are you already regretting what we just did?"

She shook her head.

"Me neither," he said.

She nestled against him once again. "Is your leg hurting yet?"

"What leg?"

"Either that means you've lost all feeling in it, or you really are all right."

"I've got feeling, that's for sure, just not the hurting kind."

She laughed softly, then grew quiet. "I don't understand you, Cad. You seem invincible to pain, or even fear. At Lattimer's ranch Sonny could have shot you without any trouble, but it didn't bother you at all. It's like you have a guardian angel watching over you, to keep you from harm."

Darned if she wasn't as smart as she was sweet. "What would a cussed man like me be doing with a guardian angel? The truth is, I'm too mean to get hurt."

"You're not mean to me."

She edged up to kiss him, putting energy into the effort. Too, she shifted around a little to remind him they were both still naked and their bodies so entwined, it would be hard to tell where one of them ended and the other began.

Hers would be the satiny skin, pale as moonlight, soft as morning mist; he was the one covered in rawhide, firm and bristled and tough.

Funny thing how the softness was getting to the rawhide. He responded to her kiss in kind, glad to leave the angel talk behind, and it wasn't long before he was feeling frisky again. Oh, well, he told himself, a man could be condemned to hell only once.

"You were saying maybe it was the whiskey that cured my problems," he said.

"And you said it was the company."

"There's one way to find out. The whiskey's worn off, but the company's still here."

Amy ran a foot down what was supposed to be his good leg, then eased her knee between his thighs.

"The company's not going away anytime soon, either."

"She'd play heck managing it."

He cupped her buttocks and pressed her against his leg until she was straddling his thigh. It didn't take much encouragement on his part to get her to rotating her hips, rubbing her sex against him, her breath coming in short, quick gasps.

He was too selfish to let her finish what she'd started without inserting himself into the proceedings.

"Ride me, Amy. I'll show you what to do."

She gave in right away to his suggestion, letting him shift her where she could settle on top of him and ease down on his erection. He liked her sitting this way; he liked touching her breasts.

Her head dropped back, and the smile of total abandon on her face, animal-like in the firelight, drove him over the edge.

Amy slept through the rest of the night. Cad spent the time holding her and counting stars, and when the stars faded he spent the pre-dawn hour telling himself he'd done her no harm. She'd come to him as willingly as any woman he'd ever known. No, more so, because she'd wanted nothing for herself and everything for him, claiming she was trying to hold off his hurting and meaning every word.

She'd liked it as much as he did; they'd both gotten something out of the night.

So why did he have those sharp little claws inside him that kept scratching away every time he told himself she'd be all right?

If this was what conscience did to a man, he maybe ought to go back to his old selfish ways.

When the first golden glow of day began peeking through the trees he forced himself to leave her. Thanks to the whiskey he needed to relieve himself. And thanks, too, to the whiskey, when he stood he got the worst headache of his life.

He held his head as he stumbled toward the bushes. Dudley didn't show up until his business was done.

"Good morning, Cadmus."

Cad groaned and held on to a nearby limb. "Why don't you just strike me down now and get it over with?"

"Because then Miss Latourre would have to deal with your cadaver, and she doesn't deserve that. Surely you agree."

It wasn't a sentimental reason for postponing his demise, but it had enough charity and good sense to it to keep Cad from protesting.

He thought of Amy, asleep under the cloak, peaceful, sweet, trusting. Beautiful, too, with the early light catching in her tousled hair, making it look like fine-grained wheat brushed with honey.

There came the fanciful thoughts again, but this morning they didn't bother him.

"Don't blame her for what happened," Cad said.

"I don't."

A thousand hammers pounded inside his skull, driving all other considerations from his mind.

"What happened to the no-pain part of our bargain?"

"Goodness, Cadmus, you have a curious way of selecting portions of the agreement that suit your nature and ignoring those that do not."

"You're not going to lecture me, are you?"

"I've done all I plan to do. Consider it punishment, if you like. I call your distress a reminder of your pledge not to consume alcohol."

"She forced it on me."

"Overpowered you, did she? Forced it down your throat?"

Cad remembered the way she'd approached him with the flask, a militant light in her eye.

"Kind of."

Cad's newest enemy, conscience, struck him with force enough to make him forget his pounding head. "All right, so she didn't force me. Like she didn't force me to do anything else."

"Neither did you force her."

"Yeah, but she's not living under a curse."

"A promise of happiness is hardly a curse."

Dudley sounded miffed, but then, so was Cad.

"You say my head is hurting because I drank when I wasn't supposed to. That's not the only condition I ignored. Seems to me other parts ought to be suffering the same."

"You refer to—"

"The part of me that makes babies."

"How delicately put."

A new and terrible thought struck Cad. "She couldn't be—"

"No, put your fear to rest, although I must say you've come to the possibility of parenthood a few hours too late. I'll try to put this in the western vernacular, which I must admit offers a charming if somewhat crude style. In your present undead state, you are, as some men say, shooting blanks."

Cad shook his head and saw right away the

mistake in the movement. "I'll be damned," he said between moans.

"It's still a possibility."

"You didn't answer my question. Why isn't my pistol—to use the western vernacular—suffering like my head?"

"Because you were thinking of someone else when you fired your blanks. Not entirely, of course, but Amy has feelings for you, and to have denied her what she needed would have brought her extraordinary pain."

A new worry struck Cad, taking its place over a hundred others. "She's not in love with me, is she?"

"How could she be, when she doesn't know who you are?"

Old Dud's reply didn't exactly answer the question, but Cad took it as a comfort. Or at least he tried to. Amy and he getting together, making vows, settling down? It wouldn't happen, not in this life and not in the next.

She needed to know what was going on with him, whether all the angels in the universe agreed with him or not. Once his brain got clear of the pitchforks—they were definitely pitchforks at work inside his skull—he'd figure out how to tell her.

And he wouldn't let Dudley know what he was doing until it was too late for him to interfere.

Chapter Eighteen

They got under way early, heading for the Thunderclap Ranch shortly after dawn. Cad had promised Amy a breakfast more substantial than fish and creek water. He promised, too, she could see the damage to the ranch for herself.

She hadn't shown much enthusiasm for anything he said, nothing like the eagerness of last night.

Instead, she'd just nodded and kept her eyes turned to the creek, the trees, the horses, anywhere but at him. Moving around the camp fire in that graceful way she had, her long legs taking her to the water, to the thick brush, she'd tested him beyond endurance.

Lordy, she could wrap those legs around a man and make him forget paradise itself. Besides, with her high, full breasts and tight sweet rear, she was as close to paradise as he was likely to get.

There wasn't a part of her that didn't claim attention and set his own parts to acting up. Physical reactions weren't the only kind gnawing at him, either. Like an addlepated boy, he wanted to carry water for her, to help her pack the bedroll, to protect her in some way he couldn't figure out. She'd done a fair job of protecting herself already, escaping a marriage she didn't want, making her way west, bringing a reprobate loner like him to heel whenever she wanted.

Heck, she probably would have escaped Lattimer's Rocking L without harm. The only thing she really needed protection from was him.

She gave no sign she noticed his agonies. He'd considered limping a little, to get her sympathy, but he couldn't bring himself to do it. Lying with her through the night had seemed the right and inevitable thing to do, but lying *to* her in the morning light was something else.

The day was clear and cold, and the mare moved briskly in her traces as they headed for the Clap. At the rear, his tethered gelding neighed impatiently at the wagon's slow pace.

For her part, Amy sat beside him in silence, hands in her lap, her hair worn loose against her cloak, the bonnet tossed carelessly in the wagon bed alongside his saddle gear. Repeatedly her shoulder brushed against his as the wagon jounced along; she didn't pull away, but neither did she cuddle next to him like she was wanting some more of last night.

He would have guessed she'd be a cuddler, but it could be she'd done all the cuddling she could handle when they were naked under her cloak.

Remembering what they'd done under that cloak, knowing things she couldn't possibly know, he renewed his vow to reveal all, whether damnation awaited him or not.

"We need to talk," he said, when they were a mile down the trail.

"We need to talk," she said at the same time.

They looked at each other and smiled, but he could see something was eating at her, the way something was eating at him.

He turned his attention to the mare's ears and on beyond to the waiting hills.

"If this is about what we did—" he began.

"It's not."

"So you're not about to say you made a mistake."

"No," she said, so low he could barely make out her words over the creak of the wagon. "I'm not about to say that. What about you?"

He took one of her hands in his. "The only thing I regretted was having to get up and make plans to leave."

For romantic talk it wasn't much, but she blushed prettily, as if she was pleased.

He ought to be more fanciful, the way he was

sometimes in his mind, but surely he'd already shown her with everything except words how she could rouse him and make him feel like a man.

Which he wasn't; not really. She had a right to know.

While he was being the coward, stumbling on a way to begin, she started right ahead.

"I was raised in a New Orleans convent by the Ursuline nuns. That was where I was teaching when Pierre showed up as my betrothed."

Cad shook his head, grateful his hangover was gone. He had others worries now. He'd bedded a virgin schoolteacher who'd led the most sheltered of lives. Worse, he would bed her every chance he got if she gave him the nod.

Which might not be likely once he got started talking.

"Amy—"

But she wasn't to be stopped. "I told you I was an orphan, but that's not true. Mama died the way I said, but I found out my father is still alive. He's not a very nice man, Cad. I've met him. He's not nice at all."

There was such desolation in her voice, he guided the mare to a shady spot off the trail and, tying the reins, took her in his arms.

"There's lots of bad men running loose," he said, stroking her hair, letting her shiver against him. He thought about setting her on his lap, spreading those magnificent legs, giving her something else to think about.

Horny coward, he called himself. She really did need protection from him.

"Lots of bad men," he repeated. "One of the worst is me."

She pushed away from him. "What are you talking about? You're the best man I've ever known. Brave and gentle and rough-talking sometimes, but kind and considerate in the ways that matter most." She ventured a small smile that tore at his insides. "I'll admit I don't have anyone to compare you to, but I'd swear you're the best kisser in the country."

"I've got you swearing now, have I?" he said, trying to be light, feeling more lowdown than ever, still wanting her when he should be showing some decency and keeping his thoughts clean.

"Swearing's not the only thing you've got me doing. I don't regret any of it."

"You might, once I get through talking."

"It's not your turn yet. I'm not finished."

"What are you going to do, tell me just how bad your papa is?"

"That's exactly right. He's—"

"Has he robbed banks?"

That stopped her. "Not that I know of."

"Or stolen money from greenhorn gamblers?"

"Maybe. I don't know."

"Has he lived his life roaming the countryside, making camp where he could, thinking of no one but himself?"

"Some of those things, I guess."

"If it's just some of those things, sugar, then he's not the worst man of your acquaintance."

"Are you trying to tell me you are? That you rob and steal?"

"Until recent times."

She didn't look in the least bit shocked. Instead, she seemed thoughtful, small lines wrinkling her brow, as if she was considering exactly what he'd said.

"So you're trying to reform."

He thumbed his hat to the back of his head and propped his foot against the brake.

"Trying. Not always succeeding."

"Have you robbed or stolen lately?"

"No." Not exactly, unless she included what he'd taken from her last night. Except she'd been willing enough, so he didn't know if that counted or not.

But his sins or lack of them weren't the point here.

"Amy, what I do or don't do isn't important right now. The fact is . . ."

Here it came, the big moment of truth, and her with her big bluebonnet eyes staring up at him, her fine chin tilted, her hair blowing in the November breeze, and looking for all the world like the sweetest, kindest creature on earth, not to mention the most beautiful.

Whatever she was doing to him, she was doing a good job.

He took a deep breath. "The fact is I'm a . . . temporary man."

* * *

Amy held herself very still. Here it came, Cad's declaration of intent, which was that sometime before long he would be moving on without her.

Her heart broke. She hadn't expected *I love you,* knew she'd never hear it, but she wasn't in the mood to hear *I don't love you* either.

What she did want to hear was *I'd like to get between your legs again.*

Or something maybe a little more romantic.

Cad wasn't a romantic man. He liked sex.

And so did she.

She licked her lips, trying to make herself look appealing, wishing she'd had some lavender water to splash on after her early morning dip in the creek. In the criminal life he claimed for himself, he must have been around women a great deal fancier than she, but she would gamble her dwindling funds he'd never met one more willing.

Her task as she saw it now was not to frighten him away too soon.

"I know last night didn't mean anything permanent to you. I'm a temporary woman too."

"It's not the same thing."

"Oh, yes, it is."

His dark eyes stared at her without so much as a blink. She could see he wasn't going to hush. He needed something else to occupy his mind. She'd learned enough about him to know what that something had to be.

Before he could say *Rough Cut, Texas,* she stood, hiked her skirts, and straddled him the way he'd shown her last night.

His flagpole pressed against her underdrawers and right away she started getting damp.

Getting his balance, he held her by the waist, but he didn't try to shove her away. Instead, he just kept on watching her, as if he was waiting to see what she would do next.

She stared down at his stubbled face and his shadowy brown eyes, his thick brows, his parted lips, his strong chin. He looked rough as tree bark on the outside, and just as dark, but she knew of slick, smooth places that weren't so visible, and gentle hands that had a magic touch.

Everything she saw and knew about him she liked. For just this moment her broken heart healed and swelled with love.

"Amy—" he said, but it didn't really sound like a warning.

"Cadmus Aloysius Rankin," she said in return, "if we don't have much longer to be together, I'd say talking was a waste of time."

Tiny lines furrowed his brow. She tossed his hat into the wagon bed and her fingers ruffled the crease in his hair until his locks were as wild as her own.

"My leg—"

"Pish tosh. If you're going to tell me it's hurting you today, don't bother. It couldn't have been broken. I haven't seen you limp even once."

She rotated her hips against him and gripped him tighter between her thighs. Yearning coiled within her like a living creature that wouldn't be denied. Judging from the glint in his eyes, he felt a coil or two himself.

"If you're going to tell me you don't like this, then get to it, because I'm right at the point where I don't think I can stop."

"You sound like me."

"Of course I do. You're my teacher, remember?"

"Yeah, I remember."

He eased his hands just high enough so that his thumbs could stroke the hard tips of her breasts. She felt each touch through the layers of her clothes.

"I was thinking about the staid young miss who threw rocks at me from a tree," he said in a voice that was satisfyingly thick.

"She's still around somewhere. Give me a hard time and you'll find out soon enough."

His lips curved into a wicked grin. "A hard time is exactly what you're going to get."

He licked her lips, and it was as if he were entering her in every orifice.

"I'm not planning to tell you I don't like it," he said.

"I'd call you liar if you did." Again she rotated her hips. "I can feel your flagpole too well."

"My flagpole?"

The old Amy from the tree would have blushed at such boldness. The new Amy grinned. "That's what I call it. Do you mind if I give it a name?"

He licked her lips again. She felt the thrill all the way to her toes.

"There's nothing you're doing right now that I mind."

Amy sighed in relief. She had stopped the *temporary* talk and started the pleasurable time again.

She glanced over her shoulder at the mare, who was cropping grass in the shade, then checked out the gelding, who was doing the same at the rear of the wagon. Around them the hills remained quiet and eternal.

"One thing about Texas," she said, "when you're alone, you're alone."

She kissed him. He kissed her right back. The two of them got so involved in the activity, what with her hands roaming through his hair and caressing the warmth at the back of his neck and his hands finding their way under her skirt, that they toppled off the seat and onto the blanket in the wagon bed.

They landed with a crash, and Amy broke the kiss long enough to ask if he was hurt.

"Just my flagpole."

"Don't tell me it broke."

"No. But it did lose contact for a second there."

There wasn't a part of her that wasn't tingling as she settled herself astride him, letting him stretch out so he wouldn't get a cramp. "It won't happen again," she promised, and the kissing commenced in earnest, their tongues and teeth and lips all getting into the act.

"My drawers have a slit in them," she whispered into his mouth when she couldn't take the building heat a moment longer.

"My trousers need to be unfastened."

He took care of her while she took care of him, and she slid down on him as if she'd been doing it for years.

With her cloak and skirt billowing around them, they made the wagon rock.

Afterwards, as the last ripples of pleasure passed into memory, they continued to hold on to each other. Amy knew not how Cad was feeling, but for her, they might as well have been in a fancy boudoir stretched out on a four-poster feather bed, with yards of filmy curtains blocking out the world.

And not in the back of an open wagon with only a thin blanket to cover the hard boards and nothing but a few trees to screen them from the wide landscape.

Amy cared not where they were, only that their bodies were still joined.

With each experience she became more addicted to making love. But only with Cad. No other man would ever touch her where he touched her, not if she lived to be a hundred. Which meant they had to do what they were doing as often as they could until their temporary time was done.

Cad didn't seem in any hurry to leave, or even to separate himself from her. Not until the horses started getting restless. She felt the tension in him right away. A horse's neigh sounded like a bell tolling the end of their rendezvous. Easing herself beside him, straightening her clothes, she watched as he sat up and studied the hills.

"Anything wrong?" she asked.

"Probably not."

But he kept on studying. Again Horse neighed. "Stay low, Amy," he ordered as he fastened his trousers, slapped his hat back on his head, and reached for his shotgun.

Amy suddenly felt as cold as she'd been hot.

"There's someone out there," she said, remembering the way they'd been shot at on the first ride into Rough Cut.

"Could be an animal. Man's not the only critter to roam these hills."

He slipped over the side of the wagon and stared toward a scattering of boulders to the west. Something glinted in the morning sun. Something like the barrel of a gun.

Amy saw it the same moment he did. Her heart caught in her throat.

"Stay here," she begged.

"Lay low," he ordered in return. "I can't protect you if you don't do what I say."

She wanted very much to be protected by

him, but she also wanted to do some protecting in return. Helpless, she watched as he walked toward the boulders.

A shot rang out, and his hat went skittering across the ground. Amy screamed and came close to clearing the wagon and running after him. Only the knowledge that she'd get in the way held her back.

"You out there, Wiley?" Cad shouted as he strode across the rocky ground. "Shooting from ambush seems your style."

Another shot hit the dust in front of his boot.

"Come on, Fike, you can do better than that."

Amy shivered in fright. Wiley Fike, the deputy Cad said had shot at them before, must be taking target practice again. Or trying to intimidate them, having what he considered fun.

He needed a woman instead of a weapon, she decided, but figuring out his problems didn't still the terror in her heart.

Why didn't Cad shoot back? She knew he could hit anything he aimed for, but he just kept on walking, the shotgun held loosely in his hand. He stopped a dozen yards from where the glint had been seen.

The deputy's cadaverous figure rose from behind the rocks, a rifle aimed at Cad.

"You got no sense, Rankin," he yelled.

"That's what I hear."

"I could take you down right where you stand, then use your gun on the woman. Claim you shot her and then I shot you. No one would be the wiser."

"You could try it."

Which was what he did, lifting the gun and firing straight at Cad. Again Amy screamed, but with Cad continuing to walk straight on without a sign of being hurt, she fell silent, too frightened to make a sound. The astonishment on Wiley Fike's face, evident even from a distance, echoed in her heart and mind.

The deputy fired again and again as Cad strode toward him. When the rifle was empty Fike pulled out a mean-looking pistol and fired some more, but Cad didn't once break stride.

He stopped when they were only a few feet apart, Fike half-hidden by the boulders, Cad standing on the open ground.

Amy couldn't hear what they were saying, but whatever it was it sent the deputy scurrying across the rocks and out of sight. Bounding over the side of the wagon, she lifted her skirts and ran toward the man she loved.

He was watching her all the way. Gasping for breath, she stopped a few feet from him and looked for signs of blood. Dizzy from running and blinded by fear, she studied him fast. He was a blur, but he was an upright one, and she saw no sign that he had been wounded.

Relief danced through her, then gave way to fury. "That was the stupidest thing I've ever seen anyone do," she yelled, her hands on her hips.

"Don't bother to get your hat. I'll make you a dunce cap instead."

"I knew what I was doing."

"You knew the deputy couldn't hit the ground if he aimed for it? Nobody could be that bad a shot."

She started to cry. Angrily, she brushed away the tears.

"You were scared," he said, taking a step forward. "I'm sorry about that."

"Of course I was scared," she fairly screamed. "Anyone in his right mind would have been frightened out of his wits. Is that what was wrong? Fear robbed you of good sense?"

Even as she said the words, she knew they weren't true. Cad was the bravest man in all the world.

She threw herself into his arms and covered his face with kisses. Dropping the gun, he held her close and let her carry on.

Hugging him tightly, she buried her face in his chest and fought for control. If she kept this up, she'd be straddling him again right here on the hard ground, tearing off his clothes, making sure his various parts were still all right.

Slowly sanity returned, and with it confusion. She pushed away to look up into his eyes. "First the leg and now this. I don't understand, Cad. I must be losing my mind."

The heat she was used to seeing in his expression had disappeared; in its place was a deep, dark stare that told her nothing of what he was thinking.

But he was thinking; she knew that well enough. The trouble was, he was thinking things she wouldn't like.

If she could take back her talk about understanding, she would. Cad could be a ghost for all she cared; she would love him just as much.

But he wasn't a ghost; he was flesh and blood and all man.

She shook her head. Maybe this was all a dream.

He rested his hands on her shoulders. The warmth and strength of him were all too real.

"Look closer at my clothes, Amy. Do you see the bullet holes?"

She saw them now, in the front of his coat, in his shirt, in his sleeves. How could she have missed them before? She'd been looking for signs of blood, that's how.

"This is crazy," she said, her mind in a whirl. "He hit you, didn't he? He didn't miss."

"No, he didn't miss."

"But you're alive."

"Yes and no. Remember how I called myself a temporary man?"

Amy's heart turned to stone. "I remember."

"Now's a good time to tell you exactly what I meant."

Chapter Nineteen

For the telling Cad settled Amy in a soft patch of grass beside the wagon and commenced to pace.

"I'd appreciate it if you didn't interrupt," he said.

"I won't," she answered in a small voice. The air was chilly in the shade. Huddled inside her cloak, she ventured a thin smile. "I won't attack you again."

Cad muttered curses under his breath. Even when he was trying to do right by her she made him feel like a rat.

He started right in, telling his strange tale in the order in which things had happened. He didn't leave out much, except the part about Michael and losing his parents, concentrating instead on his wild life after his family was gone and on Dudley's determination to set him along the straight-and-narrow path.

He left out, too, the part about no whiskey and no women; Amy would be blaming herself for leading him astray.

One more thing he didn't tell her was the part about how she was getting to him. When Fike had talked about shooting her he'd come close to planting a bullet between his narrow little eyes.

It was this last part, the part about the caring, that convinced him a confession was long overdue. Amy was unsettling him as no one had ever done, making him think things he'd never thought before. Making him . . .

Care was about the best way he could put it. He refused to use a stronger word.

Maybe she wasn't feeling the same way about him, maybe she was just waking up to the pleasures of the world, but he'd like to think maybe she was waking up to him.

Could be his ego was getting in the way. Or maybe, just maybe, he was reverting to the person he used to be, before the soldiers, before the swamp, wanting her to want him in ways that went beyond the sex.

He couldn't let that happen. Too much suffering went with the permanent kind of caring. And so he told her about being undead.

While he talked, she leaned against the tree at her back and stared into the distance. When he was done silence roared between them.

He settled on his haunches beside her. "I'm not lying to you, Amy. Everything I've told you is the truth."

She turned her wide blue eyes on him. "If that's what you claim, then that's the way it is. I just didn't know such a thing was possible."

Her voice was flat, as if she didn't catch on to exactly what he was saying. Of course she didn't. If he hadn't lived the story, he wouldn't believe it either.

She touched his hand for a moment. Her fingers burned against his skin.

"You feel so real."

"I am real."

"Not quite."

"I'm real enough."

"For some things, I suppose."

This time her voice took on a soft tremor, but he didn't think she was about to cry. Her eyes were too dry, too blank, too inwardly turned for tears.

She glanced toward the wagon, and he knew that, like him, she was remembering what had happened in the back.

"Could you always . . . do it? Was the part about your injury disabling you just a lie?"

"It was a way to keep me from pulling up your skirts. I wanted to do it the first time we met. That's the God's own truth. You were quite a sight, coming down from that tree. I thought maybe my dying was already done and I'd gone to heaven."

She paid no mind to the compliment. "The scar—"

"—was where the guard shot me outside the bank."

She pressed a hand to her cheek. "And I asked to see the wound when all the time . . ."

A new thought caused her to start. "What if I'm carrying your child? I hadn't thought about it until now, but I guess the possibility exists. Will the baby be born . . . undead?"

"You're not pregnant. Dudley says I'm shooting blanks."

"I don't understand."

"I can't have children. At least for now."

"Oh." She hugged her middle. "Then what we did was of no consequence."

Pulling himself to his feet, Cad felt a flare of anger, then told himself to settle down. She was better off looking at things in a practical way. Still, she was writing him off fast.

"You wanted a baby? Is that what you've been aiming at?"

She stared up at him without speaking right away. He thought about her carrying his child. He thought about it a long while.

She was the first to look away, making him feel empty inside.

"I didn't even think of babies until this minute," she said in a lost kind of voice. "If I had wanted a child, I'd be an even bigger fool, wouldn't I? We would have ended up as two more charges for Prudence Thor."

Before he could respond she stood and walked away from the shade, putting a dozen yards between them. After a long while, with the November sun streaking down in patches through the clouds, she turned to face him. The best of the autumn sunlight nestled in her hair, and there was a new resolution in her eyes.

"You're making this up, aren't you? Dreaming up a wild excuse to leave."

He shook his head.

Sighing, as if the spirit was going out of her, she closed her eyes for a moment. "I guess you're not." She stared at the front of his coat and shirt, at the dozen holes the bullets had made.

"What did you tell the deputy to make him run? That you had the angels on your side?"

"What I said was, if he didn't hightail it out of the county, I was going to cut off his balls and feed them to the buzzards."

"He seemed to take you seriously."

"He's not a total fool."

She thought some more. "The nuns never mentioned liaison angels."

"They're not quite up to being guardians yet. Guardian angels deal with the living, not the dead."

She blinked a time or two. "And his name . . . Gabriel I could believe. Not Dudley."

"You're trying to reason this through, Amy. I

had the advantage of seeing my blood spill out on the street and feeling my heart stop. The undertaker was ready to slice into me when Dudley suddenly appeared. Believe me, liaison angels really do exist."

He picked up the shotgun at his feet. "It's loaded. Test me. Shoot me yourself."

"Oh," she said; then, turning, she put more distance between them, the hem of her cloak dragging across the rocky ground. The day turned darker the farther she walked. At last she halted, her back still to him. A cold wind picked up, whipping her cloak about her. He gave her time to think, but he didn't take his eyes off her, off the mass of golden hair that blew wildly about her head and shoulders.

She didn't speak for a long time. It seemed an hour, but more likely it was only minutes. When she returned to stand in front of him, walking slow and steady, her eyes locked with his all the while, he still couldn't read her mind.

"You're here to clean up Rough Cut, right?"

"That's right."

"The bartender says he's not getting as many men riding through as he used to."

"They don't like losing at cards. In case you're wondering, I beat them fair and square."

"Dudley wouldn't let you cheat."

"Old Dud's got a lot of rules."

She swallowed and briefly closed her eyes. "I'm sure he does. Aren't you about done with the task set you? Most of the gamblers and thieves are gone, and the deputy, too."

"There's still John Lattimer. He's the real source of evil around here. I'll have to destroy him to make sure the job is finished right." The tightness in her expression made him want to defend himself. "He threatened to kill me, remember? He'll be killing others before long too. Anyone who gets in his way; women and children if need be."

"You're right, of course. But destroy . . ."

She kicked a stone at her feet, her gaze cast down. "How do you plan to do it?"

"I haven't decided yet. It would help if you didn't go out to his place again."

When she raised her eyes he caught a glimpse of sadness in their depths; or, if not sadness, a lost and empty look. He'd seen it there before. He still didn't know its cause.

"I hadn't planned to see him again. I'm sure he doesn't care if he sees me."

"Then he's a bigger fool than I thought."

"Maybe." She studied the cloud-crossed sky. "Is Dudley watching us now?"

"It's possible. I can't see him unless he wants me to."

She rubbed her arms. "Was he watching when we . . . were together?"

Cad shrugged. "All of Texas could have been watching and I wouldn't have known. I was thinking of other things."

"I didn't give you much choice. And you didn't answer my question. Could he have been looking down at the wagon?"

"I doubt it. But he's not a mortal. If he did see us, he wouldn't . . . well, he wouldn't get any pleasure in it."

"I see," she said, but from the blush on her cheeks he wasn't sure she spoke the truth.

She gave a last look at the sky, and a long sigh. "You may not need to eat, but I do. Let's go on to the Clap."

He reached for her. She backed away.

"Is that all you've got to say?" he asked.

"I need some time, Cad." She stood straighter, drawing strength from somewhere. "Give me time."

Cad ran a hand through his hair. The woman facing him now with her chin tilted against him and her eyes clear and without expression was not the same woman who'd wrapped herself around him and sent him crashing to the wagon bed.

But, of course, to her he wasn't the same man.

"The Clap it is," he said, and he went to untether the mare.

Within minutes they were once more on the trail, Cad's hat pulled low on his forehead, Amy busy binding her hair and tucking it under her bonnet. She was grateful he didn't push her for more talk. She would have to think in order to respond, and she was working too hard at keeping her mind a blank.

She was such an ordinary woman, and here

she was caught in an extraordinary time. How she was to handle the situation, what exactly she was to tell her heart—as if her heart would listen—she hadn't the vaguest idea.

Ever since Pierre sniffed his way to her side, talking about getting her alone in a ship's cabin, she had taken to rushing into things. This time she would think matters through before she decided on a course of action.

Undead. What a terrible word; not even a word, really, not one she had ever read. But it was better than *dead,* which Cad could be if things did not go right for him.

They must. She crushed all other possibilities. He would destroy her father and then move on. Leaving her alone.

It wasn't as if anyone cared what she did, not in the long run. If she was to have any kind of life after Rough Cut, she had better start thinking of herself, although how she was to live without purpose she didn't know. Maybe Dudley could give her some advice.

During the long ride she didn't have much else to do but consider her options. If she were a better person, she would be thinking how she could help Cad. But she wasn't good enough for that; not just yet.

Neither could she see how to help herself. The longer she pondered, the easier it was to decide on her feelings. She was furious; she'd been betrayed. It was a great deal better than feeling desolate.

"You should have left me up that tree," she said, loud and clear over the horse-and-wagon noises.

She felt Cad's eyes turn to her in surprise, but she kept on staring at the mare's rump.

"You chucked rocks at me, remember? It called for investigation."

"All right, then, you should have left me to fend for myself and ridden into Rough Cut alone. You had no right to involve me in your problems." She knew she was being unreasonable, but she was too caught up in turmoil to keep quiet.

"By then I'd got a good look at you. Whether you admit it or not, liking a woman's looks is not an insult, Amy."

She wasn't in a mood to be appeased.

"You didn't like anything else?"

"I didn't *know* anything else."

"You weren't even alive and you took me to your room." Her cheeks burned as the memories returned. "And you unfastened your trousers when we were barely acquainted."

"You asked me to. Besides, that's the way I am with women. It clears up misunderstandings between us right away."

She slammed her fists against her lap. He was right, of course. She'd pushed him into just about every advance he had made on her. After a while she hadn't waited for him to act, but had gone ahead on her own.

But he could have stopped her at any time, she reminded herself.

If she took him to task he would probably say she was so beautiful and so seductive, he couldn't control himself.

And then she would say—

Amy stopped herself. The one word that would never fall between them was *love*. Right now she couldn't let it enter her mind, or else she might lose her anger. She would be doing that soon enough.

Despair welled up in her. Cad was more special than she could ever have imagined, and she loved him more than ever. But he'd hurt her, too, by keeping his secret when she'd opened herself to him completely.

Not completely, her conscience whispered.

Yes, completely, in all the important ways.

John Lattimer? Love? These aren't important?

Of course they were; Amy's turmoil increased a thousandfold.

She fell to silence. Thank goodness, so did he. Neither spoke again until they arrived at the ranch and she got her first look at the destroyed barn. Wishing no one harm, she was shamefully grateful for something besides Cad to occupy her mind.

Amy remembered the Clap as a perfect place nestled in a neatly tended valley, surrounded by verdant hills. On this gray afternoon the valley's perfection was marred by a black, jagged scar behind the ranch house, where once had been a red-roofed barn.

Prudence Thor stood close to the charred rubble. At her side were a couple of her men and the two women who helped her care for the orphans.

Present, too, was Tommy, as lanky and freckled as Amy remembered him, his arm no longer in a sling.

The widow greeted them with a wave. "Still too hot to do much clearing. I'll rebuild, of course. Got to. Otherwise it'd be like giving in."

Amy almost felt sorry for her father, what with the strong-willed Prudence and the invincible Cad lined up against him.

For just a moment she remembered the way he'd looked at her, and the inward look he'd turned on himself. The world and its people were turning out more complex than she'd ever dreamed.

She dropped from the wagon without waiting for assistance. Prudence glanced at Cad. "What happened to you? Looks like your clothes've been used for target practice."

"They were, in a way. It's a long story, too long to go into just now."

He didn't look at Amy as he spoke. She didn't feel inclined to explain what he meant.

Prudence looked from one to the other. "Everything all right?"

"Everything's just fine," Amy said.

"We got started before breakfast," Cad said.

"Any chance we could get some grub?"

"The children are in there now. Join 'em and help yourself to whatever looks good."

Amy felt Cad's eyes on her. Did she still look good to him? Given the possibility he might not complete his assignment, was she the last chance he had for satisfaction before passing on?

She hadn't looked at their situation quite like that before. If she asked him, he would deny it, even though Dudley must have told him not to lie.

Well, he *had* lied, if only by omitting a few details about himself. Before she could put more thought behind his failing and going to hell, perhaps hurried on by her scandalous behavior, she retreated to the kitchen. Much to her surprise, she discovered she was ravenous. With little Lenoma sitting beside her and chattering on about the fire, she ate the biggest plate of ham and eggs she'd ever had.

Cad didn't bother with the pretense of joining her, for which she was grateful. When she thought about it, his not eating or sleeping sounded as strange as anything else he had said.

She and the children cleaned up, then went outside to join the others by the ruins. As always, her gaze was drawn to Cad. He stood apart from the others, talking to Tommy, gesturing toward the charred remains. They looked natural together, she thought, the strong dark man and the sandy-haired, skinny boy. Like father and son, or two brothers born years apart. A lump caught in her throat. Tommy could be her son . . . their son, or someone like him a few years from now.

Except it wouldn't happen. Tears threatened, and she felt empty inside. She pulled herself together as a carriage rumbled down the incline to join them. It was the sheriff's carriage she had ridden in on her journey out of Del Rio, the first part of her ride to Rough Cut.

Sheriff Bowles looked sober enough as he lowered his stout body to the ground. Much to Amy's surprise, he had a companion. Even more to her surprise, she saw it was Kate.

"Thought I'd help Hickok earn his salary," the madam explained, although no one had put a question to her. She was wearing a rustly green cloak and a matching bonnet atop her red hair. Her cheeks were pinked from the ride, and Amy realized what a handsome woman she was.

The sheriff's ruddy face wrinkled into a frown. "Don't know what I'm supposed to do." He stared around the ruined barn. "He sure did make a mess, didn't he?"

The widow pounced on his comment right away. "Who? You got proof who set the fire?"

"Now how in the hell would I have that?"

Kate elbowed him in his prominent stomach and gestured toward the children close by.

"Watch your language, Hickok," she said.

To Amy's astonishment, the sheriff actually looked embarrassed.

"Your problem," she went on, "is that you spend too much time alone."

"I was hired to protect the bank."

"Now who in his right mind is going to rile John Lattimer by stealing his money?"

Amy cast a sideways glance at the only bank robber of her acquaintance. He shot her back a warning look. Straightening, she turned her back to him.

Kate's thoughtful eyes took in the brief exchange. "Something going on between you two?"

"Nothing," said Cad.

"Nothing," said Amy.

"Sure clears that up," Kate said, glancing without comment at the state of Cad's clothes. She looked at Prudence. The two women shrugged.

Before Amy could think of a change in subject, two more carriages arrived. In the first were Pierre and Lilly Mae, followed close behind by the valet George and another resident of the pleasure parlor, Carmen.

They were arriving in pairs, as if they were headed for the arc, thought Amy, who was in a biblical mood.

Everyone exclaimed over the extent of the damage and the wonder that lives hadn't been lost.

From time to time Pierre cast guilt-laden glances at Amy.

"Thank you for escorting Lilly Mae," she said,

wanting to put him at ease. "She must have wanted very much to find out exactly what had happened."

"Oui," he returned, clearly in one of his less voluble moods. True to form, his companion didn't say a word. George and Carmen conversed in a polyglot combination of English, Spanish, and French that made sense only to them.

"About the target practice . . ." Amy began, remembering the last time she and Pierre had been together.

Pierre glanced sideways at Lilly Mae. "I have become convinced my skills need much work."

Lilly Mae's doing, Amy was sure. Even her French fiancé was finding comfort, and maybe more, in the West. Happy for him, she felt more desolate for herself.

While the men studied the rubble, the women went inside. Before Kate could start in with questions again, Amy asked a few of her own.

"I didn't know you and the sheriff were friends."

"He and I go back a long way. We arrived in Rough Cut about the same time, five years ago next spring. Drifters, both of us. I didn't start out that way, mind you, but a no-good man taught me I'd better take care of myself."

Carmen echoed the sentiment in broken English that held a trace of a French accent, but Lilly Mae kept her eyes on her hands.

Kate looked at her women. "Anybody minding the store?"

"Dora and Sal," Lilly Mae ventured. "Business sure has dropped off in the past few weeks."

"It's the nature of the trade. It has its ups and downs."

"*Es verdad,*" said Carmen with a laugh. Lilly Mae gave no sign she caught the joke. Try though she might, Amy saw no humor in the remark. Too well did she remember the way she and Cad had made the wagon rock.

One by one the children were driven indoors by the increasingly cold wind. Lilly Mae and Carmen turned their attention to caring for them in the front parlor. Amy wanted to do the same, but Kate took her aside, dragging her into the kitchen with the excuse of putting on a fresh pot of coffee.

"You two are sleeping together, aren't you?"

Amy started guiltily. "That's what he pays me to do."

"Hell, honey, I know he wasn't bedding you at the Pleasure Parlor. I can tell about these matters. It's my business to know. I'm talking about while you were out last night. And if I'm not mistaken, maybe this morning, too."

"I'm not charging him. And I doubt it will happen again."

"You love him, don't you? No, don't bother to deny it. If he don't know it, too, then he's a bigger fool than I've taken him for."

"He's got other things on his mind."

"That's what they all claim. Other things more often than not being a wife and kids."

"Cad's not married."

"I believe you're right. He's got the look of a loner about him, a drifter. And you're a woman for settling down."

"Maybe I used to be. Not anymore."

"Keep telling yourself that if it'll make you feel any better."

Kate said the words gently, and Amy saw the madam meant to be her friend. "Do me a favor: Tell Lilly Mae that Pierre and I truly are no longer betrothed. I don't know what's going on between them, or if he will act honorably, but I rather think he will."

Kate touched her hand. "Whores learn not to expect much. But she'll appreciate your passing on the message."

Under the kind assault, Amy almost broke down. "I need to go help with the children."

"They are cute tykes, aren't they?" A look of longing warmed the madam's green eyes. "There was a time—"

She shook off the warmth. "That was years ago. Anyway, I got a message too. For your man."

"He's not my man."

Kate went on as if she hadn't heard. "A stranger rode into town yesterday. The kind we usually get, only better-looking than most and with a calculating look in his eye, as if he was planning something. He seemed highly interested when someone in the saloon mentioned Cad. Said they were friends from way back."

"Oh?" Amy knew in her heart that whatever Kate said next would not be good news.

"Said if I saw him to let him know his old buddy Rick Marsh was camping just north of town."

Amy took a minute to figure out who she meant. Alarmed, she turned away. Rick Marsh was Cad's sometime partner who had helped rob the Galveston bank.

Chapter Twenty

Within an hour the town women went back to Rough Cut, leaving the men to start clearing the ruins. Amy didn't have a chance to tell Cad the news about his partner before she left.

Opportunity wasn't the only reason she kept it to herself. She didn't know what it would mean to Cad, or how he would react.

At least that was what she told herself. On the ride to town she admitted the truth. She didn't care beans about Rick Marsh. She was simply too cowardly and far too confused to confront Cad alone about anything. How could she possibly approach him after all he'd said to her and all she had said to him? She didn't know what to think or how to feel about his condition. She wanted to cry and rage and run away all at the same time.

It took her a sleepless night to sort things through and to understand her heart. By the time dawn cast its gray light onto Rough Cut, she was ready to talk.

She knew he had returned; from her window she'd seen him ride into town around midnight and walk into the hotel. It was strange how she always sensed when he was near, as if something or someone were guiding her thoughts.

She thrust the idea away. Next thing she knew, she would be meeting Dudley for herself and asking for the advice she'd wanted yesterday.

This morning advice wasn't necessary, and neither was chastisement. From the moment Cad had started confessing, she'd been thinking of herself, of how he'd kept her in the dark, of her reactions to him, of maybe carrying his baby.

Worst of all, she'd been angry with him. Angry! She would regret that anger until her dying day.

She hadn't come to the conclusion quickly. What he'd told her still seemed impossible. It was also impossible that although she wanted a place to belong and someone to share her life, her goal seemed farther away than ever.

Impossible, too, that the man who'd given her

life and the man who gave her a reason to live were mortal enemies.

And it was impossible that the chaste, convent-raised girl she had once been could turn so quickly into a sex-starved woman who couldn't get enough of passion.

Most impossible of all was the love she bore a man who wasn't alive.

Yet all these impossibilities were true. And there was only one thing she could do about them. She wasn't being impulsive. She was being practical.

Shortly after dawn she dressed carefully, choosing everything she put on with a critical eye, then covering her choices with a cloak and hood. Making her way across the street to Cad's hotel room, she knocked once and let herself inside.

He was stretched out on the bed, one hand beneath his head, the other holding a cigar. Somehow he'd found pillows and sheets to cover the mattress; all in all the room didn't look half bad now.

Neither did Cad. Gray light filtered through the window, allowing her a good look. He'd changed into a black shirt and trousers, but his feet were bare and his legs were crossed at the ankle. He blew a smoke ring into the air and stared at her across the room.

"I didn't know you smoked," she said.

"It's another of my vices. I thought I'd given it up."

"Some habits are hard to break."

"That's what I hear."

Amy could see he wasn't going to make this easy for her. But then, he didn't know what she had come to say.

As she looked him over, letting her gaze trail down from his unreadable eyes to the open throat of his shirt to his flat abdomen to his long, strong legs, she abandoned her plan to start out telling him about Rick Marsh.

She certainly hadn't dressed with his thieving partner in mind.

She tossed back her hood and shook out her loose hair. He flicked his cigar out the window and kept on watching her.

"Good aim, Cad. You're very skillful with your hands."

"It comes from a lifetime of breaking into safes."

A lifetime. Amy almost cried at the words.

But she hadn't dressed with crying in mind, either.

"The nuns said high arches are a sign of high birth. Did I tell you that?"

"Shows the nuns can be wrong. My parents were educated people, but they worked with the soil."

It was a detail about himself he had failed to mention yesterday. She tucked it away with her other memories of him.

Suddenly she was nervous, in ways she hadn't been at their campsite or in the wagon. Her actions then had been spontaneous. She was a calculating woman now.

And Cad wasn't helping in the least, stretched out like that on the bed and watching her without giving any sign he liked what he saw.

"I came to apologize," she said.

"What for?"

"The way I acted yesterday."

"You didn't do anything wrong."

"Oh, yes I did. I was angry and confused and hurt, not sure whether to believe you, as if you could lie about such a thing, with your clothes riddled by bullets. Mostly I was considering matters from my point of view. During the night I got to thinking about how you must feel."

"And?"

"I decided that you don't know how long you have to live"—her voice caught but she kept on—"and you have every right to take what pleasure you can. Especially when it's offered to you without question. You passed up chances with me early on, but lately you haven't seemed inclined to do so."

"I'm glad you noticed."

"I don't think you'll be so inclined today."

She slipped off her cloak and saw heat flare in his eyes.

The eyes that had been pinned to hers started a downward trail, to the red silk slip of material that hugged her body from low on her breasts to the tops of her thighs, to the black garters and flesh-toned stockings encasing her legs, to the high-heeled boots laced tightly up her calves.

This was the most seductive outfit in her mother's trunk. The neckline and hem of the silk were both trimmed in feathers dyed a matching red. They were beginning to scratch. She hoped he would decide soon what he planned to do.

He sat at the edge of the bed. "Come here."

He didn't have to say it twice.

Her boots fairly slid across the floor. She stopped close enough for him to run his palms along the outside of her thighs. His breath warmed her abdomen through the silk, tickling her skin, sending fire raging through her veins.

Her knees threatened to buckle, but the least she could do for him was keep standing where he obviously wanted her. His fingers played with her garters, then slipped to the back of her legs, edging higher until he cupped her rear.

She was naked under the silk.

"Well, well," he said.

"Nothing seemed to fit with this."

He kneaded her nether cheeks. "Nothing does just fine."

Amy had to grip his shoulders to keep standing. Under her hands, he felt solid and strong and very much alive. That was the way she must look at him. Alive, and wanting to enjoy each moment of pleasure that offered itself.

"The other night, by the camp fire, you kissed me," he said, and she knew what he meant.

"I wasn't sure you liked it."

He made a sound that was half laugh, half growl. "I liked it." He studied her pebbled nipples, outlined by the silk, then looked into her eyes. "Did you?"

She nodded. "I tasted you for a long time. I kept wanting to taste you again. Is that a terrible thing to admit?"

"It's not unnatural, if that's what you're worried about. The way it's not unnatural for me to want to taste you."

All the fire that had been coursing through her veins settled in one hot place between her legs.

"I don't know—" she began, embarrassed by the idea of what he was suggesting. Embarrassed and thrilled too.

"I do."

Her fingers dug into his shoulders. As always, Cad understood what she was feeling.

He lifted the red feathers to reveal her private hair, black as night, unlike the locks she showed to the world.

"You're beautiful," he said.

"I can't stand this much longer," she said.

"Neither can I."

With deft, sure movements he laid her beside him on the bed and covered her mouth with his. After a long while he broke away.

"Cad," she ventured, ashamed of herself for interrupting whatever he planned to do. "Would you undress me?"

"I kind of like the stockings and shoes."

"It's just that the feathers are scratching me."

He grinned, but there was more heat than humor in his expression.

"Can't have you distracted, can we?"

Slipping the silk over her head, he tossed it aside, then took time to look her over. She felt wanton and wanted and as happy as she had ever been, mindless in her joy and eagerness.

She even liked the feel of the sheets against her back, a fact she pointed out.

"They were here when I got back last night." He ran his tongue along her throat. "A gift from Kate. She must have figured you'd be visiting soon."

He made his teasing way to the tips of her breasts. Amy arched her back.

"Kate's a smart woman," she attempted to say, but it came out an unintelligible sigh. She would have tried again, but Cad got down to serious business, putting his lips to parts that turned her into a wild and writhing creature, someone who could do nothing but cry out his name again and again.

His face nudged her thighs apart, but she needed little urging to open to him. His tongue found the place that would satisfy her most. He licked her, then covered her with his lips. Small, sucking sounds drove her mad. Lightning flashed in the blackness behind her closed lids, and all the world became a tempest raging inside her, climaxing into a thunderbolt of ecstasy that seemed to have no end.

Shattered, yet deliriously whole, she thought the thrills would last forever, but of course they slowly faded, leaving her wanting more, much more. He had satisfied her, but in her frenzied state she was not satisfied at all.

When he kissed his way back to her lips she tasted herself on his tongue. Her heart pounded with love for what he had done.

His clothes felt rough and teasing against her naked body. She wanted to stroke his hot, slick skin. Rapacious fingers tore at his shirt. She sent the buttons skittering, but she'd got no further than baring his chest when he gripped her hands and kissed her fingers.

"I can't wait," he growled. Unfastening his trousers, he settled between her legs and slipped inside her with such ease, she knew that at least part of him had found a home.

Her muscles convulsed around him. He licked her lips. "You can come again. Just move with me."

As if she had a choice. Wrapping her arms and legs around him, she stroked the back of his thighs with her boot heels, with as delicate a touch as she could manage. Cad was right: He could take her to ecstasy once again. Holding him tight, forgetting the strokes, this time she soared with him into the storm.

Cad undressed, removed Amy's stockings and boots; then, with her garters tucked aside with his trousers, he pulled a sheet over them. She snuggled against him. He thought with satisfaction that she was a cuddler after all.

"You didn't owe me an apology," he said.

"Yes, I did," she murmured against his chest. "Don't argue with me. It's not an appropriate time."

"I should apologize to you."

She lifted her head and stared up at him, a wicked glint in her eye. "Not for anything you've done lately."

"Glad to hear it."

"That was a compliment, you know."

"I know. Thank you."

"You're welcome. For someone who's not quite alive, you have a very active body; did you know that?"

Cad could hardly believe he was having this conversation. "You seem mighty comfortable with my condition this morning."

He felt her stiffen, then relax once again against him. When she finally answered her voice was soft. "I decided that if you can be brave about it, so can I. After all, you're the one who's . . . in the condition."

"Amy."

"What? You sound serious."

"I might not make my way through this all right."

"Life's a challenge to everybody." Her fingers made small circles on his chest, concentrating on the vicinity of his heart. "Life . . . and death."

"Damn it, woman, I feel responsible for you."

She smiled up at him brightly, too brightly. "I'll bet you're not supposed to curse."

"*Darn it* sometimes doesn't do the job."

"Nevertheless, you mustn't push Dudley too far."

"You sound familiar with him."

"Then I'll say Mr. Dudley. Unless he has a last name."

"Nope."

"What does he look like?"

Cad described his white-bearded angel with the gentle smile and the no-nonsense stance. "He's a stubborn critter, but he has a kind of glow about him that warms the air. Don't know how he does it."

"Maybe it's his goodness. Maybe it's love." The last word came out almost a whisper.

Soft as it was, it tied him in knots. "Maybe. Love's not anything I'd know about." He spoke more harshly than he'd intended, but he couldn't let her start getting ideas. Couldn't let himself, either. For him, she'd come along too late.

"Haven't you ever loved anybody?"

Cad thought over the question. Answering ought to be easy, but not with Amy in his arms. Not with a thousand claws scratching around his heart.

"Not in a long while."

"Who was she?"

"You're getting mighty nosy."

"Then don't tell me. I guess it hurts too much to talk about it. Goodness, if I ever fell—"

"She was my mother."

"Oh," Amy said in a small voice.

"I take it you haven't been in love."

It was another strange twist in the conversation, but Cad couldn't make himself stop. He wanted to know everything about her, not just what she liked in bed.

"Except for schoolgirl crushes," he added.

"If I'd had a crush, it would have been over someone I saw from the top of the convent wall."

"You led that sheltered a life?"

"I got out on occasion, for walks with the nuns. Besides, you can observe a great deal from that wall. And I always thought . . . well, that my one true love would take care of me for the rest of my life."

"And along came Pierre."

"That's when I decided to take care of myself."

Cad ought to feel sorry for her. She wasn't like him; she wasn't meant to be alone. Instead, he felt relief because there was no one else in her life besides him. He really was a bastard. He didn't deserve to live.

"Caring for yourself is hard, especially for a woman."

"It's hard for anyone. Look at you: It took an angel to straighten you out."

He stroked her arm and tickled his fingers

across the rise of her breasts. She sighed contentedly.

"I'm not sure I'm so straight."

"What does Dudley say?"

"He's not given up hope yet, but he's definitely concerned." Cad forced his straying hand to rest on her shoulder. He knew what he had to say next, but it took some pulling to get the words out. "If this doesn't work out for me, what will you do?"

She gave him a brave smile. "The same thing I'll do if it does work out for you: probably go back to San Antonio and find a husband." Her voice was as overly cheerful as her smile.

The claws tore at Cad's insides. Like hell she'd end up in another man's bed.

But he had no right to make her his.

He didn't want to, not for all time.

But he couldn't let her go.

For the first time he could remember, he didn't understand himself. Was the pounding of his heart a sign of love? Couldn't be. So why did she make him feel so rotten when she was away from him and so good when she was near?

Something had to change. He was a loner, but he thought they might travel together for a while. If he got his life back. Sure, that's what they would do. And when one of them got the itch to travel on, the other would say good-bye in a civilized way.

Except that he wasn't civilized.

She ought to know that and stop making demands.

She hadn't demanded a thing.

That was what tore at him the most. She had him so turned around, he didn't know what to think, or do, or say. He'd never been jealous before, never bothered to care whether a woman liked being with other men, but if he ever saw a man's hands on Amy, he didn't know what he'd do.

"You're awfully quiet," she said. "Penny for your thoughts."

He let his hands and lips answer for him, finding all her precious places that kept him on edge. He found them again and again, and soon he was inside her, claiming her as his in the only way he knew how, telling himself that the one thing important to both of them was the here and now.

They didn't talk again, except with their bodies, and at last she fell into a deep sleep. He held her close, not wanting to disturb her rest. In the stillness of his room the knock at the door sounded like a cannon's blast.

Without invitation, a man stepped inside.

"Rick!"

The only visible part of Amy was a tangle of golden curls on the pillow; still, Cad held her protectively close. She stirred, then settled against him.

What the hell was Rick Marsh doing here? Not that he cared.

"Get out," he ordered.

Rick leaned against the door and thumbed his hat off his forehead. With his fair hair and even features, the slippery Virginian was an innocent-looking bastard—handsome, too, the women seemed to think—but his looks were deceiving. Like Cad, he'd lost everything in the war; like Cad, he'd taken to outlaw ways.

With eyes clear and cool as creek water, he looked at Amy's garments on the floor, the cloak, the crimson silk and feathers, the stockings, the high-heeled, lace-up boots.

His mouth twisted into a crooked grin, but his eyes remained clear and cool. "Well, well, podnah, looks like you got you another one. Never saw a man who could rope the hottest women around the way you can."

Amy snored softly.

"Must have worn the poor little lady out. What say she gets some rest and I give her a try?"

Cad could have choked the life out of Rick without a second thought. But he'd be choking out his own life at the same time, and right now he leaned toward hanging around a few years.

He summoned all the restraint he could manage. "I'll meet you across the street at the Inside Straight. It'll take a few minutes."

"Give her another poke, eh? A few minutes is all I need."

With a doff of his hat toward the bed, he exited as smoothly as he had entered.

In the silence, broken only by Amy's breathing, Cad did some thinking. Whatever happened to him, he couldn't let her go right away. It wasn't a noble decision, linking her to his pitiful fate, but he'd stick by it until he felt the fires of hell.

He glanced around the room. "Listen carefully, Dudley, wherever you are. As soon as I can get Amy safely across the street, get your invisible wings down here and be ready to talk."

Chapter Twenty-one

"Shouldn't we talk to him? He's calling us loud and clear."

Dudley shook his head. "No, Michael. There's nothing we can say that will help him now. He has to help himself. He must apply what he has learned."

The angel studied the puzzled youth. "It was always going to come down to this," he added. "Redemption must start from within."

"But he's got more to worry about than just himself."

"Yes. That's something he is now feeling in his heart, and he finds it greatly troublesome. He must change from the man he was to the man he must be. Any change is difficult; for

Cadmus, alteration of self is formidable indeed."

"He has a powerful feeling for the woman, doesn't he? Physical feelings, I mean."

"This puzzles you."

"I've watched him for a long time, just about since I arrived in heaven, and I've never known him to be so . . . I don't know how to put it. Crazy, maybe, like he can't get his thoughts in order, or his feelings, either."

"Men and women are meant to feel such craziness about each other. It is God's plan for the continuation of life, and it is one of the basic conditions of conjugal love, together with loyalty and the willingness to sacrifice. You died young, before such instincts could develop in you."

Michael smiled. "I remember a girl named Eleanor. She lived in town. I used to make excuses to see her. Cad teased me for singling out just one. He said there were too many fillies around—that's what he called them, fillies—to limit myself. He planned to be the best stud stallion in the parish and to service them all."

"Many young men make the same claim until the right woman comes along."

"Is Amy the right woman for him?"

"Goodness, yes. Now it is up to Cadmus to see the truth. If he does, we must rejoice for him, for he will have understood he needs another human the way Amy does. And in the understanding he will be led into the life he should have lived. The kind of life that you would have enjoyed."

"And if he doesn't?"

"Let's not speculate about such an eventuality. We must keep our faith in the man."

He spoke with more confidence than he felt.

Michael fell silent for a long moment. "When I asked you to help my brother I didn't imagine so many complications."

"I must be truthful with you: Neither did I."

"I care for Amy too. Almost as much as I do for Cad."

"She is a brave and troubled woman with a good heart."

"I loved my father so much, it's difficult to understand how she can forget John Lattimer with such ease. He's a bad man, of course, and he left her a long time ago, but still I'm confused."

"There are facts about her father she has yet to learn, although he is, as you say, a bad man. And do not believe that she has forgotten him. For your brother's sake she believes she has, but like him she has inner demons she must yet confront."

"Speaking of demons, what about this Rick Marsh? Will he cause trouble?"

"Undoubtedly Cadmus will be tested by his presence. Come, Michael, let us observe their confrontation. Let us also send our kind and encouraging thoughts to him, and, as always, remember him in our prayers."

Frustrated by Dudley's absence, Cad saw he had no choice but to meet Rick. He found him sitting at one of the back tables in the saloon. Close to the door, a couple of strangers were playing cards, but otherwise the Inside Straight was empty.

He nodded at Amsterdam behind the bar.

"How're things at the Clap?" the bartender asked.

"A mess, but nothing that can't be repaired," he said, and kept on walking.

A full whiskey bottle and two glasses sat on the table in front of Rick. He filled one and shoved it toward Cad.

Cad shoved it back as he sat beside him. "You'll have to drink alone."

"Now ain't that a change." Rick threw back the whiskey and poured himself another drink.

"What are you doing here?" Cad asked.

"Thought you caught the big bullet back in Galveston, old buddy."

"What with your hasty departure, I can see how you wouldn't know the way things turned out. And you didn't answer my question."

Rick scratched the bristles on his cheek, fair as the ill-combed hair on his head. Despite his scruffiness, he had an innocent look about him—except when Cad looked at his eyes.

"I'd guess I'm doing what you're doing." His voice lowered. "The Rough Cut bank's begging to be robbed."

"Don't even think about it. The money belongs to a man with more fire power than the cavalry and a hell of a lot more sense."

"Never were an army man, were you? But you never were a coward, either."

"Call me what you like. Just keep moving on."

Rick chuckled. "Shit, Cad, I've come too far not to get something out of the miles. Anyways, I've heard of this John Lattimer. I've also heard of a drunk sheriff and Lattimer's gunmen who ride into town from time to time. None of 'em here all at once, what with guarding His Lordship's ranch and all."

"You've done some investigating."

"Learned to from you."

"You should also have learned when to ride away from a job."

"And when to carry through with it. Speaking of carrying through, you leave the woman in bed?"

"Mention her one more time, Rick, and I'll shove that bottle down your throat."

Rick leaned back in the chair and stretched his legs under the table. "My, oh my, what have we here? Cupid's arrow found you? Or maybe, like the bank, you just want to keep a good thing to yourself."

"However you figure it, you're leaving."

Rick's eyes narrowed as he studied Cad. "You always did like working alone. This time, podnah, you'll have to shoot me to get me gone."

"If necessary."

"Why, you son of a—"

Rick stopped, then burst out laughing.

"Had me going there for a while. What I always knew about you, Cad, what kept you from being one of the great thieves, was not cowardice. You've got the nerve of a riled grizzly. I've seen you face down a dozen men and have 'em shitting in their trousers before you were done. But you lacked the instinct to kill."

"What I lacked was the motivation. Could be I've got it now. Push me too far and you're likely to find out."

"I'm not exactly soiling my britches, if you know what I mean."

"You've never been hard to figure, Rick. Too bad you've come to the wrong place at the wrong time. Your problem is, you have no luck. The Galveston job was your idea, but you missed the payroll by a day. And you had the misfortune—you could call it a lack of foresight—to overlook the guard. A brave man and a shootist, he was. He stopped us both cold."

"There ain't no guard on the Rough Cut bank, just one lone teller, according to what I heard. An old cuss who counts the money to stay awake. Sounds like my kind of place."

He shoved back his chair and stood. "Seems to me my luck is changing, Cad. It's about time. All I ask is you stay out of my way. For old time's sake. We've ridden too many roads together to start shooting at one another now."

He headed for the door, then turned for a final say.

"Tell you what: This may take me a week or so to work out the details. Let's make a deal. I'll stay away from your woman, like you ask, and you stay away from me."

Amy spent the next two days missing Cad. She knew he was out at the Clap, helping Prudence with the clearing and the planning, but he was also standing guard to keep the ranch from further harm. He'd asked her to stay in her room while he was gone. Agreeing came easy since he'd done the asking when they were tangled together in bed.

He had a way of manipulating her that could be a source of irritation if she didn't keep reminding herself he had more important matters on his mind than a woman he would be leaving soon.

If on occasion she found herself at the edge of desolation, she pulled herself back. Once Cad's fate was determined, she could wallow in despair to her heart's content.

She spent the days also thinking about other matters, reading through her mother's diary, finding nothing that hinted at the loving feelings she held in her own heart. Marguerite had held no real affection for the men who kept her, although it seemed that several had loved her.

Poor Mama. Whether she ever realized it or not, she had led an unfulfilled life.

Even as Amy reached that conclusion, she felt desolation return. Fulfillment came at a heavy price, as Mama must have known. Whatever happened to her after Cad was gone, she knew she would not love again.

On the morning of the third day alone, she was propped up in bed with paper and pen, working on her own diary, deciding what a sad, strange couple Marguerite and John Lattimer had been, when a knock sounded at the door and her father strode into her room.

Kate was right behind him.

"See here, John, you can't just walk in here like you owned the place," the madam said, her voice rising to a rare shout.

"Miss Latourre and I need to talk," he said, keeping his eyes on Amy.

"Talk!" said Kate. "Humph!"

Amy stared at her father, unable to speak right away. He stood straight as ever at the foot of her bed, but something was different about him, something that came from within. He didn't seem as cool, as calculating as she remembered him in her mind. Neither did he seem much friendlier than he had when she'd confronted him at his ranch.

What he seemed was tense, but about what she couldn't guess. Premonitions of disaster stirred within her. She told herself to be strong. Unfortunately, she was wearing one of her mother's filmy wrappers, which revealed more than it hid—in case Cad showed up without warning. Embarrassed, dropping the writing material on the floor, she crossed her arms in front of her and held the wrapper closed at her throat.

"It's all right, Kate. You can go," she said when she found her voice. "I'll be fine."

With a shrug and a shake of her head, Kate did as she was asked.

Amy sat huddled on the bed, wondering what to do about this sudden and unwanted confrontation. The men in her life kept surprising her, but she wasn't getting any better at knowing how to react to them.

Lattimer set his hat on the foot of the bed. His gray hair was slicked back, creased from the hat, and he was wearing his usual garb—black suit, string tie, the fancy clasp at his throat. His shirt was white enough to have just been laundered, and she wondered how he kept from picking up trail dust. He probably ordered it to stay away.

He studied her for far too long, but there was no manly hunger in his expression. Still, Amy wished with all her heart that she'd bound her hair into a tight knot and put on one of her high-necked, dowdy gowns.

She wished, too, she could feel something for this man who had given her life, could at least find a way to tell him the truth. She'd sensed a sadness in him out at his ranch, momentary though it had been. Maybe—

"You don't look like any whore I've ever seen," he said.

She swallowed her hurt. "I came out here to learn the trade."

His stare remained hard and disbelieving.

"Besides," she said, thinking of her attire, "I thought I did look exactly like . . . what you said."

"Whore. I said whore." His voice turned harsh, as if he wanted to shame her. "Most whores know a trick or two about hooking a man. You look like you'd faint if I said boo."

"It's just that my time is paid for."

"That's what I hear."

He didn't sound pleased, but still she doubted he had come to buy her favors.

She felt dirty simply considering the possibility.

He picked up the papers from the floor and glanced at her spare scribblings. "What's this? Starting a diary, are you?"

She didn't answer, grateful she hadn't gotten far in the writing.

"I knew another woman kept a diary." His gaze turned inward. "It was a long time ago."

Amy held her breath. The silence between them lengthened.

From wherever his mind had traveled he came back to her, staring at her features as if he planned to draw them. The air grew thin and cold, its iciness shivering across her soul as she saw the truth. Somewhere deep inside him, he knew who she was. Tears gathered at the back of her throat. He knew, though he'd not put the knowledge into words, but it brought him little joy.

For a moment it was as though she tumbled through space, with no one to catch her, no one to care. Once again she was a six-year-old child, separated from her papa, thrust by her mama into a place of black-robed strangers, left to comfort herself.

"You have a trace of New Orleans in your voice," he said.

"I lived there for a while," she managed.

Why was he toying with her like this, prolonging her agony?

"Who were your folks?"

"No one you would know," she whispered.

"Who are you?" he asked in a voice not much louder.

"I told you, Amabelle Latourre."

"I'm not used to being lied to," he said, moving close, as if he would intimidate her into the truth.

His arrogance snapped her out of her spell. Why should she tremble before him? He'd already done the worst he could to her, done it a long time ago. She was his daughter, though she might never admit it. It was time she reacted with some of his strength.

"You're not used to being told no," she said, trying to sit straight on the too-soft mattress. "Leave Prudence Thor and the children alone."

"Haven't you noticed? Since the fire, since your visit, I've done nothing. Nothing but think, damn you. And remember."

His face grew flushed and a wildness settled in his eyes. "Who are you?" he shouted. "Answer me or I'll—"

He took her by the shoulders and shook her. Her hands fell away and the wrapper fell partially open. Stunned by the cruelty of his hold on her, she could do nothing but stare up at him from the bed.

The door slammed open. "Goddamn," a familiar voice said.

Relief rushed through her. Cad had returned.

Dropping his hands, Lattimer stepped aside. "The woman and I were busy. Get out."

Cad looked past him to Amy, his stare sharp as a knife from beneath the low brim of his hat. Relief fled and she saw herself as he did, saw her flushed cheeks and loosely worn hair, her see-through wrapper, her bare breasts revealed in its opening.

A hardness settled in his eyes that she hadn't seen in a long time.

"Yeah, I can see you were busy. Unless the lady wants to tell me different."

She stared at him in disbelief, lost as she had been on the day of her mother's death. "You have to ask?"

"Just tell me what's going on."

He couldn't seem to take his eyes off her breasts.

This time his stare didn't heat her. Instead, it turned her cold as the air. Cold and unrelenting, like the men who had invaded her room.

In the small quarters, thick with masculine presence, she was alone in a way far worse than her most dreaded fears. And she didn't care whether Cad was alive or undead or whatever he called himself. If he asked, she would stay with him as long as she could, comfort him, share whatever fate awaited. But he was a man without faith, a man who would keep himself apart no matter how long he lived. Like John Lattimer, always thinking of himself.

She should learn from them both.

"You've found me out, dear Cadmus," she said, stifling a sob, making no attempt to cover herself. Instead, she sat higher in the bed to give him a better look. "I'm just making plans for how I'll take care of myself when you're gone. You brought up the issue yourself and got me to thinking. Sometimes I'm a little dense, the way I was about getting pregnant, but eventually I work things out."

She looked from her lover to her father and back again.

"Mama and I were more alike than I ever realized. We both have no judgment in men."

Cad looked as though she'd slapped him.

"Get on out," she ordered, "so I can get back to work."

She was so wrapped in fury and hurt, it took her a while to catch on that Cad's anger was gradually fading. Instead, he looked stunned, and then, if she had to put a name to it, satisfied.

He took a step toward the bed, his lean strength moving in on her, muddling her mind and her resolve. Lord help her, crushed as she was, she longed to throw herself into his arms.

"You said your father was a bad man. I should have figured out right away who you were."

He dropped his hat on the bed, beside her father's. "I'm the dumb one, not you. Your real name's Amy Lattimer, isn't it? This bastard is the reason you came to Rough Cut, not any plan to be a whore."

She shook her head in denial, but she couldn't speak.

Cad glanced at Lattimer. "I'm right. Had you figured it out? Had she told you yet?"

Lattimer's eyes narrowed. "I suspected that's who she was."

Cad turned a humorless smile on her. "I'm not the only one with secrets, am I? Anything else you forgot to tell?"

At the moment he looked as smug and arrogant as her father. Judging her, condemning her, keeping her at arm's length even while he took her time and time again in bed.

He held no devotion for her; neither man did. Throw herself into his arms? Not in a million years.

In that instant her heart broke into a thousand pieces. She doubted it would ever be whole again. She fought for dignity, for pride, but she found only a desolate anger that would have to suffice.

She pulled herself to her feet, standing by the bed as straight as she could manage, her chin tilted against them both. She didn't bother to cover herself; the only shame she felt was for them.

"There is one thing that ought to be said. I had thought that I loved you, that I would abandon my father to your cause even though I promised on my mother's grave never to bring him harm."

"Amy—"

Her raised hand silenced him, and she turned on Lattimer.

"Mama knew where you were. A detective tracked you down, but then he disappeared. Did you have him killed, hoping the information he uncovered wouldn't bring your bothersome wife and daughter out to your ranch?"

"His death was an accident. Sonny misunderstood what he was up to."

"And what about you? Knowing your wife was alive and wanting to know where you were, did you wait with a loving heart for her to arrive?"

Her voice almost broke. She fought to keep it strong. "No, don't bother to answer. You abandoned us a long time ago. What did you care where we were?"

He ran a hand through his hair, disturbing its neatness. "I went back for both of you, after the war, when luck finally turned my way."

"You're lying. Mama knew nothing about it."

"She never saw me, being otherwise occupied, so I figured I'd best look out for myself and head back to Texas. Don't look so shocked. You weren't around. I decided she'd given you away."

"You didn't know her very well."

"Maybe not. And she didn't know me."

He spoke as harshly as he had ever spoken, and he seemed as far away as he had ever been.

Both men did.

She glanced from man to man, her father with his cold gray distance, and Cad with his unreadable dark stare.

"I ask one thing of you both, and one thing only. You've vowed to kill each other. Please don't."

Tears burned in her throat. Unable to look at them longer, she dropped her gaze to the hats on her bed.

"Don't worry, Papa"—she said the word with scorn—"I'll make no demands on your money. Your fortune is safe."

"You think that's what this is about?"

"What else could it be? Certainly not affection. And, in case you were considering it, don't bother to defend your daughter's virtue, or make Cad do right by me. He didn't force me into anything. It was rather the reverse."

With more strength than she'd ever possessed, she forced her eyes to Cad.

"I came out here thinking I was prepared for whatever happened. I wasn't prepared for you. There must have been a thousand hungers suppressed in me. You fed them, but only after I begged you to."

She took a deep breath, but she wasn't done. "For answering those needs, whatever happens now, I'll always wish you well. But since I can't change you I'll have to change myself. If that means falling out of love, then that's what I'll do. If it takes the rest of my life."

With a low cry, he started for her. Gunshots on the street stopped him.

"Robbery!" someone shouted. "Sheriff's been shot. Some fool's trying to rob the bank!"

Chapter Twenty-two

Cad felt like someone was tearing him in half. He needed to hold Amy tight against him, let her sweet softness soothe the ragged torment she was putting him through, and, if she would let him, soothe some of her own. This defiant, passionate woman was all the heaven he could ever want, but hell was breaking loose on the street.

For the time being heaven would have to wait.

He tried to speak with his eyes, but he was never a man for subtlety. Besides, he might have to do some convincing before she went into his arms.

"Later," he said. "We're not yet done."

Before she could deny him all over again, he

rushed from the room, Lattimer close on his heels.

The stillness of the scene on the street took him by surprise: Pierre and George, the whores, Amsterdam, the rest of the town's usual residents were scattered down its length, unmoving, Rick holding an arm and leaning against a post by the bank, close by the fallen sheriff and a hand-twisting bank teller, and in the center of the street was the tall, cadaverous figure of Deputy Wiley Fike, one hand holding a bank bag, the other a gun.

"Good," said Lattimer, who started toward the deputy. "You got the money."

Fike raised the gun. "I got it all right. For myself."

Lattimer stopped in his tracks, arms lowered to his sides. "Don't be a fool."

"You hired me to watch over your town because I was the best. It's time to pay my price."

"By God—" Lattimer began as he lifted a hand.

"And don't go for your gun. You're not good enough."

Cad gestured for Lattimer to back down. The two men stared at one another in defiance, but it was Lattimer, long used to delegating his battles, who gave in and stepped aside.

Slowly, steadily, Cad began to walk down the street, his hand resting against the holstered Peacemaker. He halted a dozen yards away from Fike.

"Put the gun down, and the money," he said.

Fike's colorless eyes narrowed to slits in his gray face as he steadied the rifle. "I won't miss you this time."

"You didn't miss me before," Cad said.

The deputy took aim. "Nothing else figures. I couldn't have missed a yellow-bellied coward like you." He spat in the street. "Won't pull that gun, will you? Haven't got the guts. Consider yourself a dead man."

"I have for a long time."

All eyes on him, he took another step. Fike's gun barked fire. The bullet tore his shirt, then fell to the ground.

Something like fear crossed the man's face. "You're wearing some kind of armor, ain't you? That's what it is. Goddamned armor."

"You might say that."

"Then why don't you take me down?"

Cad's fingers itched to draw the gun. Fike was asking for it, clear enough. He got the feeling the money wasn't what this was all about; it concerned power and control. Fike had lost it once when he'd failed to riddle him with bullets; irrationally, he needed to prove he was the better man.

But killing someone, even a deranged snake like Fike, would send him straight to hell. And for the first time since the Atchafalaya Swamp, he had reason to live.

Amy gave him purpose; she'd taught him to love. The realization hit him with the power of a thunderbolt. Holding her wasn't enough; he wanted to cherish and protect her for the rest of a long, long life.

He'd felt it back in her room, but he'd been too dense to see it. He loved her. As long as he drew breath, he always would.

In that instant a weight lifted from his shoulders. For the first time in years he felt good about himself. Heck of a time to come to the realization, when he was facing a crazy killer surrounded by a crowd.

A smile split Fike's sunken face, a smile of evil proportions as he looked past Cad.

"She sure as hell ain't protected, is she?"

All pleasure fled as icy fear gripped him. He glanced over his shoulder to see Amy standing in the street in front of the parlor, wearing one of her gray silk gowns, looking as beautiful and vulnerable as he had ever seen her.

He started to order her back inside, praying to Dudley that for once she would obey, but the click of a hammer told him prayers were too late.

Whirling, he fired just as the Peacemaker cleared the holster. Fike's eyes widened enough to show his surprise. He swayed once. "I'll be damned," he said, then fell backward to the ground.

"Yeah," said Cad, with more bitterness than the world could contain. "You speak for us both."

Lattimer brushed past him, headed for the

bag of money. Turning to Amy, who stood straight and tall in her place, Cad was barely aware of the commotion around him. Amy was his all, his everything, the best that life could offer any man.

He wasn't surprised she didn't come to him. Of all the witnesses to the shooting, she was the only one who knew he'd never been in danger. And she'd already said her good-bye, said it in ways even a fool like him could understand.

She was right; their love was not meant to be. It would be a cruelty in his final moments with her to confess how he felt. He'd hurt her far too much already. He would burn in a thousand hells before he hurt her again.

But oh, how he wanted to hold her one more time.

The tears staining her cheeks were his undoing. Turning, he did the hardest thing he'd ever done in his life. He walked away, headed for the fallen deputy. Paying little attention to Lattimer, he grabbed the heavy bag of coins from his hand and strode past Kate Cassidy, kneeling on the street beside the groaning sheriff, past the nervous teller, past Rick who stared at him with curious eyes, and entered the dim interior of the bank.

"All right, Dudley. Come and get me." He dropped the money on the counter. "And see that Amy gets some of this. She's earned a hell of a lot more, but it's the best I can do for her now."

Silence and shadows met his plea. Tossing the Peacemaker beside the bag, he opened his arms. "Didn't you hear me? I said come and get me, goddamn it."

A sigh rustled like a breeze from the far corner of the room, followed by a glow of unearthly light.

"Cadmus, will you never learn? You must clean up your language."

Dudley appeared in the glow, an admonitory smile appearing within his white beard.

"I figure a man headed for hell can say what he wants."

"Why do you figure that?"

"Weren't you watching out there? I killed a man."

"You had no choice."

Cad scarcely heard him. "And what's more, I'd do it again. I wanted to pump bullets into his rotten carcass and make sure he'd never threaten anyone again. Now get me out of here. They'll think I'm a hero, and we both know that's a lie."

"You could have been killed."

"Not when I'm already dead."

Dudley shook his head. "Poor Cadmus. You haven't realized the truth yet, have you? Michael, I believe you should be the one to tell him."

From out of the misty light, a shadowy shape drifted into view, features indistinct, but Cad recognized the apparition as his brother. A sense of awe and peace settled upon him. This time, fear did not replace the gentler feelings. Unsteady on his feet, unable to reach out, he let the sensations settle the bitterness in his soul.

If this was dying, it wasn't all bad.

"You did it," Michael said.

Cad shook his head in puzzlement. "Did what?"

"Redeemed yourself."

"I killed a man."

"You saved a life. Besides, you were already alive."

"I'll be dam—darned."

"Not with Amy by your side," said Dudley.

"I couldn't have done it without her, could I?"

"A bad man is never as strong as a good woman."

Cad grinned. "Yeah. And she's the best." He looked toward his brother. "I have you to thank for her."

"She came along all on her own, as much a surprise to us as she was to you."

"She's quite a woman," said Cad.

"Whether you know it or not, brother, you're quite a man. You took care of me when I needed you. There was nothing you could have done about the snakes. I hope you have forgiven yourself."

"I'll always regret what happened."

"Regret yes, blame no."

Staring at the shadow, Cad at last accepted his innocence.

"I love you, Michael."

"I love you, Cadmus."

Even as he said the words, Michael's figure faded back into the light, at last disappearing from view.

"No!" Cad cried, not wanting to let him go.

"He must leave," said Dudley, resting a hand on Cad's sleeve, applying warmth instead of weight. "But know that you have brought him peace. Now he can take his rightful place beside your parents for all eternity."

Cad listened and understood, and a little of Michael's peace settled in his heart. He felt, too, a restlessness to get on with his life. From now until he took his place beside his long-lost family, he knew he would feel them close by.

Footsteps sounded at the door. "Talking to yourself, podnah?" Rick asked.

Cad glanced around the bank, but the light was gone, along with the ethereal figure that had governed his life for so long. He nodded a good-bye, knowing that Dudley still watched, then turned to face his former partner.

"I was talking to an angel," he said.

"Sure you were. Must have been a short conversation, since you just walked in. Guess he didn't talk back."

Cad shook his head in puzzlement. The time with Michael and Dudley must have been no more than an instant to the earthly world. He glanced at Rick's wounded arm. "You shouldn't have tried the bank."

"Lots of things I shouldn't have tried. With all the commotion outside, folks have forgotten about me. Besides, I didn't shoot the sheriff. His own deputy did. Fine town you got here."

"It could be."

"Can't wait around to find out if you're right. I'm slipping out the back door, unless you've a mind to stop me."

His eye fell to the bag of money on the counter.

"Don't even think it," said Cad.

"Want it for yourself?"

"Not this time. Not ever. Now get on out of here and change your ways."

"Damned if you don't sound like a preacher," Rick said as he hurried past him.

"I'm not that much redeemed," Cad said to the departing figure.

Alone, he thought of Amy and the wooing he would have to do. Dudley had called her a strong woman, and that she was. Her problem was, she'd made him a strong man. He smiled to himself. Fall out of love with him, would she? Like heck. Whispering a *thank you* to Michael, he grabbed the money, returned to the street, and headed for the pleasure parlor, where Amy still stood.

He came to a halt in front of her. Looking at her, at the golden hair and bluebonnet eyes, at the tearstained cheeks, at the lift of her chin, and the way her body seemed to call to him, he felt a surge of love stronger than he had ever known. And a tingle of fear that, for all his determination, his salvation had come too late.

He held out the bag. "This is for you."

Her eyes darkened. "It's not mine."

"Your daddy's got a hundred times this stashed away. Rick always was a fool. I doubt he got more'n a sampling of what's in that bank."

Her chin tilted a little higher, and a familiar urge tightened his loins.

"I can take care of myself," she said.

He thrust the bag of money into her hand. "With some resources, maybe you can. But is that what you want?"

She squeezed her eyes closed for a moment, then looked at him with a hurt and a resolution that almost broke his heart.

"Wanting doesn't seem to matter much, does it?"

Cad grew impatient. "Amy, there's something you ought to know."

"Haven't you done enough to me?"

"I've just begun, darling. I've just begun."

"I—" She stared at him with wide eyes. "What did you call me?"

Before he could respond he heard the pounding of a horse's hooves. He turned to see Sonny riding down on him, rifle raised.

The horse reared as Sonny pulled back on the reins. "I always took you for a thief. Didn't know the two of you were in cahoots. Think you're such a good shot, do you?" He flicked a scornful glance at Amy. "And she thinks I'm not man enough for her bed."

Cad slapped at his holster, then remembered he'd left the Peacemaker in the bank.

"No!" Lattimer shouted from down the street.

But Sonny was too far lost in a killing hunger to hear. "Guess I can take you both down with one shot." The hammer clicked. Cursing the absence of his gun, Cad shoved Amy aside just as two shots rang out. Fire burned in his side; he stumbled backwards, falling into what seemed an endless void, thinking with a swell of bitterness that his new life hadn't lasted long at all.

He opened his eyes to see Amy one last time. She knelt beside him, an expression of amazement on her face.

"You're bleeding," she said.

He sure as heck was. Settling his head on her lap, she touched his side. He winced. "And you're hurting," she added.

He managed a grin, then decided if he could do that, maybe he wasn't injured as bad as he'd thought. He probed his wounded side. The pain was there but, best he could tell, Sonny had managed only to graze him. He would live, after all.

He looked past her to the twisted body on the ground. That was more than he could say for Sonny.

"Who got him?"

"My father," said Amy, wonderment in her voice. She sat back on her heels. "I can't believe this day. He killed his own man to protect us, and . . . you're bleeding." She said it as if his injury was the most wonderful thing in the world.

Cad felt the same way.

"How long have you been . . . not undead?"

"No more than a quarter of an hour. Maybe less."

"You knew it?"

"Not right away. It took Divine inspiration to make things clear."

"Dudley told you?"

"Right. When I went into the bank."

She stroked a strand of hair from his face. "You risked your life to save mine. Right after you got it back."

"Love does crazy things to a man."

"Love?" She gave him a tremulous smile.

"I love you, Amy Lattimer, and I don't care what your name is. That is, I don't care as long as you change it to Rankin. Unless you've already fallen out of love with me."

She kissed him. The taste of her was like wine, and he forgot his injury.

"I never could have done that, Cad." She smiled through her tears. "I didn't even want to, but since I didn't have any rocks to throw at you, saying I did seemed the best way to defend myself."

Taking her hand, he kissed her palm. "I used to be afraid of caring for someone. Did you know that? Cad Rankin, thief and all-around tough guy, carried a load of fear he didn't want anyone to see. But caring is making me strong, Amy. There's no other reason to live."

He looked past her to the man standing by her side, staring down at them, a grim look on his face. Lying in the street, wounded, comforted by a woman, he felt more powerful than the big, bad rancher could ever be.

"Take your money, Lattimer. The lady doesn't need it after all."

Lattimer kept on staring, looking as if he wanted to say something but couldn't pull out the words.

You've vowed to kill each other. Please don't.

Amy's plea hung in the air between them. Cad knew that Lattimer was hearing it too.

Without glancing at the money, or at the man he'd just shot, Lattimer walked away.

Amy stared after him in silence, then returned her attention to Cad. He saw the sadness and regret in her eyes.

"Don't worry, darling. I've got a liaison angel hanging around without anything to do right now. After me, redeeming your papa will be no problem at all."

"Do you really think so?"

"I know it." Somehow he did.

She kissed him again, making it longer and sweeter, then backed away. He glanced at her bosom, admitting some of his bad habits would be hard to break.

"You buttoned your dress wrong."

"I put it on in a hurry. But I can take it off just as fast."

She inspired Cad to struggle to his feet.

"Get me to your room, Amy, and I'll show you just how much alive I really am."

Later, when he'd been helped up the stairs by Amsterdam, administered to by Kate, and stripped and cleaned by Amy, he lay stretched out under the covers, naked except for the bandage on his side, and watched as she put his shirt to soak in the basin across the room.

They were alone. At last. His wound was hurting, but it wasn't anything he couldn't endure. Besides, he kind of liked the pain. It came with being alive.

"Come here," he ordered.

"You need to rest."

"Rest's not what I need."

"You'll kill yourself all over again."

"But I'll die happy."

She shuddered. "Let's not talk about dying."

"I'll expire if you don't get to this bed."

A slow grin brightened her face, and Cad's heart started pounding in anticipation.

"I don't have a choice, do I?"

"Nope."

She moved slowly toward him, her silk skirt rustling with each step, then sat primly at the edge of the bed.

"You really did it, didn't you? Reforming and

saving Rough Cut, I mean. Dudley must have been surprised."

"Not when he saw I had help. Oh, I ran off the bad guys, all right, by taking their money. That usually works if you want to discourage someone from hanging around. Difference with me this time was, I did it without a gun. Took some powerful changing, I have to admit."

He pressed her hand against his heart. "You did the hard part. Reforming both me and your papa, and just by being you."

"He's not really reformed."

"He's started. The first is the hard part. Believe me, I know."

He stroked her arm and studied her gown. "The buttons are still wrong."

"I was waiting for you to fix them. When you got the strength."

She leaned close, brushing up against him. He winced despite himself, but he didn't think she saw.

"Remember when you thought I had a broken leg?"

"I remember."

"Do you also remember how you made me forget it?"

Her blush told him he didn't need to describe what she'd done, how she'd gone under the cloak and kissed her way down to . . .

He stopped himself. If he kept this up, he'd explode before she touched him.

"I need comforting again," he said.

"But—"

"Trust me."

She laughed, and even with night pushing against the window, sunlight burst into the room. "I do trust you. It's myself I'm worried about. What if I get too rough?"

"Try it, and we'll see what happens."

Staring up at her, he felt the pain in his side ease. Dudley's doing? A parting gift? He didn't know, but he thanked him all the same.

He pulled her against him, letting his hands roam across her tight-tipped breasts before settling against her shoulders. Lifting her hair, he kissed her ear, then whispered a few particulars about what he wanted her to do.

And added what he would do to her in return.

"What a wicked man you are," she said in mock alarm, but he could see the heat in the depths of her eyes.

"That I am," he said as he worked at the buttons of her gown. "In some ways, my love, I will never be redeemed."

Epilogue

On the second wedding anniversary of Cad and Amy Rankin, with their infant son Michael Dudley sleeping peacefully in his nearby nursery, Cad took his beloved wife into their bedroom to give her the gift he'd carefully planned.

He moved to the bed, but she remained by the door, eyeing the package in the center of the quilt.

"We agreed not to get each other anything."

"It's not much."

"There's nothing I need."

"Nothing?"

She walked slowly toward him. Sauntered more than walked. Graceful, seductive, slender as ever, though her breasts had swelled from motherhood, she still had the power to turn him inside out.

Her hands rested against his shirt as she brushed her lips against his. "All right, so there are a few things I'll always need."

She backed away long enough to remove his sheriff's badge. "This tends to get in the way."

"How about the rest of what I'm wearing?"

"In time, my love. Since you broke the rules and bought me a gift, the least I can do is open it."

Reluctantly, he let her go, watching as she tore into the paper. For all her attempts at being worldly, at being tough, she still kept an innocence about her that he found endearing.

There was nothing innocent about the gift.

She held up the black lace stockings and the frilly garters. She even managed to act surprised, though he'd given her the same present a year ago.

Of course he had. They went so well with the red silk-and-feathers outfit she wore for him whenever he asked. The problem was, he kept tucking the garters away, collecting them the way some men collected stamps.

Each to his own, he always said.

"I'm a sentimental man," he explained. "I can't forget the first time you wore it. When you came to my hotel room to let me know you accepted the way I was."

"Oh, I recall very well. I thought you'd be leaving soon."

"I fooled you."

"And yourself."

She looked past him to the fine, wide room, and out the window to the spread of land that John Lattimer had given them as a wedding present. Cad hadn't wanted to accept it, but since he'd been the cause of the man's redemption he hadn't figured out a way to say no.

Besides, Amy had said it pleased her very much that after so many years her father wanted to accept his parental role, and the lavishness of the gift had nothing to do with how she felt. Lattimer had already fired all the gunmen working for him; this had been another step in proving himself.

Any other woman, he might have doubted. But not his true love.

"We have a good life," she said.

Cad agreed. When Hickok Bowles moved on west with Kate Cassidy, he'd been reluctant to take the job as county lawman. But understanding the criminal mind the way he did, he'd found it easy to convince the drifters and would-be thieves who passed through on occasion to keep on moving. That left him time for raising horses, the job he loved the most, right after caring for his wife and child.

The *banditos* still turned up from time to time, but they did nothing more than fire a few harmless shots in the air and keep Amsterdam in business running the Inside Straight. In the past two years he hadn't heard from Rick Marsh, which was just as well, considering the badge he now wore.

He'd told Dudley that given his success with Lattimer, he ought to take on Rick, but the angel had yet to respond.

As for the pleasure parlor, Dora and Sal were the only women left. They had enough trade to keep them going, especially with Amsterdam visiting Dora the way he did, and when they weren't at work they studied the reading lessons Amy gave them in the school she'd opened in town.

The Professor, keeping a tenuous hold on sobriety, took on her teaching chores when she found her young son making demands. The school was filling fast, not only with the parlor women and the children from the Clap, but with the families of settlers who were moving into the county and into town. New businesses were springing up just about every week, and a new church was going up behind the bank.

Pierre had married Lilly Mae and settled in Del Rio, opening up a French restaurant for the passengers on the new train line that had recently been laid. Cad hadn't seen how he could make much money, but that didn't seem to concern Pierre.

His valet George had taken Carmen back to

his homeland, but Cad didn't know if they'd ever been wed.

Not so his father-in-law. A month ago, after breaking up the Rocking L into smaller spreads and selling them off to the newcomers, he'd taken Prudence Thor as his bride, promising to care for the orphans as his own.

"Got some making up to do," he'd declared. "Prudence can keep title to the Clap."

Amy had cried at the wedding, but she'd sworn the tears came from happiness.

Cad's happiness came from her.

Sitting at the edge of the bed, he watched as she slipped out of her gown.

"Close your eyes," she ordered.

He did as she bade, listening to the rustle of her clothes, growing hot and hard as the seconds dragged by.

"All right," she said. "I'm ready."

So was he.

Studying her as she walked toward him, letting the sight of her deliciously familiar body taunt him, he started to unbuckle his pants.

"Let me," she said as she stood between his legs, so close the feathers at her thighs tickled his nose.

Cad grinned and fingered one of the garters. For the time being he'd let her have her way. He'd let her keep the garter too . . . for a while. After all, as a wise angel had once told him, a bad man was never as strong as a good woman.

Amy Lattimer Rankin proved old Dud right every day of the week.

An Angel's Touch
Longer Than Forever
Bronwyn Wolfe

"A wonderful, magical love story that transcends time and space. Definitely a keeper!"
—Madeline Baker

Patrick is in trouble, alone in turn-of-the-century Chicago, and unjustly jailed with little hope for survival. Then the honey-haired beauty comes to him, as if she has heard his prayers.

Lauren has all but given up on finding true love when she feels the green-eyed stranger's call—summoning her across boundaries of time and space to join him in a struggle against all odds; uniting them in a love that will last longer than forever.

_52042-7 $5.99 US/$7.99 CAN

Dorchester Publishing Co., Inc.
65 Commerce Road
Stamford, CT 06902

Please add $1.75 for shipping and handling for the first book and $.50 for each book thereafter. NY, NYC, PA and CT residents, please add appropriate sales tax. No cash, stamps, or C.O.D.s. All orders shipped within 6 weeks via postal service book rate. Canadian orders require $2.00 extra postage and must be paid in U.S. dollars through a U.S. banking facility.

Name____
Address____
City ____________________________ State______ Zip______
I have enclosed $______ in payment for the checked book(s).
Payment must accompany all orders. ☐ Please send a free catalog.